The Final Blitz

A Grumpy Sunshine, Enemies-to-Lovers Football Romance

CK Franco

Blurbs

When star defensive lineman Brick Turner becomes the headline no team wants, the league sends in damage control.
Enter Natalie Brooks—sharp, disciplined, and immune to charm.

Natalie doesn't babysit egos. She controls narratives.
Brick doesn't follow rules. He breaks them.

Assigned to manage the most volatile player in professional football, Natalie steps into a locker room crackling with tension, resentment, and unspoken loyalties. Every move is watched. Every word could end a career. And Brick? He makes it clear he doesn't want saving.

But beneath the anger and defiance lies a man pushed to the edge—by pressure, expectations, and a past that refuses to stay buried.

As the season spirals toward its breaking point, boundaries blur, trust is tested, and control becomes a dangerous game. One wrong step could destroy everything they've worked for—on the field and off it.

The Final Blitz is a grumpy-sunshine, enemies-to-lovers football romance about power, discipline, and choosing growth when walking away would be easier.

Perfect for readers who love:

Sports romance with emotional depth

Strong, career-driven heroines

Redemption arcs and forced proximity

Closed-door romance with high tension

To the ones who stayed
when walking away would've been easier.

And to those learning that control
isn't about silence—
it's about choosing what matters most.

Discipline isn't punishment.

*It's the courage to hold steady when everything demands
you break.*

Prologue

"The stadium wakes before the sun."

Floodlights slice through the dawn like warning flares, illuminating press vans clustered at the gates—hungry, waiting. Natalie Brooks feels their presence before she sees them. Cameras. Questions. Judgments already written.

She parks, smooths her jacket, and exhales once.

Inside the locker room, tension hums beneath steel benches and damp concrete. Headlines glare from the walls. Careers hang in the balance. This isn't just a team in trouble—it's a narrative spiraling out of control.

Then the door opens.

Brick Turner's laughter cuts through the room—raw, careless, dangerous. The sound of a man who refuses to be managed.

Natalie steps forward anyway.

She wasn't sent here to be liked.
She was sent here to stop the collapse.

And for the first time, Brick Turner meets someone who won't flinch.

The game—on the field and off—has officially begun.

Contents

Damage Control

The sun was a pale promise behind the stadium's towering silhouette as Natalie Brooks's rental car hummed onto the gravel lot. Press vans crowded the main entrance like sharks sensing blood in the water, their antennas bristling. Floodlights highlighted the gleaming sides of cameras and tripod legs. A strobe of flashes burst as she eased the car to a stop.

The air held a crisp edge—the faint metallic scent of early morning dew mixing with warm diesel fumes and fresh-cut grass from the nearby field.

Her phone buzzed quietly inside her leather bag. She pulled it out, the screen casting a pale glow in the dim morning light. Unread emails stacked up: league directives, sponsor queries, and urgent memos. Then she froze at a terse text from her boss: *Good luck. You'll need it.* The words hit her like a cold splash of water.

Security staff materialized instantly, their crisp uniforms a clean break against the chaotic swirl of reporters. They parted the crowd with practiced efficiency, forging a path to her passenger door. She opened it, the sharp click of her heels ringing against the pavement. A chill wind teased at her jacket's collar, and she instinctively pulled it tighter. Distant whistles and shouted questions prickled her skin like static. Her jaw tightened, but her stride didn't falter.

"Ms. Brooks! What's the plan for Turner?" Voices rippled ahead, relentless.

"Will the team discipline Brick this time?"

"Is the league going to suspend him again?"

She pushed forward, nodding curtly but not slowing. A camera lens whirred too close. Flashes popped like gunfire. Every muscle coiled behind a polished facade.

The crowd's din dimmed behind heavy steel doors. Natalie stepped into a cavernous corridor where echoes bounced off cold concrete walls—the soft shuffle of papers, the tap of pens, and conversations stretched tight and thin.

Staff huddled in knots beside locked storage, their faces tight with nerves. The sharp scent of disinfectant mixed with sweat-caught hosiery filled the air. Rookie players leaned against lockers, their eyes darting from her to the ceiling like frightened birds trapped in a cage.

She understood then what they all felt: the weight of waiting, the uncertainty crackling through the building like electricity before a storm.

Natalie's gaze swept over the plastered posters lining the hallway—headlines splashed in red and black: *Turner's Temper Threatens Team. Disaster on the Gridiron: Damage Control Needed. Is the Defensive Lineman Beyond Redemption?* The words thrummed with accusation. Somewhere, muted by the steady pulse of time, the league's clock counted down. Answers were due.

She slid her hand along the cool steel doorframe, feeling the scratches and faded signatures that traced the stories of seasons past.

Her other hand tightened into a loose fist. The sound of voices crescendoed inside—rough laughter from a man who owned the room, the slap of gear slamming against metal. This was the heart of the storm she had been sent to calm.

Her boss's text felt like a spotlight burning straight through her chest. There was no hiding from this. She swallowed hard, already bracing for what lay ahead.

The corridor narrowed, compressing the charged atmosphere until the only thing left was the door ahead. Her breath stuttered. Every step forward took her deeper into the fray—a crucible where reputations would be forged or shattered.

She pressed her palm to the door, feeling the weight of every pair of eyes waiting on the other side.

There was no turning back now.

A ragged burst of laughter cut through the murmur outside the locker room—loud and raw, unmistakably Brick Turner's. The clatter of cleats against metal lockers followed. Equipment dropped with sharp slaps. Natalie stalled beneath the flickering fluorescent light above the door. Her breath caught. The air thickened—heavy with tension, a faint, familiar musk of sweat and leather wrapping around her like a warning.

Beneath that bravado, something brittle waits: anger, perhaps. Defiance. Exhaustion that runs bone-deep. She recognizes it because she has learned to read what lives underneath the noise—the small fractures that precede collapse.

The door swings open, and the room hushes like the eye of a tempest. Half-dressed bodies gleam with damp skin and grime. Jerseys drape over muscles earned through grinding hours. Heads snap toward her entrance. Eyes flicker—curiosity mixed with skepticism, wariness threaded through calculation. The silence curls between rows of lockers, broken only by the quiet drip of a leaking faucet somewhere in the corner.

Natalie threads through the narrow aisle, her heels muffled by the tension hanging heavy in the air. Every pair of eyes tracks her measured steps.

She stops beneath pale, flickering light and folds her hands in front of her. Taking a slow breath, the words come steady, crisp against the electric quiet: "I'm Natalie Brooks. I'm here because you need someone to handle the storm for you." Her gaze sweeps the room, settling with quiet authority. "I'm not here to punish. I'm here so you all get to keep playing football."

Her voice settles like oil atop restless water—calm but firm, unyielding.

A ripple of chatter swells. Tight jaws clench. Eyes dart toward each other, then quickly away. Fingers tap restlessly on benches. A few players exchange loaded glances, heat flaring beneath their exhausted faces.

Natalie holds up her hand, palm outstretched. "Phones. Everyone."

The command is simple and non-negotiable.

Reluctant hands emerge from pockets and benches. Phones land on the metal bench with a series of thuds. Sharp sighs and low grumbles echo in their wake. The faint buzz of screens fading to darkness fills the space—an invisible barrier shutting off the outside world.

At the back, Coach Marcus Hale leans against the locker banks, arms crossed over his broad chest. His quiet strength saturates the room like gravity bending space. His gaze never leaves Natalie—sharp and appraising, his eyes unreadable but laced with approval. The crease of his brow deepens, lines of age and experience sculpting his face into an unspoken warning: this is the line. No more second chances.

For years, Hale has held this program together through sheer force of will and consequence. These boys know him and fear him, even. Now they're watching to see if he trusts her. That trust is the only currency that matters in a room like this.

Players shuffle. Bodies straighten. Shoulders square like recruits forging resolve in the crucible of command. The room tightens. Breaths sync into a held cadence. Silence thickens—a taut wire ready to hum.

"We're done here," Natalie says, concise and edged with control.

It is not a question or a request.

The locker room feels cavernous and confining, humming with restrained energy. Damp sweat and leather mingle with a faint trace of eucalyptus from the showers. Stale ozone from the harsh, artificial lights hangs heavy in the air.

In a low voice, carried only to the nearest bench, a conversation crackles between two players:

"Think she's really got the balls to keep us straight?"

"Nah. She's just polishing our mess for the brass," the other snaps back, eyes narrowing.

A younger player shifts, unease flickering across his face. "But if Coach is backing her—"

"Coach backs the team. Don't expect him to throw you a life jacket if you're sinking."

Natalie catches the tail end of the conversation. Her eyes narrow subtly, and her lips press into a calm line. She hears the question beneath their words: Who holds the real power here? And more importantly—will she?

A storm is brewing beneath polished speeches and forced cooperation. Fragile. Simmering. Waiting.

Coach Hale steps slightly forward. His presence fills the room like gravity itself, silent but absolute. The unnamed jitters settle. Players incline their heads, and bodies tilt toward the unspoken promise and threat that come with his leadership.

Natalie senses the fracture line beneath the surface: loyalty tangled with skepticism, hunger fighting hesitation. The weight of every lost opportunity and the burden of past mistakes hang like smoke in this confined air.

Yet here, in this pressure cooker of ambition and doubt, the first threads of order are woven. Phones are collected, and eyes are cautiously fixed on this unexpected outsider. Their quiet resistance is held at bay—for now—by authority and necessity.

The locker room settles into a fragile harmony, a taut silence ready to fray under the weight of truths yet to unfold.

The game, both on the field and off, has just begun.

###

Natalie stepped forward. The fluorescent lights cast a harsh gleam across scattered jerseys and bare arms stretched over benches. The locker room smelled thick with musk—sweat, leather, and liniment clinging like a second skin to uniforms worn thin by season after season.

Half-dressed men shifted their weight. Water bottles flew between hands. Shoulders rolled and stretched. Eyes flickered toward her—curiosity mixed with suspicion in equal measure.

"Let's get this straight," Natalie began, her voice even but carrying a crisp edge that sliced through the low murmurs. "The league is watching. Our sponsors are watching." She gestured to the smeared newspaper headline on the wall, mocking the team's recent scandal. Last month alone had been catastrophic—viral videos, fines, and sponsors threatening to bail. The damage was quantifiable and public.

"Everyone outside that video screen expects us to crash and burn, or worse—spin the truth this way and that. We've lost control of the narrative."

She paused. "Let that land."

"Now it's time to take it back."

A few players cast sideways glances, their brows knitting together. Tension tightened between them—palpable as a charged wire strung taut. Natalie met each gaze with steady calm, the kind of presence that didn't need volume to command attention.

"Every public statement—no exceptions—goes through me first." The hint of dry humor softened the room's edge. "I know you all have opinions. Lots of them. You'll share those opinions with me first."

Reluctant smiles flickered here and there, quickly swallowed by the weight of the moment.

Caleb leaned against the cold metal of his locker, his thumbs moving rapidly across his phone beneath the table. His eyes flicked up—sharp and wary. Nearby, Eli folded his arms across his broad chest, his jaw clenched tight like a door slammed shut. His dark eyes watched every move.

Natalie shifted her weight, unfolding the page in her hands that held the new communication protocol—the game plan for damage control.

"My philosophy?" Her voice softened, almost conspiratorial. "Calm. Disciplined. Fair. But absolutely uncompromising. Discipline isn't punishment—it's a form of care. You protect what matters by controlling your reactions and your message. That's how we break the cycle."

A ripple ran through the group, accompanied by low murmurs and whispered exchanges between players struggling to digest rules none had asked for, let alone wanted.

"What's fair about this, Natalie?" came a voice from the back. It was barely more than a murmur, but it was loaded with resistance. Others nodded in agreement. A slow chorus of skepticism rose beneath the surface.

Natalie didn't flinch. "This isn't about control for control's sake. It's about protecting your future—on the field and off the field. Every interview, every tweet paints your story. This pact keeps that story yours, not theirs."

She reminded herself of her own stake in this matter. It wasn't just the team's reputation hanging in the balance; Brick's career could unravel, along with her own sense of purpose.

Caleb's fingers tapped a quick rhythm against his phone. His eyes darted from the packet she slid across the bench to his teammates' faces. Eli's silence was more defiant than any protest—his hardened stare drilled into Natalie's calm presence like a challenge.

"Looks like you're coaching us off the field now," Caleb muttered, low enough for the nearest few to hear. "I didn't sign up for this game."

Natalie shot a glance his way—sharp, but not unkind. "Off-field matters always exist. Do you want to control it, or do you want it to control you?"

A slight stiffening rippled through the benches. Caleb's jaw tightened, and someone exhaled sharply through his nose.

Natalie continued, her hands moving deliberately to distribute sealed crisis packets across the benches. The rustle of paper was sharp in the thick air. "Don't think this makes you a prisoner. This is your shield—your blueprint for what we say, how we say it, and when."

A player's sleeve brushed against the cold floor as he shifted restlessly, his eyes scanning the detailed rules reprinted inside each packet. Another player sneered, but it faded quickly as Natalie's steady gaze swept the room, demanding attention without raising her voice.

The faint tick of a clock echoed off the concrete walls.

Time dripped in this crucible of raw, half-baked resolutions.

Caleb pocketed his phone and clutched the packet, his lips pressed into a hard line. Eli's arms unfurled slowly, his palms resting on his knees, but tension clung to him like a second skin. Each breath in the room tasted metallic—sharp with sweat, grit, and unspoken challenge.

Natalie lifted her head, the faintest crease between her brows softening slightly.

"Questions?"

Her voice opened space for confrontation. No one moved. The storm simmered beneath a fragile surface.

"Just make sure we're not losing the playbook for the season in the shuffle," Caleb called out quietly—careful, honest.

"We'll keep the playbook," Natalie replied without missing a beat. "And we'll build the plays that matter most."

A few chuckles broke the stoic silence. The room shifted. Faint crescendos of acceptance wove quietly through the resistance.

As the last packet landed on a bench near the door, uncertain compliance threaded through the locker room. Players exchanged looks—some resigned, some still daring to question.

Natalie folded her arms lightly, her eyes sweeping over the squad. She knew the real test hadn't begun.

Not yet.

The faint adrenaline hung in the air. The whispered doubts beneath it spoke louder than any promise.

She had laid out the rules.

Now, all eyes would watch how they held.

The heavy locker room door creaked open. Brick Turner stepped inside, a towel draped across his broad shoulders like a cape of defiance.

The chatter died mid-sentence. Heads snapped up. A dozen pairs of eyes narrowed, measuring him the way predators size up rival territory.

Natalie stood at the front, packets in hand—the calm eye in the brewing storm. Brick's gaze locked onto her and held.

His voice cut through the silence, low and edged. "Babysitter and spin doctor, huh? I didn't know we hired a nanny to parade around the locker room."

The jeer ripples outward. Players shift, their shoulders tensing.

He pushes forward, that sardonic grin pulling at the corner of his mouth. His scarred jaw is set, muscles coiled beneath his skin—a tempest barely contained. "Hope you packed a helmet, Brooks. Damage control is a contact sport—and I'm the first hit."

The room holds its breath.

Natalie doesn't blink. Her voice slides out, calm and steady—an unyielding line drawn in the turf. "I'm not here for a fight, Logan. I'm here to keep you all on the field. That means playing by the rules—both on and off it."

Their eyes meet. Fire against ice. Neither wavers.

From the sidelines, Eli's smirk creeps forward, tinged with sarcasm. He leans into the moment like a loyal shadow. "Sure, Brick, show them how sweet damage control tastes. Maybe she'll spin gold out of this mess—if we're lucky."

Caleb's fingers tighten around his phone. A shadow creases his brow as his eyes dart between Natalie and Brick. Doubt flickers there—a nerve stirring beneath his calm exterior.

Brick cranes a weary glance toward Coach Hale, who stands like a sentinel across the room. Arms crossed, imperious yet watchful. The old man knows exactly what Brick is doing; he has seen it a hundred times before—the defiance wrapped in a thin coat of respect. A slow, deliberate eye-roll escapes him. *Here we go again.*

But he refuses to shrink back. His feet remain planted. His voice never softens. His body stays taut like coiled steel wire.

The locker room hums with electricity—defiance and duty locked in silent collision. Sweat mingles with the faint antiseptic tang of the benches. Cleats echo distantly against the tile, a heartbeat beneath the raw nerves and quiet menace. Brick Turner holds the floor, unyielding. The storm gathers force, no closer to breaking than before.

Coach Marcus Hale's footsteps echoed off the concrete and tile as he stepped from the shadowed back of the locker room. The air tightened. The unnecessary noise folded into a hush so tense it felt like a held breath.

His voice unspooled, low and deliberate. Each word landed heavily: "This is the last chance for some of you—you know who you are."

The rumble settled beneath the weight of those words, hanging like a noose just out of sight.

He waited. The silence stretched. Then he pressed on without raising his tone. "We're not here to play games with your futures. One slip. One more reckless move." He paused. "And it's not just your career that's on the line; it's everything around it: families, reputation, livelihoods."

Coach knew these weren't just careers burning away—these men carried the hopes of their families, with entire neighborhoods counting on this moment.

Steel glinted in his eyes as he scanned the players. Some looked away, while others squared their shoulders like soldiers bracing for orders.

The murmurs that had threaded through moments before vanished, replaced by a brittle quiet. Coach Hale's presence filled the room—his controlled intensity hollowed out dissent before it could form. "You don't have to like it. Hell, you might hate it." His voice remained firm but fair. "But this is how we save this season."

He nodded once toward Natalie, steady and unyielding at the front. "And that starts with listening to the woman who's been put here to clean this up. All public statements—every. single. one.—goes through her." His gaze sharpened. "Because it's a damn mess out there, and if you think you can outrun it on your own, you're wrong."

The line of players shifted. Some clenched their fists against their thighs, while others crossed their arms tighter across broad chests. Caleb's side-eye flickered between Brick and Natalie, skepticism etched on his face like the clock ticking toward game time. Eli remained still and stoic, his lips pressed into a thin line. His folded arms became a fortress against the rising pressure.

Brick's jaw clenched tightly. Veins stood out like taut cables beneath his skin. His gaze flared—smoldering embers barely contained—as his eyes rolled with a sharp edge of contempt. But no words escaped. He sized up Coach Hale. The coach's authority pressed against his defiance, and the silence swelled with unspoken challenges.

Coach Hale let the moment stretch without breaking eye contact. Then he folded his arms across his chest. Around him, the energy shifted—a reluctant surrender to the reality of the stakes.

The locker room breathed tension—a dank mix of leather, sweat, and liniment that was heavy and almost suffocating in the cramped space. The metallic sting of impending discipline hung in the air like dust.

A player's foot tapped against the scuffed floor. Another exhaled sharply, shaking out simmering frustration. The rattle of tape and the faint clinks of water bottles punctuated the stillness as players began to absorb the gravity beyond their usual game-day worries.

A quiet ripple passed through the room—from the end of the benches to lockers lined like sentries—signaling the slow diffusion of flaring tempers. Coach Hale's steady gaze provided an anchor, drawing the frayed threads of focus back into order.

From somewhere near the back, a low murmur flickered. Tentative shifts in posture. No rebellion. Even Brick's shoulders twitched. A single, grudging nod folded some semblance of acceptance into the tight coil of his stance.

Coach Hale stepped back a pace. His voice dropped another notch so that only those closest could hear—an intimate warning wrapped in the authority of years. "For some, this is the crossroads. You can fight the system. Punch holes in the wall. But some walls will break you if you aren't careful."

His words lingered. The weight of consequence pressed down like the humid air before a storm. The locker room waited, caught in a fragile balance between defiance and discipline.

Eventually, the coach stepped aside, giving a silent command for movement. Slowly, like soldiers ordered to their posts, the players began to shift. Their scattered murmurs dimmed into practical compliance.

Natalie caught the glances. The guarded expressions tightened just a degree less, sensing the moment's shift from confrontation to reluctant truce.

Brick pulled his towel tighter around his neck, making adjustments slow and deliberate. His glare, still pointed toward Natalie, didn't waver as he steeled himself for the battles ahead—not just on the field, but in every negotiation and every confrontation this season promised.

The locker room thrummed with the sharp scrape of benches and worn leather as players rose. The collective tension folded quietly into a shared understanding: the remaining time to prove themselves was perilously thin.

Coach Hale's final nod closed the moment like a judge's gavel. Words unspoken—but heard loud and clear—pressed on every shoulder in the room.

Without a sound, the players turned and began to disperse, stepping toward showers, lockers, and the uncertain road ahead. The stakes smoldered in the air like a half-quenched fire. Consequences settled firmly like dust on cleats. Unavoidable. Real.

The last crisis protocol packets slipped through Natalie's fingers, passed methodically to the waiting staff. Tension rippled through the locker room—quiet, contained, like a kettle just beginning to hiss. Mutters slipped through clenched jaws, rough and cautious, like suppressed growls echoing off metal lockers slick with sweat and exhaustion.

"Outsiders never get it," Caleb said, shoulders hunched as he laced his cleats with deliberate, measured movements. His gaze flicked sideways toward Natalie—sharp and skeptical.

Eli folded his arms, jaw clenched. "Yeah. Like these rules fix what's actually broken."

DeShawn leaned against the metal locker, dark eyes scanning the wrinkled faces of the packets in his hand. "Discipline's a joke when it doesn't come from inside. We aren't puppets."

The air thickened with their whispered frustrations—an electric pulse beneath the steady fluorescent hum. Sweat hung heavy, a damp proof of hours spent in battle, layered over leather and mesh. Fluorescent lights cast sharp lines across bruised skin and turbulent expressions.

Caleb bumped Eli's shoulder, feeling reluctant yet curious. "Do you think she's really going to last through Brick's storm?"

Eli snorted, rolling his eyes. "About as likely as hell freezing over. That guy's all lightning... and thunder." He let out a rueful chuckle.

DeShawn shook his head slowly, a corner of his mouth tugging into a smirk. "A storm is one thing. It's the wreckage afterward that has me worried."

Natalie stood a few steps away, listening carefully—not interrupting, but memorizing every twitch and every glance. Her boots made soft scuffs against the polished concrete as the last players vanished toward the showers and lockers, dissolving into the maze of the team's sanctuary and battlefield. Footfalls and low grumbles faded, swallowed by the cavernous room.

Coach Marcus Hale remained—a solid anchor amid the drifting chaos. He stepped beside Natalie, his presence deliberate and grounded. Behind that calm exterior, something deeper stirred: the weight of protecting his players while maintaining order, the impossible balance between loyalty and accountability. He had worked too long with this team to let them fracture now.

His voice came low but firm. "We can't let this fester."

His eyes scanned the scattered debris of packets and smoldering resentment.

"Immediate media briefing tomorrow. Full transparency, controlled. We set the story before someone else writes it for us."

Natalie nodded, matching his steel. "I've drafted a timeline for the next seventy-two hours. Close monitoring of Brick and key players. We tighten the narrative here, then ripple outward."

Marcus folded his arms, his brows knitting in thought. "Good. Contain the leaks. The phones collected are just the start."

A pause hung between them, the weight of the challenge settling in.

"We're a team, all of us," Marcus said, gesturing broadly to the locker room. "This is ours to fix."

Her lips pressed into a firm line. "I'll watch the fractures closely. United front."

One shadow remained beside the lockers.

Brick Turner moved with slow, deliberate steps. His hands tugged at the waistband of his sweatpants, the fabric bunched where his fingers clenched tightly. His gaze swept the room—cold, precise—and latched onto Natalie with the force of a snare. His broad shoulders tensed, muscles coiled beneath bruised skin.

As he pulled on his jacket, his voice dropped, rough as gravel on pavement. "Good luck, Brooks. You'll need more than discipline to clean up this mess."

Natalie's shoulders didn't flinch. Her eyes met his—steady, unmoved by the simmering storm he wore like armor.

Brick didn't wait for a response. The scrape of his cleats echoed sharply against the tile as he turned away, swallowed by the narrowing corridor beyond the locker room.

The door sealed the tension behind him.

Natalie retrieved her phone with a practiced swipe, her fingers dancing over the screen. Her voice came low and deliberate.

"First impressions: significant resistance from core players. Caleb, Eli, and DeShawn each show their own brand of skepticism. Brick's volatility simmers just beneath the surface, ready to strike."

She paused, her breath steady despite the pulse pounding in her veins.

"Coach Hale's support is critical, but the battle lines are set. Immediate focus: control the narrative. Stop the leaks."

The memo sealed with a soft click, echoing through the empty locker room. She tucked her phone into her jacket pocket and straightened her spine, drawing in the cool air that carried hints of aged leather, antiseptic, and raw determination.

Natalie stepped forward, her boots clicking sharply against the tile as she exited the locker room. The corridor stretched ahead—a gauntlet of shadows and flickering lights. The stadium beyond waited, immense and unyielding.

Her jaw tightened, her eyes clear.

The path was set. The fight had just begun.

The Problem Player

T he sky is still bruised with the dark purple of early dawn as Natalie pulls into the stadium lot. The engine of her rental car hums beneath swelling floodlights that slice through the mist like searchlights. She cuts the ignition.

The clipboard is cool in her hand—steel-edged and purposeful. She straightens her navy blazer with practiced efficiency. Around her, the echo of shouting breaks against a wall of press vans, their satellite dishes perched like alien appendages, serving as a visual reminder of the media machinery that feeds on scandal and volatility.

Before she can fully inhale the damp morning air, scented with cut grass and diesel fumes, voices reach her. Sharp. Invasive. Relentless.

"What's the team doing about Brick's behavior?" a reporter shouts.

"Any comment on the risk of suspension?"

"Is Turner really out of control?"

The cameras flash like strobe lights. They swarm around her, hungry.

Natalie steps out. Her heels click on the cracked pavement. The sharpness of her stride cuts through the cacophony as she pivots the clipboard before her like a shield. Heat presses against her back—eyes, lenses, questions without mercy. She sidesteps rolling wire cages of equipment, her jaw set and her breathing controlled. A clammy breeze stirs a strand of hair across her temple, but she doesn't brush it away.

Her heartbeat echoes in the hollow of the stadium: slow, deliberate—a drum in a pit of tension.

A vibrating buzz tugs at her pocket. She pulls out her phone. Unread emails from league officials glow on the screen, each one a coded demand, a warning wrapped in corporate language. One message blinks with cold brevity: "Good luck. You'll need it."

Her teeth nearly grind together. She swallows hard, muscles taut beneath her skin, and stows the device away. The faint crispness of the morning air mingles with the subtle bitterness of anxiety. The stadium is waking to a new reality—one she has been summoned to manage.

The front gates yawn open, cavernous, echoing with the ghosts of games past.

Her footsteps reverberate down tiled corridors. Stiff echoes bounce between sterile walls clad in the sharp scent of disinfectant and polished metal. Rookie players drift nearby, their hushed whispers curling like smoke. Heads tilt her way; eyes weigh her—a silent code of curiosity mixed with wary judgment.

She catalogs the murmurs beneath her breath. National headlines spin like dark pinwheels in her mind: "Turner's Temper Flare," "PR Crisis Deepens," "Fractured Team Image." The ticking clock of media scrutiny pulses under her skin, relentless and unforgiving.

She knows what most of them don't—that Brick's volatility is a shield, a way of pushing back against the weight of expectations and the suffocation of being America's golden boy with a fracturing seam.

But empathy won't fix this situation; professionalism will. Distance will. That's what she's here for, even if it means compartmentalizing the human beneath the liability.

A young staffer passes, nodding briefly. His gaze flickers like a nervous signal flare. She senses the careful tightrope she must walk—fragile alliances and unspoken rules balanced on either side.

Finally, she arrives at the heavy oak door of the administration office. Its surface is cool and unyielding beneath her fingertips. She pauses, taking a slow breath that fills her lungs. The dull ache of weariness settles like sediment in her bones. The weight of the day crystallizes in that still moment—every fractured headline and every whispered doubt coalescing into a singular challenge.

A voice cuts through the gathering tension—sharp and low.

"You ready to clean up the mess he's made?"

Natalie doesn't turn immediately.

"I didn't come here to play babysitter; I came to fix a liability."

The reply comes quickly, taut with restrained frustration.

"Believe me, you're walking into the eye of a storm. Brick's been more trouble than any of us cares to admit."

Natalie finally meets the speaker's eyes—a familiar figure in this fractured arena. Her voice is clipped and steady.

"I don't have time for trouble. I clean up messes."

She squares her shoulders and turns the handle. The door swings open, and the hard click of the latch echoes like the first beat of a battle drum.

Natalie spots Nina Alvarez outside the admin office. Early light paints the sprawling stadium behind her in shades of amber and gray.

Nina's tired eyes flicker to life. Her lips press into a steady line as she steps closer, her hand settling lightly on Natalie's arm like an unspoken promise.

"Brace yourself," Nina murmurs, her thumb brushing reassuringly across Natalie's arm. "A storm's coming, but you aren't standing solo."

The words land like ballast. Natalie feels the quiet strength radiating from the athletic administrator's stance. Around them, the crisp morning air carries the scent of fresh-cut grass and the lingering tang of locker room sweat. Somewhere down the corridor, footsteps echo. A locker door slams in the distance.

Natalie's jaw tightens. She swallows hard, gripping her clipboard like an anchor. Her breath clouds in the cold.

"Brick's routines are rigid." Nina glances around, checking for invisible watchers. "Weight room mornings—six to seven, like clockwork. He's laser-focused then. His temper spikes right after, though, especially if someone interrupts his flow."

Natalie's pencil moved across the paper. Each word stitched together an image: a man built of discipline and defiance, with cracks barely visible beneath that unyielding shell. She was constructing a map of his moods, his triggers, and his breaking points.

"During warm-ups, he's with DeShawn and Caleb. But watch how he keeps his distance from Jaxon." Nina's voice dropped. "Steady. Sure. But there's an edge there."

"Grudges?" Natalie's voice barely broke the quiet. "What sets him off?"

"Loss of control. Disrespect. Being surprised—those make him snap like lightning." Nina's smile was faint, touched with caution. "Once you're in his circle, he's loyal as hell. But that loyalty flips fast when he feels cornered."

She pressed her phone into Natalie's hand. "I texted you a list of players to watch. Keep today low-key. We don't need headlines about the PR manager stirring the pot."

The weight of it settled in Natalie's palm—the glowing screen a tangible whisper of the storm brewing beneath the surface. Her fingers hesitated for a fraction of a second before sliding the device into her blazer pocket. This wasn't just reconnaissance. One wrong move, one careless word, and Brick's fragile reputation—and her credibility—could shatter. The media was already circling, waiting for any slip.

"Thanks, Nina. More than you know," Natalie said, her voice steady despite the pressure building behind her ribs.

Nina squeezed her arm once more. "It's a marathon, not a sprint. You'll find your footing."

The two women exchanged a glance heavy with understanding—a fleeting alliance forged in the early hours before chaos unfolded. Nina stepped back, the clack of her sneakers against the tiled floor punctuating the moment.

Natalie drew a steady breath. The sharp tang of paper and leather mingled with the crisp morning air. Her fingers tapped the phone in her blazer pocket once, twice. Then she stilled them.

Ahead, the corridor stretched out, humming quietly. Somewhere beyond, the stadium stirred to life.

She adjusted her blazer at the waist, tilted her chin up, and pushed open the door to the main facility. Filtered light flooded the threshold, chasing shadows into corners. She stepped inside.

Players moved with purpose. Staff wove between schedules and strategy. The charged energy of anticipation folded tight. Beneath the surface, a network of alliances and tensions pulsed—unseen but potent.

Natalie gripped her clipboard, one quiet ally in a tempest of fury and expectation. She walked forward, Nina's text a quiet beacon in her pocket.

One day. One careful conversation with Brick. One chance to understand what was unraveling before the whole thing came apart.

She disappeared into the controlled chaos of the facility, ready to listen.

The weight room buzzes with a steady clatter—iron plates striking iron, a metallic percussion underscored by heavy breaths and scattered shouts. Chalk and sweat hang thick in the humid air, warping the morning light that slants through high windows. The rhythmic thud of weights hitting the floor reverberates like a heartbeat.

Natalie stepped inside. The echo swallowed the scrape of her shoes on the rubber mats.

Her eyes scanned the room until they settled on a towering figure hunched over a barbell: Logan "Brick" Turner at the deadlift station, lips pressed tight, earbuds sealing him inside a private world. Even from across the room, she recognized his reputation—a man both feared and respected, his volatile nature a constant voltage running beneath the team's surface.

His workout shirt darkened with sweat. Muscles bunched. Veins like ropes on his forearms flexed as he hoisted the punishing weight.

She waited for a break in his set, a pause sharp enough to carve space between the grind of his breath. The barbell settled back onto the rack with a satisfying clang.

Her hand twitched, briefly clutching the clipboard as if it could steady her racing thoughts. She squared her shoulders and stepped forward, smoothing a crease in her blazer.

"Logan Turner," she began, her voice steady but clear above the ambient noise. "I'm Natalie Brooks, the new PR manager. I'll be shadowing you today."

His eyebrows drew together. A storm darkened his eyes. He snorted—a short, dismissive grunt—and pivoted on his heel so that his back faced her. No greeting. No invitation. Yet as he reloaded his grip, he made no move to shoo her away.

The room shifted. Brick's presence cut through the chatter like an iron beam through smoke—cold, unyielding, and impossible to ignore.

His gaze snapped to DeShawn Price across the room. DeShawn leaned on the leg press, a casual grin twisting his lips. Natalie recognized the exchange immediately—a rivalry fraught with respect, the kind that could trigger Brick's volatile side. It was exactly the type of moment she needed to catalog, a litmus test of his mood and control.

"You're moving like you don't want the ball next game. Quit loafing," Brick called out.

DeShawn fired back, playful but edged. "Says the guy who's still sulking about last week's whistle."

The exchange crackled. Neither man ceded ground. Natalie noted the quick flicks of their glances, the terse humor masking simmering rivalries beneath half-smiles and clenched jaws.

Brick cut a commanding figure elsewhere in the room, barking terse instructions at Caleb Monroe, who nodded with a mix of respect and caution. The words were clipped—almost grating. Yet Caleb didn't flinch; he licked his lips, fingers tightening on the dumbbell as he moved to the next rep.

Jaxon Reyes steered clear, his posture relaxed but distant, eyes darting briefly toward Brick before retreating to his phone. Brick acknowledged him with a curt nod but kept his distance, a firewall of unspoken tension hanging heavily between them.

Natalie scribbled swiftly, cataloging every nuance—the way teammates hesitated or leaned in, the subtle shifts in weight, the buried resentments lurking beneath half-smiles and clenched jaws. The hierarchy hummed beneath the surface, revealed through these endless micro-dances.

She stepped closer to the squat rack, where a line of players rotated through sets. The low murmur of encouragement or challenge echoed off the walls—a mix of brotherhood and battlefield. Some avoided Brick's space as if stepping into shadow, while others nudged near, testing boundaries.

At one bench, Caleb caught Brick's glare after a sloppy move and straightened instantly, shoulders rigid. DeShawn lobbed a dry remark about focus, and Brick's eyes narrowed, lips tightening as he surveyed the room like a sentinel guarding fragile peace.

The grating scrape of a weight plate sliding onto a bar broke through the background hum. Brick's breath came in measured huffs, his jaw clenched, and his fingers were white where they gripped the iron.

Natalie's pen paused, then resumed—notes filling pages with clinical precision: body language, tone shifts, triggers. Each detail was a thread in the tangled web.

"You mind if the lady shadows the legend?" a voice muttered nearby.

DeShawn chuckled low, his eyes glinting under furrowed brows. "Brick don't care who's watching. She can learn something."

Brick's reply was rough. "Don't get in my way."

Natalie caught the exchange without breaking stride.

She moved closer, observing Brick's methodical routine—the controlled aggression in every rep, the quick surveys of the room, and the silent messages sent and received through half-glances and brief nods.

Between sets, his shoulders tensed at a whispered comment from a rookie approaching too fast. The swift flicker of menace. His quiet warning: *Back off*.

Yet just minutes earlier, he had shared a rare half-smile with DeShawn, a private jab that cracked something in his rigid facade.

At the far end, Jaxon's eyes flicked toward Brick again, lingering longer this time: shadowed, uncertain. There was no warmth—yet something like acceptance, grudging but present.

Natalie closed her notebook, the pages thick with observations but lacking neat conclusions. The air vibrated with unspoken rules and loyalties, carved not in words but in endless micro-interactions.

She exhaled, pressing her lips into a thin line. Keeping a low profile wouldn't be easy, but proximity was the only way forward.

She stepped silently to the edge of Brick's circle and folded her arms loosely, sinking into the rhythm of the room, determined to learn the language of tension and trust beneath the clang of plates.

Natalie trailed the swarm of players into the cafeteria. Trays clattered, and hungry voices hummed low, filling the cavernous room with the percussion of morning appetite.

The scent hit her first—burnt toast and bitter coffee, thick and suffocating, mingling with the sharp chemical bite of cleaning products. It was the early morning rush, the smell of controlled chaos.

Brick moved through the crowd with deliberate purpose, his shoulders parting teammates like water. Without a word, he cleared a narrow spot at a crowded table, shoving the bench aside. He pulled Natalie down beside him before she could settle elsewhere. The chair scraped against the floor—a sound that seemed to cut through every conversation at once.

All eyes flicked toward her.

Some were curious; others were wary. The room seemed to lean in, the hum thickening around her like a held breath. Natalie had heard the whispers before she arrived—Brick Turner's latest target, the corporate suit come to catalog their sins. She straightened her spine, gripping the clipboard like a shield.

"Well, well." Brick's voice cracked across the table, loud and rough with sarcasm. "Look who's sniffing around again. Corporate snooping harder than ever, huh?" His grin was crooked, filled with dark amusement and the promise of trouble. The table rippled with quiet chuckles.

DeShawn leaned back in his chair nearby, flicking a finger toward the coffee machine. His smile was teasing and sharp-edged. "Speaking of snooping—you remember what Brick did to that coffee maker last week? It still smells like a burnt apology."

Brick snorted, his chest heaving. "That damn machine had it coming. It brewed water hotter than the refs' tempers on game day." His gaze slid to Natalie, sizing her up as if he were calculating exactly how many barbs she could take.

Natalie's lips twitched, but she didn't let them break into a smile.

"If coffee is the greatest casualty today," she said, her voice cutting clean through the banter, "I'd say the team's in better shape than last Thursday's press coverage."

She didn't back down. She didn't look away.

Brick's expression shifted—not exactly softening, but something in it changed. The hostility lost its sharp edge.

Troy Maddox slipped into the crowd, his tall frame cutting through the congregation like a shadow. His fingers flew across his phone screen as he muttered something indistinct about "family stuff." His eyes were shadowed with concern. Distraction.

Emma Caldwell watched him from across the room, her brows knitting tightly. She caught Natalie's eye and offered a small, knowing frown. No words passed between them; none were needed. The signal landed deep—something was wrong with Troy, and Emma was worried.

Natalie filed that away.

"You bring the noise, Brooks," Brick said, leaning back. "I'll give you that."

DeShawn shot a wink in her direction, grinning as if she had just been invited into some private game. She barely cared to play.

Natalie lifted her coffee to her lips. The bitter tang of black coffee coated her tongue, grounding her against the tide of eyes still flickering her way. She sipped slowly, letting the caffeine brace her nerves. Her gaze moved from player to player—mapping alliances and charting the silent fractures beneath casual words. Who leaned in. Who pulled back. The rhythms of power disguised as banter.

Brick jerked his chin toward a teammate across the room. "Do you see them all circling? Like sharks smelling blood. The team's more like a pack of hyenas half the time."

Natalie's eye twitched. She kept her voice level. "Hyenas are loyal to the pride. It sounds like your pack just needs leadership."

"Leadership?" Brick's grin was as sharp as wire. "That's rich coming from the woman with the clipboard." He flicked an irritated glance at her notes.

"I keep score," she said, meeting his gaze unblinkingly. "It's my job to know the numbers you'd rather hide. And Brick? That includes your messes and your merits."

A low chuckle rumbled from DeShawn nearby.

"Messes and merits," DeShawn said, shaking his head. "Sounds like a memoir title."

Brick settled back, his eyes narrowing. He was less hostile now, almost considering.

Troy's exit carved a brief silence in the cafeteria. His retreating figure was swallowed by the chatter and clang. Natalie watched as Emma's eyes lingered on his disappearing back, worry blooming like a shadow behind her composed face. She would have to check in with her later. Emma seemed to know more than she was saying—about Troy, about the team's internal fractures, about what might be splintering beneath the surface.

The thought that Troy's distraction could derail the entire operation flickered through Natalie's mind. She would need to watch him more closely.

The banter swelled again around the table, a patchwork of teasing and testing. Players circled around Brick's volatile core, each one calculating their position and their risk.

Natalie closed her mental file with a deliberate snap. Every smirk, every glance, and every jab was cataloged as data for the battles ahead.

She finished her coffee, the warmth slipping from the ceramic cup between her fingers before she set it down gently. The liquid still steamed faintly at the bottom. She watched Brick's profile for a moment—muscles tensing beneath his shirt, jaw clenched against some unseen frustration.

She stood, gathering her notes and her resolve.

Ready to shadow the storm that was Brick Turner for the rest of the morning.

The afternoon sunlight filtered unevenly through the gaps in the towering stadium stands, casting long shadows over the emerald-green turf. The sharp tang of fresh-cut grass hung heavy, mixed with the metallic clang of weights settling on the racks. Somewhere, a whistle pierced the air, undercut by low grunts and the scrape of cleats against turf worn smooth by relentless drills.

Natalie fell into step a few paces behind Brick, clipboard tucked firmly under one arm. Her ears tuned to the rhythm of the team's drills—the pivot of bodies, the collision of muscle and will. The air itself seemed charged. Players coiled and released in orchestrated bursts, each movement a calculated strike.

Brick's broad frame cut through the chaos like a breaker. His shoulders were tight, and his eyes narrowed with unmistakable intensity beneath a furrowed brow. When a rookie stumbled, fumbling the snap during a rapid play drill, Brick's reaction snapped too—a sharp bark of rebuke slicing through the air.

"That's on you! Focus like your career depends on it, because for some of you, it damn well does!" His voice cracked with a raw edge, his words as hard as stones thrown into still water.

The rookie shrank back, his shoulders tightening. Murmurs rippled around them, and the tension thickened—almost tangible enough to taste.

From the sideline, sharp footsteps cut through the mounting storm. Coach Marcus Hale emerged, his presence immediately shifting the atmosphere. His voice rose, calm but commanding, halting Brick's protest before it could erupt.

"Turner, cut it out. Now." The authority in his tone brooked no argument. "Protocols exist for a reason. Public dressing-downs are separate from practice. We keep it professional."

Brick's jaw clenched, and his nostrils flared. The simmering fury didn't fade; it just held back, locked under Hale's steady gaze.

The coach's eyes swept the group—measured and unyielding. Even the rookie straightened, relieved by the intervention.

Natalie inched closer, her clipboard balanced between steady hands. Brick's gaze drifted toward her more often now—furtive, simmering with grudges neither spoken nor masked. She caught the slight clench at the corner of his mouth. His fists curled briefly, fingers flexing against the fabric of his sleeves. His shoulders squared, then dipped just a fraction—a silent battle being waged beneath the surface.

Around them, teammates exchanged glances weighted with familiar hierarchies. DeShawn leaned slightly away, his fingers drumming rhythmically on his thigh. Caleb watched with careful neutrality. Jaxon frowned briefly before focusing on the playbook in his hands. The air folded and refolded with syncopated tension—a battlefield of wills as much as of bodies.

"Keep it moving!" Coach Hale called, breaking the silence.

The team scattered back into formation. Whistles and shouted calls rose again like a storm reshaping its course.

When the drills wound down, players retreated beneath stretched canopies. The sharp scent of cooling sweat mingled with the faint bitterness of spilled energy drinks. Low conversations hummed, jerseys rustled, and the occasional cough crackled in the dry air.

Natalie pulled out her notes, her eyes scanning her tidy lists and scribbled observations: verbal arcs, body language, and subtle frictions. Her fingers traced the names—Brick, DeShawn, Caleb—pausing on key moments: the glare Brick threw when her clipboard appeared, the flash of frustration when the rookies hesitated, and the guarded way he locked eyes on her more than once.

She updated her schedule in the margins, rehearsing the firm but measured tone she would need for the media training session—an intervention he was already bristling against. She knew what this meant: managing optics was one thing; holding fire in her hands without getting burned was another entirely.

A hand clapped down on her shoulder. Solid. Brief. She looked up to meet Coach Hale's gaze, steady and approving.

"Natalie, you've got this." His voice was low, edged with challenge but filled with trust. "Keep steady. Brick's a fighter. You'll see that."

"Understood," she replied, her voice controlled, even as adrenaline pinned her lungs tight. She met his eyes. A silent accord passed between them—this wasn't just about managing optics.

Brick shifted nearby, his eyes flickering in her direction again. Guarded. Unyielding. The weight of unspoken battles lingered between them.

Later, as the team reassembled for a strategy meeting, Brick's restless energy hummed beneath the surface, coiling and ready. Natalie's presence was a sharp edge against his storm, her clipboard a silent witness to the uneasy truce they shared in this charged space.

The promise of a media session hung unspoken. It was the next move in a game where trust was earned in whispered seconds and iron discipline.

"Your tape's coming," she murmured under her breath. Not a threat, but a warning.

His jaw twitched. He said nothing—only the tight-set line of his mouth and the flicker in his eyes that she knew well.

Challenge accepted.

The corridor thrummed with footsteps and distant locker room banter. Natalie cut through it all—her focus sharp and unwavering. She spotted Brick before he rounded the corner: a massive frame, his soaked practice jersey clinging to muscles still taut from drills. His brow furrowed the moment he caught sight of her clipboard.

"Brick."

He stopped short. His eyes were sharp, but impatience flickered through them like a warning light.

She stepped closer, her voice firm. "We're scheduling media training this week. You're a high-profile target after the last few incidents. The league is watching. The team's reputation is on the line."

His jaw tightened. The sharp click of his teeth was audible even over the echoing walls. "Media training? What, do you think I'm some kind of rookie? Babysitting doesn't suit me."

Natalie's gaze narrowed but remained unflinching. "It's not about what suits you. It's about controlling the narrative before it controls *you*."

Brick scoffed. He crossed his arms—his broad shoulders blocking the hallway like a fortress wall. "Sounds like another hoop to jump through."

Heavy footsteps fell behind them. Coach Hale slid alongside Natalie, his chest puffed out like a general on parade. He gave her a brief, approving nod. Then his eyes locked onto Brick with the no-nonsense seriousness that had turned many players around.

Brick's shoulders sagged, and the fight leaked away. "Fine. Whatever."

Natalie masked her relief with a tight nod and pulled out her phone. "I'll reserve the media room. You'll attend with two rookies—Caleb and DeShawn. We will record the session, review it, and improve."

Brick jerked a thumb toward the locker room, his voice rough. "Yeah, great. Lights, camera, babysitting. I can't wait to get in front of the cameras."

Natalie let the comment slide as they moved. The walk felt tight, and tension hummed in the air like static before a storm. Brick flung an irritated glance her way but said nothing more. The rookies trailed behind, their eyes wide, caught between curiosity and dread.

At the media room, Natalie flicked on the overhead lights. The sterile glare washed over the sleek space. She set up a camera on its tripod—its lens a cold, unblinking eye—and arranged cue cards with crisp, printed questions: "Tell us about yesterday's game." "How do you handle pressure?"

The faint scent of electronics and polished wood filled the room, mingling with the low hum of fluorescent lights and the ghost of stale coffee from earlier meetings. A distant keyboard clicked somewhere down the hall. Natalie ran a hand over the cue cards, anchoring herself. The quiet click of her pen broke the silence as Brick lumbered through the door.

His stare was dark—resistant.

She met his eyes, steady and unyielding despite the disdain simmering just beneath. Here, amid the hum of machinery and empty seats, the game changed. The fight wasn't on the field; it was a battle for control, for image, for redemption.

Brick loosened his jaw into a thin scowl but didn't argue. The roar of the stadium felt miles away. In this tight, practiced arena, players became vulnerable actors.

"You're looking at this all wrong," he muttered, slumping into a chair near the camera. "This is just corporate babysitting."

"You're not the only one on the line." Natalie's voice was smooth but edged. "One slip, and the headline writes itself. You want to control that? Then this is the only way."

He sneered, but the simmering defiance in his gaze faltered beneath the steady weight of her conviction.

Coach Hale's nod echoed in her mind—a silent promise that she wasn't alone. He had made it clear: Natalie had his backing, and Brick knew it. That support shaped everything here. It shaped Brick's grudging compliance and her confidence.

The bitterness curled on Brick's lips, but the grudging nod he offered as he settled signaled a small, hard-earned victory.

Natalie's fingers brushed the camera lens. A slight tightness gripped her chest as she prepared to turn the invisible spotlight onto them all. The session was about to begin, bringing with it the first real test of control, discipline, and the thin line between public spectacle and private truth.

The media room hummed with artificial light and stale air, a plastic sheen glossing the pale walls. Cameras perched on tripods, with wires spider-webbing across the low carpet. Natalie adjusted the clipboard under her arm, scanning the setup once more before looking up at the trio seated across from her. Logan "Brick" Turner slouched in the center chair, restless energy radiating from his broad shoulders. The two rookies glanced between Natalie and Brick, their nerves as thick as the scent of burnt coffee lingering in the small space.

Natalie cleared her throat, her voice even but firm. "Alright. We'll run through some interview questions." She paused. "Keep your answers clear and concise. Tone matters. This is how you build positive rapport." She flipped open her notes, her eyes steady on Brick.

His dark eyes flickered with amusement, and his shoulders shifted as he leaned back. "Discipline?" The word dripped with sarcasm. "Yeah, sure. Maybe if we had a coach who liked to throw a punch or two, things would get sorted out faster."

Natalie's jaw tightened as she pointed to the camera, the red recording light blinking steadily. "Remember, keep it professional. This isn't the arena."

One rookie shifted awkwardly. Brick snapped at the other, "Relax, rookie. We're just playing dress-up for the cameras." His lips curled into a mocking grin as he waved an exaggerated hand toward the screen. "News flash—press eats villains like me for breakfast." His gaze landed on Natalie, sharp and daring. "Think they'll love me or hate me today?"

Natalie's fingers tightened around her pen. "This isn't a game, Brick. Words don't just bounce off—not like they do on the field."

Brick chuckled, defiance sharp in the confined stillness. "Fine." He straightened, eyes narrowing and voice dropping to a theatrical growl. "Here's my official statement: 'If you don't like how the game's called, maybe next time I'll punch the ref. That'll teach 'em.'" He leaned back, smirking, the joke hanging heavy in the air—half menace, half challenge.

Natalie's breath hitched and steadied. Her fingers curled tighter around the clipboard, her knuckles paling. She stepped forward, gaze locked on Brick, forcing the calm she didn't feel. "That's not the message we want out there. It's irresponsible, and it's not funny."

From the corner, a young staffer leaned against the faded wall, phone poised casually in his hand. His bored expression betrayed an eagerness for distraction. Without announcement, he tilted the phone, capturing Brick's mimicry in crisp digital clarity. The glow flickered against his face as he pocketed the device, his eyes gleaming with the potential for chaos.

Brick paused at the door, dropping his bag with a thud. His smirk widened. "You know," he called back over his shoulder, "the world is going to love that clip."

Natalie stood frozen for a moment, her clipboard clenched so tightly that the edges bit into her palms. Her breath slowed, shifting from frustration to sharp clarity. The ripple had been cast. The calm they fought for? Shattered. Her mind raced—already drafting damage control—as Brick's words echoed like static in the sterile room.

By late afternoon, the air in the stadium had grown heavier. Sweat and turf dust mingled with something else—an invisible storm crackling across glowing screens everywhere. A staffer's phone buzzed relentlessly. A snippet of Brick's media training had surfaced on social media, his voice laced with sarcasm: "Maybe punch the ref next time." The clip spread like wildfire. Hashtags pulsed through Twitter—#GridironGaffe, #TurnerTrouble. Memes bloomed: pixelated versions of Brick's narrowed eyes and smirking lips. Instagram reels stitched together replays with the insult, the crowd's roar buried beneath digital fury. In today's game, a viral blunder was more dangerous than a fumble—instant, unrelenting, and impossible to outrun. Fear rippled through the fandom. Some scoffed at the joke, while others murmured their worries. Would Brick's explosive past finally choke this season's fragile hope?

Inside the compact conference room, sharp afternoon light fought against a creeping tension. Natalie's eyes flicked to her phone, and her brow tightened. Nina and Emma leaned in, their faces drawn but steady. Beyond the door, voices hummed with confusion and rising speculation.

"We've got a problem," Natalie murmured. She tapped her phone screen, confirming the clip's viral reach. Every second counted. "I'm taking Brick. We need to get ahead of this."

Nina's gaze flickered to Emma. "He won't just roll over. But if anyone can de-escalate, it's you."

Emma nodded, her lips pressed thin. "We need a tight narrative—something he'll let us craft."

There was no time for debate. Natalie rose and strode out, her heels echoing down the hallway with brisk intent.

She found Brick near the locker room entrance. His broad frame hunched forward, arms crossed—a fortress of defensive scowl. His dark eyes flicked up as she approached, sharp and unamused. With a clipboard tucked beneath one arm, his voice was calm but unforgiving.

"We need to talk. Now."

Brick's shoulder twitched in a half-shrug, and muscles rolled beneath the tight fabric of his shirt. "Let me guess—they're blowing a joke way out of proportion."

"Not just any joke," Natalie replied evenly. "People are as soft as a marshmallow these days." She paused, letting the silence settle. "That line crosses a line. It's blowing up online. You're a target."

He smirked, defiance sparking. "It's humor—sharp, yeah, but humor." His weight shifted, unconvinced. "I'm not apologizing for telling the truth about discipline."

Natalie held his gaze steadily, matching fire with ice. "It's not about shrugging off consequences. Words stick around, Brick. One dumb line, and they write your whole story for you."

His jaw tightened. The storm behind his eyes flickered—frustration, maybe even fear. He hated feeling so exposed, as if every misstep was a spotlight pinning him down.

"So what? You want me to put on a show for the cameras? Fake sincerity?"

"I want you to understand the fallout before it burns us. This isn't about putting on a show." She stepped closer. "It's about controlling the narrative before it controls you."

Brick's gaze dropped to the floor. His fingers tightened into small fists at his sides, knuckles whitening. A subtle tremor ran beneath the surface of his bravado.

"You're not just a player anymore," Natalie continued, her voice steady. "You're a story they'll tell one way or another. Let me help write it with you."

He grunted, his voice low and rough. "Don't think I'm buying in just yet."

Natalie didn't flinch. "You don't have to buy in."

She held his gaze. "Just ride the wave. Don't let it capsize you."

A charged silence stretched between them, heavy with unspoken truths. Then Brick's arms folded again, but with less edge. A reluctant nod passed between them—not exactly agreement, but a truce.

Natalie exhaled quietly, brushing past him without another word. The door clicked softly behind her, shutting out the heavy thrum of turmoil and defiance within.

Back in the empty hallway, she pulled out her phone. Her fingers tapped furiously as fragments of a plan crystallized. The clock ticked like a drumbeat in her ears—minutes stretched thin to smother a wildfire before it burned the whole season down. Her breath hitched suddenly, and a heavy tightness settled in her chest.

No time to hesitate. No room for mistakes.

The hum of distant voices, the clang of lockers, the sharp scent of leather and liniment—it all grounded her. Her jaw set once more, and her shoulders squared. She moved through the hallway with purpose, already composing the first line of Brick's redemption.

Fluorescent lights buzzed overhead. The cramped PR office felt claustrophobic, with walls plastered with framed headlines—some triumphant, others tarnished. Stale coffee lingered in the air, sharp with the bite of stress that nobody bothered to mask anymore.

Natalie didn't pause at the threshold. She moved toward the glossy table with purpose, her jaw set. Nina was already there, her warm eyes steady, fingers poised above her phone like a pianist before the opening chord. Emma slipped in beside them, each movement deliberate, calm but coiled—her fingers flexing as if ready to weave words into something solid enough to shield against the coming storm.

"We need a statement that flips this." Natalie's voice sliced through the thick silence—brief, steady, like a blade honing focus. "Brick's comment has to sound like what it is: a joke twisted out of context. We own the mess before it owns us."

Nina's fingers flew across her phone, pulling images with practiced efficiency. "Last month's kids' charity event. Best shots of Brick smiling and interacting—nothing like this 'loudmouth' image circulating." She exhaled, a faint smile crossing her lips. "I'll prep these for posting: timed, tagged, full engagement angle."

Emma tapped notes into her tablet, her brow furrowed. Her voice was softer than Natalie's, measured. "I'll reach out to the guys for short quotes—genuine ones about Brick's character, his work ethic, and the way he grounds the locker room." She glanced toward the door and then back. "I'm checking in with him myself first. Wellness before strategy—we can't spin if he cracks under the weight."

Natalie nodded, but her stomach twisted into knots. The viral clip swirling through social media was a wildfire, consuming context and fueling verdicts with each share. Her fingertips hovered over the keyboard, trembling slightly before pressing forward. The viral clip's impact rippled through the locker room in whispers and sidelong glances—players were uncertain whether to stand with Brick or distance themselves. That uncertainty was its own kind of damage.

She swallowed hard. "Timing is everything. Charity content goes live before the afternoon spike—followed immediately by the quotes.

We overlay positivity beneath the outrage. Squeeze the oxygen out of this thing."

The screens scattered across the table were splattered with tweets. Disparate voices swirled into a cacophony of amusement, fury, and mockery. Every ping jabbed at the tension like a countdown none of them could stop.

Nina's thumb hovered over the post button for the photo series. "Ready."

Natalie exhaled. "Do it."

Minutes stretched thin as they watched the numbers climb: likes, shares, and retweets ticking upward in real time. The dissonance was immediate—some applauded the charity work, while others doubled down on cruelty. But a tide had begun to shift, fragile and uncertain.

Emma's footsteps returned softly against the floor. Her brows knitted, lips pressed tight, but her eyes held steady—a quiet promise beneath the exhaustion. "Brick's bruised. Not just physically." She sank into the nearest chair. "He knows the clip is everywhere, but knowing we're fighting for him... it helped. He'll engage. Slowly. But he'll do it."

Natalie's jaw clenched. "That's all we can ask right now. Discipline over impulse. Control over the chaos screaming for attention."

Her fingers moved again, scheduling posts for teammate quotes—short bursts of sincerity. Jaxon's calm steadiness. DeShawn's laid-back loyalty. Each bite-sized message was another brick in the wall they were hastily building around a reputation teetering on the edge.

The phone notifications became a rhythmic drone, a reminder that the battle was far from won.

Yet, in the measured flurry of faces and words, a fragile order began to anchor the storm.

Natalie slumped against the cool edge of her desk. Hours pressed into her bones like a physical weight. Fear gnawed at her—the fear of failing Brick, of letting the team down when they needed her most. This job stretched her limits every single day, emotionally and mentally, in ways she would never admit aloud.

She flicked her eyes to the screen, watching positive content thread carefully through the noise.

"This won't fix it overnight." Her voice came out rough with exhaustion. "But every little win pushes the needle forward."

Nina folded her arms. Her gaze was sharp but steady. "It's a marathon, not a sprint. Brick's not just fighting the media—he's fighting himself right now. That's the harder battle."

"Yeah." Natalie drew a slow breath, letting it fill her lungs. "And so are we."

The locker room hummed with low voices and the scrape of cleats on tile as the team filed in, shedding sweat-soaked jerseys like armor after battle. DeShawn grinned wide, lobbed an elbow toward Brick, and shook his head with mock pity. "So, how long do you think Ms. Clipboard over there lasts? Five minutes? Maybe thirty tops before she crumbles under all this chaos?"

Laughter bubbles around the group—easy camaraderie mingled with skepticism. Nods and murmurs ripple beneath the ribbing, like an incoming tide. Brick catches the teasing but doesn't rise to defend himself—not yet. His arms fold across his chest, and his eyes scan the room with a shadowed edge. Natalie balances her clipboard on one arm, flips a pen between her fingers, and lets the moment wash over her. This is the pressure cooker she stepped into. If DeShawn's bet carries weight here, she's already got a mountain to climb.

Troy Maddox stands near the lockers, scrolling through his phone with careless ease. His voice cuts in, casual but holding an invisible weight. "I gotta jet soon. More family drama waiting on my side." He shrugs, flashing a half-smile that barely conceals the weariness tugging at his eyes.

"So, what's going on?" someone asks, curiosity pricking the air like static.

Troy waves the question off with a breath and pockets his phone. "You know how it is. Stuff that doesn't mess with your game but doesn't let you forget it's there."

Emma Caldwell watches Troy, her eyes narrowing slowly like storm clouds gathering. Her lips press into a thin line. That distant look in his gaze—she knows it too well. Whatever's pulling at him won't stay quiet for long, and it'll affect the team before he's ready to admit it. Her silence speaks louder than any question could.

Natalie's gaze flicks between players, scanning this shifting map of alliances and unspoken burdens. DeShawn masks sharp instincts behind laughing impulses, while Troy carries quiet storms behind distracted smiles. Emma watches like a lighthouse, steady and perceptive. And Nina—usually the quiet support—always holds a tether to sanity in the chaos.

A shift in position brings Nina Alvarez closer, her tone low and steady, meant only for Natalie's ears. "Brick's been through worse, you know. This isn't the first storm he's weathered."

The team knows how to ride these cycles with him. Years of volatility have taught them the rhythm—when to push, when to let him breathe, and when to remind him he isn't fighting alone. It is a language written in shared locker rooms and hard-won trust.

Natalie nods, her eyes thoughtful as she absorbs the undercurrent. Nina's voice carries more than reassurance; it holds the history no one else dares to voice aloud.

DeShawn zeroes back in, his tone teasing but affectionate. "Man, Brick's gone viral now. Think we should start hustling autographs before he thinks better of it?"

Brick's jaw clenches so tightly that the muscles twitch. His mouth dips into a shadowed frown that doesn't quite reach his eyes. He doesn't shoot back a retort but lets the ribbing wash over him like a cloudy tide—there's a sullen kind of acceptance in his posture, raw and honest. Natalie scribbles quickly, closing her notebook with a soft snap. She's not just managing a temper; she's navigating a web of loyalties, histories, and fragile egos tangled tightly beneath the locker room's fluorescent haze.

The air tastes thick with sweat and the faint metallic bite of liniment, mingling with the distant rumble of traffic beyond the stadium walls. It's a heady perfume of grit and endurance—the scent of lives spent in the relentless pursuit of a fragile dream.

"Look, Brick, you gotta admit, the 'punch the ref' line?" DeShawn elbows him with a grin. "Classic you. It could've been worse—like 'throw my helmet into the crowd.'"

Brick's eyes flicker with something close to humor. A ghost of a smile teases the corners of his mouth before retreating. "Yeah, 'cause that's exactly the kind of headline we need."

Nataly's breath catches in her throat for a second, then escapes in a quiet sigh. The weight presses deep but steady, rooting her resolve. This gig isn't for the faint of heart. Brick's battles won't be won with rules alone. Trust, patience, and a few key allies will be the currency of progress.

Nina sidles up beside her, her voice low but firm. "You're not alone in this. Emma's got an ear on the team, and I'm watching your back when you need it. It's a long game."

Natalie meets Nina's steady gaze, gratitude flickering beneath the surface. It's more than professional courtesy—it's a rare hand extended in this battlefield of temper and reputation.

The buzz of lockers slamming and distant shouts begins to fade as players drift toward the exits. The day's friction cools but never quite dissolves. Natalie shoulders her clipboard, determination settling like armor against the fatigue pressing into her bones.

Outside the cacophony of the locker room, the late afternoon light shifts toward dusk. Shadows stretch long against the concrete walls as Natalie steps through the door, her mind already calculating moves on a board most wouldn't see—alliances to nurture, tensions to tame, and the heart of a man who might just be worth the fight.

She's tired, yes, but she's far from done.

Sparks in the War Zone

Natalie leans forward at her desk, her eyes tracking the flickering images on her laptop screen. The latest social media clip of Brick Turner's outburst plays on loop, frame by frame, with every explosive moment dissected beneath the stark fluorescent light.

The hum of servers fills the PR office like a distant storm brewing, while low chatter drifts from adjoining rooms. On the desk beside her keyboard sits a thick stack of papers—a stapled disciplinary record worn at the edges and heavy with history. She taps her pen against a crisp legal pad where lists of timestamps crawl in neat, determined handwriting.

The clip freezes as Brick's fist slams onto the turf. His sneer twists his jaw—an instant that ignited a thousand fiery comments online. Natalie scrawls "00:37" beside a note: "Repeated aggression pattern." Two previous infractions flicker through her mind: the press release she fought tooth and nail over and the suspended game no one wants to revisit. She marks another timestamp, feeling the weight of the work pressing around her, concrete and uncompromising.

A sudden thrum of raised voices drifts upward through the open office door—a charged conversation from the locker room beneath. The words are muffled, but the rising edge of frustration is unmistakable. She flinches at the sharp, accusatory tone, then forces her jaw to relax and holds firm. Her fingers pause on the clipboard, and the paper rustles faintly beneath her grip.

Upright, she straightens her blazer, the fabric stiff around her shoulders. Her palm presses flat against the clipboard's cool surface. A tight knot clenches in her stomach, and her breath catches for a heartbeat. A flicker of cold resolve sparks behind her eyes—sharp and brittle, as if she is already bracing for the storm to come. It is time to face it.

The polished stadium corridor stretches ahead, glossy beneath the dying light of the setting sun filtering through high glass panes. Her steps echo—a measured rhythm against the hollow walls. Through the window, the sprawling practice field resembles a deep emerald canvas fading into shadow. A few players trudge toward the locker room, their bodies heavy with exhaustion, jerseys clinging damply to muscular backs.

Emma catches her gaze in the glass. A quick, subtle nod. An unspoken lifeline in this swirling chaos. Natalie returns the gesture with a faint smile, the tension in her chest rippling but slightly softened. They have weathered worse together—years of quiet battles far from the spotlight, standing firm when everyone else wavered. The nod carries all of it.

Approaching the locker room door, heat rises in waves. Stifling. Sharp. The tang of liniment and leather mingles with the mustiness of worn tile and damp towels. Natalie pauses, her hand reaching out.

Her fingers tighten on the cool steel doorframe, knuckles blanching as the voices behind it rise. Her breath deepens, catching the humid air in a slow, steady inhale—mingled with sweat, resolve, and the faint metallic hint of adrenaline.

Every second feels taut. The weight of expectation presses down like dusk settling deep into the stadium's bones. This moment is hers to command.

She steps inside.

The locker room's air vibrates with a mix of sweat, leather, and the sharp tang of eucalyptus from the distant showers. Metal lockers line the walls—scratched and scarred—and overhead fluorescents flicker sporadically, casting sharp shadows. Natalie steps through the door, her heels clicking softly against the cool tile. With her clipboard tucked firmly against her hip, she scans the room with swift precision.

There. Brick Turner, the center of the chaos. His broad frame is slumped over the bench, a soaked towel draped lazily across his shoulders like a cape. His grin is loud and brash, a storm waiting to break, surrounded by teammates trading jabs and laughter. The murmur of voices feels like an undercurrent ready to surge.

Natalie tightens her grip on the clipboard. Not now. Not again. Her heels echo, purposeful and steady, as she crosses the room without hesitation. Brick's sharp eyes catch hers.

"Clipboard management, huh? You writing fan mail?" His voice spills out, dripping with mockery, the grin widening—cocky, untouchable.

She doesn't blink or sway. With her feet planted firmly and her spine straight, she raises her voice so the cluster of players turns, curiosity flickering across their faces.

"Logan." Her tone clips the air with ice. "I'm here about the latest social media leak." She taps the clipboard, the sound crisp. "Time-stamp: 3:47. That moment when you slammed the quarterback after the whistle." Her eyes hold his, steady and unflinching. That play had detonated across every sports outlet by evening—commentators seizing on the unsportsmanlike conduct, the recklessness, and the question mark it placed over the team's discipline. One moment of aggression rippling outward, casting shadows over franchise credibility and corporate partnerships alike.

Laughter bubbles from a few corners, but it dies under the weight of her gaze. Brick's comrades fall silent, their glances flickering between Natalie and him.

"You've been here before, Logan. June 12th—after the game against Detroit—and then again last month during the charity event. Each time, you ignored the protocols we hammer into the team." She flips open a few printed pages, the rustle sharply clear in the quiet. "Your disciplinary record isn't just a series of mistakes; it's a pattern that puts the entire team's reputation—and your career—at risk."

A low murmur rises at the edges of the crowd, breaths held, tension thick enough to taste. The usual dirty locker-room jokes falter; the room shrinks, drawn in by her words.

"No one here is above the rules," Natalie continues, her voice cool but unwavering. "Especially not you."

Brick shifts under the spotlight, his eyes narrowing and lips twitching into a half-smile—not from amusement, but from challenge. The laughter that once peppered the air evaporates like mist, replaced by a charged hush as every player focuses on Natalie's precise, unyielding call to account.

The stark fluorescent light highlights beads of sweat on Brick's forehead, and the scar above his brow tightens as his jaw clenches. Around him, teammates' faces harden or flicker with uncertainty. Some avoid his gaze; others—like Jaxon—watch with quiet calculation.

Natalie's breath steadies, her heartbeat a measured drum beneath her calm exterior. She senses the storm gathering in the room, the fragile line between respect and rebellion thinning. Yet she holds the floor, unbowed, a command center of logic and resolve amid the chaos of bruised egos.

The clipboard slips into her hand like armor. Beneath the veneer of professionalism, exhaustion threads through her—the weariness of treading this same ground again, of watching brilliant talent sabotage itself through arrogance, and of being forced into the role of enforcer when what she craves is collaboration. But her face betrays none of it. Her eyes trace the faces before her, locking on Brick's once more.

"This isn't personal; it's about responsibility. You're not just playing for yourself; you're carrying everyone's career on that field. So yes, the social media gaffe—because no matter how good your game is, the last impression matters."

She lets the silence stretch, the weight of consequence settling over the room like a heavy fog.

Brick's smirk flickers but doesn't fade—a silent dare, a war cry without words. The rest of the players barely breathe, the room steeped in electric tension as all eyes settle on the woman who has just turned their locker room into a spotlight stage.

Brick pushes off the bench with a lazy grin curling the corner of his mouth, his towering frame unfolding as he steps forward. The towel hangs heavy around his neck, sweat-darkened and rough against the sharp lines of his jaw. His eyes lock on Natalie, slow and deliberate, as he closes the gap between them—almost close enough to touch, but never quite. The air thickens, charged like the quiet before a storm.

"You're always watchin', huh?" he says, his voice low but slicing through the buzz of the locker room. "Can't miss a thing. It's like you're just waitin' for me to slip so you can pounce."

His words hang in the air—half a tease, half a challenge.

A few players nearby chuckle, their eyes darting between the tension and the next volley. The leather cleats scuff against the tile. Somewhere past the lockers, showers hiss and drip. The musk of drying sweat settles thick in the air—this is a place where tempers flare after practice, where emotions run close to the surface, and where a single word can ignite or defuse everything.

Brick twists the towel in his hands—a deliberate, lazy motion that draws attention to the taut muscles along his forearms. "Discipline," he murmurs, dragging the word out like a secret. "Punishment." His voice dips darker, almost playful. "Guess you like keepin' me on my toes. Or maybe you're just into the... consequences."

Snickers ripple from some teammates, and a few nudge each other with knowing grins. Brick's smirk widens. He shifts his stance, cocking one hip forward—a dare thrown to the room.

"You know," he continues, his voice rising enough for everyone to catch every word, "there's a fine line between control and... enjoyment. I figured you'd know all about that, Miss Clipboard."

Natalie stands rooted in place. Her fingers tremble around the edge of the clipboard, her knuckles whitening, but she meets his stare unflinchingly. She feels his eyes roving, the weight of his gaze like heat pressed to bare skin. His words drip with double meanings that tickle the edges of propriety. She doesn't flinch.

Brick wrings the towel tighter and lets it fall slack. The tension spirals as he laces his taunts with swagger.

"Maybe you're the real enforcer around here," he says. "The iron fist behind the fancy talk. I can hear you now, setting rules, doling out rewards... and punishments."

His smirk dims into a sharper edge as he fixes her with a long, unblinking stare. "Don't worry," he whispers, just loud enough, "I can take whatever you dish out. Maybe even... relish it."

The words hang in the stale locker room air between them like smoke from a slowly burning fuse.

His gaze flickers across the crowd—teammates caught between amusement and unease, a split that mirrors the fracture running through the team itself. Some admire his swagger, his refusal to bend, while others respect Natalie's authority and her unshakeable control. The room itself seems divided, holding its breath, waiting to see who will fracture first.

His gaze settles back on Natalie. The space between them contracts to a taut wire of electricity. Every person in the room feels the raw, undeniable charge pulsing in the silence that follows.

The locker room quiets. Breaths catch in throats.

Brick's gaze holds firm, daring her to break first.

The locker room hums with low murmurs, underpinned by Brick's lingering smirk and scattered chuckles from his teammates. Natalie steels herself, her feet rooted firmly on the cold tiles.

"You want me to play your game?" she says, her eyes sharp not with anger but with precision. "Fine."

She inhales slowly. Seconds tick away between her pulse and the thick, sweat-heavy air. The pause sharpens her focus.

"But let's get something straight—those comments about discipline and punishment?" Her voice cuts clean and clinical. "They don't get a pass here. They're not clever. They cross a line."

Her gaze slides across the cluster, landing on furrowed brows and twitching lips. Some players exchange wary glances, loyalty fracturing in the silence. Brick's glare flickers, but she doesn't flinch.

"This isn't private." Natalie's fingers twitch against the edge of the clipboard. She straightens her shoulders. "It's public. It threatens every one of your careers."

Harsh fluorescent lights buzz overhead, casting sharp shadows across sweating skin. The sting of stale sweat mingles with the faint metallic scent of lockers. Distant sneakers scrape against the tile as murmurs ripple toward silence.

"That clip at two minutes and nineteen seconds?" She continues, her voice steady despite the rush beneath her skin. "It's not isolated. It's a pattern—one that's already cost the team goodwill—and yes, it's costing you personally."

The room tightens. Sweat gleams on Brick's collarbone. Damp strands stick to his temple. His jaw works, tension radiating through his shoulders as he shifts, the towel slipping.

Natalie's chest tightens. She channels it into control, her voice unwavering.

"Suspension. Damaged contracts. Loss of sponsor trust. Fans who stop shouting your name with admiration." She lets each consequence land. "That's what continues."

Brick's mouth opens, but she cuts through before he can throw another barb.

"This team isn't just athletes showing up on game day." Her tone sharpens, driving home every syllable. "It's a network. Fragile. Every reckless act unravels it."

She had stood in locker rooms before, faced this same resistance, this same testing of boundaries. It had steeled her then. It steadies her now.

"You want to bait me into a fight?" Her voice drops to something quiet and icy. "Don't."

Brick narrows his eyes. "Oh, Clipboard Queen's got rules now?"

"Discipline isn't a game," Natalie says, meeting his gaze evenly. "Crossing the line has consequences." She taps the clipboard once, crisp and final. "And I'm here to hold this team accountable. If that means standing alone, so be it."

Her hand firms around the clipboard like a shield and anchor. The words hang heavy in the thick air. A few players exchange uneasy glances. Phones are still. Eyes lock.

Brick's gaze holds hers for a beat longer, the challenge still flickering there. However, the fire in her eyes doesn't dim. It burns steady and unwavering—an unspoken promise that she means every word.

The room waits in stillness. Breaths falter throughout the locker room. Natalie lets the moment settle like dust before the storm.

DeShawn, Caleb, and Troy lean against the lockers. The sharp clang of metal pierces the murmur of the locker room. DeShawn's broad shoulders tense as he exchanges a glance with Caleb, whose brows knit in cautious watchfulness. Across from them, Troy shifts his weight, arms folded tightly, lips pressed into a thin line that barely conceals skepticism. Their eyes flick to Natalie and then to Brick, as if weighing the air for danger—or perhaps entertainment.

DeShawn's smirk fades into a quiet sigh. His eyes scan the tension stretched tight as a wire between Natalie and Brick. Caleb scratches the back of his neck; even his calm gaze flickers with unease. Troy glances over his shoulder, jaw clenched. None of them move, but their stances speak volumes—curiosity mingled with doubt, amusement laced with discomfort.

Jaxon steps forward from the cluster. The thud of his cleats on the tile feels louder somehow. His lean frame moves with effortless authority, a calm force settling over the charged room. He slides quietly between Natalie and Brick, grounding the space with his measured presence. The edge in Brick's glare sharpens briefly—a warning unspoken—but Jaxon's steady eyes don't waver.

"Alright, let's keep it PG in front of the kids," Jaxon says, his voice laced with gentle humor. His smirk serves as half a shield and half a peace offering.

Brick's grin tightens, a slow curl of his lips that doesn't quite reach his eyes. With a towel still draped around his neck, he steps back just enough to give Jaxon room—a calculated recoil—and folds his arms, watching.

Jaxon's hands raise slightly, palms open but calm, the universal signal to ease up. His tone cuts through the tension like a cool breeze on a heavy afternoon.

"Brick, man, you know better than to let this get out of hand," Jaxon says smoothly. "Remember the last time you lost it? You nearly cost us all."

The eyes on Brick sharpen. The weight of history hangs between them—that incident last season when his fists had found a locker instead of an opponent, when the team had held its breath, waiting for suspension papers. Everyone knows the wreckage left in the wake of his temper. The silence shifts, thick and palpable.

Jaxon doesn't let his gaze drift; instead, he focuses squarely on Brick's chest, his voice dropping just enough to be both confidential and commanding.

"She's not your enemy."

The declaration hangs in the air, more than a simple statement—almost a lifeline. For a moment, nothing shifts. Then Jaxon turns his head briefly, his eyes catching Natalie's in a glance that holds an unspoken nod of respect. Not warmth—too soon for that—but respect nonetheless, an acknowledgment of the difficult role she's stepped into.

Around them, the room's energy stirs. Some of the younger players exchange quick glances, uncertain whether to trust this moment. A few nod slightly—the ones who have seen Natalie work and know she is not the enemy that Brick's glare suggests. Others linger near their lockers, shoulders hunched, their skepticism etched in the set of their jaws. One or two whisper something low and tight, their doubt audible in the breath of it.

Players start to stretch and shuffle. The clatter of cleats on tile grows softer as the crowd begins to thin. Chatter dims before murmurs flicker like wary flames, hesitant and uneven. The weight in the room eases just enough to breathe. The glare between Brick and Natalie dulls but does not vanish—an ember beneath the ash, simmering.

Jaxon steps back, his broad frame easing away but still remaining central, a silent reminder that the balance must hold.

"Let's wrap this up," he mutters, his voice low but carrying. "There is plenty more work ahead without us tearing each other apart."

As teammates begin to drift off, some exchanging quick, tight-lipped smiles and others casting guarded looks over their shoulders, the locker room exhales. The sharp edges dull but linger—a promise that this battle is not over, just paused.

DeShawn nudges Caleb, who chuckles softly but without any real mirth, while Troy watches the resettling players file out, the tension scratching under his skin. The pack fractures into smaller groups, the sticky residue of confrontation settling into cautious silence.

Natalie adjusts her grip on the clipboard. The cool plastic bends slightly beneath her palm. She catches Jaxon's eyes for a moment—a flicker of alliance that steadies her. His expression conveys something more than support; it's a confirmation that she is not alone in this.

Brick remains seated a moment longer, shoulders squared and jaw tight, his gaze locked on the spot where Natalie once stood. The locker room hums around him, but the space between them feels electric—charged with rivalry, perhaps, but also with something else. Something unspoken and raw.

Slowly, Brick stands. The towel shifts on his neck. He rubs a heavy hand over his face before pushing off toward the showers. The others disperse with a mixed chorus of grunts and half-hearted jokes, the locker room resuming its usual rhythm but carrying the aftertaste of something unresolved.

The crowd parts enough for Natalie to step back toward the exit. Her footsteps are light but steady on the cool tile. The murmurs follow her like shadows, a whispered chorus of skepticism and silent bets on what comes next.

Jaxon watches her go, his lips pressed tight in that rare, serious expression. His glance slides to Brick, who is now looming near the showers, before the gravity of the moment pulls his gaze to the floor.

The locker room empties. The echoes of their words linger like footprints on windblown sand—faint but impossible to erase.

The locker room buzzes with settling tension, murmurs curling like smoke around clustered players. Natalie presses her clipboard tighter under her arm, the glossy papers crinkling faintly. She walks with careful strides toward the exit, her shoes scuffing against the cold, cracked tiles.

From her left, a drawled mutter breaks through—sarcasm sharp as a blade. "PR ladies."

Natalie's steps falter. The words scrape at her ears.

The scent of sweat and damp fabric hovers in the air, mingling with the metallic tang of lockers and faint disinfectant. She pauses beneath the harsh fluorescent lights, their flicker casting angular shadows on the gleaming pipes overhead. The ventilation drone fills the silence behind the departing voices. She inhales slowly. The dry, stale air burns her throat as she exhales—long and deliberate—her shoulders sagging with the weight she had held taut moments before.

Her gaze drifts over the dispersed group: half-turned backs, loosened jerseys, and the dull gleam of cleats. A pair of teammates exchange glances, their eyes tracking her retreating form. She senses the pull of their judgment like an invisible thread. Her fingers curl around the edge of her legal pad, smoothing the corners of her notes before she forces each step to be steady, measured, and controlled.

The tightening in her chest claws beneath her ribs. Her heartbeat quickens, but she wills her expression into a calm mask, her lips pressed into a thin line.

The fluorescent corridor swallows her as she slips through the door. The sudden quiet presses against her ears. Her heels echo faintly—the only reminder of her presence in the sterile hallway. She stops at the junction where the locker room opens into a narrow, windowless passage. A chill rises from the concrete floor beneath her feet.

There, she leans against the cool wall surface, the rough paint transferring its faint grit to her palm. Her breath comes out shaky at first, mingling with the faint hum of distant stadium fans fading into the early evening. The tang of sweat lingers on her skin—a stubborn reminder of the charged space she had just left. She closes her eyes, pressing a palm against her forehead, willing her racing pulse to slow.

The locker room still holds the residue of confrontation—sharp words hanging like unsettled smoke. But here, in this desolate corridor, tension coils tighter around her ribs, twisting into loose knots of doubt and defiance.

Her shoulders sag just a little. She tugs her blazer tighter and shifts her weight from foot to foot, avoiding the sidelong glances that might come if anyone passed. The fluorescent lights hum above her, relentless and cold.

"They don't get it," she murmurs, her voice barely more than a whisper.

A soft shuffle echoes down the hall. Jaxon's chuckle drifts faintly from inside, breaking the suffocating hush like a warm breeze. Natalie's hands twitch against her clipboard. She runs her finger along the edge of her notes—scribbled headings and timestamps etched with purpose.

"I know they're difficult," she whispers, her voice resolute now, each word a challenge cast into the empty corridor. "But they need to see what's at stake. They don't want promises; they want proof."

Her lips curl into a subtle, tight smile. The hallway's chill seeps beneath her blouse, but the flame igniting inside her flares hot and precise. Each breath grounds her. The quiet power of her own conviction hums beneath the surface—sharp and steady.

"I'm not here to be liked," she breathes. "I'm here to change the game."

The door to the locker room remains slightly ajar behind her, a sliver of warmth spilling into the stark hallway. She dares to glance back.

Brick stands alone amid scattered gear and discarded towels, his massive frame silhouetted against the harsh fluorescent light. His eyes lock onto hers through the narrow gap between them—dark and unreadable. Something flickers in that gaze: anger layered with a hesitant something else, a fragile glimmer of recognition or challenge. He doesn't move; he doesn't turn away as the last of the team's presence fades into shadow around him.

Natalie's throat tightens at the sight. An electric pulse threads through the lingering tension between them. There's history in that look—years of unsaid things, of him seeing her when others dismiss her, and of complications neither has dared to name. She holds his gaze a moment longer, then draws her clipboard closer and turns fully away. The echo of the closing door seals her resolve.

She inhales deeply, her back pressed against the cold wall, steadying herself for the battles yet to come. The murmurs from inside still whisper behind that door. Out here, beneath the unforgiving glow of fluorescent lights, Natalie claims the quiet moment to breathe steadily and prepare—for the fight, for the change, for the man she's meant to reach.

The corridor waits, empty and expectant, as she steps forward again.

###

Emma's hand slips lightly around Natalie's elbow, guiding her gently aside near the dull gray door of the supply closet. The harsh hum of fluorescent lights overhead makes the quiet between them feel sharper, but Emma's voice drops low and steady, soothing in contrast to the residual tension trailing Natalie from the locker room.

"You kept your cool in there," Emma says, her eyes steady and warm with understanding. "I've been where you are—the new face walking into a boys' club that's seen too many outsiders come and go. It's brutal at first."

She pauses, her jaw tightening at the memory. Years of proving herself. Years of swallowing doubt.

"You just have to hold onto that calm," Emma continues, her hand still steady on Natalie's arm.

Natalie's shoulders slacken just a fraction as the lingering heat from the locker room soaks into her blazer. A slow exhale escapes her lips. The faint scent of liniment and sweat still clings to her clothes, reminding her how raw the room was behind that door.

"Calm has to be my weapon," Natalie admits, her voice tight but honest. The weight of the day presses into her bones. "But it doesn't feel like enough sometimes."

Emma nods, a knowing smile ghosting her lips. "With this crew, talk's cheap. We have to show them. Words don't mean much until they're backed by action. You'll hear their skepticism. You'll feel isolated." She leans against the wall, her clipboard tucked against her ribs. "But persistence—that's what changes the game. I'll back you up when it counts."

Natalie meets Emma's eyes, grateful for the rare offer of solidarity. The buzz of activity drifts past them—players moving down the hall, lockers sliding open and shut, sneakers scraping against the tile.

"Thanks, Emma," Natalie says. She unfolds her legal pad from the strap over her shoulder, her pen scratching against the paper with urgent precision. The action steadies her, shaping structure out of the chaos—rules and rituals to corral the wild edges of behavior that threaten the whole team.

Emma leans in, watching the beginnings of a plan take form.

"Weekly check-ins. Social media drills. Clear, enforced accountability," Natalie mumbles, her handwriting neat but urgent. She underlines something and then pauses. These rules would feel sterile and impersonal. But they had to mean something. They had to prove to the team that respect wasn't given—it was earned through consistency and consequence, not exceptions or excuses.

"Step one: no more surprises," Natalie continues, the words shaping themselves as she writes. "Step two: consequences must be real. Step three: trust has to be earned."

Emma's fingers tap against her own clipboard—steady and thoughtful. She knows what it takes.

"That's the way forward," Emma says. "Keep the pressure consistent, and don't let the distractions win. Call me if you need someone in your corner."

Natalie pauses, her eyes trailing to Emma's quietly fierce expression. "It helps to know I'm not alone in this war."

"Never," Emma replies softly, then glances toward the glowing edge of the locker room doorway. "No matter what it looks like."

As Natalie turns to walk away, the corridor stretches ahead, fading into the golden tint of the late afternoon sun spilling through narrow windows. She stops, caught by a flicker at the edge of her vision.

Her gaze darts back through the open locker room door, where shadows pool and teammates move in slow disarray—jerseys tossed, cleats being tied. Brick stands apart, his massive frame rigid. His eyes lock on hers, blazing with a storm barely masked by fury and something else: curiosity? Pain? The line blurs.

He doesn't move and doesn't look away.

The others drift past like waves pulling away from the shore. The air crackles—a promise and a warning tangled into that unwavering stare.

Natalie swallows the tight pulse in her throat. She lets the doorframe slip behind her, clutching her clipboard tighter. Her footsteps echo down the tiled corridor—steady and measured. Each step carves space for the battle ahead.

Brick Turner's defiance lingers at the edge of her vision, sharpening her resolve like a blade.

She walks on.

Rules and Consequences

The stadium sat swallowed in pre-dawn shadows when Natalie pushed through the heavy glass doors. Her heels tapped against the polished floor—brisk and deliberate. The manila folder in her grip was heavier than it looked, its bold label catching the low light: Turner—Conduct Protocol. She didn't hesitate.

The locker room breathed in silence. Players clustered in scattered groups, shoulders tense, eyes flickering like shadows avoiding the folder in her hand. Jerseys hung half-heartedly. Cleats were untied. The faint musk of sweat mixed with worn leather hung thick in the cool morning air—a quiet accusation.

Natalie moved to the glass desk by the lockers, setting the folder down with deliberate calm. The cold surface mirrored her composed expression—the sharp set of her jaw and the faint tension in her steady hands.

From across the room, Emma caught her eye. Calm and reassuring. A quick nod passed between them. *We can get through this.*

Near the end of the lockers, Jaxon leaned against the metal frame, arms crossed loosely but eyes sharp. Caleb stood nearby, shifting his weight from foot to foot. His phone was clutched in his palm, thumb twitching over the screen as if he were trying to decipher something he couldn't quite read. The younger player struggled with more than just game day pressure—the media storm brewing outside these walls, the fallout from last night's chaos, the weight of being tangled up in something he hadn't caused. It showed in the tightness around his mouth and in how he couldn't meet anyone's gaze for long.

Jaxon nudged Caleb's shoulder, breaking the ice with a half-grin. "So, are you ready to slug it out with the media, or are you just here for the caffeine fix?"

Caleb swallowed, his voice tight. "Honestly? I'm stuck in a quiet storm brewing inside."

Jaxon laughed, dry and low. "Yeah, quiet storms sometimes drown out the loud ones."

Natalie watched from her desk, arms crossed. The exchange felt familiar—players wrestling with more than just the game. But Brick's absence was a missing pulse, an empty locker that spoke volumes.

Minutes stretched thin. The overhead lights hummed, washing the room in unforgiving white. Natalie smoothed the crisp stack of protocol copies beside the folder, the paper whispering under her fingertips.

"It's going to take more than last night's noise to shake us," Emma said quietly, stepping to Natalie's side. Her sneakers tapped softly against the tile. "We hold the line."

Natalie nodded, her eyes scanning the restless faces. "We get through it by keeping the line clear. No one is above it."

Caleb broke the quiet again, his voice barely carrying across the lockers. "Last night messes with your head, huh?"

"It's why you don't mix bourbon and football," Jaxon said.

"Yeah?" Caleb looked down the length of the room, a thread of reluctant amusement weaving through his voice. "I figured it was just Brick's special recipe for chaos."

Natalie allowed herself a small smile—the first crack in her armor. "Chaos doesn't win games," she said, her voice smooth but firm. "Discipline does."

Soft laughter rippled around her, but beneath it lay something dogged and serious. The air loosened its grip, if only slightly. Emma met Natalie's eyes again—steady and knowing—and the room exhaled, ready to face whatever came next.

Natalie slid the folder closed one final time, lifting her chin against the crisp morning light flooding the room. The hum of the facility settled into a steady rhythm—a pulse beneath the tension.

Here, in this charged silence, the battle lines were drawn.

The day began.

The conference room buzzed with restless energy. Boots scuffed the polished floor. Lockers scraped. Chairs grated softly against the cold tile.

Overhead fluorescents hummed, casting a clinical glare that sharpened the edges of everything—and everyone. The tension thickened like smoke.

Coach Marcus Hale stood at the head of the room, a sturdy figure framed against a wall-sized display. Behind him, team statistics and mottos blinked quietly. His reputation preceded him—fifteen years of building championship teams and commanding respect without raising his voice. The players knew his silences carried more weight than most men's words.

"Take your seats," Hale said.

His voice cuts through the murmurs like a whistle piercing a crowded stadium. The room settles. Some players slump low, while others stare straight ahead, muscles coiled in silent resistance.

Natalie Brooks strides forward, her silhouette slicing through the murmur. She sets a manila folder labeled "Turner — Conduct Protocol" squarely on the podium. Her fingers smooth the edge. The weight of it—the weight of what it represents—sits tangible between them all.

Brick's absence leaves a hollow gap, amplified by the thick silence.

Her gaze drifts slowly from one anxious face to the next, pausing briefly where unease tightens like a knot: DeShawn, Troy, and Eli, with his fingers dancing nervously over his phone.

"This isn't just about image," Natalie begins, her voice steady and clear. "It's about earning the right to play, about the trust we build, and the standards we uphold—on the field, in the locker room, everywhere."

The scent of sweat and stale cologne lingers. Players exchange sidelong glances, their eyes narrowing and flickering with restrained defiance.

Natalie opens the folder. She extracts a stack of printed sheets and begins passing copies forward with deliberate care. Glossy pages reveal the "Personal Conduct Protocol" in stark black type. The list reads like a creed:

No physical or verbal altercations.

Mandatory weekly therapy check-ins.

Punctuality for PR and media events is required.

Strict social media restrictions are in place.

Immediate incident reporting is necessary.

Daily anger-management journaling is expected.

DeShawn snorts softly. A smirk flickers at the corner of his mouth—quiet rebellion masked by humor. Troy, seated near the back, lets a slow eye roll carry his dismissal, irritation rustling beneath his composed facade. Eli's fingers twitch, his eyes flicking between the protocol and the room, swallowed by apprehension.

The room ripples with whispered murmurs. Boots shuffle. Questions hang unspoken in the stale air.

Natalie's gaze remains unmoved, steady as a captain steering through rough seas.

She knows what this moment costs—presenting protocols tailored for one player, making them public, and forcing the team to witness discipline dressed as standardization. The line between accountability and humiliation blurs thin. But boundaries exist for a reason; they always do.

"Look," Natalie says, her voice firm, with an undercurrent of intentional resolve. "These protocols are tailored to address specific risks and lay out clear expectations. But today, we present them to the entire team—not to single anyone out, but to underscore the culture we demand: accountability, respect, and discipline."

Coach Hale steps forward. His shadow broadens across the wall. He lifts his chin, his eyes sharp, delivering the silent weight of authority without a word.

Minutes stretch. The only sounds thread between barely contained exhalations and the faint tap of nails against wood. A chair leg scrapes across the tile—sharp, metallic, jarring in the stillness.

Then Hale nods. Once. Grave and unyielding.

The nod is a seal, a declaration carved into the team's collective conscience.

The tension eases just enough to breathe. A brittle calm wraps around the room.

"You all know what's on the line," Hale finally speaks, his voice low but firm. "This isn't a negotiation; it's an expectation."

DeShawn leans toward Troy, whispering with a grin, "If Brick's journaling all that anger, it'll be a damn bestseller by season's end."

Troy shakes his head, smirking. "Tell him to toss in a glossary—a whole dictionary of how not to screw up."

Eli's fingers hesitate over his phone. His thumb twitches but remains still, caught between retreat and resolve.

Natalie's eyes flicker across the group, catching the subtle dance of resistance and budding acceptance. She meets Eli's gaze briefly and draws a small, encouraging nod. The moment is faint but real—a lifeline tossed in storm-tossed waters.

Coach Hale shifts his weight, clearing his throat. "We're here to win—not just games, but respect. Every name on that list means something. Every step off the line has consequences. That's the playbook now."

The room exhales collectively. Some stiffen, while others lean back. The weight presses in but, paradoxically, also offers structure. Natalie folds her hands, feeling the smooth plastic of the folder beneath her fingers—a tangible reminder of the fragile order they seek to rebuild.

A low murmur of assent sneaks through the room: muted, uncertain, but growing.

No one says it aloud yet, but the message lands like a hush between them all: this day marks a turning point. The standard isn't just in print; it's alive in the heavy eyes, the taut jaws, and the clenched hands struggling to find calm.

Natalie slides the last protocol copy into the folder and locks eyes briefly with Coach Hale. His nod is the final beat in the symphony of command.

The room begins to shift. Players rise as the silent directive settles deep, tempering flames and staking ground in the ever-churning battlefield of discipline and redemption.

###

The door swings open with a casual thud.

Brick strides in late, legs stretched wide and arms folded like armor across his chest. His boots thump softly against the polished floor as he moves toward a vacant seat near the back.

The silence in the briefing room presses down like a weight. Overhead, the lights hum faintly—that electric buzz before a storm breaks.

He pulled the "Personal Conduct Protocol" from the table and ripped it open with exaggerated flair.

Flipping through the pages, Brick's voice rose, dripping with sarcasm. "Let's see here. No verbal or physical altercations?" He let the words hang like an accusation. "Oh, really? That's rich." His gaze swept the room like a searchlight, cataloging every flinch. "Mandatory weekly therapy sessions."

A pause—sharp and deliberate.

"What, is this a middle school sleepover? Do we all get coloring books and juice boxes too?"

A few teammates cracked smirks. Others stiffened, their gazes fixed on the room's outlines, unwilling to fuel the fire but unable to ignore it. Brick began pacing—each step deliberate, each sneer timed to draw laughter from scattered corners. "Punctuality for PR and media stuff. Like I'm supposed to bow and curtsy for them." His voice bounced off the stark walls. "Social media restrictions? Can't post what I want? What's next, 'No eating pizza on the sidelines'?"

His booming laugh echoed.

Then his hand moved to his back pocket—smooth, practiced. He angled his phone toward the doorframe.

A shutter clicked.

Natalie stood poised at the front beside Coach Hale's empty chair, her sharp gaze pinning Brick like a wary falcon. She watched—cool and methodical—as he took the shot. Her fingers tightened briefly around her clipboard before relaxing.

Her hand moved with the precision of a scalpel.

She reached out and plucked the phone from his grip as if it weighed nothing. No shout. No snap. She set it on the podium with clinical care, then flicked a note into her tablet: "Unauthorized social media during briefing — phone confiscated."

Brick's breath caught. Heat simmered behind his sharp eyes.

Thirty minutes later, the PR media prep session rippled with tension as Brick strolled in, exuding a relaxed swagger that dared her to react. His smirk was lazy—a crooked challenge. The faint scent of sweat and cut grass clung to him, mixing with the sterile air inside.

Natalie glanced up from her clipboard, her gaze steady as steel. "You're late. Again. We start on time—no exceptions." She tapped a note without breaking eye contact.

Brick slid into his usual spot near the edge of the circle, chuckling softly, like a storm crouched but unrestrained.

Jaxon leaned back against his chair, arms crossed, lips pressed into a thin line. His eyes didn't leave Brick—disappointment layered deep beneath the surface, barely masked by years of shared battles. Across the room, Emma offered Natalie a barely perceptible nod, the kind that said: *You're holding steady. Good.*

The subtle exchange drew no attention, but its weight folded tighter into the air than any spoken reprimand.

Brick's grin widened. He sensed the gathering unease like a hunter smelling the wind shift.

He leaned back in his chair, flipping through the protocol packet once more. His voice remained low and mocking. "You want me to journal my anger? Babysit my feelings?" He let that hang. "Hell, I'm supposed to be the monster in the middle. Now I'm therapy's poster child?"

His chuckle was sharp-edged. A few uneasy half-laughs rippled through the room.

Natalie's eyes narrowed, but they held a calm that dampened any eruption. Her fingers tightened briefly around the clipboard before relaxing. The faint scrape of pen on paper echoed through the charged silence—an anchor. She remained rooted, quietly logging each moment as if taking stock of wild weather.

The room tightened further. Even the murmur of breath was measured. Cautious.

Then Brick stood. Slow. Deliberate.

He threw the folder on the table. "You can keep your rules," he snapped. "I'll play my game my way." His gaze flicked toward Natalie—sharp, loaded with every unspoken resentment.

She flipped a page on her clipboard. The pen moved across the paper in steady strokes: "Defiance noted."

Brick turned on his heel. His boots echoed down the hallway with a brazen swagger that filled the space like thunder. Doors swung softly closed behind him.

A residual charge buzzed in the whispers that followed. The tension didn't dissipate; it hovered—thick, electric—swelling in the wake of rebellion.

Back in the media prep room, Brick slid in again, late as if timing were his weapon. The hum of equipment and quiet chatter stopped as he asserted his presence with a crooked grin. He owned the moment.

Natalie looked up without blinking. She assessed him like a strategist marking a battlefield.

"You're late. Again," she intoned. Her voice was steady, her eyes calm pools of unyielding resolve.

"I'm making an entrance." His retort cut sharp enough to slice through the sterile air.

Jaxon's gaze pinned Brick with the weight of years—friends turned wary sentinels. Emma's quiet nod braced Natalie's posture like reinforcement: strength in silence, patience in discipline.

"Control's an illusion," Brick muttered as he slid into his chair.

The corners of the room seemed to tighten like a noose.

Natalie's pen hovered, then moved across the paper in deliberate strokes.

The morning's rebellion crystallized in that quiet sound—official and unyielding. Brick leaned back, smirking but contained, a storm restrained only by the battles yet to come.

The late afternoon sun bleeds orange across the practice field, casting long shadows over the emerald turf. Brick storms forward, boots pounding the grass. His eyes lock on the bulky tackling dummy—the rookie gripping it like a lifeline.

He drives. Brutal. Unstoppable.

The impact shatters the dummy. Splinters of hard plastic explode outward, raining down on the green like shrapnel.

The rookie stumbles, arms flailing. His cleats slip against the turf, and for a moment, he's falling, falling—then he catches himself. His face drains white. The pressure of being seen, of failing in front of the team, of standing inches from raw violence—it all crashes through him at once.

Coaches cut off mid-shout, their mouths parting in surprise. Players pause, cleats scraping the grass, breaths held in a collective intake.

The air tastes of crushed rubber and fresh-cut turf, thick with a simmering quiet that feels dangerous.

Brick's chest rises and falls in sharp, defiant bursts. His gaze narrows as a slow, brutal smile tugs at the corner of his mouth.

Without missing a beat, he strides past the media tent. Cameras swivel like predatory eyes, lenses trained on his retreating figure. Flashbulbs pop silently, trying to puncture the veil he throws around himself. Brick's mouth quirks into a smirk, daring anyone—media, coaches, teammates—to give chase.

The tent remains ominously still. No calls. No shouts. No attempts to stop him.

His footsteps echo down the corridor into the locker room, where a group circles in a tense huddle. Strategies whisper beneath the surface. Plays are dissected under breath. The weight of last night's conflict chokes the air—who still backs Brick, who is turning away, and who can't decide if loyalty means staying silent or finally speaking up. The fractures are deeper now, sharper, turning teammates into something fragmented and raw.

Brick barges in, his broad frame cutting through the quiet like a thunderclap. A ripple of startled looks meets him. Some eyes brighten with something like relief. Others harden with resentment. Most just flicker with uncertainty—the same uncertainty that has been festering since the night before.

He leans against a bench, his voice low and laced with mockery. "Guess I gotta add 'dummy demolition' to my resume now. Who knew my tackling skills turned destructive?"

A few loyal teammates chuckle nervously, their laughter tight and uncertain. Others shift uneasily on their feet, their eyes darting toward the door. The room's air thickens, charged with that awkward mix of fear and reluctant amusement, the undercurrents of fractured loyalty pulling taut.

Natalie sits just beyond the locker room, her eyes trained on her tablet. Each violation is logged with clinical precision: the splintered dummy incident, Brick's deliberate media skip, and his disruption in the locker room. All time-stamped. All tagged with discreet notes. She taps her stylus efficiently, her voice and heart detached from the chaos as she compiles an unyielding record.

Later, in the softly lit media office, Natalie steps to the whiteboard, clipboard in hand. With careful strokes, she pins succinct bullet points summarizing the day's infractions. The notes stand stark against the white surface: "Broken equipment—reported; Missed media session—logged; Locker room conduct—documented." The sharp scent of dry erase markers mingles with the sterile atmosphere, creating an unspoken ledger of consequences building in silence.

Outside the office window, the practice field stretches out, empty now except for the lone tackling dummy's shattered remains. Splintered plastic and torn padding litter the turf like scattered bones, silent witnesses to Brick's escalating storm. Players drift away in clusters, their conversations muted. The day's energy has drained into something fragile and unsettled—as if the field itself holds its breath, waiting for the next explosion.

Natalie finds him near the lockers, his jaw clenched tight. His fingers grip the edge of the bench, knuckles whitening.

"Maybe you're proud of breaking *stuff*," she says quietly, "but you're breaking the team, too."

Brick's eyes flash. A storm brews beneath his skin. "Don't act like you understand. This isn't about the team. It's about control."

She meets his gaze evenly, unflinching. "Control is earned, not stolen. You think you're bulldozing the world, but you're just crashing into your own walls."

He snorts, shaking his head with a bitter laugh. "Yeah? Well, maybe chaos is the only thing that makes a damn lick of sense around here."

"Maybe," she whispers. "But chaos doesn't win games. Discipline does."

Around them, the locker room is enveloped in a heavy silence. The tension is palpable, with neither willing to blink first.

Brick rakes his fingers through his hair and stalks away, his footsteps leaving echoing trails of something unsettled in his wake.

The practice field's broken dummy remains sprawled on the turf, stark beneath the fading sun. Its shattered pieces tell a story of resistance and reckoning. The team's fractured unity teeters, fragile and raw, caught between the man who breaks things and the woman who records every shattering moment.

The media office sits quietly. Natalie's fingers tap the tablet screen—steady, rhythmic, purposeful. Her eyes skim timestamps and terse notes. Each one marks an incident, each one cracking the fragile order she's fighting to restore. Brick's name appears over and over, a stubborn shadow refusing to fade. Instead of words, she chooses documentation—the cold precision of recorded truths.

She slides the tablet onto the glass desk and lifts a magnetized note. The peeling comes with practiced ease—a small resistance, then release. Her fingers press the printed summary to the whiteboard hanging outside the locker room. The words are clinical, devoid of judgment—terse but unmissable:

— Splintered tackling dummy: 3:45 PM

— Missed media session: 4:20 PM

— Locker room disruption: 4:30 PM

No shouts. No threats. Just quiet accountability pinned in plain sight.

The hallway buzzes. Fluorescent lights hum softly beneath the muffled sounds of late afternoon—cleats scraping against tile, lockers slamming shut. Sweat still clings to the air, mingling with the sharp bite of liniment and the leather-and-metal tang of drying gear.

Footsteps echo. Slow. Uncertain.

Natalie tucks the folder under one arm and moves down the corridor. She finds the rookie pressed against the lockers—a kid with wide eyes and hands wrapped so tightly around a water bottle that his knuckles have turned white. His shirt bears a faint splash of mud and a bruise blooming purple beneath his collarbone. She remembers the cracked plastic of the splintered dummy breaking further under Brick's fist, the rookie's startled yelp, and the way he had staggered back, frozen, his entire body braced for a storm. The kid idolizes Brick and has followed him since preseason, yet Brick had nearly taken his head off.

Natalie sinks to one knee. The cold tile settles beneath her. She meets the rookie's wide eyes. The fluorescent glare strips away shadows, but the shaky flicker in his gaze holds stubborn fear.

"What happened wasn't your fault," she says. Her voice remains steady and gentle. "Do you hear me?"

The boy's shoulders shift. A breath loosens somewhere deep inside. His eyes flicker down, then up again. He is less anxious now. Still raw, but less anxious.

He nods—small, shaky.

Natalie stands and brushes a stray lock of hair from her face. Her heels tap lightly against the polished floor as she crosses to the adjacent office. She pulls Brick's conduct folder from the stack. Her fingers glide over the surface. She writes—clinical, detached, precise: broken equipment, missed media session, locker room disruption. Each incident is logged in the folder's sterile history.

She taps the entries into the secure team system. The progress bar crawls forward—slow, steady. A digitization of consequence.

She could confront him now. She could summon him to her office, raise her voice, and demand accountability the way coaches do. But Natalie has learned something harder: that silence carries more weight than anger. Documentation transforms frustration into fact. Facts don't argue; they simply exist. And when the time comes to act—truly act—those facts will speak with the authority of undeniable truth.

Her eyes drift back to the whiteboard across the hall. Players and coaches glance at it as they pass. Their gazes linger, and their steps slow. The bullets stand bare—undeniable. No raised voices, no dramatic pleas—just unembellished truth, plain enough for those willing to read it.

Muffled voices rise from the locker room. The rhythm is tentative—a fragile truce after Brick's daily storm. She knows the quiet defiance still simmers beneath the surface, but for now, this quiet counter of hers is enough.

"Brick's not twelve," Natalie mutters, tapping a line on her screen. "He knows the score."

Emma's voice glides from the doorway: calm, cool, edged with exhaustion. "No argument there. But getting through to him feels like chasing smoke."

Natalie's lips twitch into a thin smile, her eyes fixed on the notes. "Maybe it's not about chasing. Maybe it's about waiting for the smoke to clear."

Emma steps fully into the light and folds her arms. "And meanwhile, we're just supposed to sit on our hands?"

"No," Natalie's voice drops. "We hold the line quietly, documenting every misstep so that facts speak louder than anger."

Emma nods, her shoulders releasing a fraction of their tension. "You're building a case here." She pauses, her eyes softening briefly. "And maybe a bridge."

Natalie taps the last entry. The sound is small but final. "Discipline doesn't always roar; sometimes it whispers."

A door creaks down the hall. The rookie pauses near the whiteboard, his eyes scanning the list. His finger trails absent-mindedly over each bullet point. The entries are like small scars—proof that missteps leave marks, even when no one shouts, especially then.

From the glass office, Natalie watches him for a moment. Then she turns away. The folder closes with a soft snap.

The late afternoon sun pools against the tinted windows in long, cold fingers. Shadows sharpen edges as the day tilts toward evening.

No confrontation. No raised voices.

Just the steady, deliberate pulse of accountability marked in ink and light, waiting for the next move to come.

The door to Coach Hale's office closes with a muted click behind Logan "Brick" Turner. The afternoon sun filters through the blinds, splintering gold and shadow across the polished floor in sharp, deliberate lines. Brick leans against the doorframe, his jaw tight and arms folded—a wall of muscle and history.

His chest still heaves from the meeting. Sweat clings to his collar. He can taste the metallic tang of his own anger, sharp and bitter on his tongue. The weight of past mistakes presses down on him, a familiar ache he can't shake. One more misstep, and it's over. He knows this. The fear of it gnaws at him, mixing with the rage that never quite stays buried.

"So, what's this? A tea party?" His voice carries a sarcastic edge, brittle laughter threading beneath it. "Or do you just want to lecture me on keeping my temper in check?"

Coach Marcus Hale sits behind his desk, his eyes narrowed but steady. Authority fills the room like an unyielding drum. With deliberate calm, he pushes a neatly typed folder toward Brick—a paper boundary drawn in black and white.

"This isn't a game, Turner." Hale's voice cuts through the stillness, low and unflinching. "This is your line. Step over it again, and you're done. No appeals. No hero's exit." His eyes lock on Brick's, unwavering, infusing every word with resolve.

Brick's smirk flickers. Hale's stare strips it away like ragged cloth exposed to flame. He tries again, a joke curling at the corner of his mouth—light enough to deflect, to break the tension.

"What, so you want me to be some kind of saint now? Save the world with spotless conduct? Please."

His voice rises slightly—a gambit, a last reach for control.

But Hale doesn't move. The silence stretches between them, dense and unbending.

"Your talent won't cut it if your head's not in the game." Hale leans forward, his voice edged with finality. "Grow up. Or watch this team move on without you."

Brick's grin dies. His shoulders lock tight, and his fists curl so hard that his knuckles blanch. A flush blooms beneath his skin—hot, stubborn, pulsing with rage he can barely contain. Without another word, he swings around and storms toward the door.

Heavy boots thud against the floor. Each step thunders with restrained anger.

The hallway swallows the sound, but his pace remains sharp—fast. He's a man on the verge of breaking.

Around the corner, Natalie Brooks rounds the bend. Every step carries calm precision—the deliberate stride of someone who never loses control, unlike him.

Their paths collide. Bodies brace just long enough, then their eyes lock.

Silence crackles between them: raw, brittle, electric.

Brick's chest heaves. His storm-tossed gaze conveys everything he won't speak. There's history between them—the kind that cuts both ways. She knows how to set him off; she knows exactly where his defenses crack. And he knows she does it on purpose.

Natalie's eyes hold steady, a cool flame meeting his heat. She doesn't flinch; she never does. Her breath comes evenly, controlled, while his rasps jagged and sharp.

For a heartbeat, the world contracts to the space between them: fierce, dangerous, a wire stretched so taut it might snap.

Then Brick turns, pushing past her. A storm simmers beneath his skin. Words remain swallowed, trapped behind clenched teeth and the weight pressing down on both of them.

The corridor echoes with all that remains unsaid. He disappears down the hall, leaving a shiver of volatile energy lingering in the air.

Natalie exhales softly, her shoulders sinking just a fraction. The faint scent of cut grass and sweat clings to the fading light—a reminder that nothing between them is ever finished. The silence stretches after him, a promise folded in tension.

Waiting.

The locker room still hums with yesterday's tension, quieter now, but the air is thick with it. Caleb leans against his locker, fingers trembling as they scroll through the comments beneath his photo. The screen's glow cuts sharp lines across his face—lips pressed tight, nails biting crescents into his palm. Some comments praise; others wield fancy words like knives.

Heat crawls up his neck. Unseen eyes press in from every typed word, every share.

He swallows hard, his jaw flexing. The sounds of the room fade to a dull backdrop—locker doors sliding shut, distant laughter, the occasional clank of cleats on tile. His heart ticks out an uneven rhythm.

A shadow drops beside him.

Troy's grin comes slow and knowing, his eyes tracing the tension in Caleb's jaw before flicking to the phone screen. "Photo's blowing up, huh?" His voice drags easy, like a Sunday afternoon. "The big leagues have their eyes on you now. Better start working on that killer smile for the cameras."

Caleb's breath hitches. Heat deepens the flush creeping across his cheeks, nearly crimson. He glances up, away from Troy's gaze. "Yeah, well... I'm already dreading the questions."

"You'll knock 'em dead."

Before Caleb could respond, another presence slid in—DeShawn, carrying the easy swagger of someone born to ease tension. His hand landed heavily and warmly on Caleb's shoulder, anchoring him.

"The press doesn't get to mess with your head," DeShawn said, half-grinning. "You're more than a snapshot or some tired headline.

Hell, half the time I barely survive halftime snacks, and I'm just trying to run the ball."

Caleb exhaled, slow and shaky. The tight line of his mouth twitched, then softened—just enough for a fragile smile, barely there. But the tremor in his eyes didn't quite dissipate.

"It's just..." His voice came out quiet, almost swallowed. "What if I mess up?"

"Hear that?" DeShawn's teeth flashed bright under the harsh locker room lights. "Fear? Every player in this room eats that for breakfast. You just gotta chew it up and spit out confidence."

Nate's heels clicked sharply against the tile. Natalie stepped closer, her soft footsteps muffled on the floor. She caught Caleb's trembling fingers clutching the cold phone and let her gaze settle, steady and warm.

"I see the worry creeping in," she said, her voice calm and unflappable despite the stress humming between them. "You don't have to face the media alone. I'll prepare you—we'll run through questions, responses, everything. You'll be ready."

Caleb blinked. Surprise flickered through his eyes like flames at dusk. The tightness around his mouth loosened.

"When?" His voice was hesitant but hopeful.

"Right now, if you want. Media room. Quick session—just enough to steady you for tomorrow's interviews."

He nodded, a quiet surrender.

Around them, the mood in the locker room shifted. Teammates shrugged off tension and returned to the rhythms of evening prep—the shuffle of cleats, the rustle of jerseys, and distant banter knitting into normalcy.

Caleb slid his phone into his shorts pocket. His breath came steadier now. His shoulders rose and fell in a controlled manner. He followed Natalie out, each step quieter and more deliberate, as the door swung shut behind them—sealing away the stifling weight, at least for a while.

The hum of quiet chatter threaded through the corridors and locker rooms of the stadium's innermost sanctum. Players clustered in low voices, some brushing past with forced grins, while others lingered in tight circles as if weighing allegiance and doubt on invisible scales. Brick's name slipped through the air—half spoken, half swallowed.

A few let their defenses harden around him. "The guy's got heart," one voice insisted, fingers tightening around a phone like a lifeline. "He's our line of fire."

Others turn away, shoulders angled inward, their silence louder than words.

The fracture runs deep. Some teammates still believe Brick can pull himself back from the edge, while others whisper that his spiral will drag the whole team down with him. The uncertainty hangs between them—thick and suffocating.

Nearby, Jaxon leans against a steel column, arms crossed and his jaw clenched tight enough to fracture stone. Across from him, Emma's hands fidget with the hem of her shirt, her eyes sharp and drawn with worry.

"He's spiraling," Emma says, her voice almost brittle, wary of the walls that listen. "I don't know if he can pull back without breaking everything else."

Jaxon's eyes dart to the distant groups, his jaw tightening before he turns back, his lips pressed into a hard line. "Maybe it isn't about if," he mutters, flicking a hand. "Maybe it's when—or if he even gives a damn."

Emma exhales—a slow breath weighted heavily with stalled hope. The silence between them stretches.

"We're all holding on by threads," she says finally.

The tension tightens, a fragile web stretched between belief and fear, stitching the room with silent questions no one dares voice aloud.

Far above the field, on the stadium's executive level, Natalie and Nina sit side by side in the media office. Glowing monitors cast their pale light across desks stacked with folders and press releases. The walls wear headlines—victories, scandals, echoes of battles past. The faint tang of stale coffee hangs in the recycled air, bitter and familiar.

Between them, the manila folder with its stark label—Turner—lies open, sheets bristling with logged infractions, timestamps pressed like cold evidence.

Nina taps a pen lightly, her eyes tracing each entry as if searching for the spark that might ignite change. "He's not just breaking rules; he's shattering trust. Do you think consistency will be enough to reel him in?"

Natalie's voice is steady, a quiet ripple cutting through the sterile stillness. "It has to be. Control fights fire with fire. Consistency fights fire with bricks—slow, deliberate, unyielding bricks. This isn't about crushing him; it's about building something that lasts."

She pauses, her fingers drumming once against the folder's edge. The weight of what she's about to enforce settles across her shoulders—the professional mandate clashing against something harder to name. A sense that Brick's trajectory matters beyond statistics and protocol, that this moment, if handled wrong, could break him entirely.

Nina nods slowly, absorbing the weight of those words and the subtle defiance beneath the clinical surface. "So—repeat the message every day, every play, no exceptions?"

"Exactly. Discipline isn't a punishment; it's the only way out."

They share a look, full of hard-earned resolve, their fingers already poised to schedule the next steps.

Down below, near the training tables scattered with towels and water bottles, Jaxon catches Emma's arm as she passes, pulling her into the shrinking space between sweat-streaked benches.

"We can't keep pretending Brick's going to flip the switch overnight," Jaxon says, his voice low, almost lost beneath the distant echo of closing lockers.

Emma studies his face as if she's reading a play too complicated to interpret. "Yeah, but what if the switch never comes? We need him, Jax. The team needs him. But if his rage wins out—"

Jaxon's laugh is rough and humorless. "Then the team's dead. Or it's just us pretending it's alive."

"But what about loyalty?" Emma presses. Her voice softens, becoming almost pleading. "Is that just an excuse to enable? Or is it a rope we throw to someone who is drowning?"

Their eyes lock in a battle of hope against uncertainty that swells beneath their words.

Jaxon's shoulders drop. "I don't know." His voice cracks just enough to shatter the hard edge. "Maybe loyalty is the only thing we have left."

Emma nods, her shoulders tightening against the weight of a question with no easy answer.

Outside, the stadium's lights blur into a murmuring background as Brick's truck rumbles through the winding access road. The cold leather of the steering wheel presses into his palms, slick with sweat beneath the fading sun.

His jaw is a hard line, clenched as if it could contain all the turmoil inside.

He repeats Coach Hale's words under his breath, the warning echoing like an ominous drumbeat: "Line crossed. One more time, you're out. No second chances."

The phrase tastes bitter in his mouth—dry, acrid, seeping into every nerve. Shame prickles beneath the bravado, a shadow that gnaws at the edges of his defiance. The thrill of rebellion falters, revealing something hollow—something like fear.

A fragile crack in the armor.

His eyes flick to the rearview mirror. The bright taillights of the stadium shrink, swallowed by the gathering dusk. The engine rumbles under his hands, a steady pulse in the quiet cab. It marks the end of today's fight and the uncertain dawn of what comes next.

The lights of the facility blink off one by one, folding the stadium into shadow as Brick's truck fades into the night, leaving behind the residue of tension, raised stakes, and a battle only just beginning.

Anger Isn't Power

The late-afternoon sun flickered through the stadium's steel skeleton, casting long shadows across the emerald turf. Brick's cleats hammered the field in a measured rhythm. Thud. Thud. Thud. Each step was a pulse of restrained tension. His jaw was locked tight, muscles rippling beneath the sweat-darkened jersey. Shoulders rigid as if bearing an invisible weight, he prowled through the drills—a tempest barely contained.

From across the field, Caleb fumbled the blocking assignment. Again. His hesitant stance contrasted sharply with the brute certainty that Brick demanded.

Brick's low voice cut through the drone of snapping tackles and shouted calls. "You're breathing too shallow, rookie. Anchor your feet. Stop flinching like you're already losing."

Caleb blinked and tried to reset. The next snap revealed panic clinging to his movements. The blocking slipped.

Brick's frustration surged like a lightning strike.

"Hell, Caleb! What the fuck are you doing?" His voice climbed, rougher now, slicing past the line between coach and something darker—something dangerous.

He closed the distance with heavy strides. His hands shot forward, fingers twitching near Caleb's chest, ready to shove him upright. The air tightened. Anger radiated in waves—then suddenly, he pulled back. His hands trembled, frozen in the space between them. A storm held in check by sheer will.

Caleb's shoulders stiffened, and his breath came shallow and quick.

A whistle cut through the heated air—sharp and enduring, snapping the tension like brittle wire.

Coach Marcus Hale strode onto the turf, his boots echoing through the charged silence. His gaze drilled into Brick. Players halted midsnap, their breaths hitching. Murmurs rolled like distant thunder through the ranks.

Then—heels. Clicking crisp and detached, slicing across the grass.

Natalie appeared from the sideline, her face a calm iron beneath the late sunlight's glaze. The practice rush faded, and the air carried the sharp tang of sweat and cut grass.

"Logan." Her voice rang low but was edged with unmistakable steel, pulling every eye like a taut wire.

Brick turned, his eyes flashing fire beneath thick brows. But Natalie didn't waver. She moved directly between him and the stunned cluster of teammates, her stance radiating undeniable authority.

"Leave practice. Now."

The command hammered through the field like a gavel—final and uncompromising.

Heads swiveled, and eyes darted between Brick and the space she had claimed. Natalie raised her voice just enough to slice through the static. "Brick will issue a public apology—to Caleb and to the fans—for violating the conduct protocols. This is not negotiable."

Stiff silence followed, heavier than the humid air. Caleb's shoulders tensed beneath Jaxon's steadying hand—one anchor in a world suddenly rattled.

Brick's chest swelled with a harsh intake of breath. His eyes ignited with raw, flickering flames. His stride became predator-like as he moved toward the tunnel. Every step shook the turf beneath him, his shoulders squared like a blockade against the world's judgment.

No words. No arguments.

Just a cold, sweeping retreat as his teammates watched in stunned silence.

Murmurs rippled like a spreading tide. Players' shoulders stiffened. Jaxon's hand remained firm on Caleb's shoulder as the drill's steady rhythm stuttered, then fractured beneath the weight of silent judgment.

Brick's footsteps echoed hollowly through the tunnel mouth, swallowed by the darkness beyond the floodlights. His fury tightened into compressed silence—coiled, lethal.

The field held its breath. The afternoon shifted—uneasy, fractured.

The narrow hallway buzzed with cleats on tile—sharp, rhythmic. Natalie led the team directly from the field into the media room, her stride purposeful and commanding.

The space hummed with sterile brightness—icy-white walls and crisp overhead lights that cast no shadows. The heavy scent of polished wood and faint disinfectant settled thick in the air, a smell Brick associated with institutions and consequences. Nina stood behind the bank of cameras, her fingers flicking buttons with practiced efficiency, positioning them to catch every angle. The microphones gleamed on their stands, cold and impersonal.

Natalie pulled Brick aside near the entrance, her voice low and edged with steel. "Here's the wording for your apology. Keep it short. Keep it formal. No deviations." She slid the printed page across the podium's glossy surface.

Brick's jaw clenched so tightly that it ached. His fists balled at his sides, knuckles paling as he fought the urge to explode. But he nodded—no protest, just the storm gathering behind his eyes—coiled and waiting.

The reporters shuffled into place, lenses pivoting and pens poised. The room fell into hushed expectancy. Brick closed the small distance to the podium. Each step echoed in the sterile chamber. His shoulders squared, and his eyes narrowed. He gripped the edges of the wood like a drowning man gripping a raft.

"Cameras rolling," Nina's voice hummed softly from behind the equipment.

Natalie slid into her seat off to the side, a clipboard balanced neatly in her lap—poise wrapped in quiet control.

Brick inhaled sharply. The words tasted foreign as he forced them out.

"To Caleb Monroe, our rookie, and to the fans who support this team: I want to apologize for my behavior during practice today. My actions were unacceptable, and I recognize how they affected my teammates and those watching. I am committed to earning back your trust through discipline and respect."

The words felt clipped and heavy in his mouth, grinding against the raw edges of his pride. His gaze flickered briefly to the edge of the podium. Muscles trembled beneath the surface. The silence that fell afterward was thick. Taut.

A reporter leaned forward, her voice sharp through the microphones. "Logan, can you explain what triggers these outbursts? Are you struggling to control your temper on the field?"

Brick's eyes hardened. His answer came cold and flat. "No further comments."

Another reporter pressed in. "Do you think your suspension history jeopardizes your season, both on and off the field?"

"Not at this time."

He glanced toward Natalie. Her fingers tapped the clipboard with precise impatience—a warning. She stepped forward, her voice smooth but firm.

"That'll do for now. Let's wrap it up."

Clicking sounds and murmurs whirled as the reporters began packing up. Natalie signaled to Nina, who dismantled cameras with brisk efficiency. The atmosphere shifted from public spectacle to backstage urgency.

Brick wedged past the clustered chairs, his steps heavy and deliberate. The weight of the room pressed against his back. He didn't look at Natalie. His anger roared like an inferno muted beneath a veneer of cold resignation. She watched him go, letting the distance widen without reaching out.

At the door, Brick paused.

His breath came harsh and fast, swallowed by the chaos of the hallway beyond—flickering screens, camera flashes, the scent of electronics, sweat, and something darker brewing beneath it all. His chest rose and fell: shallow, hurried.

Without a backward glance, he strode away into the maze of corridors.

Natalie straightened the scattered papers on the podium, smoothing the edges with deliberate care. Her eyes tracked Brick's retreating figure through the partially opened door, steady and watchful. The thin line of tension etched across her brow softened imperceptibly. Calm amidst chaos.

"Did you mean that?" A voice broke the charged silence.

The last reporter lingered near the podium, pen still poised.

"You heard what I said." Brick's voice cut like steel beneath the hum of dismantling microphones. His eyes flashed, defiant. "No more questions."

"You're dodging." The reporter pressed forward, unyielding.

Brick's glare slammed into the lens like a sudden storm.

"You want a story?" His voice dropped low, icy. "Try harder."

Natalie's hand nudged him gently backward, a razor edge beneath the touch. "Brick, that's enough."

He snarled under his breath but fell silent, swallowing back the tempest behind thick walls of bruised pride.

The crew whispered and packed up. The room emptied like a battlefield after a truce. Natalie folded the last sheet of paper with meticulous care, her lips pressed into a thin line.

The hallway's charged murmurs swelled outside the closed door, voices rising and falling like restless waves. She lingered in the fluorescent hum, her eyes fixed on the space Brick left behind. The echo of unresolved fury hung thick between them.

The stage was set. The lines were drawn. The war of wills had only just begun.

The weight room swam in harsh fluorescent light. The clang of metal bounced off cold concrete walls. Brick's arms coiled tight, sleeves rolled above his elbows, sweat tracing rivers down the hollows of his temples.

The fluorescent lights buzzed overhead, casting sharp shadows across his slick skin. Cold sweat slicked his palms. The rough bar bit into his calloused fingers. The smell of rubber mats and stale sweat clung to the air—a battle-worn scent he had come to know all too well.

Each breath tasted sharp, tangy with iron and resolve.

He slammed the loaded barbell onto the rack. The echo cracked through the still air like a gunshot. He glared at the weights, muscles trembling, then lifted again.

Rep after grinding rep. His face hardened—distorted with frustration, shame flickering beneath the surface like a wicked blaze. The barbell quivered in his grasp. His hands shook, threatening mutiny. On the next lift, failure came suddenly and brutally. The bar halted mid-air. Brick's chest heaved. His knees buckled. He collapsed forward onto the bench, his forehead nearly grazing the scuffed vinyl. His breath hitched in ragged gasps.

From the doorway, Natalie stands frozen, files clutched loosely in her hands. The sharp staccato of heavy breathing cuts through the quiet hum of the office. Then—a harsh thud reverberates as something heavy smacks against the floor. She exhales slowly and steps inside, a silent observer on the threshold, watching Brick push through another punishing set. His knuckles whiten, and his face twists in silent battle.

The barbell rises again, muscles coiling and veins straining. But the weight becomes a mountain. Mid-rep, his arms betray him. Brick folds forward, burying his face in his hands, shoulders shaking with a tremor that is not just physical.

"I always mess up..." The words escape like a raw whisper, ragged and bitter.

Natalie moves forward, closing the space between them. Her voice is low but unwavering. "You don't have to carry it alone." Her eyes hold steady, unblinking—the kind of quiet challenge that dares him to trust her.

Brick jerks his head up, his glare sharp enough to cut glass. "Get out. Just get the hell out." His voice breaks on the word, trailing off as his hands tremble against his knees, breath hitching in a harsh, uneven rhythm. Then silence swallows the room.

With trembling hands, he presses them to his knees, folding into himself. The rage bleeds away, replaced by something far heavier—guilt that sinks into the marrow like ice. He stays bent over, muttering fragments tangled with regret.

"That night... I almost destroyed everything." His voice barely rises above the pulse of his own heartbeat. "I almost ended someone's future. The hit that nearly shattered a young teammate's entire career—mine too. Everything I had built."

Natalie seats herself on a nearby bench, leaving a generous distance but staying close enough to be present. The weight room's sterile fluorescent glare casts long shadows around them, stark and unyielding. She doesn't move. She doesn't speak. She just waits with the kind of patience that doesn't require words.

Brick's eyes refuse her invitation—dark pools of anguish and self-recrimination. His breath rattles, breaking into uneven sobs swallowed deep. The bench creaks beneath him.

Time drags slowly. Natalie sits steady and silent, her own jaw tight, fingers gripping the edge of the bench just hard enough to make her knuckles pale. The quiet between them thickens but remains unjudging.

Then his voice rasps again, fractured like glass.

"I keep punishing myself, as if that's supposed to fix anything."

She leans in slightly, her voice steady. "Discipline—it's not natural for everyone. Your anger—that's armor. You've been defending yourself for a long time." She pauses, and for a moment, her own composure flickers—a shadow crossing her face, her jaw tightening almost imperceptibly. She knows this armor too; she wore it so long that it became her skin. "These protocols—they're not cages. They're chains we need to snap, not a spotlight to shame you."

Brick's jaw tightens, the weight of her words settling on him like a fresh bruise.

"I don't want forgiveness. Not yet." His voice cracks, raw with the edge of something barely held back. "I'm just—tired of hating myself. Like I'm a ticking time bomb waiting to explode."

Natalie's gaze softens, but her voice remains calm. Unyielding. "Self-loathing isn't atonement. It's a prison. Power isn't anger; it's the choice to control yourself—even when it's hardest. That's strength."

He scoffs bitterly. "How are you so damn calm when I'm at my worst?"

A shadow flickers across her face. For a moment, the controlled exterior cracks. "Control is my armor too. Not because I'm fearless, but because I'm terrified." She exhales slowly, as if releasing words she's kept locked away for too long. "Sometimes, control is the only thing standing between us and chaos."

The confession hangs between them, bridging a silent understanding.

Brick's breath hitches. The hard edge of his face softens. Silent tears carve trails down his cheeks. His fingers unclench. The invisible chains slowly loosen. For the first time, raw grief spills forth—no bravado, no fire. Just brittle vulnerability laid bare in the unforgiving fluorescent light.

He nods once—a small, fragile surrender.

Natalie rises, her voice gentle but resolute. "Whether you break down or break through next time, you don't have to do it alone."

She steps away, leaving the empty bench creaking softly in her wake. The harsh glare of the weight room presses down. But within the stillness, Brick sits slumped, his chest heaving with exhausted breaths. The first real crack appears in his armor—fragile but undeniable. Real.

The weight room hums with the low echo of dropped plates and distant footsteps fading into the stadium's vast corridors. Natalie slides onto the metal bench a few feet from where Brick sits slumped, his shoulders hunched but rigid despite the exhaustion pooling in his frame. She leaves space between them—neither too close nor coldly distant—as if respecting some invisible boundary he has drawn around himself. Her voice breaks through the dusty stillness, calm and steady.

"I saw what almost happened out there today," she says quietly, watching him out of the corner of her eye. "I noticed you fought it—you stopped yourself before it got worse."

Brick laughs, a harsh rasp that scrapes against the silence. He spits onto the weight-worn floor, the gesture sharp as a knife. "Fought it? There ain't nothing to fight, Natalie. I'm a walking disaster. Every time I breathe wrong, I'm on the edge of blowing up. I can't control my temper; I never could."

The words tumbled out, bitter and jagged as broken glass. In the fluorescent glare, she watched his jaw clench, the cords of his neck straining beneath sweat-dampened skin.

Natalie leaned forward slowly, her elbows braced on her knees. "Discipline—it's not natural for everyone. Anger has been your armor. I understand that." She paused, letting the words settle. "These conduct protocols? They're not about breaking you down or humiliating you. They're there to break the cycle."

"And what if the cycle is all I know?" Brick's voice came out coarse, barely above a whisper. His hands trembled as he pulled his arms tighter around his knees. "What if the anger is all that's kept me from falling apart because way back last year..." The crack widened. His breath hitched. "I nearly destroyed someone's whole damn future. And ever since... I haven't been punishing them. Hell, I've been punishing myself."

The metal bench felt cold beneath him. Everything felt cold except for the shame radiating from his chest.

"Self-loathing is all I'm good at. It isn't accountability. Just this... sickness that eats me from the inside out."

Natalie's gaze softened, but her tone remained firm, refusing to trace easy forgiveness. "Self-loathing isn't atonement, Brick. It's a prison you built for yourself." She let that land. "Real accountability? It's about choice and control. Not your anger. Power isn't in the rage—it's in mastering it."

Brick looked up slowly. His eyes caught the light like storm clouds brewing just beneath the surface—wet and shadowed. "How do you... stay so calm? Even when all I've got is my worst self on display?"

Her lips pressed into a thin line. She chose her words carefully, speaking a truth she rarely offered lightly. "Control is my armor, too." A pause, long enough to matter. "But it's not because I'm fearless.

No. It's because I'm scared—every damn day." Her eyes flicked to his clenched fists and then back to his face. "It's just that I chose to put on the armor instead of breaking down." She inhaled slowly. "We're not so different when you strip it all away."

The tension shattered then—soundless, sudden—like a crack splitting stone.

A tear slipped free down Brick's cheek, tracing a dark rivulet over the dust on his skin. His fists unwound, fingers curling loosely against the bench's cold metal. The fluorescent lights hummed overhead. Somewhere distant, a door slammed. But here, in this corner of the weight room, he wasn't the ironclad storm on the field anymore. He was raw, stripped bare beneath the weight of old ghosts and new burdens.

When Natalie spoke again, her voice was soft but steady. "The next move? It's yours. Whether you break down or break through... you don't have to do it alone."

She rose with slow grace, her footsteps measured as she crossed the room. Her silhouette faded into the half-light, swallowed by shadow. Brick remained seated, his chest heaving in an exhausted rhythm. The first fissure in his armor had opened—shaken, yet somehow lighter. The weight of his silence now held something fragile: a promise. The faint scent of sweat and leather lingered in the space where she had been, a reminder that he was not entirely alone in this.

The Night Line

The worn leather of the couch creaks beneath Brick's weight. Sleep is a distant country. His eyes stare ahead, unblinking, caught in the undertow of the weight room confrontation with Natalie. Her words—sharp and unyielding—circle like a predator. Lightning-quick anger and regret that tastes like copper. The ghost of his own fury lingers in the air, thick and suffocating.

He carries the weight of what he said, of what he couldn't take back.

Sliding off the couch, his feet hit the hardwood, cool against his sneakers. Each step is restless and rhythmic—a counterpoint to the hammering of his heart. His hand rises to the jagged scar arching above his right eyebrow. His fingertip traces the toughened skin where the past whispers in a voice he can't silence. The familiar roughness should ground him, but it doesn't. Tension knots in his jaw and spreads down his neck.

A buzz cuts through the silence—sharp and insistent. His phone vibrates on the battered coffee table.

Brick snatches it up.

The screen glows. The words arrive like a fist to his throat:

"Eli Brooks involved in an accident. Details pending."

His chest tightens. Pressure clamps around his ribs, cold and un-yielding. The protein shake beside him slips from his fingers. Crimson spills across the table—sticky and spreading. The scent of strawberry powder and milk mingles with something acrid rising from inside him: panic, raw and suffocating.

His hands tremble. The flood returns—old trauma, old helpless-ness. That hospital. Those lights. The faces gone stiff with loss.

This can't happen again.

His breath hitches. One hand shakes as he fumbles with the phone, pulling up contact after contact like a man clutching at straws in a hurricane. Each call goes to voicemail. That hollow ring echoes, haunting. His voice pitches higher, cracking as he leaves terse messages.

"Eli... call me back. Please."

Again. Another name. Another hollow ring.

His voice grows hoarse and desperate. Frustration sharpens into something rawer. Anxiety crushes down, a fist around his hope.

Without thinking, something in him rebels. He dials Natalie.

The line clicks. Breathes alive.

"Natalie... it's Brick. Eli's in an accident." The words stumble out, breath short, as if each one costs too much. Panic drips between syl-lables. Guilt presses under his ribs, widening the fissure in his chest.

Silence. One beat. Two.

Then Natalie's voice cuts through—calm, urgent, stripped of its usual polish.

"Brick, listen. I'm on my way. Stay put, alright? Don't move until I get there. Get ready for the hospital. Keep your phone close."

Her tone is steady. No fluff. No empty reassurance. Just hard facts wrapped in something softer.

"Where exactly?" Brick barely breathes the question.

"Main ER entrance. I'll meet you there. Drive carefully."

Her words come swiftly—sharp orders that somehow soothe the chaos spiraling inside him.

Before he can say more, the line goes dead.

His fingers snap the phone shut. No hesitation. He yanks on his jacket, zipping it up with jagged, angry motions. The phone presses hard in his fist—as if it might splinter. Keys jangle sharply as he grabs them. Footsteps pound through the apartment like a drumroll into the unknown. The cold outside seeps in as he storms through the door, adrenaline thrumming through his veins.

—

"I should've seen it. Should've known."

Brick mutters the words as he paces, his voice rough. The apartment's shadows flicker with the glow of the streetlamp. Each step is jittery. Raw nerves are stretched tight.

He stops and swallows hard. His fingers drag across the jagged scar again—tracing back to himself. Back to something steady.

His heartbeat drums louder than the city's hum outside.

His mind spirals into places he thought he'd buried. Memories sting like teeth. The hospital's fluorescent lights. The helplessness. The faces gone rigid with loss. That same suffocating pressure now presses on someone he cares about. Someone still fighting.

"Damn it, Eli," he breathes.

His phone vibrates—just a notification, nothing more.

Brick lets out a ragged breath and steels himself. Everything else falls away. There's only the hospital, only Eli, only hope—fragile and thin as a thread.

—

His truck rumbles to life. Tires bite into the asphalt as he tears through the dark toward the hospital.

"Brick, you need to slow down. Talk to me." Natalie's voice comes through the Bluetooth, steady, pulling him back from the spiral.

"I'm trying," he snaps, frustration raw-edged. "I'm sick of waiting. Nobody's answering."

"When you get there, check in with intake. Wait for me. I'm coming."

"Don't keep me waiting," he pleads, his voice cracking.

"You're not alone."

His grip tightens on the wheel, and his breath stutters.

"I'm... I'm sorry," he chokes out, words tumbling free like ragged pieces of himself.

Natalie answers without hesitation. Her voice carries a warmth that catches him off guard.

"The past is heavy, Brick, but this is now. You can't carry it all."

His shoulders sag as exhaustion and fear converge in a silent tremor.

With her voice still in his ear, he pushes harder on the gas. The night stretches ahead, dark and waiting. He chases the fragile thread of hope beneath the city lights, toward a future that isn't written yet.

Behind him, the apartment goes dark.

Brick's truck thuds into the hospital parking lot, tires crunching over scattered gravel. He kills the engine. The sudden silence presses against the roar still pounding in his chest. His hands tremble on the wheel for a moment, then he swings the door open. The cold night air bites at his face as he staggers forward, muscles taut beneath the weight of dread. Fluorescent light leaks from the automatic glass doors, stark and unforgiving, pooling onto the cracked pavement like liquid ice. Brick pulls his jacket tighter, his jaw clenched so hard that it is a test of will to keep his teeth from grinding.

Inside, the harsh light stabs at his eyes. Heat from too many bodies, mingled with the odor of disinfectant and stale coffee, wraps around him like a shroud. He hates hospitals—too sterile, too exposing—but Eli needs him. He swallows the lump tightening in his throat and moves toward the ER desk. His boots echo sharply against the linoleum floor, a hollow percussion in the tense hum of murmured voices and the beeping of monitors.

The nurse at the counter looks up, her face shifting from tired to guarded in an instant. "Family only. Are you family?" Her voice is clipped, a barrier as much as a question.

"I'm here for Eli Brooks." His voice catches, then roughens. "Eli Brooks. He's under your care."

The nurse holds up a hand, directing him toward the intake paperwork piled to one side. "We'll need patient details for the intake process." Her eyes flick to the thin line of sweat on his brow.

Brick's heartbeat hammers. Each breath comes ragged and shallow as he glances over the forms without focus. Around him, the ER swirls—a confusing torrent of hushed footsteps, the distant wail of sirens, and the steady beeping of a monitor somewhere deep inside. His size makes him impossible to ignore, yet internally, the panic scrapes away at any sense of presence, shrinking him into something fragile.

He paces the space between the vending machine and the elevator, flexing his hands desperately, his ears straining for any word, any sign.

As he spins in that anxious orbit, a brisk rhythm joins the chaos. Natalie strides in—her heels clicking with controlled purpose on the tiles, her stance steady despite the undercurrent of urgency in her glance. She moves with the calm mastery of someone accustomed to navigating storms. At the intake desk, she introduces herself sharply. "Natalie Brooks, team PR manager, here with Logan Turner." Her pen glides across the forms in a practiced motion, signatures tight and purposeful. Her voice balances authority with urgency as she negotiates quietly with the hospital staff, threading through privacy protocols and contact chains.

Brick watches her with a tangled mix of resentment and grudging dependence twisting tightly inside his chest. The familiar set of her jaw and the way she commands even this sterile silence serve as a reminder of battles fought and alliances forced. She finishes speaking, folds the paperwork neatly, and then gestures toward the seating beyond the kiosk.

Together, they move to the sterile waiting area—rows of mismatched plastic chairs under the glare of fluorescent tubes that leave no corner soft. Natalie claims a seat next to him, her posture an impassive shield, but her eyes flick carefully to all the comings and goings.

Brick slumps into the hard plastic chair beside her, his breath shallow and uneven. A tremor jolts through his fingers, which twitch like sparks against his thighs. The faint buzz of a muted TV in the corner offers a strange, unwanted soundtrack: headlines about wildfires blazing, unconnected to the electric ache filling the room.

The sterile scent of the hospital air—sharp antiseptic mixed with the faint trace of someone's unwashed clothes—wraps around him. The distant clang of a gurney and the sharp voices nurses use to cut through the noisy chaos all weave into a tapestry he can't unravel. He closes his eyes briefly, fingers curling into fists before loosening, as the awful dance of panic settles just enough for him to breathe.

In the dull glow of that waiting room, he and Natalie sit side by side, divided by space yet tethered by fear, each lost in the silence that screams louder than words.

"How long..." His voice catches, then roughens, "How long is this going to take?" Brick glances sideways at Natalie, his eyes dark and restless, arms folded tightly across his chest like armor.

"They don't run on our clock," she says with a dry edge, her eyes scanning the empty corridor. "But I've got a line open to the admins. We'll know as soon as they do."

He snorts, not quite a laugh. "Seems like you have everything under control." His tone is sharp but undercut with something fragile—wanting to believe it is true.

"It doesn't feel like control." Natalie's voice softens. "Just managing the chaos." She taps her phone, her fingers flying as she drafts messages and monitors streams coming across the team channels.

Brick bites his lip. His fingers drum a staccato rhythm on his knee. The noise of footsteps and distant carts rolling by—every small sound is a trigger for his rising tension. "How do you stay so calm? I feel like I'm falling apart."

Natalie finally turns, her gaze steady, betraying no pity—just presence. "You don't have to hold it all up. Sometimes, you just have to stand there and let it sway."

He exhales a shaky breath, his body coiled tight against the waiting. The tension jitters beneath his skin, raw and reckless. His glance catches her reaching out, a calm hand settling on his forearm, grounding him in the flood. He doesn't pull away.

The hospital TV flickers with unrelated news—a politician's speech, sports highlights he can't focus on. Yet amid the sterile buzz of this place, the weight shifts—a strange, fragile tether between two fractured pieces trying to hold steady.

Brick collapses deeper into the chair, his limbs trembling, every muscle screaming for relief in a song of silent desperation. The waiting presses on, cold and relentless, as outside, the night stretches on, indifferent.

The harsh lights above cast sharp shadows across Brick's rough hands. He stares at them as if they hold answers, his fingers twitching as if the weight of the world might slip through his skin any second. His knee bounces erratically, tapping the floor with a restless rhythm.

Every footstep echoes like a bomb ticking—sharp, invasive.

The distant scrape of a wheeled cart grinds against the linoleum. His jaw clenches. The sterile smell of antiseptic and bleach hangs thick, pressing in on him like a second skin—suffocating, clinical, utterly wrong. It's the smell of places where bad things happen, where control slips away. Brick's chest tightens. The walls seem to close in, all those gleaming surfaces reflecting his panic back at him like mirrors he can't escape.

"I should've noticed," he mutters, his voice low and rough, the words scratching at the silence.

Natalie sinks down beside him, her posture steady yet softening the sterile chill between them. Her fingers tap out urgent texts—quick and clipped—each message a lifeline thrown into the swirling chaos around them. Her expression is tight, her eyes scanning incoming messages, absorbing the flood of digital anxiety without breaking. The faint hum of the ER wraps around them like a fragile bubble, barely holding the panic at bay.

She's not just managing the crisis for the team; she's here for him. That complication—that tentative trust built under pressure—settles between them like an unspoken promise.

Brick tries to muster stillness, but it slips away. His voice cracks when he finally dares to speak: "How... how the hell do you keep it together? Every second feels like it's stretching, and I'm just—" He swallows, raw and rattled. "I can't just sit. I'm the guy who's supposed to look out for everyone. And I missed it. I missed Eli."

Natalie's gaze holds him, steady and unmoving. She stretches her hand, light and deliberate, settling it over his forearm. He shudders—not from the cold, but from the invisible tremors rattling beneath his skin. She doesn't speak immediately, letting her presence do the quiet work of steadying him.

When the words come, they are spare, stripped of clichés.

"You're not in this by yourself."

Her hand is warm, a tether in the clinical chill. Brick's shoulders tense, then slowly unwind, the knot loosening just enough to breathe. He won't meet her gaze; instead, his eyes fixate behind her, trying to peel away the shadows clawing at his mind.

Suddenly, Natalie's phone buzzes sharply. The screen lights up with Caleb's name, cutting clean through the silence. She slides a thumb over the display and answers. Her voice is clipped but protective, the shield she wraps around Brick.

"He's stable for now," she says in a low tone, her eyes flicking to Brick quickly. "No fatal injuries. They're keeping him under observation. I'll update you as soon as I know more."

Brick's jaw tightens, every line on his face carved from raw tension. He watches her, awash in a cocktail of resentment and reluctant relief. She fields the questions he can't answer—not yet—her voice a calm anchor amid the chaos.

"Thanks, Nat," he manages, his voice rough like sandpaper.

Natalie's focus swings back to her phone as she types out notes, her fingers moving fast but with purpose. Brick folds his large hands into his knees, his fingers lacing tight—trying to hold himself together. A ragged breath slips out, sharp and uneven. The storm inside him is just beginning.

She rubs his forearm once, lightly—a single gesture heavy with unspoken promise and certainty. Then she glances back down at her phone, tapping out another message, the words private between her and the quiet glow of the screen.

"I don't know how much longer I can sit here," Brick admits after a silence, his voice bitter with exhaustion, the weight of guilt pressing down like a vise. "It feels like I'm drowning, and everyone's depending on me to surface first."

Natalie's eyes flick up, softening but resolute. "You're not drowning. Not while I'm here."

He lets out a humorless laugh. It's thin and hollow.

"You always sound like you've got it figured out. I get so damn lost."

She doesn't argue. Instead, her hand squeezes his forearm again, warmer now—steady and real.

"No one has it all figured out, especially not in waiting rooms like this."

Brick takes a slow breath, his muscles relaxing incrementally as the crushing weight eases, paced as if measured by the rhythm of her touch. The sterile walls and flickering fluorescent lights fade a little. The hum of monitors and soft murmurs around them settle into a background buzz rather than a crescendo.

"Why do you stick around?" His question slips out more vulnerably than he intends, and for the first time, his gaze catches hers—raw and unguarded.

"Because someone has to." She shrugs, a half-smile flickering—tired but genuine. "And this mess isn't just yours to carry."

Her clarity bolts a sharp line through his chaos. Brick's fingers unfurl from their tight grip, his hands resting limply on his knees as he exhales—slower now, closer to steady.

Natalie's phone buzzes again—another wave of updates to manage, messages to send, plans to draft—but she has found a different rhythm now. One that balances the whipping storm inside Brick against the calm she is determined to bring. Her eyes slide up from the screen.

"You're not alone here," she says quietly, her voice almost a whisper amidst the vague clamor of the ER.

Brick nods, a slow surrender in the tense set of his shoulders. The first cracks of fragility show beneath the armor he has worn so fiercely. The waiting stretches ahead—long, uncertain, and jagged—but for now, the hold of her presence is enough to keep him anchored.

The minutes drip by—slow and merciless. Brick folds deeper into himself, his hands sinking into his knees as Natalie taps notes onto her phone, her touch on his forearm a steady pulse beneath the sterile glow. A lifeline threading silence between them.

###

A buzz shatters the hospital waiting room's quiet hum. Natalie's phone vibrates sharply against the plastic armrest. She snatches it up, slipping into a hushed whisper.

"Hey, Emma."

"Status?" Emma's voice cut through, low and urgent. "What's the word on Brick? And Eli?"

Natalie leaned back. Shadows pooled beneath the harsh fluorescent lights. Her throat tightened. She inhaled shallowly, fingers curling around the phone like a lifeline.

"Still waiting. No news yet." The words came out thin and uncertain. "I don't know what Brick needs right now, Emma. Not just someone sitting here with him—something more."

The silence stretched between them—patient and unhurried.

"Nat, there's no perfect fix here." Emma's voice softened, layering warmth beneath the clinical hum. "Just show up. Let yourself care, even if he fights it. Even if it's messy. Sometimes, it's the bare presence that heals."

Natalie closed her eyes. The dim flicker of monitors cast a pale glow over her face. She drew in a slow, steadying breath. The tension knotted in her shoulders eased, just a little.

She shifted her posture, sitting taller. Her feet found purchase on the cold linoleum floor. The rigid role of "team PR manager," protector of images, faded for a moment. Something softer took its place—something human.

She pulled the phone away from her ear and typed with her thumb: *Thanks. I'm here.*

The screen dimmed. She set the phone in her lap, fingers brushing its smooth surface almost reverently, then turned her whole body toward Brick.

The chair creaked beneath her weight—a subtle, anchoring sound.

The waiting room pressed in around them with starkness. A television murmured distant news, a cold drone in the background. Antiseptic air filled the space. The chill of exhausted linoleum permeated the atmosphere. The faint scrape of a nurse's shoe across the tile added to the ambiance. These details crumbled into insignificance.

What mattered was Brick.

His fingers twitched against the armrest. His gaze flickered to the door and then snapped back. His jaw was clenched so tightly that she could see his pulse throb at his temple. He looked less like the explosive force she had battled with and more like a man grasping for footing on an unstable ledge.

Natalie felt a prickling rush in her chest. This was no longer a task to contain a crisis; it was something far more fragile: the tenuous thread of trust, stretched taut in the silence between words.

She caught his glance and offered a small, deliberate nod—steady and unwavering. Not a command. Not an expectation. A tether.

"That's all I've got for now," her whispered voice broke the quiet. "I'm not going anywhere."

The words were bare, stripped of euphemism or spin, weighted with intention.

Something flickered through Brick's gaze: a shift, an acknowledgment.

Natalie's hand twitched, almost reaching out. She pulled it back, waiting for permission in the tense air between them.

The night outside deepened. Somewhere, a faint echo of distant footsteps could be heard. The patience of the waiting room was measured and unyielding, pressing in around them. But here, in this shared stillness, a quiet accord began to take shape.

###

The hallway breathed a hollow chill as the surgeon slid into view, his coat flapping softly with careful, measured steps. Light flickered harshly off polished shoes. Brick sat hunched in the waiting area, every muscle taut beneath the sharp hospital fluorescents.

The man's voice struck like a cautious drumbeat in the quiet space.

"Eli is stable. He remains unconscious, but there are no fatal injuries. We're monitoring him closely—intensive observation is necessary for now."

Unconscious. The word detonates something in Brick's chest—a phantom memory of another hospital, another waiting room, another moment suspended between life and death. His breath catches. Then, just as suddenly, it releases. No fatal injuries. Eli is stable.

Brick's shoulders sagged. Relief broke over him.

It coursed through his ribs, dragging his breath heavy and ragged. His knuckles whitened around the edges of the plastic chair, skin stretched tight over trembling fingers, the sharp corners biting into his palms. The air tasted metallic in his mouth. His legs trembled beneath him—an unsteady foundation for the fortress of rage and fear that had held him upright for days.

He rose without thinking. His boots scraped the tiled floor, too loud in the near silence.

"Thanks," he muttered, his voice cracked and tight—like he was holding back a storm.

His throat burned. Hot, stinging tears pricked behind his eyelids, each one a silent confession. Swallowing them down felt like swallowing fire.

Natalie stepped close, her presence steady in the chaos. As they walked toward the hospital doors, Brick felt the weight of her calm orbit around him—the way she didn't demand anything, just offered her steadiness like an anchor. Part of him resented needing it. Most of him couldn't survive without it. The automatic panels slid apart with a hollow sigh, and he shoved past into the biting night.

Cold air stabbed at his lungs, sharp and clean. He leaned hard against the truck's fender, the rough metal grounding him even as adrenaline unspooled raw beneath his ribs. His fists wrapped around the steering wheel, fingernails pressing crescent moons into the worn leather.

Natalie moved after him carefully, leaving space—a distance measured not in feet but in trust. Her eyes traced the fragile, fraying edges of his quiet storm. She watched the shallow rises and falls of his chest, the way his shoulders sagged and twitched under the weight of everything unsaid.

Slowly, ever so gently, she reached out. Her hand floated near his—a question hanging in the chill night air. No demand. No expectation. Just an offering wrapped in quiet strength.

His breath caught in his throat. He swallowed hard. His fingers twitched, tracing an unsure line before settling over hers. Their digits tangled, trembling bursts of unspoken need and fragile hope threading between calluses and warmth. Her thumb brushed soothing circles across the back of his hand—an endless loop, a silent promise.

The streetlight splashed stark white onto the cracked pavement beneath them. Their joined hands cast long shadows, tangled but steady. The low hum of distant traffic murmured around their solitude.

"You're allowed to feel this," Natalie whispered, her voice a soft current against the brittle quiet. "I'm here."

Brick lowered his gaze. His shoulders rounded inward like a wilting reed. Silent tears pricked and fell, tracing warm lines down his rough skin. His fingers tightened their hold—the fragile line between strength and surrender.

They stood still, two broken shapes held together by the tenuous thread of touch, the heavy, steady silence wrapping around them like a quiet shield against a world that demands hardness.

Brick blinked past the sting in his eyes, his throat tight. His voice came low—a rough rumble that barely scratched the silence between them. "Thanks... for tonight. For, y'know—being here." He lifted his chin, barely nodding, as if loosening the iron grip squeezing his chest. His shoulders slumped just a fraction, like a fortress cracking but still standing. "You gonna check in on me tomorrow?"

Natalie's gaze settled steadily on him, her voice firm but softened by the weight of the night. "I'll text. See how you're holding up." She shifted her stance, her fingers brushing a stray strand of hair from her face before folding them into a simple offer. "Need a ride? Or... company at your place?"

He shook his head, his lips pressed into a hard line that masked something gentler beneath. "I got it. I appreciate it, though." The words lacked any edge—just a quiet thanks, raw and honest in its own way.

Her phone lights up. With deliberate care, she taps a string of digits into his device. The screen glows faintly as she hands it back—a gesture more personal than they have allowed themselves so far. "Call anytime," she says, her voice dropping the polished tone she usually wears. "That's not a PR line."

Brick takes the phone, his thumb lingering over the screen. Giving her his number feels like handing over a piece of armor he has worn for years—an exposure he has long avoided. But something in her eyes, steady and unflinching, makes the risk feel less like surrender and more like trust. The way she watches him is a tether stronger than any professional protocol—a silent promise in the fluorescent glow of the lot.

He watches her move—graceful steps carrying her to the car. The soft click of the door echoes in the crisp night air. Pale light washes over him, and his fingertips, still warm from that brief contact, prick with a strange mix of vulnerability and strength. Exposure and refuge are tangled in an unspoken truce.

The truck's low rumble swallows the city's distant sirens and chatter. Taillights blink, shrinking into the night's black canvas. He leans heavily against the truck's rough metal, his breaths deep and uneven. Cold air fills his lungs, and for a moment, he lets himself wonder if maybe—just maybe—the weight he has carried for so long doesn't have to crush him alone. It's a fragile thought, barely formed, but it settles somewhere deep.

Long after the last glow disappears, Brick remains rooted, the silence around him thick with quiet electricity. Then, with a slow inhale that steadies the tremor caught beneath his ribs, he turns the key. The truck growls to life. The road ahead is empty—uncertain—but somehow less daunting.

He pulls away from the hospital, the weight on his shoulders a fraction lighter, carrying a fragile sort of promise he is not quite ready to name.

The Game That Tests Him

The gray light of dawn sifts through the high apartment window, pale and reluctant, touching the walls with a cold promise. Brick's fingers twitch against the quilted blanket, his muscles knotted tighter than the laces on his cleats. His jaw clenches hard, teeth grinding behind closed lips.

Coach Hale's voice echoes—stern and unforgiving—the warning crackling like static electricity: one more slip, and it's over. The bench looms ahead, not just a place to sit but a marker of failure, a sentence handed down with no appeal. To Brick, being benched meant erasure. It meant becoming invisible to scouts, to the league, to himself—another body taking up space instead of claiming it.

He pulls the threadbare hoodie tighter around his broad shoulders, the fabric worn thin along the cuffs, the team logo cracked and faded like the trust he's struggling to rebuild. Sweatpants hug his legs—black, loose, but damp at the knees from restless tossing. His gaze burrows into the indifferent cityscape beyond the pane: rooftops shadowed under steel-gray clouds, streets still empty save for the occasional car's distant hum. An unshakable tension coils in his chest, a tight band squeezing each breath, making the quiet apartment feel smaller, too vast, like a cage.

His eyes catch the faint dust motes drifting in the chill morning air, flickering like ghosts of past mistakes. The window fogs where his palm presses against the glass, warmth splintering the cold but failing to soften the weight settling deep in his gut. The rising sun is a sliver behind the horizon, beginning to color the sky with weak yellows that feel almost cruel—a reminder that daylight betrays every hidden flaw and every crack in the armor he keeps locked tight.

The clock ticks—steady and unforgiving. Nothing will change. The team bus will come. The eyes will watch. The whispers will follow. Brick's hand curls into a fist and then unclenches, his knuckles pale beneath calloused skin. A tightness clenches his throat. His Adam's apple bobs, but no sound comes. The words press heavily behind his teeth, biting silence into the chilly air.

When the first hum of the engine rumbles down the street, Brick moves with calculated deliberation, dragging on the damp hoodie and sliding a leather duffel over one broad shoulder. The bag feels heavy—not with gear but with all the weight he drags behind him: the roster threats, the past bruises, and the fragile hope threading his fingers. Outside, the wet pavement gleams faintly, cold mist curling up from cracks like ghostly fingers reaching for his ankles.

Footsteps echo softly and measured as he walks, the city waking around him in slow rhythms. He slips earbuds into his ears, but music offers no refuge—only a brittle barrier against the noise inside and out. The sharp scent of rain lingers after an early morning drizzle, mingling with the faint bitterness of burnt coffee wafting from a nearby café. Brick's jaw flexes again, swallowing the taste of bile and frustration.

His pace doesn't falter as he crosses the parking lot, eyes fixed ahead yet seeing nothing but shadows flickering at the edges. No words rise to meet the knot in his throat, and no calls distract him. He resists the pull of dialing a voice he wants to hear—someone who might understand or soothe—because this time, there's no safety in reaching out.

The team bus waits on the curb, its glossy black sides reflecting the dawning sky, a beast ready to swallow the squad whole. Even from the parking lot, Brick feels the weight of the stadium beyond—that looming concrete cathedral where thousands will watch, where every stumble is magnified, and where one mistake becomes a legend of failure. Game day. The atmosphere already crackles with tension, thick enough to taste. This is where it matters. This is where he either proves himself or disappears.

Brick slides inside with practiced quiet, the rubber soles of his sneakers thumping softly against the metal steps. Teammates trickle in around him, their chatter low and halfhearted, shots of early caffeine and grim focus settling the morning tension.

He settles at the rear, the last sanctuary in the long, narrow cabin, sinking into the worn leather seat as if it might somehow swallow the rising storm inside him. Thick cables of headphones plug into his ears—sound barriers sealing out the hum of engines, the scrape of cleats, and the glances that photographs cannot catch but nonetheless convey. He spreads his legs wide, his hands curling and uncurling on his knees in a silent fight against the tide of anger and dread.

Faces drift past his peripheral vision—Jaxon's easy grin, DeShawn's sideways glance—but Brick doesn't look up. They catch his eye and quickly look away, reading the stubborn set of his jaw and the hard line of his gaze against the window. Unspoken words cluster between them like static.

Two voices rise low, barely audible beyond the thrum of the engine.

"He's gotta get it together—or he's gone."

"No doubt."

The words land like stones against Brick's ribs. His chest tightens further. His breath catches. He doesn't answer—not with words, not with a glance. Instead, he watches the first light crack across the empty road, the city's steel bones waking beneath his steady, clenched fists.

The bus rumbles forward, its tires humming against the wet pavement, carrying the weight of unspoken threats, battered hopes, and a man caught somewhere between fury and fragile resolve. Brick leans back, tension settling into a brittle armor once again as the world outside edges inexorably closer—the stadium, the crowd, the fight.

All around, the team moves like shadows in the dawn, scattering behind him. Brick holds tight to the silence, the music, the pulse of his own breaking will. Eyes forward. Hands tight. Every muscle coiled for the storm to come.

The bus rumbles forward, a low, steady hum beneath the tension thick enough to choke on. Brick slouches toward the rear, settling into the worn leather seat with his broad legs splayed, a fortress of muscle and simmering quiet. Headphones over his ears drown out the world—or at least, that is the plan. His hands twitch, clenching into tight fists before uncurling against his knees, fingers restless with the fight that won't fade. Around him, murmurs rise and fall like whispers in a church, eyes flickering his way, measuring, diagnosing the storm barely contained.

A few rows forward, Jaxon and DeShawn lean toward each other, their voices hushed but sharp. They had come up together, the three of them—Brick, Jaxon, and DeShawn—bonded by the streets and the field, by promises made in youth that felt unbreakable then. Now, that bond is frayed under the weight of Brick's mistakes. Jaxon's lips move, shaping words without sound: "He's got to get it together—or he's gone." The weight of that unspoken ultimatum hangs in the air, an invisible noose tightening.

Brick's gaze remained steady on the fractured cityscape racing past the window—dark outlines of buildings softened by the dawn's first light. These streets had raised him. They had made him. Now they threatened to claim him back. He swallowed the words like bitter pills, the sting settling heavily on his tongue. Not a flicker, not a twitch betrayed his inner tempest. The silence between them fed the ever-looming pressure, and Brick let it wash over him, isolating himself as the murmurs rippled behind his back.

The bus's wheels thudded rhythmically against the pavement, each heartbeat marking time closer to the arena's iron gates. The stale scent of leather and faint sweat clung to the air, mingling with the crisp bite of early morning coffee and the lingering bitterness of yesterday's frustration. Brick felt the hum of his own heart pounding—not just from the adrenaline but from the knot of expectation tightening in his chest. His fingers curled against his thighs, nails digging in, grounding him.

DeShawn caught Brick's eye briefly, his expression a mix of cautious support and hard truth. But no words came.

Brick didn't turn. The world outside slid by—a blur of concrete and the fractured glow of streetlamp halos fading with the morning's first light. In here, on this moving island of whispered tension, every glance felt like a test. Every breath was measured and counted.

"Look," Jaxon murmured low enough for only DeShawn to hear, his voice rough with unshed frustration, "we all want him with us on the field, but if he slips again—it's game over for him. No second chances, not this time."

DeShawn nodded slowly, his eyes shadowed but steady. There was a weight in that nod, a shared understanding of how close the edge really is.

Brick's jaw clenched until the scar above his eyebrow pulled taut. Muscle and memory surged beneath his skin. He hated being managed—this cage of quiet warnings and loaded looks. He hated it. But he knew the truth: he was walking a tightrope stretched thin over a chasm of past mistakes, ready to swallow him whole. His fists balled against the fabric of his sweatpants, knuckles white, fingers trembling despite his efforts to stay still.

Behind him, more sidelong glances drifted. The soft footsteps of teammates boarding, the sliding creak of bus doors closing, and low voices behind closed curtains. Some carried hope; others, a silent judgment. Brick folded into himself, cocooned by his hoodie. The world filtered through the thrum of music pulsing in his ears—his barrier, his shield.

The bus slowed, tires crunching on gravel beneath the stadium's cavernous silhouette rising ahead like a titan waiting to be challenged. The city's pulse quickened—distant cheers already spilling, carried on the cold breeze that slipped through cracked windows. Brick's breath quickened. His shoulders pulled tight in stiff determination, or maybe defiance. He lifted himself with slow, deliberate motions, the muscles coiling beneath his skin like restrained thunder.

Without a word, he edged past his teammates, their eyes following him. No nods. No greetings. Just the press of shifting bodies and the hum of expectations. The cold metal rail bit sharply beneath his fingers as he stepped off, the ground solid and real after the bus's insistent rolling motion.

Jaxon caught his eye again, now direct and unguarded. Brick offered a tight, almost imperceptible nod—the shaky truce of a soldier heading into battle.

"Ready?" Jaxon's voice was low, nearly swallowed by the racket of distant cheers.

Brick's only answer came as a flat murmur, his voice tight as a drawn bowstring. "Yeah. Gotta be."

They fell into line, the group moving toward the stadium doors like a pack of predators on the scent—each man carrying his own burden, but Brick's felt the heaviest of all. The air tasted faintly metallic, sharp with anticipation and the distant promise of battle.

Footsteps echoed against the concrete as they entered the cavernous arena, the faint scent of turf and sweat awaiting them inside. Brick's fingers twitched at his sides. The battle had not yet begun but was already raging beneath his skin. His eyes locked on the tunnel opening, swallowing light and hope in equal measure.

No one said a word as they disappeared into the shadows. The silence was thick and electric, nothing but the sound of the stadium breathing around them.

The door whispered shut behind Natalie. Morning sunlight stabbed through the floor-to-ceiling windows in sharp beams. The PR office held its usual hum—quiet and electric with the kind of urgency that came from managing crises before they broke wide open.

She set her laptop down with care. The screen flickered to life, revealing spreadsheets and crisis protocols stacked like armor against whatever the day would throw at her. Three years of this work had taught her that in professional sports, the real battles weren't fought on the turf; they were fought in soundbites and headlines.

Natalie slid off her coat. The sharp scent of freshly brewed coffee mingled with the stadium's sterile chill—a combination she had come to associate with controlled chaos. Every morning felt the same: clinical precision stretched thin over simmering volatility. She had learned to move within that space carefully, reading the room's pulse before anyone else could.

Her eyes found the printout on her desk: talking points from last night, black ink smudged where her grip had tightened. She smoothed the wrinkles with her palm, steadying herself.

Movement caught her eye beyond the glass partition.

A figure leaned against the team entrance archway, notepad poised with the ease of a predator: Victor Cross. His too-slick smirk and cold eyes had a way of making people forget he was just a journalist. He tapped his pen—sharp and deliberate—scanning each player who filed past. Each arrival was another potential story in his calculation, another angle to exploit.

Natalie's nails bit into the edge of her desk, and her breath hitched. Victor's presence here, this early, meant he was hunting for something specific. She had learned to recognize that particular focus of his; it was how he operated—patient, relentless, and utterly without mercy.

She typed quickly, her eyes never leaving him: *"Victor spotted near entrance. Monitoring."*

Sent.

Her phone buzzed faintly with Emma's acknowledgment, their silent code for the front lines.

Natalie closed her laptop, the soft click sounding too loud in the quiet office. She rose, the leather of her chair creaking as she pushed back from the desk. The hallway outside stretched narrow and muted, alive with distant echoes of pregame chatter and cleats scraping against the tile. She moved toward the media room, her heels tapping a measured rhythm against the floor.

The sidelines hummed with activity. Players gathered in clusters, their energy coiled tight with anticipation. There was Brick Turner, pacing like a caged animal. His jaw was clenched so hard that his knuckles had turned white. Muscles corded in his shoulders and arms, every line of his body screaming with restless tension.

Flashes erupted across the field as the press pool snapped photos. The humid scent of cut grass and sweat mixed with something metallic—the tang of anticipation hanging thick in the air. Camera shutters clicked like insects swarming a wound.

Natalie pressed her fingertips against the doorframe. The cool metal grounded her. She surveyed the room, tracking Victor's position and watching how his eyes moved across the assembled crowd as if he were weighing secrets on an invisible scale.

"She's on edge," a colleague's voice came from behind her. The words cut through the silence like a warning flare. "Victor's not here for pleasantries."

Natalie didn't turn. "He never is."

"Whatever he's looking for—"

"He won't find it." Her voice came out cooler than she felt. "Not on my watch."

The colleague stepped back into the rising tide of pregame chaos.

Natalie exhaled slowly, taking one measured breath, then another. The night's residue eased from her chest. Her gaze slid across the field, where the first members of the team moved like currents in restless water, each step weighted with hope and dread.

Victor tapped his pen again. His focus had narrowed entirely on Brick—on that hard-shelled figure pacing by the sideline.

She understood what he was hunting for. She had always understood.

Her thumb moved across her phone screen. Another message to Emma: *"Keep an eye on the press room. Victor's circling."*

No response was needed. It was always understood.

The fight wasn't just on the field today; it never was.

Natalie turned away from the window. Her steps were light but purposeful as she moved toward the edge of the field. Her presence would be a shield—steady, deliberate, a counterweight to whatever chaos was building.

Victor remained at the entrance, a dark silhouette sharply carved by the rising sun. His shadow stretched long across the morning, a thread weaving through everything.

At the threshold of the media room, Natalie's fingers curled around the door handle. The polished metal was cool against her skin—a stark contrast to the heat coiling in her chest.

The crowd outside swelled. Voices rose. Electricity crackled through the air. But all her focus remained fixed on the lone figure standing guard at the entrance: Victor Cross, a predator in a suit.

"Storm's brewing," a nearby reporter muttered.

Natalie met his eyes. Her voice was low but firm. "Storms always come. The question is whether you're ready."

She slid the door open and stepped into the light. The barrier between calm and chaos was thinner than a breath.

Outside, the game waited. Inside, the war had already begun.

The locker room fell silent as Brick stepped inside. His shoulders slumped, and his head dipped low, weighed down by the walls closing in with expectations.

Conversations died mid-sentence. A wave of stillness rippled across the rows of lockers, their worn wood etched with names and numbers—stories of battles won and lost. His cleats scraped softly against the scuffed floor, a steady thrum barely disturbing the quiet. Sidelong glances flickered toward him: curious, wary, some tinged with guarded sympathy. Then they shifted back to scattered gear and tape waiting for the night's clash.

Coach Marcus Hale stood tall on the raised platform at the center of the room, clipboard in hand, eyes sharp beneath the brim of his cap. In this league, public benching during the pre-game lineup announcement was rare—a statement, not just discipline, but a public marking.

His voice cut through the hush: measured, unyielding. He read the starting lineup, each name landing like a hammer on the anvil of anticipation.

"Brick Turner will sit out the first half. Disciplinary action for the recent infraction."

The air twisted. A collective exhale rippled off the walls like disturbed water. Some murmurs of disbelief echoed in the silence. The disappointment was audible—a low rumble mingled with unrest. A few players shifted their weight, exchanging looks that said everything without words: this changes everything.

Brick's jaw tightened, a coiled spring. Muscles twitched beneath taut skin. His breath hitched—bitter, shallow. He tried for a quick smirk, a cracked mask to hide the fissures beneath, but it faltered under the tension coiling in his shoulders like a spring on the verge of snapping. His eyes sharpened, glinting with silent promise.

Jaxon nudged DeShawn just a row ahead, his voice low but carrying enough to pierce the quiet.

"If he doesn't fix this, he won't be sticking around much longer."

The words hung heavy and cold, wrapping around Brick like a noose. He didn't flinch or respond. His gaze remained fixed just past the row of lockers, absorbing the room's shifting currents—the tentative votes cast in his favor and against him.

The door creaked open. Natalie stepped in, her heels clicking softly against the tile. Her entrance was quiet but commanding—a contrast to the charged atmosphere. She scanned the room just long enough to find Brick.

"Turner," she said, her voice smooth yet edged. "I need a quick quote for the social posts. Outside."

He didn't meet her eyes. His shoulders braced as he followed her out. The door whispered shut behind them.

The hallway narrowed. The scent of linoleum and stale sweat gave way to cooler air, tinged faintly with the metallic tang of freshly cut grass from the field beyond.

Natalie folded her arms, her presence filling the narrow space between them. For a moment, neither spoke. Brick's mind flickered—a flash of what had led to this infraction, a blur of anger he couldn't quite take back, and beneath it all, the gnawing doubt that maybe she was right. Maybe he was the problem.

Her voice dropped—low, steady, with no hint of softness.

"This isn't about your temper or us managing your image. You need to play for your pride, your future. Not for me, not for the team's social media stats. For you."

Brick's lips parted, but no words came immediately. His eyes darkened, the fight simmering beneath a veneer of calm. His fingers pressed silently into the cool plastic of his helmet—a question he couldn't quite ask.

Then, in a voice that was rough but resolute, he answered, barely above a whisper but firm enough to carry.

"I want to play. I'll control it."

Natalie studied him for a long moment—the hard line of his jaw, the set of his shoulders, the quiet fire in his gaze. She nodded once, subtle, almost a secret pact, and then led the way back inside.

As they reentered, the locker room hummed with renewed energy. Players shuffled pads and tape, and helmets thudded onto benches like distant thunder. Brick stood apart, helmet in hand, the cool plastic smooth against his fingers. His breath settled into a measured rhythm while the weight of benching pressed down—not as punishment, but as a challenge carved into bone.

The chatter resumed, softer now, cautious, as if the storm had passed but left its chill behind. Brick's eyes scanned the room—not meeting anyone, yet deeply registering the looks tinged with curiosity, respect, and wariness. Each breath he took steadied him further, the heavy air thick with anticipation and unspoken promises.

The benching wasn't a sentence; it was a crucible. And Brick, despite everything, felt the heat.

Brick's boots scuffed the cracked concrete. The afternoon sun beat down, searing through the thin mesh of his worn sweatshirt. His muscles twitched—restless and coiled. His fists clenched tight enough to blanch his knuckles, and his breath came jagged and shallow.

His replacement anchored the line ahead, solid but hesitant, fumbling assignments as the defense unraveled play after play. Brick's gaze darted to every snap and every missed gap. The taste of frustration sat sour and sharp in the back of his throat. He had not yet stepped onto the turf.

He paced back and forth, like something caged, caught between impulse and restraint.

Natalie stood near the boundary, her shoulders squared beneath her crisp team jacket. The scent of fresh-cut grass mingled with the iron tang of sweat and the sharp metallic ring of shouted instructions. Her gaze snapped between the frenzied field and the press box looming above. There, Victor Cross scribbled endlessly, his fingers tapping against the spine of his notebook, his eyes narrowed beneath the brim of his hat.

Each glance in his direction tightened the line in her jaw. She knew what he was waiting for—any crack, any slip. She gripped the cool metal railing, needing something solid to anchor against.

The defense faltered again. An ill-timed blitz. A missed tackle sent the offense spiraling downfield like a rolling storm. Whispers rippled through the sideline. Brick caught the layered glances cast in his direction—some edged with irritation, others calculating. Could he save this? Or would he just make it worse?

An assistant coach's voice sliced through the din, sharp and commanding. "Pick it up! Eyes on the ball; Turner's watching!"

Murmurs followed. Suspicions ripened among the crowd of players.

Natalie pulled her phone from her jacket pocket with a practiced flick. The screen glowed. A message from Emma: *You holding up?*

The simple inquiry felt weighted. She knew what was really being asked—was she holding up under the pressure of being near Brick while the media vultures circled? Could she maintain her professional distance while the whole stadium waited to see if he'd explode?

Her reply came without hesitation: *Barely. He looks ready to combust.*

She tucked the phone back and stepped closer to Brick. No words—just a presence steady and solid as a rock beneath the storm, offering a rare tether to sanity.

Brick's chest heaved. Sweat traced cold lines beneath his hairline despite the sun's heat. His fists unclenched slowly, the burn of adrenaline fading only as coaches barked final orders and the referee's whistle cleaved the field.

The crowd's roar simmered as the clock ticked down. Each failed tackle was another nail in the team's dwindling chances. Brick's boots scraped rhythmically on the gravel. The fire in his chest burned but remained contained. His broad shoulders rose and fell with ragged breaths, sweat slick beneath his hoodie.

Around him, murmurs softened into a solemn hum, a blend of hope and doubt. The defense shuddered under pressure. Teammates exchanged looks—some fiery and frustrated, others resigned yet watchful, calculating the impact of Brick's absence and his looming return.

Natalie crossed her arms, her jaw clenched. Her eyes were unwavering as she caught Brick's guarded glance. The tension between them crackled—not with anger this time, but with a fragile thread of trust and unspoken possibility.

"You think you need me out there, or not?" Brick's voice rumbled low during a rare quiet pause, barely more than a growl.

Natalie held his gaze steady. "I think the team needs the right Brick, not one who loses himself."

"Not losing it today." His jaw tightened. "Just gotta hold tight and keep things steady."

"It's not patience I'm asking for," she stepped closer, her voice low. "It's a smarter play—for you."

Brick swallowed hard, muscles coiling beneath his hoodie. He let out a slow breath that tasted of defiance and necessity.

"They're watching," he muttered, nodding toward the press box, heavy with scrutiny.

"We both know it," Natalie whispered. "Victor's counting on you to slip. Don't give him the satisfaction."

"Easy to say when you're not stuck on the sideline." His tone hardened, shadows crossing his features. "I didn't get benched because I'm broken. I'm being punished."

"A punishment isn't the end," Natalie replied, her voice firm. The weight of care threaded through her words. "It's an opportunity—to prove you're more than your mistakes."

Brick's eyes narrowed, and his lips pressed into a line. The sun caught the sharp angles of his face, illuminating the jagged scar above his brow—a map of battles fought both inside and out.

He loosened his fists, a whisper of surrender escaping his lips. "I want to play. I'll control it."

"You better," Natalie said, stepping back. Her fingers brushed a stray strand of hair from her face. The stadium hummed around them, electric and alive. "Because this half isn't over."

The shrill clang of the halftime whistle sliced through the tension—sharp and final.

Brick exhaled, letting his fists fall open. The hardness in his eyes melted into something quieter, more resolute. The sideline emptied as coaches called the team back to the locker room. Brick moved with measured steps, shoulders squared beneath the weight of all eyes and expectations.

The first half ended with the team trailing. The taste of defeat was bitter but not yet final. Brick breathed in the sharp air, the scent of turf and sweat mingling with heavy anticipation.

Tonight, the field waited. And so did he.

Coach Hale's clipboard cracked against the bench.

The sound split the locker room like a starting gun, drawing every eye from tape rolls and open lockers to the rigid set of his mouth. He scanned the room slowly and methodically before his gaze locked on Brick—a weight behind it that felt less like a challenge and more like a reckoning.

"Discipline." His voice cut sharply through the stale air. "Unity. Those two things decide this game. This season."

He let the silence linger.

"You want to win? You want to be the player this team needs, not the one tearing it apart? Then that starts now."

The fluorescent lights buzzed overhead, amplifying the sweat prickling along shoulders and palms. Chairs creaked as bodies shifted—fidgeting fingers drummed on dirty benches, breaths held and released in uneven cadences. Murmurs fluttered, tentative and sharp, threading through the stale air like whispers chasing mounting dread.

Brick sat rigid, ragged and raw, a storm waiting to break or be harnessed.

Jaxon's voice cut through the murmur, steady but urgent. "We need Brick out there. But we need the right Brick."

His words rippled through the room. Eyes flicked toward Brick—answers waited in the stiffening set of his jaw and the hard grip of his gaze.

Coach Hale stepped forward, his voice low and lethal. "Turner. This is your shot. No more warnings. No second chances." He paused. "One slip. One loss of control. You're done."

The room felt as if it were narrowing, the walls closing in with the weight pressing down.

Brick's fingers curled white-knuckled around the edge of the bench. His breath hitched once before settling. He rose—controlled, but the faint tremor in his hands spoke louder than the calm in his voice.

"I want to play. I'll control it."

Near the door, Natalie watched quietly, her pressed blouse and tailored trousers a sharp contrast to the sweat-stained chaos around her. Her eyes caught Brick's in a brief, unguarded moment—soft but fierce, a shot of steady confidence. She nodded—small, almost invisible—but charged with more meaning than words could hold.

A crackling current surged through the room.

Helmets snapped into place, chinstraps clicking tight and sealing the tension. Players rose with new urgency, their movements sharp and deliberate.

Brick shrugged into his pads, each movement fueled by resolve and a gnawing, quiet edge of fear.

He turned toward the tunnel, each step measured, his head held high despite the storm in his gut. The locker room hummed behind him—scattered shouts, the distant clang of metal lockers slamming shut, the collective intake of breath.

His fate hinged on the next sixty minutes of controlled fire.

Coach Hale's declaration settled into the room like sediment. Players chewed over the ultimatum, the line between redemption and expulsion thinner than ever.

Jaxon leaned closer to DeShawn, his voice tight with the edge of truth. "He's walking a razor's edge. But if he stays steady, Brick's the one who can turn this around."

DeShawn nodded, his eyes tracking Brick as he collected himself—silent and focused.

"It's been a long time coming. Let's hope he's got that grip."

A faint metallic scent leaked from the corner—sweat mingled with liniment and the residue of leather. In this claustrophobic crucible, the weight of consequences pressed on everyone's skin.

Outside, the stadium lights flickered suddenly, announcing the start of the second half. The distant rumble of the crowd murmured through open vents, a living beast in wait.

Natalie's voice found him as they walked toward the tunnel, low but unmistakable. "Do you think you can hold it together?"

His jaw clenched, his eyes steady on the barrier ahead. "It has to be that way. No screw-ups."

She tilted her head, wary yet not unsympathetic. "It's not just for the team. It's for yourself. Control isn't weakness."

He cracked the barest of smirks. "Control is the hardest damn thing I've tried to learn."

She laughed softly—a brief, bright sound cutting through the tension.

"Then start proving it."

Brick's gaze flickered back, a spark lighting deep inside those storm-dark eyes.

Jaxon's words echoed in his chest, steady as a heartbeat: *We need the right Brick.*

That Brick—coiled, sharp, and restrained—rose from the ashes of doubt beneath the blistering lights.

Brick paused at the mouth of the tunnel, the sounds bleeding in—chants, the sharp snap of cleats on turf, and the heated pulse of anticipation.

He inhaled.

Grass. Sweat. Adrenaline. Steel sharpened in his lungs.

The locker room's cold fluorescent glow faded behind him as the stadium's roar swallowed the corridor whole.

He stepped into the fray—a man remade at the halfway line, the game's fragile momentum balanced on his self-restraint.

Behind him, Natalie lingered in the doorway, her eyes not leaving him until the stadium consumed him entirely.

His promise hung on the edge, fragile but fiery—a test that would either remake him or break him.

Either way, there was no going back.

Brick's cleats slapped against the turf. Each step rang sharply against the cold slice of night air that caught in his lungs. From the stands, the crowd fractured—cheers tangled with skeptical murmurs drifting like static over the emerald field. His eyes scanned the horizon, then flicked to his teammates. His lips moved silently as he mouthed the defensive call, a ritual performed with measured precision. The stadium floodlights blazed down, spotlighting the grit and weight settling on his broad shoulders.

The whistle shrilled.

Brick shifted into rhythm, moving from assignment to assignment. Each tackle was textbook—precise muscle memory carved into bone and sinew. He remained disciplined, resisting the bait of late hits, that invisible line between ferocity and foul. When a rival player launched a cheap shot, his face twisted with antagonism, Brick absorbed it like stone. His body tensed. His hands stayed low. The crunch of pads, the metallic clang of helmets—it all blurred into a restrained tempo where restraint became his quiet rebellion.

After the whistle, the same rival sidled closer. His voice snaked, prodding.

"You gonna lose it, Brick? Or are you going to play like a man tonight?"

Brick's jaw clenched so hard that his teeth ground together. His eyes darkened, a flicker of fire barely contained beneath his gaze. His breath steamed in visible puffs as he stepped back deliberately. Muscles coiled with every painful urge to snap back. The roar of the crowd surged, hungry for a fight. Instead, Brick folded himself away—a statue carved from willpower—and walked off the bait.

Up high in the press box, Victor Cross leaned forward, his eyes sharp as a hawk's. His pen hovered above the notepad, poised to capture every twitch of emotion that might betray Brick's fragile control. The journalist's gaze flickered over the man's clenched fists and the rigid set of his shoulders, cataloging potential fuel for headlines. Victor had built his career on Brick's downfall, on the assumption that control was just a mask waiting to crack. Every twitch, every fleeting shadow fell within his careful scrutiny—a predator marking his terrain, waiting for the slip that would justify every article he had written.

On the field, the offense set up near the red zone. Tension stretched taut like frayed wire. Brick's mind sliced through the noise, reading formations and predicting plays with lethal clarity. His experience had taught him to see three moves ahead—a discipline born from countless film sessions and the hard knowledge that one mistake meant giving ammunition to men like Victor. No room for error. No room for rage.

Then—in a burst of controlled energy—he exploded through the line. His arms wrapped around the running back in a textbook tackle, chest pressed solid, knees driving backward in perfect timing. The crowd held its breath. The opposing player crumpled short of the goal line. Brick sprang up. No flourish. No showmanship. Just the steady inhale of a soldier returning to ranks.

Caleb's hand slapped his back, firm and sure—the kind of contact that conveyed trust earned and deferred.

"That's how it's done, Turner. Patience isn't your usual game, but I'm here for it."

Others clapped helmets, quick and warm. The energy shifted in the air like a crack in a gray sky. Skepticism yielded to relief. Grudging respect infected the huddle's tight circle.

Brick stood there, lungs burning. A slow cascade of sweat traced rivulets down his neck. His breath hitched. He forced it to be steady. The weight of fresh respect settled heavily—a new armor he wasn't sure he was ready to wear. The huddle hummed softly, a breath amidst the storm. Across the sideline, Natalie's eyes caught his. They shone sharp and bright, threaded with worry and something softer beneath the professional mask.

The stadium noise faded beneath the pounding of Brick's heart. The fate of the game, the fragile balancing act of trust and discipline—it all coalesced in this moment, breathing with him from the field to the press box where watchful eyes waited.

"You were damn near perfect out there."

Caleb leaned in, his eyes bright with anticipation. Brick's voice came low and steady, the familiar roughness softened by the weight of meaning.

"Don't start hyping me up like I'm some angel now. Are you sure you have the right guy?"

Caleb smiled, unrepentant.

"If this is the guy, I'm all in. Let's just hope Coach remembers the new Brick, not the old wrecking ball."

Brick shook his head. A shadow of a smirk lifted the corner of his mouth before settling back into guarded resolve.

"Winning is the only way I prove I'm still playing for keeps."

From the sideline, Natalie stepped closer. Her voice was calm but edged with steel.

"You kept your edge, just under control. Don't test me next time."

Brick's gaze flicked to hers. The tension between them wove from unspoken challenges and cautious trust.

"Don't get used to me playing nice just yet."

Natalie shrugged, her eyes catching his with a spark that spoke of battles fought and won within quiet spaces.

"Maybe not. But today? It's a start."

The huddle tightened. The moment stretched and folded. Brick's breath slowed, deliberate. He stood tall beneath the stadium lights—no longer just the volatile force he once was, but a steady pillar amid the chaos. His teammates glanced at him anew. The hesitant nods and pats carried unspoken admissions: this might just be the turning point.

Natalie's gaze lingered, a silent prayer sent across the field. Her heart thudded hard in the pressurized air.

Brick breathed in the noise, the expectation, and the fragile thread of acceptance weaving itself through the roar around him. The battle was far from over. But tonight's second half, shaped by control and quiet courage, seeded the hope of redemption.

The clock's final seconds dripped away like thick syrup from a spoon. Slow. Viscous. Inevitable.

Brick crouched low, his fingertips digging into the turf as a bead of sweat trickled beneath his helmet. His breath snagged, and his heart drummed a steady beat inside his ribcage. Every nerve screamed, but his gaze stayed locked, unmoving. Around him, the crowd's roar crested and dipped—a living tide swelling as the offense ground down the remaining yards. The air thickened with sweat and the electric pulse of something approaching victory, mingled with the sharp snap of adrenaline cutting through exhaustion.

The quarterback snapped the ball one last time.

Brick lunged. The tackle landed clean—textbook, controlled, disciplined. A strike that flushed the rival's hope into the grass.

His teammates erupted behind him, their voices raw and jubilant. The final whistle sliced through the evening air.

The score leaned the way they had prayed—just enough to lift them from the mouth of defeat.

Amid the hurricane of celebration, Brick stood off-center, his helmet loose in one hand like a sobering anchor. His chest rose and fell in a steady, deliberate cadence, sweat slicking his skin with the scent of iron and relief. His stat line spoke volumes in the cold light: no flags, no fouls, the stops that mattered.

Grit. Restraint. Stitched into every play.

The weight of it hit him then—not the victory, but something quieter. The astonishment that his own hands had stayed clean. That he had held it together when the noise wanted to shatter him. His eyes swept the field, measuring rather than searching. No loud cheers passed his lips. Beneath that calm surface, something fragile flickered in the depths of his gaze.

Across the scrambling chaos near the sidelines, Natalie slipped through the crowd, the hem of her blazer catching faint glimmers of floodlight. She stopped at the edge, her heart hammering beneath her cool exterior. Their eyes locked—their own silent exchange stretching tighter than any spoken word.

She lifted her hand for the briefest moment, her thumb rising in a slow, steady thumbs-up.

It carried everything: pride, relief, and the unspoken knowledge of battles fought and barely won.

Brick's lips twitched imperceptibly, a shadow of a smile breaking through his stoic mask.

From the gathering shadows near the tunnel, Victor Cross emerged—a man moving with the casual ease of someone who knew exactly what damage he could inflict. He fell into step beside Natalie, his voice low and sharp as a blade cutting through the stadium's roar.

"Seems your problem child picked up a few tricks," he murmured, his eyes flicking to Brick, who was still basking in the team's fragmented adoration. "For now. Do you really think he can keep it together?"

Natalie tightened her jaw. Victor's presence was a weight she had learned to carry—a looming threat not just to the team but to her fragile control over the media narrative. The professional burden pressed down, heavy with personal stakes. The crisp click of her heels maintained a controlled tempo against the stadium's roaring backdrop.

"Brick's more than tricks," she said, her voice courteous but laced with steel. "He's earned this chance. You'll see if he can keep it."

Victor's smile twitched—a razor-thin line of challenge. Then he let the subject drop, vanishing into the fluorescent hum of the tunnel lights like a shadow devoured by brightness.

Behind them, Brick peeled away from the yelling crowd, his shoulders tight as if holding back the storm inside. His eyes flicked upward, catching the harsh glare of the stadium lights, unblinking. The cheers pressed in around him like distant thunder—welcome, yet foreign.

The buzz of adulation swirled around him. Hands slapped his back, and helmets clanged in celebration. But his face carried that stunned quiet—the expression of a man who had tasted respect for the first time and wondered how long its sweetness could last.

Natalie watched him retreat. The lines in her face tightened, not from joy but from the sharp edge of impending scrutiny. Each step Brick took into that locker room shadowed the fragile truce between past storms and the hard-won calm of the present—the pressure that could ignite or extinguish the flame entirely.

Somewhere in the distance, Victor Cross's footsteps faded, but his threat lingered like the bitter aftertaste of something not yet confronted.

The tunnel swallowed Brick in its cool, shadowed expanse. Behind him, the stadium's muffled roar faded to a dull drumbeat. He steadied his breath when a heavy hand crashed onto his shoulder—the grip firm, more brotherly than casual.

DeShawn's voice broke through the low clatter. "Man, I didn't give you much credit, but damn—you pulled it off."

Brick turned and swallowed a knot tight in his throat. The words latched onto his ribs—awkward, raw, closer to a lifeline than praise. He blinked and nodded before he could think better of it, his voice caught somewhere shy of sound. The heat of DeShawn's hand lingered—a silent truce formed in the lingering tension of hard-fought yards and harder-won control.

"I had no choice," Brick says, his jaw tight and his voice low. "I couldn't let that punk get in my head."

DeShawn's eyes gleam. "Yeah, but you didn't snap a single time. That's new for you, Brick. Really new."

"I'm done burning bridges."

"Good," DeShawn says, stepping back. He nods toward the locker room entrance. "Because the team's watching now. And so am I, brother."

As Brick moves past, Jaxon drifts close. Their eyes lock with an electric flash. No words—just a quick nod, charged and heavy with promise. The weight of it settles: *you're part of this now, in a way none of us could say before.*

Jaxon's voice drops low and urgent. "You showed up. That's all we wanted. Now don't mess this up."

Brick exhales. The words bruise but are honest. He offers a small, almost sheepish grin—fragile but sincere. "No promises," he says, half-joking, but the tremor in his breath betrays him.

Inside the locker room, sandalwood and sweat swirl beneath the harsh fluorescent lights. Brick peels off his pads. Every snap and clatter echoes in the cavernous space. His skin prickles beneath the release, and his muscles unwind with reluctant relief.

By the doorway, Natalie lingers. Her fingers tighten briefly on the hem of her jacket. Her gaze locks with his—steady and warm—yet the slight furrow between her brows casts a shadow across her face, betraying the tension beneath her calm. Between them hang years of conflict, fragile trust, and unspoken hopes neither wants to name.

The silent dialogue pulses between them, full of promises and fears neither dares voice aloud. Her slight nod is a tether, a wordless acknowledgment that this moment, this fragile shift, is as much hers as it is his.

Then she steps back, shoulders squared, retreating to her realm of schedules and damage control. The click of her heels and the rustle of papers mark her departure like a closing chord.

Brick's eyes linger on the spot where she last stood, tracing the soft curves of hope and caution she has become. The scent of her—clean, faintly floral—hangs like a whispered secret in the air.

Motion from the corner catches his attention. A shadow detaches itself from the doorframe. Victor Cross, phone pressed to his ear, has an expression that is unreadable but sharp as a blade. The call ends abruptly as he meets Brick's gaze. The tension stiffens—silent, palpable. Brick feels that familiar chill—the shadow of Cross always lurking, waiting to strike where he is weakest. This isn't over. Not by a long shot.

The locker room hums with life. Players peel off their gear, and laughter rises and falls like tides. But Brick stands still amid the flux, caught between the fragile bloom of acceptance and the invisible chains of scrutiny. His hands clench briefly at his sides, knuckles whitening, before relaxing.

A slow, steady pulse beats behind his ribs.

He's here, for now.

And the game has only just begun.

Crossing the Line

Brick towers at the heart of the locker room, steady as a mountain. Bodies spill around him. Hands slam into his back. Thick palms slap. Fists pound. Teammates shout praise like fuel for their drained spirits.

The air thickens: sweat sharp under harsh fluorescent lights, mingling with the metallic tang of liniment and the staleness of old towels hanging in the corner. Breaths come ragged, and voices are hoarse but loud in victory's aftermath. A collective heartbeat thrums against the locker room's concrete walls.

Jaxon slides up beside him, a grin wide and easy. "Miracle on the line today, Brick? Bet the whole team's still shaking their heads."

His tone ribs but holds respect—a rare nod to Brick's hard-won control.

Brick smirks, a flash of teeth brightening his rugged face. "Yeah, miracle and all," he mutters, his voice gravelly but pleased.

Caleb leans in with devilish teasing. "Hey, lighten up, tornado. Thought you'd blow a gasket in the fourth quarter."

DeShawn chuckles, his eyes glinting with mischief. "Guess someone's finally figuring out the brakes."

The locker room shifts. The air loosens. What started as jabs tightens now into guarded camaraderie, like grudging respect threading through the teasing. Brick nods at each, his smile lingering just enough to soften his usual edge.

The door swings open.

Natalie steps into the buzz, clipboard in hand, her heels clicking softly against the tiled floor. Her dark eyes scan the room—quick, calculating, professional. Then they drift to Brick, an unspoken pull drawing their gazes together.

Across the room, their eyes catch and hold. His breath hitches slightly. He feels the heat of her stare like a jolt beneath his skin.

She moves toward Coach Marcus Hale, her voice calm and certain against the backdrop of celebration. Marcus, solid and steady in his team jacket, listens with measured nods. A few players hover nearby, their faces open but tired. Through it all, Natalie's awareness never strays far from Brick. Her posture remains tight. Ready.

One by one, players peel away—a trickle turning into a wave—leaving behind the fading echoes of the thinning crowd. Brick hangs back, a towel pressed to his neck, water droplets tracing paths down his broad shoulders.

The locker room hums with a different energy now. Lower. More insistent. The adrenaline fades, replaced by something heavier—an unresolved tension coiling in his chest, his guarded anticipation about what comes next. The air charges with anticipation rather than release.

Natalie steps forward, her voice clipped but carrying an edge. "Brick, the media's waiting for a sound bite. Just a minute."

His gaze locks onto hers, sharp and unreadable beneath the fading adrenaline. "Sounds like you've got your hands full."

She shrugs, the hint of a smirk tugging at her lips. "You're part of the problem. Or the solution." Her tone holds a balance of challenge and invitation.

Brick's jaw tightens. He closes the scant space between them, his hand sliding to click the locker room door shut. The latch echoes like a starting gun.

The sudden quiet presses in. Their eyes break contact only to find each other again moments later—this time raw and unguarded.

He looks at her then, not like a man with a reputation to protect, but like a man stripped down to something urgent and fragile. His voice is almost a whisper beneath the heavier quiet.

"You don't have to play it safe with me."

Natalie's breath catches. Her shoulders stiffen briefly before easing into the tension that coils around them both. Neither takes a step back. Neither dares.

The sounds of the emptying stadium fade to a distant murmur beyond the thick door. Between them, the air thickens with something old and new all at once—want, uncertainty, and desire threaded with the hard promise of boundaries yet to be crossed. They stand inches apart, a silent standoff breathing slow and deliberate in the dimming light.

The locker room's roar fades behind them, muffled beneath the steel-and-glass shell of the stadium. Brick's fist brushes the door handle of the press box before he turns. His voice drops low. "I'll drive you home."

Natalie's breath catches. Her eyes widen just a fraction. The weight of those four words settles over her like a coat she didn't know she needed. She tightens her grip on the bag strap, her fingers worrying the fabric. The hum of the sidelines and the distant chatter of the departing crowd feel distant now, like noise from another world.

Her professional armor flutters, worn thin by the rawness of wanting something she shouldn't want.

She looks away. "If… if you don't mind."

He shrugs. A corner of his mouth twitches—barely a smile, but there. "Got a ride for me after?"

"No." Her voice steadies and grows crisp. "You'll have to take me." They both know the line that hangs between them—threadbare, tense, electric. Neither is ready to cross it outright, nor willing to step back.

Without a word, they part ways.

Natalie steps into the cool night. Her boots echo across the concrete. Brick moves toward a matte black SUV, shadowed beneath the stadium lights. He waits, engine off, breathing steady, though his muscles coil tight beneath his leather jacket.

Minutes later, the sliding door clicks. Natalie slides in beside him. The leather seat is cold against her palms. Outside, the scent of rubber and faint smoke from nearby grills drifts through the open window, mingling with the metallic pulse of the night air. Ahead, city lights blink like distant stars—indifferent and relentless.

The silence inside the cabin stretches taut as a bowstring. Natalie twists her hands together in her lap. Brick's knuckles whiten as he grips the steering wheel, his thumbs tapping an erratic beat. Restless. The rearview mirror catches the briefest exchange—a spark of nerves, something unspoken flickering there—before each turns away again, locked inside their own cage of thoughts.

The dashboard hums. Brick starts the engine. Tires crunch over loose gravel. Around them, the stadium's roar has dissolved into whispers of wind and distant traffic—a world asleep or on pause, waiting. Except for these two, caught in orbit just beyond reach.

Brick's voice breaks the quiet. Rough. Low. "You sure?"

Natalie exhales. A ghost of a smile curls her lips. Her fingers still twist together in her lap. "Yes. I'm tired of fighting it."

Her words settle in the small space between them, heavier than the night air itself. Brick shifts gears, his eyes flicking to the rearview mirror. More question than confirmation. Natalie meets his gaze with a nod so slight it might have been missed—if they weren't both watching every subtle motion like a code written in body language.

The car tires purr against the asphalt as they glide through the stadium lot, folding into lanes shadowed beneath towering floodlights. Inside, the world shrinks: the pulse of the engine, the rhythm of breaths, her calm breath, his measured inhale, and the fragile cadence of two people grappling with the gravity of simply being close.

Minutes stretch by in tacit truce, and the city's glow softens the boundaries around them. Tension coils tighter—the pull between control and surrender—something electric, tentative, humming beneath skin and bone.

At last, they slow outside a towering structure of slate and steel: Brick's apartment building, stark against the starless sky, with windows glinting sharply like shards of glass. The engine cuts, and the headlights die. Brick unbuckles, his body stiff but movements deliberate.

Natalie steps out, and the cold bites softly through her coat. Brick's hand brushes the pocket of his jacket, fingers curling around the key fob before he opens the door. The scent of cold concrete and distant rain greets them—urban, clean, a threshold to something private and unexplored.

Inside the lobby, the elevator hums to life with a muted ding. Natalie leans back against the cool wall, her shoulders sinking slightly as if trying to anchor herself against what's coming. Brick stands opposite, arms folded tight, but beneath the stoicism, a subtle tremble betrays the storm he's holding in check.

The air thickens. It is not quite spoken but palpable, heavy with unspoken words and restrained desire. Their eyes catch—quick, furtive—flitting away as nerves ripple beneath the surface.

The elevator ascends, clicking softly between floors. They stand enclosed in this bubble of charged silence that clamps tighter the closer they get to the upper levels. The walls seem to close in, swallowing the noise of the world beyond. Only their breath remains, along with the distant hum of the city below. They have shared looks across crowded rooms, stolen words in hallways, and pretended indifference during staff meetings. But never this. Never alone like this, with nowhere to hide.

Brick finally breaks the quiet. His voice is low enough to be a murmur but edged with fragile resolve. "You good with this?"

Natalie manages a small, wry smile—sharp and genuine despite the tension. "Yeah. Better than I thought I would be."

Their silent agreement tightens the air further, a mutual admission without the need to speak it aloud. When the elevator dings again, the doors slide open smoothly, revealing the quiet corridor where fate waits in the shadows.

They step forward together, two silhouettes swallowed by soft hallway lights. Their footsteps muffle against the thick carpet. Neither glances back as the door closes behind them with a muted click. The world outside fades to a distant echo.

In that moment, the choice hangs between them: uncharted, reckless, inevitable. The night envelops them, thick with the promise of crossing the line—a boundary dissolved by shared glances and quiet consent.

The elevator hums shut behind them, thick, still air settling into Brick's apartment like a living thing. The door swings open, revealing a space as raw and unyielding as its owner: charcoal gray walls, sleek black leather furniture, and a few stark metal accents catching the low light. No fluff, no soft edges—just the bare bones of a man who has learned to keep things tight and controlled. Every sharp corner and shadowed wall mirrors the man who guards himself fiercely, as much a fortress as a home.

Brick steps in first, the faint scent of cedarwood and leather trailing in his wake. The familiar smell floods Natalie's senses—one she has memorized in stolen moments, now wrapping around her with dangerous familiarity. She steadies herself against the weight of it, against the pull of him in this space where his control is absolute.

He moves to the counter and unscrews the top of a whiskey bottle. "Drink?"

Natalie sets her purse on the polished ebony table. The sharp clink of leather against wood breaks the quiet. She shakes her head, her voice clipped but steady. "No... not tonight."

He studies her for a flicker—something tighter than refusal, more deliberate. He nods. "Okay."

No words fill the room after that. The silence doesn't feel empty; it's heavy, charged, as if the air itself is holding its breath. They stand an arm's length apart—two figures carved from different stones, both wanting to break but neither daring to go first. The ache between them spins invisible threads, tugging tight.

Natalie's gaze drifts to the crease beneath Brick's jaw and catches the flicker there—something raw, unguarded. Her fingers twitch—barely a tremor—as they edge forward, brushing lightly against the firm fabric of his shirt, where his chest rises and falls beneath.

Brick freezes.

The noise around them fades, replaced by a roaring pulse in his temples. His breath hitches, and his eyes lock on her hand, searching for a command. He doesn't move away, doesn't breathe out; he just stays caught, waiting, needing her to make it real.

"It's me," she whispers. Her voice drops low, uneven, and urgent, as if the words catch on the edge of her throat.

Her touch lingers, palms warm against the hard line of muscle. Brick's shoulders drop, a slow exhale releasing years of tension in a breath carried between them. Then her voice cuts through the heavy quiet again.

"I want this, but I don't want us to crash and burn—not because of foolishness." Her eyes catch his, fierce and unblinking. "I need honesty and boundaries. If this costs us, then at least it won't be because we didn't know the risk."

A flicker of something familiar crosses Brick's face—guilt, maybe fear—before his jaw hardens. "We'll stop whenever you want. No second-guessing."

He doesn't just say it; he means it. His body tightens with the promise, every muscle taut with restraint and raw need. Then he closes the distance, hands rising slowly to rest near her waist—not yet holding, just testing.

He brushes his lips against hers, tentative—like testing cold water before the plunge. The first touch is featherlight, almost a question. Natalie's breath hitches as her fingers thread through his hair, and the kiss deepens—slow, deliberate. The hunger simmers beneath, a coil winding tighter with each linger.

They break apart, chests heaving, skin flushed with warmth and the shudder of proximity.

Brick's voice is rough, low, but steady as stone. "Are you sure? Tell me to stop, and I will."

A breath, shaky yet assured. "Yes."

The kiss returns like a magnet, fiercer this time. Their lips trace bold, demanding lines—hunger mixed with hesitation. When they pull away again, Brick's hand cups the side of her face, his thumb stroking her cheekbone, grounding her in the present moment.

One more whisper. More necessity than question. "Still sure?"

Natalie's voice emerges raw, thick with need—a surrender she's never allowed herself before. "Yes... don't stop."

His touch grows bolder, hands moving with measured reverence over contours he's memorizing in a fever of attention. The room melts away; the cool steel and gray walls shrink into insignificance beside the heat simmering between them.

Neither speaks. The silence is full of promises unspoken but understood. Brick's fingers tremble as they trace the line of her jaw down to her neck, drawing shivering breaths from her.

With gentle authority, he presses his forehead to hers, eyes heavy-lidded and sparkling with fierce devotion. Slowly, deliberately, Brick turns, leading her from the center of the room. Every step is weighted by the gravity of the choice hanging between them.

His voice is a rough murmur against the back of her ear. "This is ours—on our terms."

Her hand slips into his, fingers curling tight, warm against the chill of the night beyond the windowpane. Together, they walk toward the bedroom—the threshold of something new, terrifying, and utterly necessary. The hard edge of public restraint falls away, replaced by a fragile bridge stretching between hearts daring to trust.

Brick's fingers trembled as they traced the outline of Natalie's blouse. The buttons were delicate, almost fragile—he moved around them with the care of someone defusing something precious. She took his hands, quiet but sure, guiding them with soft, warm pressure.

"Here," she breathed, her voice low and steady. "Undo this slowly. Nice and slow."

The sharp scent of her perfume—something woody, almost sandalwood—wafted up as she leaned closer. The heat between them was thick enough to taste.

His pulse hammered against his ribcage like a warning. Every move weighed heavily with caution. His hands paused at the hem of her blouse, trembling under the weight of memory—his size, his strength, the scars he carried like ghosts. He had broken things before. He couldn't break this.

She was watching him. Waiting.

Brick moved forward. Unwrapping her like a secret, he let his fingers brush her skin. Never rushing. His breath mingled with hers in the quiet—only the faint rustle of fabric and the occasional hitch in his own breathing.

"Is this good?" His voice was rough, barely louder than a whisper. "Can I keep going?"

Natalie's lips curved into a reluctant smile, her eyes brighter than the low lamplight. "Yes. Please." Her voice trembled with more need than she would like to admit. The walls she had built around her heart crumbled one careful touch at a time.

His hands learned the language of her body. They ebbed and flowed—sometimes tender, sometimes urgent. Each touch was a question; every pause was an invitation to speak without words.

There was a desperate edge beneath the gentleness, as if he were holding back a storm contained within his chest.

"You okay?" His eyes searched hers, raw and open, vulnerable in a way she'd never seen.

Natalie's fingertips traced a slow path down his arm, steadying him without a word. "Don't hold back," she murmured, her breath warm against his collarbone. "I want to hold on to this—the feeling that I'm the one you're choosing, not just the fight you're running from."

A fragile confession slipped through her voice, soft as a prayer. "I'm not usually like this. I don't let go easily. But this—" She paused, as if the admission itself cost her something. "This is different."

Her hands became a map, directing, coaxing, and shaping the pace between them. Consent here was a dance—spoken in touches, glances, and shared breaths. Their bodies negotiated boundaries with careful devotion.

The urgency surged. Brick's grip tightened, his slow exploration sharpening with intensity. Tension and release swirled like a tempest, fierce and fragile. His lips brushed hers—his tongue gentle at first, then more demanding, searching for a harmony neither expected.

She answered in kind, trembling beneath him—every inch a surrender and also a declaration.

"Tell me if it gets to be too much," Brick said between heated kisses, his voice thick with need and tenderness entwined. "If you want me to stop, just say the word."

"I won't," Natalie whispered fiercely, her body arching instinctively toward him. "Keep going."

At the peak, everything slowed. Time stretched those moments between gasps and heartbeats. Natalie's hands cradled his face—soft and strong, grounding him. His heart felt as if it might break under the weight of her touch, the tenderness she offered without hesitation. His mouth found hers again—more delicate this time. Gratitude wove through each kiss.

Her chest rose and fell beneath him, her breath uneven. A shiver rippled down her spine—not from the heat, but from something raw and unspoken between them. She melted into his arms, fragile and steady all at once.

Brick pulled her closer, his muscles taut as he held her like a lifeline. "Thank you," he murmured against her temple, his voice raw with earnestness. "For trusting me."

Her fingers threaded into his hair, the movement gentle and grounding. "I'm okay," she said, her voice steady despite the tremor running through her. "Did you ever want it to stop?"

He shook his head slowly. "Never. But I swear—if I saw any hesitation, even a flicker—I'd stop. Right away." His lips brushed against her forehead, a vow and an anchor in the uncertain night.

They lay tangled in the quiet dark, breaths mingling, hearts thudding in tandem beneath the sheets. His hand found hers, fingers weaving together—a silent promise held in that simple contact.

The storm between them hadn't passed; it had settled into a steady flame—one neither knew how to name yet, but both felt deeply.

The room held its breath alongside them. The shift beneath their skin was tender and irrevocable.

The room breathes around them, shadows pressing softly and darkly against the slate-blue walls. Brick's fingers trace idle, almost reverent paths along Natalie's arm. The slight tremble beneath his touch is confession enough—no words needed.

"I'm scared," he admits, his voice just above a whisper. The city hums outside, but here, it's quiet. "Not of what we just did. That wasn't the hard part." He pauses, his eyes searching hers. "It's what you make me want: to be careful, to be gentle. I thought I lost that somewhere."

His chest rises and falls in a hesitant rhythm, rawness threading through his voice like a fragility he usually buries deep beneath muscle and fire.

Natalie's breath catches—a fragile gasp caught between hesitation and need. Her fingers twitch, brushing lightly against his wrist. "I've never crossed this line before," she admits, her voice barely more than a cracked whisper, trembling like ice melting on skin. "I never expected it to matter this much or to be this complicated."

Her fingers find his—tentative, seeking—and the familiar ache of control loosens with each passing second. "I'm scared, too. Not just because..." She gestures vaguely between them. "But mixing desire with work? It's dangerous."

Brick's gaze flickers down to their entwined hands, his jaw tense as he fights the urge to run. "That line? Hell, it's crossed," he growls, his voice rough but low, almost soft. "And this isn't no fling. Not for me. Not with you."

They don't try to name it—the precarious, blazing thing kindled in the dark. No reckless promises. No half-hearted ones. Just the weight of truth, silently shared, settling like dust motes in a slant of moon-light.

Natalie squeezes his hand, a breathless gesture that speaks volumes. Then she curls against his side, her forehead resting against the curve of his shoulder. The heat between them doesn't cool; it lingers, a steady pulse beneath skin and bone.

Brick's rough palm tilts her chin, tracing the line of her jaw as if memorizing every doubt and hope nestled there. "You okay?" His voice is softer now, cautious. "We can stop. I'll stop. Anytime you say."

Her lips part. The faintest tremor in the nod she offers says everything. "I want this," she whispers, her voice trembling. "But I'm scared—scared of losing myself. Losing... us."

He pulls her closer then, the weight of his arm draping protectively over her shoulders, anchoring her in the fragile sanctuary of his quiet.

They lie tangled in the crystalline stillness. The aftermath folds around them—a fragile truce hung between tenderness and uncertainty.

Outside, the night presses in, indifferent and vast. But here, in the dim glow of Brick's apartment, two hearts sync against the silence, beating in a rhythm that neither dares to name yet dares not deny.

Their breaths soften and slow. Limbs entwined. Skin warm and steady. The world beyond the window slips away as sleep gathers its gentle claim.

Holding Natalie like the most precious fragment of order in the chaos of his life, Brick lets go of all the storms inside.

And in the quiet dark, they drift—safe for now—on the fragile edge of whatever comes next.mes next.

Morning After Rules

The slate-blue wall caught the morning light—soft and cool. It pooled in a stillness that made the world feel suspended, held in amber.

Natalie blinked awake on Brick's sectional, the fabric cool beneath her bare arms. A shirt lay tossed across the coffee table, wrinkles like whispered secrets of a night spent before dawn peeling back the city's edge. Faint musk tangled in the air with the sharp tang of espresso long gone cold.

Her fingers traced the marks blooming across her skin—tender constellations she couldn't quite bring herself to regret. Her gaze shifted to the indent of Brick's handprint pressed deep into the pillow beside her.

Satisfaction flickered through her—quiet and fierce. The kind that only comes when night's heat still hums beneath cool morning light.

Then panic seized her chest, a cold coil of tension threading through certainty.

The bathroom door creaked open.

Brick stepped through, hair wet and spiked like storm-swept grass. Droplets clung to his bare shoulders like dew. The towel around his waist hung damp and heavy. His eyes found hers—dark pools with a glint of mirth. "Coffee's on me," he said, his voice low and rough from sleep.

The smirk didn't quite touch the heavy lines of last night sprawled between them. There was no apology, only the quiet claim of a man who owned every second.

He brushed past her, his fingers skimming her wrist—light, casual, almost involuntary. The touch sent warmth shooting down her arm.

She pulled back gently, like a tide retreating.

Her hands moved quickly, gathering scattered clothes: the smooth blouse, the curve of her skirt, the cool slide of stockings. Each layer was a silent fortress she built.

She tightened her expression like armor—control, a shield in a room still charged with electricity.

Her voice fell low and measured. "Last night can't happen again." The weight behind the words pulled the air taut. "And whatever this was—we don't mention it at work."

Her gaze met his—firm, careful. Not anger, but something sharper, quieter: a warning wrapped in wounded honesty.

Brick's jaw clenched, a muscle twitching beneath taut skin. He didn't speak, but his silence filled the room like a held breath. Then he nodded—the barest flicker of concession—and folded into the shadowed doorway, his silhouette dark against the soft light.

Natalie stepped toward the door, her fingers fumbling with buttons stubbornly tangled in their threads. Each snap was a tiny declaration. She didn't look back as the blouse closed over her chest.

The apartment hummed with unspoken tension, too small for all the things left unsaid.

"Can't just walk away like it means nothing," Brick said. His voice was rough but steady, vulnerability artfully hidden beneath the gravel.

"I'm not walking away," she replied, her voice clipped short. "I'm protecting myself. This is chaos dressed as a mistake."

Her heels clicked sharply on the hardwood as she moved past him, each step marking the distance growing between their worlds.

Outside, the city waited—already loud and indifferent.

Brick watched from the doorway, the weight in his chest heavier than the steam rising from his damp hair. The light shifted, catching the jagged scar above his eyebrow—a permanent reminder of battles fought and fences built around a heart beginning to crack. He'd survived worse than this, but he knew he hadn't.

The room quieted, then filled again with the ghost of last night—the electric charge dissolving into the mundane hum of early day.

Natalie's breath drew in sharp and steady, bracing for the storm yet to come, willing herself to walk away from the man who had already stolen pieces of her control.

On the table, the tossed shirt lay still, a silent witness to a moment neither of them could quite own yet.

Natalie's fingers traced the worn strap of her bag as she moved to the kitchen counter. Her eyes scanned the scattered papers with cool precision—the kind that never quite reached her heart. The pale morning light spilled through the window, casting sharp lines across the slate-blue walls. But inside her mind, words rehearsed themselves on a loop: *No exceptions. Brick must call me Brooks again. No favors, no slips.* The bitter taste of last night lingered beneath the sweetness of something far more dangerous.

Brick stood tall by the doorway, muscles tensed beneath his rumpled shirt. He watched her with those storm-dark eyes, the ones that flirted with rebellion.

She looked up and met his gaze—steady, unwavering.

"You're calling me Brooks again," she said, her voice low and controlled. "At work. No nicknames. Nothing casual."

Brick's jaw snapped shut. His Adam's apple bobbed sharply as he swallowed. "I don't see why that matters."

"It does." Natalie's hands pressed firmly against the countertop. "I'm the team's PR manager. My job is to keep things clean and professional. One slip-up, one word out of place, and everything burns. You know what a scandal costs me."

The faint scent of last night's cologne lingered in the air, sharp against the cool morning breeze drifting through the cracked window. She noticed it and hated that she noticed it.

Brick stepped closer. The tension prickled between them like static before a storm. He didn't blink.

"We can't just sweep last night under the rug," he growled softly, his voice rough with something unsaid. "It wasn't a mistake. It mattered."

His words caught her off guard. Vulnerability threaded through the hardness in his voice, and she felt her resolve waver—just slightly. She pressed her lips together, swallowing the flutter of surprise that bloomed inside her. Professional alarm won out. It always did.

"You don't get to rewrite the rules just because you want to," she snapped, her eyes flashing. "I have a strict line: never mix professional and personal. Ever."

Six months ago, she had watched another manager's career implode when boundaries blurred. Chaotic press conferences, headlines screaming betrayal, and a young athlete's future became collateral damage. She had promised herself then—never again. Never on her watch.

"I won't watch that nightmare repeat," she added quietly.

Brick's shoulders sagged. The fight bled out of him as disappointment settled in his eyes. She could have softened then. She should have, maybe. Instead, she twisted on her heel and strode to the door. Her heels tapped firmly against the hardwood, breaking the silence that had hung too long between them.

Brick reached out impulsively, his fingers grazing the sleeve of her blazer. She jerked away as if stung, then crossed the threshold with disciplined finality.

"You're setting terms now," he said, his voice low and rough. "Don't think I'm just going to fall in line."

Natalie paused in the doorway, one hand on the frame. She didn't turn around.

"I'm not asking for obedience," she said quietly. "I'm demanding that you respect the lines that keep us both standing."

The door clicked softly behind her.

The spaces between them yawned wide, stark as the morning light pooling cold on the floor. Outside, the world spun without mercy. Inside, the apartment felt suddenly hollow—walls closing in with the weight of things unspoken and boundaries freshly drawn. Brick lingered by the doorway, his breath shallow, watching the emptiness she had left behind like a phantom wound he couldn't reach.

Brick eased through the glass doors well before the usual rush. The sterile hum of morning settled into every corner. He drifted near the

PR office, his shoulders squared, back straight like a sentry. His stance was casual yet deliberate.

Each time the hallway emptied, he moved forward a few paces, lingering in doorways and along corridors. His eyes never stopped scanning. He didn't cross the threshold. Instead, he marked the space with the weight of his presence—an unspoken claim.

Across the lunchroom, voices ripple as staff shift between meetings and calls—a fluid tide of oversized lattes, paper stacks, and half-muted conversations. Brick's gaze locks on Natalie as she rises from her seat, the glow of her laptop catching the edge of her face. Papers are clutched in one hand, and a phone is pressed to her other ear.

Time scratches at the edges of their small world.

Their eyes meet—icy, sharp, charged. The energy flips—subtle but electric, enough to make heads swivel in passing. The space between them hums with an unspoken challenge. Brick doesn't speak, but the weight of his stare is a challenge unto itself.

Natalie's fingers snap open folders. She answers calls with clipped efficiency—the voice of a woman guarding fragile ground. Her face is a blueprint of professionalism, each gesture carefully controlled. But beneath that surface, the faint tremor in her jaw tightens—a quiet war waged in whispered breaths and clenched teeth. She breathes in the sterile mix of printer paper and stale coffee, swallowing back the ripples of doubt.

Outside, the parking lot catches shards of sunlight, creating sharp contrasts of light and shadow over the concrete. Natalie strides toward her car, her heels clicking on the pavement. The faint scent of freshly mown grass hitches on a distant breeze. Her steps falter when a figure slides beside her. Brick presses his weight against the cool metal of the door.

He leans in, his voice low and steady, embodying both demand and confession.

"I don't care about your damn rules." His breath carries heat. "I want something real. You said it was a mistake, but I know you felt it too."

Natalie's shoulders square, and her jaw locks so tightly that it threatens to crack. Her eyes narrow—a flash of fire igniting beneath her steady exterior. The breeze carries the sharp aroma of his sweat from the morning workout, undeniable and raw. She circles her arms as if wrapping herself in armor.

"They're watching, Brick." Her voice doesn't waver. "Coach Hale's eyes don't miss a thing. One leak, and it's not just your career—it's mine. Boundaries exist for a reason."

The words slice through the air. Brick's mouth tightens, and his eyes flicker, simmering. The weight of wanting and fearing warps his posture—shoulders tense, fists clenching briefly before he forces them open. He turns away without a word.

His stride toward the locker room thuds with silent fury. Each step echoes the rage he can't express.

Natalie watches him go. The distance yawns wide, and his heat still lingers in the air between them. Her breath catches—just once. Then she turns toward her car, swallowed by the swirl of staff and the dull roar of everyday bustle.

The crackle of tension remains, a static pulse that neither can ignore, marking the fragile line between what is ruled by caution and what beats beneath with reckless urgency.

Brick slumped against his locker. The cavernous room swallowed him whole—shadows pooling in corners, fluorescent lights humming their thin, industrial song. Stale sweat and leather dust mingled with eucalyptus drifting from the showers down the hall, sharp enough to coat his tongue.

His broad shoulders curved inward, and his fingers pressed into the worn wood, tracing grooves he had memorized in better days. The metal was cold against his palms, unforgiving.

Caleb and DeShawn drifted over, their steps crunching on scuffed tile with the ease of routine.

"Hey, Brick, did Brooks slam the door on another interview or just ghost you today?" Caleb's grin landed sharp and teasing, the kind meant to hit hard.

DeShawn snatched an imaginary phone from his pocket, thumbs flicking theatrically through the air. "Man, I got all her press secrets—whispered them when she thought no one was listening." His smirk stretched wide, mischief flickering in his dark eyes. "Bet she'd spill yours too if you played it right."

Brick's laugh tumbled out rough and jagged, dying on his lips before finding air.

His jaw clenched like steel against stone. A shadow flickered across his eyes—the kind that nobody else caught. "Yeah, hilarious. Just peachy." His voice trailed off, the edge dulling into something tight and tired.

Caleb stepped closer, lowering his tone. "Nah, man, we get it. The spotlight's a beast. Sometimes you want to hide from it. It's not just you, you know?"

DeShawn leaned against a bench, his eyes catching something distant. "I'll tell you, juggling all this—team, work, kid... It's a lot." His glance found Brick's. A silent nod passed between them, a crack in the usual armor. "It keeps you running."

Laughter bubbled in the background. Teammates bantered in a circle nearby, their voices overlapping, but Brick barely heard it. The usual rituals—slapping backs, jokes, the wet imprint of a sweat-slick handshake—all seemed distant now, like a radio playing from somewhere out of reach.

While his teammates ribbed him, it wasn't just teasing. It was a complex, awkward thing—the way they showed care, even if Brick struggled to accept it. The banter only sharpened the loneliness clawing at him beneath the surface. He hid behind their laughter, but isolation tasted bitter, sharper than the metallic cold of the locker against his skin.

Brick pushed off the locker. His shadow stretched long across the fluorescent glare, a dark blade cutting through the sharp light. The banter trailed after him like thin wisps trying to hold onto something solid, but he was already moving—head down, eyes heavy with battles his teammates only glimpsed but never quite saw.

"Don't let Brooks get you spinning, Brick," Caleb called, his voice firm but softening. "We've got your back, man. You're not alone in this game."

Brick paused. His jaw tightened, but he didn't turn around. The cavern's hum and chatter swallowed the unspoken promise as he slipped past, leaving the locker room behind him—a fortress of rough camaraderie unable to close the gulf spreading inside.

###

The quiet break room offers a refuge from the relentless hum of the team facility—the thrum of distant footsteps, the faint clatter of cleats on tile, and the low drone of conversations filtered by thick walls. Natalie slips inside with Nina and Emma. The door clicks softly behind them, sealing off the chaos.

The air conditioner hums. A coffee maker buzzes faintly, releasing the grounding scent of roast and cream. She lowers herself onto the scratched wooden chair and unclips her badge with a subtle exhale.

The metal lands against the table—cold and solid. A reminder that the professional world still waits outside this small sanctuary. The stakes press against her ribs. One misstep, and everything crumbles.

Her voice falters. A hushed confession slips out, fragile against the calm she fights to maintain. "Last night shook me more than I thought it would."

She let the words hang in the air. Her fingers drummed an erratic rhythm on the worn wood, her breath shallow. She forced her gaze downward, unwilling to meet their eyes—afraid that the tremor inside her might become visible.

Nina and Emma exchanged brief, knowing glances. They waited.

"I'm afraid I want him too much," Natalie admitted. Her eyes were sharp yet vulnerable. "If this explodes... I lose everything." Her gaze flicked between their faces, searching for judgment, reassurance, or maybe just a flicker of understanding.

The muted fluorescent light felt harsher now, pinning her fears to the small table.

Emma's eyes softened. She leaned forward, her gaze unwavering—offering something steadier than words. Her own past had taught her how to hold space for cracked hearts in places where professionalism demanded silence. "Look, wanting something doesn't make you weak. Desire and professionalism? They don't have to cancel each other out." A quiet smile tugged at her mouth, warm and knowing. "You're not fragile because you want. You're human. And you need to be kind to yourself."

Nina folded her hands. Her dark eyes were reflective, steady like burnished stone. "Trust your judgment, Natalie. Fear is a gut punch, but it isn't the whole truth." Her tone was deliberate, layered with hard-won experience. "I had a complicated crush once. A line blurred, and I thought I'd lose myself in it." She leaned in a little more, a conspiratorial tilt to her mouth. "But I learned to take it slow, listen to the warning bells, and—" The corners of her eyes wrinkled with humor and sincerity. "—keep the boundaries sharp. You've got the tools. The trick is to use them, not to run from them."

Their voices mingled with the faint drip of a leaky faucet somewhere behind the walls. A worn clock ticked softly. Time slowed and stretched—the room breathed with them.

Natalie's fingertip traced the grain of the table, mapping a path back to herself.

"Okay," she said quietly. "Slow down. Document everything—keep things transparent. Ask for help if I start to lose control." The words were a lifeline thrown into turbulent waters.

Emma nodded firmly. "You're not alone in this. We're here for you." Soft yet resolute, it was a quiet promise wrapping around her.

Nina smiled—brief and steady. "One step at a time. Keep your heart cautious but not closed." Her fingers brushed a stray lock of hair behind her ear, the motion casual yet deliberate. A small affirmation that restraint doesn't mean isolation.

Charged silence followed, thick with everything unspoken: the looming media glare, the fragile balance between private desire and public consequence, and the stormy complexities swirling beneath the team's polished surface.

Natalie straightened and slid her badge back onto the ribbon. A sharp clack punctuated the fragile truce she had built with herself. The tension diffused slightly from her shoulders—a subtle thaw after hours of ice-thick restraint. She stood, her chest rising and falling with measured breaths, pulling strength from Emma's steady gaze and Nina's calm reassurance.

In the doorframe, the familiarity of support lingered as she stepped out. Her shoes made a soft patter against the tiled floor, creating a quiet rhythm of resolve. The hurried pace of the facility resumed beyond the door, but something had shifted inside her. Something fragile and fierce had taken root.

She carried Emma's promise woven into her spine, with Nina's counsel threading through her thoughts—light against the night ahead. She moved forward, lighter but braced, the weight of what was at stake folded carefully into the margins of this moment.

Outside, the afternoon sun slanted through narrow windows, casting long, uncertain shadows over the team facility's worn floors. The storm waited, but for now, Natalie held onto this fragile calm—a quiet defiance against the chaos to come.

Brick's fingers curled tightly around the cold rail. Numbness crept across his fingertips where skin met rough metal. He leaned forward, muscles taut beneath his worn jacket, watching.

Across the asphalt expanse outside the team facility, Natalie stepped away from the building. Nina and Emma flanked her closely, their voices a low hum beneath the distant thud of a football hitting turf and the scrape of cleats on concrete. The late afternoon sun sank behind the practice field, casting long shadows that creased the complex's sharp lines.

This place—the practice field stretching emerald and vast—had become the crucible where Brick battled himself daily. Every drill, every rep was a test of control he barely passed. Today felt no different, except that she was here, and he was unraveling.

Natalie moves with purpose in her stride, but even from here, doubt flickers across her face. She glances back over her shoulder. Her eyes catch the field where the afternoon light wavers like flame. Her lips tighten. A raw ache blooms there, softening the usual guard she wears so well.

She hesitates, taking one breath longer than she should.

The weight of it settles hard on Brick's chest.

He blinks. His jaw flexes, fighting down the impulse rising like a tide. But his body defies him. His first step is away—turning his broad back to her, muscles coiled in reluctant retreat.

Then he pivots back. The motion is silent, charged with magnetism and unsaid words. Half-burned desire flares bright.

Teammates round the corner, talking and laughing. The hunger to chase her down falters. It shrinks, swallowed by the necessity of self-control, especially here. Especially now.

Brick swallows the raw pull in his throat and squares his shoulders, forcing the fire down into a simmer he barely trusts.

Across the asphalt, Natalie threads her way toward the parking lot with Nina and Emma. The three women move like dancers stepping through a crowded floor, weaving between scattered vehicles. Her steps falter only slightly beneath the weight of tired resolve.

She has spent the day wrestling with her own boundaries, terrified of what happens when they crumble. One mistake—one public moment—and everything she has built collapses. The fear tastes metallic in her mouth, thick and suffocating.

Then a glance flickers to the side. Sharp. Deliberate. Her gaze catches Brick's across the open space.

Their eyes lock. A standoff of longing and restraint, heavy with a conversation neither dares to speak aloud.

Nina's hand brushes lightly against Natalie's arm as they cross. Emma shifts her bag on her shoulder and casts a quick look at Brick before they turn toward their cars.

Natalie's glance lingers. Just a moment longer. A silent message is carried in the fierce vulnerability hidden beneath her poised mask.

Brick's chest tightens. Forty yards of empty space stretch between them. Each step is a reminder of rules still unbroken and bridges still unsaid.

The parking lot falls quiet, save for distant traffic and muffled cheers drifting from the stadium. Nina disappears behind a black SUV. Emma slides into a silver sedan—the door closing with a soft click that feels like finality.

Natalie remains the last silhouette. Her spine curves subtly as she pauses again before crossing toward her sleek black sedan, which gleams beneath the fading light.

Brick's voice grits behind clenched teeth, as if he is willing his body to move on its own. But his feet stay rooted, the ground beneath him steady against the storm inside.

He wants to call out, risking the humiliation of public pursuit for a chance at truth. Instead, he inhales cold air heavy with grass and exhaust and exhales slowly, surrendering to the silence.

"You're serious about those rules, huh?" His voice is low, gravel and frustration wrapped around something softer, something vulnerable.

Natalie doesn't turn immediately; her hand tightens on the door handle, fingers flexing like a silent plea for composure.

"I have to be," she replies, her voice steady and tinged with that distant professionalism he's battled all day. "This. Us. It can't happen again, Brick. It's too dangerous for both of us."

He steps a pace closer. The distance narrows yet remains barred by invisible walls.

"Dangerous? It's real. You can't just pretend it didn't mean something."

"Meaning something and losing everything aren't the same." Her eyes flash steel beneath the fray of emotion. "You think I don't want what you want? But this job, this team—it's fragile. One mistake, and it all comes crashing down."

Brick's laugh is harsh, brittle against the tension.

"You sound like Coach Hale right now."

"I'm saying what he won't." Her gaze needles him, unwavering. "We're both playing with fire, but I'm the one who has to clean it up when things burn."

A silence stretches between them—charged, aching.

Brick lets his hands fall from the rail and steps back. His voice softens into something desperate, a warning wrapped in quiet surrender.

"Just don't push me away, Brooks."

She doesn't answer; she only lifts the door and slips inside, shutting him out with the faint click of the lock. The engine hums to life, and tires crunch on gravel. The black car slides forward, leaving Brick standing alone, watching the taillights fade like a slow pulse retreating into dusk.

He's left with the raw taste of longing, the bitter scent of restraint, and all the burning possibilities edged into that suspended moment before the next storm breaks.

The Article Threat

The stadium's media room hums with restless energy, a swarm of voices rising and falling like waves in the cavernous space. Flashbulbs burst with dizzying frequency, incandescent pulses illuminating both sharp suits and casual jerseys. Natalie's heels click with purposeful urgency on the polished floor. With a clipboard pressed firmly in one hand, her other hand gestures crisply toward the waiting PR staff and reporters, her voice clipped and exact.

"As we discussed, focus on the recent training milestones. No comment on the off-field incidents. Keep it tight. Next player, please."

She steps up to the podium, her eyes scanning the throng of eager faces and pointed lenses. Cameras jostle, and microphones bob and twitch inches from the players' mouths. Logan "Brick" Turner stands to her right, his broad shoulders tensed, the scar above his eyebrow cutting a jagged shadow under the harsh lights. She notices the tightness in his jaw, the way his fingers curl and uncurl against his thigh—tells she has learned to read over months of navigating his moods. A flicker of concern threads beneath her professional composure. Whatever is eating at him today, it will take more than talking points to contain it. Natalie's gaze remains steady despite the chaos, her words streamlined like a dam holding back a storm.

"Ladies and gentlemen, thank you for coming. Brick has made significant progress on the field this season—"

A sudden flash blinds her for a moment. Microphones sway like insects drawn to heat, some thrusting forward without invitation. She cocks her head slightly, exchanging firm but subtle gestures with a nearby assistant. PR staff hustle, passing out precisely worded talking points wrapped in shiny blue folders.

Natalie threads her way between clusters of journalists and players, a conductor weaving through an unruly orchestra. The press room smells of old carpet, stale coffee, and the faint metallic tang of electronics. Her heels tap against the ground, a rhythmic counterpoint to murmured questions and clicking cameras.

Stopping at the sponsor-board backdrop, she crouches briefly to adjust a microphone stand that has slipped to an awkward angle. With steady fingers, she checks the digital display on a nearby tablet—numerical stats flickering in electric blue.

"That stat is off, by the way," she says to the nearest reporter, her tone clipped but not unkind. "Brick recorded thirty-five tackles, not twenty-eight, in the last game."

The reporter blinks, surprised, then nods before the camera clicks again. Natalie straightens and moves on, slipping through narrow gaps with the grace of someone who has done this a thousand times.

At the edge of the crowd, Victor Cross leans against a cool wall, his hands tucked in the pockets of his dark jacket. His eyes, sharp and calculating, track Natalie with calm intensity. He doesn't push into the limelight; instead, he catalogs her movements—the way she sidesteps questions with surgical precision, the brief pauses she makes near players, and the seconds she steals alone to reevaluate her next move. They crossed paths before, three years ago, when he had been digging into the team's financial dealings, and she had blocked him at every turn with polished smiles and redacted documents. She won that round, ensuring his story died in editorial. But he learned something valuable then: Natalie Voss didn't just manage crises; she orchestrated them. And right now, standing in this pressroom, she was orchestrating something bigger than the usual damage control.

He makes a mental note of her route through the gauntlet, the timing between each interaction, and how PR staff cluster and disperse in her wake.

"She runs a tight ship," he murmurs to himself, his thin lips curving into a slow, unreadable smile.

The Q&A rattles on—fast, precise, and demanding. Microphones rotate between players; the speakers' voices rise over the relentless hum of the room. Brick's responses, clipped and watchful, reflect the tension edging beneath the formal surface. The crowd hungers for a slip, a flame to ignite scandal, but Natalie's steel nerves smooth every jagged edge.

Finally, the session edges toward its close. Natalie steps back to the podium, clipboard tucked under her arm. Her eyes sweep over the remaining questions, and then she raises a hand.

"That concludes our Q&A. Thank you for your time and professionalism." Her smile is tight, the kind that doesn't quite reach her eyes but masks fatigue like a well-oiled machine.

She pivots away from the crowd, her heels clicking a retreating cadence as she cuts through clusters of lingering reporters and staff. The noise swells behind her—the murmur of speculation, the distant clatter of cameras resetting—but she pushes forward toward an exit corridor, the clamorous pressroom receding.

The sterile corridor feels cool, almost sacred after the crush of bodies and sound. Her breath steadies as she reaches the doorframe, the stale scent of recycled air mingling with faint ozone from nearby monitors flashing game highlights. For a brief moment, she allows herself a flicker of respite—a single exhale of controlled release—as the press room's chaos becomes nothing but muted echoes behind her.

The corridor hums with muted chatter beneath the chorus of stadium echoes—footsteps tapping on polished concrete, murmurs drifting like restless ghosts. Screens flicker along the wall, providing fractured snapshots of the game: slow-motion tackles, triumphs frozen mid-air, faces taut with focus. Natalie strides forward, her clipboard clutched tightly, navigating cables and equipment cases with steady grace.

A shadow detaches itself from the quieter edge. A figure slips into her path with the precision of a hunter.

Victor Cross steps closer. The space between them shrinks.

His voice drops low, just above her breath. Sharp as a scalpel. "We need to talk."

No one else is nearby. Just the flicker of screens and the faint pulse of pressure building like static in the air.

From under his arm, he pulls out a manila folder, its edges worn soft from handling. He fans it open. Contents spill into the dim light—grainy photos and police reports yellowed at the corners. His thumb glides over a booking photo: Brick's face, caught in some frozen moment. Eyes distant. Hard. Vulnerable. His finger taps a list of names stapled beneath witness statements. Crisp. Damning.

Natalie's chest tightens like a vice. Each breath comes fragile, as if the air itself weighs too much.

Victor leans in. His eyes gleam with that unmistakable blend of calculation and hunger that only a man chasing a story knows. The media ecosystem turns ruthless and unforgiving—today's hero becomes tomorrow's headline, and no one escapes the cycle once it begins.

"Natalie Brooks," he murmurs, his voice tinted with eerie amusement, "you know how fast the spotlight turns. Brick—your Brick—he's closer than you think to falling." He taps the folder with a deliberate finger. Not a threat. A warning wrapped in silk.

His grin tightens. "I'm planning to go public soon. Unless..."

He lets the word hang—heavy, sharp.

Natalie squared her shoulders. The tremor in her fingers intensified as they curled around the edge of the folder. "What do you want?"

Victor smiles. He folds a crisp sheet from the folder—a printed teaser line already polished and ready to ignite—and slides it smoothly across the narrow space between them.

His gaze never leaves hers.

"You can shape the story. Give me something—a comment, a denial. Control the narrative before it controls you." His eyes flick to the end of the corridor, where muffled voices and distant camera clicks remind them of the world waiting just beyond.

He steps closer. "That—or refuse. And watch the story break on my terms."

His voice turns almost soft, but the cold edge beneath it cuts through the space between them like a blade.

Natalie's fingers twitched at her side. She met his stare, unblinking, even as her throat tightened.

"I'm going to need some time," she whispered. "This—this isn't just a story to dismiss."

Victor's hand moves like a closing trap. The folder snaps shut, the sound echoing louder than words ever could.

He steps back into the shadowed edge. The predator fades, but the threat lingers like a stain.

"Tick tock, Natalie."

And with that, he vanishes, leaving her to bear the weight of the ticking clock and the fragile silence of a battlefield waiting to explode.

Natalie slips quietly into the cramped supply closet. The shrill murmur of media day fades behind the steel door. She leans back against the cold metal shelves. The chill seeps through her blazer—icy fingers pressing against her ribs, anchoring her to grim reality.

Her breath comes shallow yet rapid. Her pulse hammers against her temples.

The manila folder Victor pressed into her hands rests heavily on her lap. Its weight pulls at her thoughts like a stone tether.

She flips through the pages again. Each report is a jagged shard cutting through the veneer of calm she has cultivated all day. Grainy booking photos stare back from the pages—smeared with static and shadow. Witness statements clutter the margins, splotched with ink and legal jargon. She grabs the crisis checklist from her clipboard. The paper feels rough and familiar beneath her fingertips.

Her pen scratches out frantic notes: names, dates, phrases flagged in angry red ink. Her hand trembles just enough to betray the controlled mask she wears—a staccato rhythm of scribbles that battles the tight knot twisting in her stomach.

Her eyes linger on a photo of Brick—tense, with rigid cheekbones clenched beneath a furrowed brow. This version of him—the arrest, the accusation—doesn't match the man from last week's session. She remembers the slow, careful breaths she'd heard, the hesitant softness in his eyes when he finally let down his guard around her, the faint brush of his calloused hand against her skin, and the raw, careful way he traced her name with his voice. It was a fragile moment nestled in the storm of his chaos.

That image pulls tight against the sharp edge of the folder in her hands. These two versions of Brick crash against each other inside her chest—irreconcilable yet both real.

Her phone buzzed, and she swiped open the team group chat. Messages blazed across the screen—rumors of police reports, whispers of Victor Cross lurking nearby. Fingers flew over keyboards as players speculated and coaches kept their distance. Even here, far from the field, tension hung thick and suffocating.

Victor Cross wasn't just another journalist; his exposés had dismantled careers before, leaving players radioactive in the league's eyes. If he had real ammunition, if those photos meant what she feared they meant, this wasn't just a crisis to manage. This was a reckoning—for Brick, for the team, and for her own judgment.

Her thumb hovered over the screen. She typed rapidly:

"Call legal. Alert Coach Hale. Need a holding statement ready—fast. Urgent meeting. ASAP."

Each line burned with the weight of impossible choices: trust, fragile, fractured easily. The team, brick, me—all balancing on this knife's edge.

She closed the folder slowly. The crisp snap echoed louder in the stillness. Her breath steadied—slow and even—as she tucked the checklist into her pocket. Her fingers curled around the edge of the door.

She straightened her shoulders and smoothed the corners of her blazer. Forceful composure settled like armor against the storm waiting beyond.

The door opened with a muted creak. Natalie stepped back into the press corridor. The pulse of flashing cameras and snapping questions washed over her like a tide. Her gaze sharpened, and her lips tightened into a thin line as she reclaimed the professional mask, ready for the chaos that would follow.

The stadium's hum faded as Natalie stepped into the weight room. The air hit her thick—metal and sweat, heavy and close.

Brick dominated the center of the space, muscles coiled tight as he slammed plates onto the barbell with measured brutality. The clang echoed sharply, vibrating through steel and concrete. She closed the heavy door behind her. The metallic clatter died, swallowed by sudden, electric silence.

Steel eyes met hers—dark and smoldering beneath the jagged scar above his brow. His breath came heavy, tinged with rubber and chalk dust, hanging between them like a warning.

She didn't need to speak yet. The weight of unspoken words pressed down—heavier than the plates stacked on that barbell.

Natalie set the manila folder on the worn bench with practiced calm and flipped it open. Police reports, grainy booking photos, and Brick's face caught mid-defiance in stark black and white—raw, vulnerable, and damning. She met his fierce gaze evenly and didn't look away.

"Victor Cross has these," she said, her voice low and clipped. "He threatens to run the story unless we give him a comment. Soon."

Her fingers traced the folder's edges, pressing cold paper into scarred wood. The room's stillness amplified her words, turning them into a hammer striking unyielding stone.

Brick's jaw tightened. His dark eyes flicked down to the open folder, scanning the images and wary words printed beneath them like a trap. His chest rose with a quickening pulse, and the air thickened between them.

She stepped closer. Her tone softened, at least for now. "I want you to trust me. Let me handle this. Legal's on standby. I'm preparing a denial, and we'll have a player statement ready within hours. We control the narrative."

He laughed—bitter, sharp as breaking glass. "Trust you? Nah. You suits are all the same, waiting for me to screw up so you can sell me out and look good."

Her gaze sharpened. The room seemed to cool as tension stiffened her shoulders. "This isn't about me; it's about protecting you. Plain and simple."

Brick's laugh twisted into something rawer. "Protecting me? You don't know what that word means. You all talk about 'second chances' like it's some game, as if you can just reset the scoreboard and pretend the last play never happened."

He leaned in, his voice low but rough with accusation. "Pick a side, Natalie. Are you with me, or are you with them? Because right now, it feels like you're standing on the fence, watching me fall."

She searched his face, noting the sharp edges of pain and fury, the fracturing lines beneath that tough exterior. She pressed her palms flat against the bench, her fingers trembling just enough to betray the calm she wore like armor.

"I'm on your side," she said firmly, urgency threading through her voice. "But I need you to meet me halfway."

A snarl escaped him as he yanked a weight free with a vicious jerk. Metal scraped harshly against concrete—a brutal punctuation slicing through their fragile connection.

Without a glance back, Brick stormed toward the door. Each step thudded like a hammer blow. The door shut behind him with a sharp, reverberating slam.

The sound echoed through the weight room and then died.

Natalie remained frozen beside the open folder, her heart pounding in sync with that final slam. The space between them hung shredded, raw, and cold. Sweat and iron lingered in the air, mingling with the heavy silence that now filled the room.

She straightened, swallowing back the knot of frustration and helplessness tightening in her throat.

Outside, the distant roar of the stadium pressed in again—oblivious and relentless. But here, in this weight room, every breath felt heavier. It was a battleground of trust, anger, and fragile hope suspended in the quiet aftermath.

Jaxon leaned against the locker room doorframe, his voice low. The scrape of his cleats on the concrete disappeared into the clamor around them. His eyes flicked toward the practice field, where players jogged in broken rhythms, tension folding across their shoulders like a heavy cloak.

"Brick just slammed the door," he murmured to Emma, who stood beside him, her clipboard clutched like armor.

Her brow furrowed, and her eyes narrowed as she watched the players stumble through their drills, the usual focus missing like a ghost in the room. "He's never stormed out like that before. Something's wrong."

Emma's nod was barely perceptible. She shifted her weight, and the faint scent of eucalyptus from the distant showers mingled with the musk of leather and sweat—the locker room's signature perfume, heavy and suffocating today.

At the locker bay, Caleb tossed a towel over his shoulder, grinning in a way that didn't quite reach his eyes. DeShawn smirked beside him, the joke landing with an uneasy edge.

"Man, he's off today," DeShawn muttered, the casual quip barely masking the worry threading through his voice. "It's like something's buzzing under that skin."

Caleb's grin slipped into a crease of concern. "Do you think it's that serious?"

"Brick's not the type to hide anything unless it's bad." DeShawn's eyes slid toward the weight room door that Brick had just left.

The air between them tightened. An invisible current buzzed with unspoken fears.

Coach Marcus Hale stood at the locker room's edge, his broad shoulders squared like a wall against the storm. His sharp eyes scanned the shifting formations—players whispering in clusters, others stretching with distracted precision.

Brick's corner caught his gaze: empty except for a worn football and a solitary water bottle.

Then Marcus's glance flicked across the hall.

Natalie moved past, pale-faced, her lips pressed tight into a thin line. The calm mask had slipped. Marcus's jaw clenched hard. The sudden absence, the tense silence, and the fragile danger only he could read pressed heavily in the air.

He understood what others couldn't yet see: how quickly trust could fracture and how one scandal could splinter a team held together by nothing but faith in each other.

Emma caught Nina's gaze near the row of lockers. Their eyes locked in a silent exchange weighted with concern. Emma stepped off the threshold, her footsteps echoing softly on the tile as she moved toward the training field entrance, her presence a quiet sentinel for the team's well-being.

The locker room hum dimmed. Whispers threaded through tight clusters of players. Words brushed past like quick shadows—"police reports," "Cross"—fragments carrying heavier meaning than their syllables could hold. Eyes flickered, lingering too long on one another as if seeking reassurance in shared uncertainty.

The usual scent of sweat and leather hung thick, mingling with the faint sting of antiseptic from last night's cleaning, pressing in like a weight.

Caleb shifted, his voice dropping to a mutter as he exchanged a glance with DeShawn. "Did you hear about that Cross guy? What's he digging up on Brick?"

"Stuff that could blow us up," DeShawn replied, swallowing hard. "And fast."

Jaxon stepped forward, his hands tracing a slow arc over his face, rubbing the crease of worry etched there. "If this leaks, it's not just Brick. It's us—all of us. Trust shatters. Fans turn. The media claws deeper."

Emma returned, her steps measured yet brisk. She caught Jaxon's eye—a flicker of understanding that spoke of pressure beyond the physical strain.

Coach Hale exhaled slowly and controlled, though the lines around his eyes deepened. He moved deliberately among his men, his voice low, carrying authority that was part warning and part reassurance.

"We hold together," he said quietly.

The words almost got lost beneath the hum of speculation.

Natalie's shadow passed at the corridor's edge. Her shoulders were squared, but fatigue tugged at the corners of her sharp jaw, and the usually steady cadence of her stride faltered—just enough to set nerves on edge.

The whispers gathered speed, weaving through the rows of lockers like a creeping vine.

"Did you see the folder Cross showed her? Cops. Photos."

"Brick's past bleeding into the present…"

"Do you think Brick will fight it? Or fold?"

The locker room shivered beneath the weight of those questions. Body language shifted—fists knotted, eyes darted, and shoulders tightened as if bracing for impact.

Jaxon pulled Caleb aside, his voice low but urgent.

"This isn't just about the game anymore. We've got to be ready for what comes next."

Caleb nodded, swallowing dryly. "Yeah. And we've got to have Brick's back. Whatever happens."

DeShawn leaned against the locker, his jaw clenched as he glanced toward the empty space Brick always occupied—the absence a loud declaration.

The murmurs softened, replaced by heavy, shared silence. The team breathed as one, holding fast to a fragile thread that bound them even as it trembled.

In that stillness, everyone knew: the storm was on the horizon. The fallout could fracture everything they had fought to build.

No one dared to speak it aloud. But beneath the layers of loyalty and fear, the truth hung in the air—this scandal could break them.

The door clicked softly behind her, sealing out the relentless clatter of the stadium's media day chaos. Natalie's heels whispered a measured rhythm over the polished floor as she crossed to the corner office perched high above the field. The glass desk waited, immaculate and cold. Its surface reflected the gray light filtering through the floor-to-ceiling windows that overlooked the rough emerald gridiron below. She dropped her clipboard onto the smooth surface, pulling open a worn leather-bound crisis playbook—the edges softened and creased from years of unease and quick decisions.

This space was her control center, her fortress. Yet today, it felt like a lonely battlefield where loyalty and ethics were locked in combat she couldn't resolve.

The legal team's emergency contact numbers were scrawled across a sticky note in the corner. Next to it were hastily drafted talking points she'd started that afternoon. Her fingers traced the list, but the words blurred. Every possible response felt like a trap tightening around her.

With her eyes closed, she pressed her fingertips into her temples. The scent of cut grass drifted in from the open window, distant chlorine mixing with it. When she opened her eyes, the manila folder from Victor Cross rested heavily before her, its corners worn from her restless grip. She unfolded the sheet containing police report details. The names of witnesses were printed with clinical detachment. Yet each one was a silent accusation, a thread threatening to unravel everything.

Her eyelid fluttered involuntarily before a single tear slipped free, trailing molten heat along her cheek. She brushed it away quickly, biting her lip to still the tremble. The office's chill bit at her skin, but inside, panic boiled, threatening to spill out despite her calm mask. Brick—the man behind the headlines and skirmishes—anchored her thoughts. His recent moments of vulnerability flickered painfully in her memory: the way his guarded eyes had softened just enough to make the night between them more than just a fleeting advantage. And now, with Victor gunning for a public takedown, every fragile thread risked snapping.

She pulled her phone free and scrolled through the team's group chat, the screen alive with whispers of reckoning. Rumors flashed like distant lightning. In a locker room this close-knit, secrets had a half-life measured in hours. The speculation rippled outward—even players unconnected to the scandal felt the tremor of impending fallout. Everything Brick had built, everything the team had worked toward, hung suspended over a chasm.

Natalie made swift notes on the back of her checklist: call legal immediately, alert Coach Hale, and prepare a holding statement strong enough to withstand the first shock but vague enough not to inflame the situation. Every decision felt like stepping further into quicksand.

Her fingers hovered over the keyboard, trembling slightly. She typed the first draft: a preemptive acknowledgment of the investigation, meant to control the narrative before Victor's venomous version saw the light of day. She reread it. The formal tone stiffened into a wall that felt more like betrayal. Deleting it, she typed out another—a flat denial, an ironclad shield to protect Brick—but the words tasted bitter, like ash on her tongue. That one vanished with a sigh.

"My hands are tied," she whispered to the empty room, the silence pressing in with the weight of every choice she feared.

Her phone buzzed. An incoming call ID lit up the screen—Coach Hale. "Coach," she answered, her voice steady despite the turmoil coiling beneath.

"Natalie, got a moment?" His deep tones carried calm authority, a harbor amid the storm.

"I just got the green light to alert you," she said, careful not to reveal more than necessary. "Victor's pushing something hard. We don't have much time."

A pause. "We prepare for the worst. No surprises. Don't let panic dictate the team's message." He sounded resolute, yet the undercurrent of worry was unmistakable. "Legal?" he asked.

"Briefed. I'm looping them in fully. They'll advise on the next steps."

"Good. Keep your head. Keep his."

She let out a breath she hadn't realized she had been holding. "Will do, Coach. I'll update you as soon as I hear more."

"Thanks, Natalie. We're counting on you." The line went dead.

The room felt colder now, the growing dusk dimming the skyline beyond the glass. She closed her laptop with deliberate slowness, the faint click serving as a final punctuation to hours of tension. Her hands folded over the manila folder, fingertips brushing the edges worn soft from turning pages she wished she could forget.

The loneliness of leadership settled like a stone in her gut. Integrity tugged her one way, while protection pulled fiercely in the other. Somewhere between them, she had to find a foothold—not just for the team, but for Brick, the man who thought no one could stand beside him when the storm broke. The weight of that choice pressed down harder than any pressurized spotlight, a quiet reckoning waiting just beyond the office door.

She breathed in slowly, the scent of paper and leather grounding her as the night whispered promises of battles yet to come.

Rage Regression

The thin sliver of dawn sneaked past the blinds, casting pale lines across the hardwood floor. Logan "Brick" Turner's eyes flickered open—dry and heavy as ash. The room smelled faintly of sweat and stale tension, the lingering residue of a night spent tangled in restless thoughts. He didn't want to open his eyes all the way; the pressure inside his skull wouldn't ease.

The argument with Natalie replayed behind his eyelids—sharp and merciless—a tight knot coiling deeper in his gut. Her voice, steady but fierce, echoed with every tick of the ceiling fan. The word "control" was a hammer, pounding down where his defenses once stood. Then Victor Cross's threat reared—cold and clinical—snaking into his mind with the promise of ruin.

Legs swinging over the bed's edge, Brick's feet hit the cold floor, numb to the chill slipping through the cracked windows. He paced, the scrape of soles against wood sharp and relentless in the quiet. His fists clenched so hard that his nails bit angry crescents into his palms. Visions flickered—his past mistakes warping into monsters.

The smell of disinfectant rushed back, the sterile cold of that hospital corridor, and the sharp copper taste of guilt that had never quite faded. He could still see the machines, hear the monitors, and feel the weight of what he'd nearly destroyed.

A sudden buzz sliced through the silence.

His phone blinked on the nightstand. "Victor Cross" glared from the screen. Brick hesitated, then swiped.

Something big is coming for the Reign's most volatile star.

The words stung—brazen and accusing. Heat flared across his chest, muscles coiling like snarled rope. His nails dug deeper into his palms, tiny pinpricks grounding the storm inside.

The air in his apartment hung thick, almost suffocating. Brick grabbed his jacket and stepped out into the thin dawn, the cool air biting at his collar as he headed toward the stadium. The city's hum was muted at this hour, shadows stretching long between streetlights and empty sidewalks.

Inside the cavernous locker room, the scent of aged leather and musky sweat wrapped around him like a second skin. The fluorescent lights hummed overhead—too bright, too unforgiving—casting stark shadows that clawed at his thoughts. He dropped onto a bench, the hard wood unforgiving beneath him. He exhaled slowly, letting his mind spiral.

The latest incident replayed relentlessly: the explosion on the field, the snap, the shouts, the flash of the referee's flag. Every stare from his teammates felt like a verdict; every sidelong glance from the coaches was silent condemnation. He could almost hear the whispers slicing through the air—subtle and piercing—proof that they had already decided what he was and what he would always be.

The door creaked.

Caleb slinked in, his eyes flicking cautiously toward Brick. Eli followed, the unspoken tension thick between them—a careful measurement of the shifting terrain separating them from the man turned storm.

DeShawn's voice cut through with forced levity: "Man, Brick, you look like you wrestled a grizzly last night and lost." Yet even as he joked, his eyes tracked every twitch of Brick's jaw and every tightened muscle. Brick caught the watchful gaze and twisted it into a sharpened blade, perceiving avoidance and betrayal hidden beneath forced smiles and careful words.

The door opened again.

Natalie slipped inside like a ghost, her presence humming with exhaustion and brittle edges. She crossed the room with deliberate steps, avoiding his space like a minefield, but when their eyes met—raw and unguarded—her expression was a mosaic of fatigue, guilt, and accusation. A silent rebuke was spoken in the crease of her brow and the tight line of her mouth.

Heat flared across Brick's chest, his muscles coiling like snarled rope. His fists clenched at his sides, nails digging crimson crescents into his skin. The air around him buzzed with simmering temper, a storm held back only by a desperate will not to appear weak. Behind his clenched teeth and narrowed eyes, a cavernous loneliness yawned—a stark emptiness starved for connection yet too guarded to reach out.

"Why bother showing up at all?" His voice cracked through the thick silence, low and rough.

Natalie's gaze flicked away, her voice tight. "'Cause if I run, it stays broken."

"And here I thought you came to point fingers." His hand jerked, hitting the edge of the bench with a sharp crack.

She met his glare, her eyes glistening with unshed exhaustion. "Maybe I am. Maybe I'm done pretending we're on the same side."

Caleb cleared his throat, his voice gentle but firm. "Brick, this... this isn't helping anyone."

"Yeah," Eli added quietly, "we're all stuck in the same storm."

Brick let their words wash over him—sharp pebbles against raw skin. He didn't trust their sympathy. Not yet. Not after the cold distance creeping into their looks over the last few days. To him, it was betrayal wearing polite faces.

He stood slowly. The rough scrape of leather on tile echoed in the vast room. "I'm tired," he admitted, his voice hoarse. "Tired of everyone acting like I'm their problem."

Natalie's breath hitched, her walls cracking ever so slightly. She didn't answer. Instead, she cast a glance between him and the others—a silent plea tangled with frustration.

Brick's fury bristled, folding over into a hard shell of defiance. "I'm not the weak one here."

But inside, the ache deepened—a raw wound bled dry by isolation. Alone in a sea of faces, he clenched his fists tighter—a silent vow that whatever came next, he wouldn't unravel. Not now.

The morning sun slices through the tall netting surrounding the practice field, casting long, rigid shadows across the freshly striped turf. Shadows claw at the ground. Crisp air carries the scent of cut grass, sharp and earthy beneath the sterile hum of distant stadium lights still fading with dawn. The sharp slap of cleats against the turf echoed like a war drum, the cold morning air biting at exposed skin.

Coach Marcus Hale gathers the team in a tight semicircle, his broad frame unmoving at the center like a guardian standing sentry. His eyes, dark and unwavering, scan the faces before him—every one bracing for words they do not want to hear.

"Look, everybody," Coach's voice cuts through the quiet, low and steady but edged with unspoken warning. "We all make mistakes. But it's how you respond to those mistakes that defines you—defines this team." His gaze flickers to Brick Turner, sharp and undeniable, though he never says the name. "Anger's a fire, and it can burn clean—or it can consume everything. You choose which it is." Fingers point, deliberate and slow, not accusatory but precise—directed at the man standing apart, fists clenched tighter than steel.

Brick's knuckles blanched white. His breath came shallow, heat flaring behind his eyes as the words pressed against him like hands trying to hold back a tide he couldn't contain. His jaw worked. Nothing could tether the tempest inside.

Coach Hale's voice dropped just a notch. "Discipline wins games. Control wins respect." The team held its breath, the words hanging over the grid like a challenge, a promise, and a threat. Not by name, but absolutely aimed.

The whistle cut sharply through the air. Players spilled into regimented chaos—a dance of power and precision. Brick burst forward first, eyes blazing as he snarled through blockers. His hits shattered arms and tossed linemen with bone-crushing force. Each movement screamed raw, unyielding fury. Coaches shouted warnings alongside whistles, but Brick ignored every caution—pushing, crashing, bellowing, as if to break the world before it broke him.

"Turn it down!" a coach yelled. "Brick, temper it!"

His reply was a twisted grin, teeth bared beneath heavy brows, a growl scraping his voice as he shoved past another obstacle. "What's the point if I don't?"

The offensive line gritted its teeth as Brick crashed through again, knocking a teammate to the ground. Jaw clenched. Frustration burning. The slap of feet on turf mingled with the sharp crack of bodies colliding—an unrelenting percussion driving the practice forward.

From the sideline, Jaxon Reyes threaded through the swarm. His lean form breathed calm into the storm, eyes steady and voice dropping low when he reached Brick's side.

"Brick, man." Jaxon's fingers brushed against a shoulder, brief and hopeful. "You gotta ease up a bit. You know how this road ends."

Brick shrugged the hand off like a flicker of irritation—a shield wound too tight to relax. "I'm fine. I don't need you babysitting." His tone cut like ice. His eyes flickered away before refocusing on the next target—a defender scrambling to set up.

"You're not fine," Jaxon pressed, his voice steady but not insistent. "Everyone's watching. You don't want to lose yourself again."

Brick gritted his teeth, refusing to meet Jaxon's steady gaze. "I'm not losing. I'm surviving." Then, without another word, he charged back into the fray, a whirlwind of force and defiance.

Coach Hale's eyes narrowed, shadowed beneath the brim of his cap as he watched from across the field. There was talent in that fury—raw, explosive talent. But there was also danger. A coach knew the difference between controlled fire and a storm edging toward destruction. Muscle knotted tense beneath his shirt. His fists clenched and unclenched with silent calculation. Brick had the gift. The question was whether the gift would destroy him first.

A sharp nod, barely perceptible. Coach Hale signaled the defensive units to maintain formation, watching every twitch of Brick's aggression—as if holding it at bay with sheer willpower alone.

The air vibrated with urgency, every player caught in the pulse of competition tinged with something darker—something unspoken but palpable. The whistle barely blared before Brick's body surged again into the blockers, crushing through with reckless abandon as the drill spun onward.

Coach Hale's gaze never wavered, following the tempest known as Brick—his eyes alight with resolve and apprehension—letting the practiced rhythm hum louder and harder while the weight of unspoken consequences hung heavy over the field.

###

Coach Hale's voice cut through the whistle blows and the rhythmic pounding of cleats on turf. "DeShawn, you're up. Run the next play against the starters." His gaze was sharp and unwavering. DeShawn hesitated for a flicker—his heart tapping a nervous tattoo beneath his ribs—not from doubt but from the electric tension hanging thick between sweat and adrenaline. He jogged in, the ball cradled tight as the offensive line locked into formation. A solid wall of gritted teeth and broad shoulders flexed beneath the morning sun.

The field hummed with taut anticipation. A low murmur rippled through the ranks. The ball snapped—a metallic crack against the slick turf.

Brick explodes off the line like a live wire. His eyes blaze with burning intensity. Every muscle is wound tight, a coil ready to snap. His surge isn't just force—it's an eruption, a power that bends the air and distorts the world in the blur of his charge. The world narrows until only DeShawn stands in the path of the storm.

DeShawn shifts. His instincts are edged sharp. A split second's hesitation carves a gulf between survival and impact. Brick's frame barrels forward, relentless, snapping through blockers with an uncaring force that hums in the air like a thunderclap. The collision shatters the moment—the crack of bodies meeting, muffled by gasps and grunts. DeShawn's feet leave the turf. His balance erases. Brick's raw power lifts him, a ragdoll flung onto the field's unforgiving green.

The breath whooshes out of DeShawn in ragged bursts. The air tastes sharp, almost metallic on his tongue. His limbs splay in a graceless sprawl; fingers clutch his ribs where fire blooms hot and jagged beneath his skin. The world twists. Colors and sounds smear at the edges as pain tightens its grip. His vision blurs, the whistle of wind through his ears becoming a drone beneath the rising shout of silent alarm.

From the sidelines, a collective intake—the swift inhalation before chaos. Coaches freeze mid-step, eyes wide and jaws clenched. The usually brisk chatter slips into a thick silence weighted with dread. Players halt, a string of breath caught and held. The competitive edge flickers out under the heavy shadow of brutal reality.

DeShawn's chest heaves. Another breath won't come easily. A rookie body shouldn't break like this—shouldn't fracture under the weight of real contact. The thought spirals through him even as pain drowns it out. One bad hit, and everything changes. One moment, and it's over.

Brick lingers over DeShawn like a tempest. His chest heaves in harsh, wet pulls of air. His fists curl so tightly that his knuckles blanch, fingers trembling—not from exhaustion, but from pure, simmering fury that makes his whole body quake. The tension coils in his frame, a living thing waiting to snap. Sweat drips down his furrowed brow;

his jaw tightens, creaking against the torrent of rage drowning out the world.

One of the assistants calls out, breaking the stunned quiet. "Brick! Get back, now!" But Brick's eyes are locked in a tunnel toward DeShawn, fierce and unreadable.

DeShawn groans, his voice rough as his hand presses harder at his side, trying to anchor a breath that keeps slipping away. He dares a glance upward. Pain twists his features as he marks Brick's silhouette a few steps away—the rage coiled so tightly that it threatens to fracture the cold air around them.

"Too damn hard," Jaxon mutters from the bench, his voice clipped but laced with worry. He scrubs a hand over his face, muscles taut beneath his skin as he watches Brick, waiting for the storm to break—or worse.

DeShawn drags in a shaky breath and manages a strained, almost defiant snarl. "I'm fine. Just... catchin' my breath."

Brick steps back just enough. The fire in his eyes dampens to a simmer but never quite extinguishes. His voice, low and ragged, breaks the silence.

"You think that's fine? You're takin' hits out here like it's practice, but that's real. You could get hurt. You hear me?"

DeShawn swats weakly at the turf, a grimace curling his lips.

"Easy for you to say. You're built like a damn tank."

Brick's glare sharpens. Thunder rolls beneath the surface.

"Damn right. And tanks don't limp around actin' like punches are a joke."

The line between reprimand and concern thunders loudly in the charged air. Around them, the team exhales. Coach Hale's face is a storm cloud looming, fists clenched near his hips. His voice cuts through the tension like a whip.

"That's enough." His tone brooks no argument—commanding yet pained. "Brick, cool down. We're not here to see anyone broken."

Brick's shoulders jerk as if caught in an internal storm, but he pulls back, fury folding into cold resolve. DeShawn's body trembles with every breath, yet the defiance in his eyes stubbornly refuses to dim.

Jaxon moves closer. His voice is softer now but edged with steel.

"You're losing it, Brick. This isn't how we win. You're tearing us apart."

"Maybe I don't want to be part of this anymore," Brick snaps, tension unraveling in sharp exhalations. "Not like this."

"No," Jaxon says firmly. "You're better than this. We're better than this." He pauses. "You have to be."

The practice field stretches beneath a pale sky. Sunlight cuts sharp reflections off helmets and sweat-soaked jerseys. The hum of tension lingers, thick and electric—the heat of fractured trust burning in every harsh breath.

DeShawn groans again, curling tighter. Pain radiates through ribs that throb beneath trembling fingers. Brick stands over him, a volcano barely contained—angry, raw, and more alone than ever.

###

The sharp blast of Coach Hale's whistle slices through the charged air, a piercing shriek that halts every moving body on the sun-drenched practice field.

His broad frame marches onto the turf like a storm breaking, eyes narrowing beneath the brim of his cap. Brick strides toward the edge, chest heaving, muscles taut with fury and exhaustion—ready to bolt. But Hale's stride closes the distance with authoritative force.

"Turn around, Brick," Hale's voice rumbles, uneven but firm. The edge of panic threads beneath the usual sternness. "You're done here. Effective *immediately*, I'm suspending you."

Brick spins. The world tightens in his chest like a fist. Rage snarls low, claws sinking into every muscle like a living weight. *Suspended?*

"Yeah." Hale's gaze pins him, unyielding. "Because you lost all control today. That hit? Reckless. Dangerous. You're a liability."

A low growl curls from Brick's throat. His fists clench. Nails dig shallow hollows into his palms—skin tightening, trembling under the weight of what this means. One suspension and scouts stop calling. One misstep and scholarships evaporate. The field pulses with every heartbeat. Distant shouts and whistles fade into a dull hum.

Jaxon moves—swift and smooth—stepping between Brick and the coach like a human shield. His hands rise, palms aimed to steady the storm rising in Brick's eyes.

"Brick, you're sliding off the rails," Jaxon's voice cuts through, low and clipped. "And if you don't stop, you'll take the whole team down with you."

Brick's jaw tightens. "You don't get it, Jax."

"That's because right now, you're not listening to anyone."

From the sideline, a sudden surge of footsteps—a stampede of urgency. Emma and two interns come sprinting, their expressions sharp under the stadium glare. They drop beside DeShawn, whose breath hitches beneath the weight of the brutal hit. His body curls inward, protective. Ashamed.

In this sport, a player gets hit like that—leaving the field on a stretcher or not at all. Either way, the hit spreads through the locker room like a contagion, feeding the collective anxiety that one moment of recklessness can spiral into career-ending consequences. DeShawn brushes off the concern with a shaky shrug, his lips tugged tight in embarrassment, but both his hands tremble—slight, uncontrollable shivers that betray him.

Emma's fingers move deftly, scanning and probing. The smell of fresh-cut grass mingles with the faint metallic tang of sweat and tension.

Natalie's heels click across the turf—a deliberate rhythm that cuts through the chaos. She pauses just yards from the cluster, and her eyes lock with Brick's.

Raw. Exhausted. Deeply weary.

Brick's gaze flickers, searching her face for a crack—anything—to soften the wall she has built. But her jaw tightens, and a shadow of exhaustion darkens the spaces beneath her eyes instead.

She steps closer to Coach Hale. Her voice drops beneath the tension, low and edged with quiet finality. "I have nothing left to say to Brick."

A flicker of something unspoken hangs between them—a weight shared, then abandoned. She turns sharply. Her shoulders rigid as a board, she strides away with deliberate resolve. The team watches—some frozen, some hollow-eyed—the silent fracture expanding with every step she takes.

Coach Hale stands there, the whistle clenched tightly between his teeth. His gaze flickers between Brick and Natalie's retreating form. Jaxon remains rooted as a buffer, fists clenched but composed, eyes locked on Brick, trying to keep the storm contained.

The sun beats down—harsh and indifferent.

The once rhythmic thud of cleats against turf slows, replaced by the heavy breaths of a team unraveling, stitched together by the growing chasm where trust once thrived. The field hums with unspoken words and fractured loyalties, every player caught between the past's bruises and the uncertainty of what comes next.

The locker room hums with a hollow quiet, a stark contrast to its usual roar—voices, clanging metal, the percussion of a team in motion. Now? Nothing.

Brick sits on a chipped wooden bench, shoulders slumped. His fingers trace circles in the palm of his left hand. The faint musk of sweat and old leather clings heavily in the air, but there's no soundtrack here—no jabs, no laughter, no clatter. Just the dull, steady drip of a distant faucet and the occasional scrape of cleats on tile from lingering teammates.

His gaze remains fixed on his hands. The raw calluses are prominent—roadmaps of years spent grinding, fighting, and failing. Scar tissue is etched deep, physical proof of every mistake, every moment he couldn't hold it together. He studies them as if memorizing the damage might somehow undo it.

Beyond the thick glass of the locker room windows, sunlight stretches across the city skyline. He feels stuck in this grim limbo, the silence pressing against his ears. Suffocating.

Jaxon's footsteps break through the stillness—measured and purposefully slow. He stops a few paces away, shoulders squared but tense. His eyes flicker—hard to read yet carrying a weight Brick hasn't faced before. When Jaxon speaks, his voice cuts through without heat, cold and sharp in the softened air.

"You can't keep pointing fingers everywhere but the mirror, Brick." He pauses, allowing that to sink in. "Bottom line? It's on you. You've got to own it if you want to fix this."

Brick doesn't look up. He doesn't say a word. The words sink like stones into his exhaustion.

Nearby, Caleb and DeShawn lean against the lockers. Their voices are hushed but weighted with something unspoken—the kind of tension that fractures when one player can't be trusted to control his own rage. Fear and loyalty twist together, creating unspoken alliances that shift by the hour.

DeShawn's eyes dart around, betraying a nervous edge despite the grin he forces. "I'm fine. It was practice. It's not like he was trying to hurt me."

Caleb's voice holds softer skepticism. "Doesn't feel like 'practice' when you're flattened like that. Are you sure you're good?"

DeShawn shrugs. His shoulders remain tight. His hands fidget with the hem of his jersey.

"Yeah, yeah. It just stung, that's all."

They glance back at Brick together. Their eyes meet, sharing an unspoken worry—the kind that lingers in silence and steals easy breaths.

Brick shoves himself to his feet. The bench groans beneath the sudden weight. He moves into the narrow corridor. Around the corner, Emma stands by the water fountain. Her posture is calm and professional, her eyes sharp but guarded.

He clears his throat. His voice comes out rough. "Hey... about DeShawn. Sorry I scared him out there."

Emma looks up. Her lips press into a thin, practiced line as she nods slowly.

"I accept your apology. But scaring him isn't something we can sweep under the rug."

Her words aren't a scolding, but they are firm enough to remind him exactly where the line is and where he crossed it.

Brick shrugs, feeling awkward and uncertain. He moves on before the silence can swallow him whole.

Later, in the soft glow of her office, Natalie sits slumped forward. Her head rests face down on her desk, as if she has lost the fight to hold herself upright. The faint scent of cold coffee creeps under the door, overlaid with the subtle hum of fluorescent lights—too bright for her mood.

A gentle knock, barely audible. The door eases open.

Emma steps in. Her eyes flick to Natalie's bowed form. Without a word, she places a steaming cup on the desk. Warmth sends a shaky tendril of steam upward. She rests a hand softly on Natalie's shoulder—a silent offer of solidarity. Then she steps back, giving space for the cracks to show.

Natalie's breath catches. The quiet hum deepens.

Back in the locker room, the fractures stretch like tension lines drawn too tightly. Brick's fists curl into trembling knots. Anger and isolation coil beneath his skin—an invisible fire ready to spill over.

"I'm damn near tearing this whole thing apart," he mutters, barely audible, like a confession to the empty air.

Jaxon's voice stays steady—quiet but unwavering.

"We're the team, man. We don't fall apart because one guy's losing his grip."

"No one's losing their grip but me," Brick snaps, his voice low and strained. "Everywhere I look, I see them pulling away, like I'm poison."

"You're not poison," Jaxon shoots back. The usual warmth is gone, replaced by resolve. "But you gotta stop acting like it."

Brick's shoulders shake. His breath catches under the weight of everything unspoken. The silence thickens again, pushed aside only by the distant echo of footsteps fading down the hall.

Natalie raises her head slowly from the desk. Her eyes are rimmed with exhaustion. Moisture glints in the corner like spilled glass. She blinks away the sting and focuses on a speck of dust dancing in a stray sunbeam cutting across her desk.

Somewhere beyond her door, the world keeps turning—loud and relentless.

Back in the locker room, the absence of chatter stretches wide. The usual hum of camaraderie is smothered under thick layers of mistrust and fear. The fractured trust between Brick, his teammates, and Natalie hangs like a weighty fog—heavy and slow-moving.

Emma's hand lingers briefly on Natalie's shoulder, a quiet note of strength amid the heartbreak. Then she retreats softly, leaving the room to its silence.

The locker room and the office breathe the same charged air, filled with unspoken fractures and the sharp edges of broken trust and wounded hopes. Alone on his bench, Brick's gaze remains glued to his bruised hands—the battleground and the burden he carries—while Natalie's silent tears mark the distance growing between them both.

Victor Cross's fingers tap the final keystrokes on his laptop, a digital scalpel poised to slice open simmering tensions. On his screen flashes the headline: "Reign's Volatile Star Faces Brewing Storm," followed by a chilling promise: *Something big is coming for the Reign's most volatile star.* The words crackle like electricity, each phrase weighted with secrets yet to spill.

Outside, the stadium premises shift from quiet tension into a roiling hive. Reporters flare their camera lights, and voices weave over one another like gathering storm clouds. Microphones hover like hawks near the entrances while camera crews tighten their formation, focused on capturing any hint of upheaval. The air thrums with the sharp scent of rain on concrete and the metallic tang of early autumn wind—an undercurrent to rumors spreading like wildfire through social media.

Inside the PR office, Natalie Brooks leans closer, her eyes flicking rapidly over jagged headlines cascading across her laptop screen. Her fingers hesitate over the keyboard, trembling. Her breath catches, and her shoulders sag as a tight knot twists low in her chest—guilt tasting bitter on her tongue. The weight of what is coming etches deeper lines around her eyes than any headline could. She presses her palm to her forehead and then closes the laptop softly. The room falls into a strained hush.

A quiet hum filters through the floor-to-ceiling windows—the city breathing just beyond, reminding her that the storm has only just begun.

Across the facility, vibrating phones interrupt the growing quiet. Player group chats ignite with cascading notifications: speculation, emojis, and anxious chatter bleeding into one another. Players glance up, their faces tight with worry as the digital pulse quickens. Caleb and Eli exchange uneasy looks near the locker room, their movements sharp and measured, as if mapping through invisible webs of tension. Somewhere in the distance, cleats clack against tile, and staff voices murmur. The creeping unease settles like dust.

Brick's apartment is a cavern of shadows bisected by late afternoon light slicing through half-closed blinds. He slumps on the worn charcoal sectional, the fabric catching the rough scrape of his skin. His phone is gripped tightly in one hand. The glow reveals Victor Cross's post staring back at him. The words spiral into his mind, ringing louder than the stillness around him.

His jaw tightens, and his knuckles whiten as fury simmers just beneath the surface. Then his fist shoots forward, smashing into the plaster wall. The sharp crack jolts up his arm—a brief release. But the slow burn returns, sharpened and brutal. His breath stutters—a flash of vulnerability before the weight drags him down. He collapses sideways onto the floor, his muscles tight as wire, trembling beneath the thin fabric of his shirt.

Pain and weariness mingle with crushing knowledge: the walls around him, both literal and metaphorical, are crumbling. Regret cuts beneath his skin, sharp and bitter. His chest heaves with ragged breaths. The silence swallows him whole. Each exhale is a confession no one hears.

A sudden knock at the door snaps him partially upright. No one is waiting. The echo fades, leaving only the heavy, stale scent of sweat and old leather. Brick's eyes close, and his lashes fan against dust motes dancing in the dying light.

"This isn't how it goes down," he mutters, his voice raw and shadowed. "I'm not going to let them drag me under."

From the stadium, the low drone of cameras and microphones seeps through his locked windows, an ominous reminder that the world outside won't stop turning—or listening.

Natalie rises from her chair, stretching her arms above her head. The solid press of muscle beneath the cotton anchors her momentarily. With her feet steady on the hardwood, she stares out at the distant stadium lights flickering on in the dusky sky. She's caught between loyalty to Brick and the inevitability of what's coming—a tension that coils tightly in her chest.

Her voice is low, brittle with fatigue, but determined.

"We've got to get ahead of this," she says, her voice tight as she locks eyes with her assistant.

"But Brick..." the assistant hesitates.

Natalie shakes her head slowly.

"He's our storm to weather. And we're not standing down."

At the facility entrance, a reporter nudges a colleague.

"Do you think Brick's done?" someone whispers, the camera lens focusing sharply. "This teaser's nuclear."

"No way. If Cross has dirt, he'll drop the bomb soon. The team's reputation is on life support."

Inside the locker room, players huddle, thumbs scrolling, faces pale. Overlapping notifications pile up—tweets, videos, mentions—each ping feeding the anxious chorus that hums beneath their layered uniforms. DeShawn clears his throat, his voice low.

"We have to keep it tight. No letting this shake us."

Caleb nods, his eyes flickering to Eli.

"The pressure is on every one of us now."

Eli's fingers tap nervously on the phone screen.

"If Brick folds, what happens to the rest?"

The question lingers, thick as the settling night.

Back in the apartment, Brick's hands curl into fists at his sides, his nails digging into his palms until the sting pulls him back from the edge of dark spirals. He breathes in sharply—the faint smell of stale sweat and the cold bite of late afternoon air mix with distant city noise.

From his phone, the screen's light dances against his shadowed features—fragmented, fractured, like his thoughts.

A text from an unknown number flashes: *You think you can outrun your past? Think again.*

His lips tighten. The room shrinks. The walls inch closer, like predators circling.

He grinds his teeth, his breath rough.

"This ends," he vows, his voice low enough to be only his own. "No more running. No more ghosts."

The heaviness within him swells. Yet somewhere beneath the rubble of anger and fear, something fragile stirs—a delicate ember fighting to ignite.

But for now, the night is dark. Brick lies crumpled on the floor—a fortress breached, a man laid bare by the coming storm.

What Control Really Means

Brick slumps into the hard plastic chair, his shoulders curling inward. He's trying to disappear inside his own skin. The waiting room smells sterile—too clean, with a faint trace of antiseptic that claws at the back of his throat, making it hard to swallow. His palms slip against the frayed edge of his jacket sleeve. He twists the fabric between his fingers, the rough cotton sticking to skin slick with sweat.

Every few seconds, his eyes dart to the door. He's plotting a silent escape—ready to bolt the moment reluctance turns to panic.

The quiet space hums with muted footsteps and distant murmurs beyond the sliding glass doors. Each sound makes his shoulders tense tighter. Somewhere, a phone rings. Somewhere else, a receptionist's fingers clack against keys. He catalogs it all, hyperaware and exposed, despite being surrounded by strangers who don't know his name or his failures.

Plastic magazines lie scattered on a low table, their colors washed out and pictures faded. A half-dead fern droops in the corner, its brittle leaves forgotten in this place of waiting. He hunches forward, tugging his knees up, his arms wrapping tightly around them like armor. It doesn't stop the restless buzz rising beneath his ribs—a storm of shame and raw nerves.

His mind lurches backward, dragging him into the chaos of practice. DeShawn's wide eyes flash in his memory—a mirror of raw fear. The way his teammate's smile faltered, replaced by tight lines and hesitant shuffles away from his storm. Coach Hale's voice echoes, low and rumbling: "One more slip, Brick, and you're done." The words press down like a lead vest across his chest.

Then there's Natalie—the hollow ache behind her eyes, the slight tremble in her hands as she turns away. She didn't shout or slap a label on him or yell ultimatums. No—it was worse. The quiet devastation in her glance tore open something brittle and exposed inside him. His chest clenches, breath hitching as the memory slams into him—raw and unrelenting. His nails dig shallow grooves into his jacket.

The clock on the wall ticks in muted monotony—its face large but pale, hands barely moving in the stale air. He fixes his gaze on it, willing it to speed up, to swallow the waiting time. The seconds crawl between imagined whispers just out of earshot, voices layering over one another like leaves rustling, dry and brittle.

"He's a ticking bomb," someone mutters.

Another voice sneers, "Can't handle the heat anymore."

A third whispered, barely audible, "I'm not sure the team's worth the headache."

Each imagined sentence twists somewhere low in his stomach. The thought of being seen here—sitting in this clinical silence—fills him with suffocating nausea. It is the same nausea that had exploded inside his apartment hours ago, the collapse that shattered more than just his body. It cracked the armor he wore like a second skin.

His head drops, and his hair falls forward, catching the sterile light that flickers overhead and casting harsh shadows across the scuffed floor. The rough thread of his jacket brushes against plastic. A shiver runs up his spine—a fragile line of vulnerability he's unsure he's ready to cross.

Then the voice cuts through.

"Turner?"

His name slams into his chest like a starting whistle. The stiffness in his spine battles with the impulse to duck away. Slowly, painfully, he rises, every eye he imagines on him, every judgment crowding his mind. He shrinks into himself, shoulders folding inward as if pulling armor tight—careful to hide every crack.

His feet move toward the reception desk, heavy and uncertain. His heartbeat hammers in his ears. The chill from the linoleum creeps through his thin sneakers, grounding him in the moment. His palms are clammy, shaking just enough to betray his control. The door to Dr. Greene's office glides open silently ahead, light pooling into the hallway like a fragile promise.

A flicker of something unspoken catches in his chest. Hope? Fear? Both. He steps across the threshold, swallowed by calm shadows and the soft glow of a lamp. Behind him, the waiting room shrinks away. The antiseptic scent lingers like a tether to the life he is determined to confront.

The door closes behind him with a soft click—a barrier sealing off the waiting room and the uncertain past as he faces what comes next.

Dr. Greene's office feels like a refuge swallowed in muted light. A soft amber glow from the slender table lamp casts long, gentle shadows across the worn leather sofa and the single armchair. The faint scent of chamomile tea and old wood lingers in the air, calm and steady. Brick lingers at the threshold, fingers twitching with reluctant energy. The door closes behind him with a soft click.

"Please, take your pick," Dr. Greene says, her voice smooth as velvet. She nods toward the sofa and chair, her calm blue eyes meeting his without pressure.

Brick shifts his bulky frame toward the sofa and sinks down stiffly, his arms folding across his chest like armor. His jaw clenches hard enough to dull the ache lurking beneath—something sharper than frustration, something that tastes like regret. He won't meet Dr. Greene's eyes, staring instead through the window at shadows pooling beneath the trees.

Dr. Greene takes the chair opposite him, her hands resting lightly on her lap. "You've had a rough few days," she begins carefully. "That last practice session... what was going through your mind?"

Brick chuckles, low and sharp, the sound brittle around the edges. "Mind? Probably a mix of 'don't screw this up' and 'God, get me out of here.'" He smirks, but it doesn't reach his eyes. "Coach was practically foaming at the mouth. I guess I gave him more material."

Dr. Greene nods thoughtfully. "It sounds like it wasn't just simple frustration. What do you think sparked the outburst? The moment you lost it?"

Brick shifts, his shoulders stiffening. His voice drops to a guarded murmur. "I lost it, alright. Hell, I may have even put a guy on the ground harder than I should have. Rookie." He pauses, his jaw working. "The guy's probably nursing bruises and a bruised ego this morning. It could have ended worse."

She leans forward slightly, the corners of her mouth softening into gentle encouragement. "Tell me about that moment. What did it feel like?"

A flash of memory—the sharp crack of impact, the reverberation through his shoulders, the roar in his ears that wasn't cheering. The rookie's face, shocked and bleeding. Brick's fists clenched and unclenched.

For a heartbeat, his lips press into a thin line. His hands curl into fists but loosen just as quickly. "Like a switch flipped," he mutters, his jaw tightening. "My body just... went haywire. I thought I was in control, but..." He trails off, his gaze flickering to the floor. "It went sideways."

Dr. Greene nods and straightens, her voice lowering into a quiet rhythm. "Let's try something. I want you to follow my breathing."

Brick's eyes snap up with an edge of resistance. He's bristling—being told what to do is an itch beneath his skin. Yet something in the steady cadence of her voice tugs him toward compliance.

"Inhale slowly for four counts. One, two, three, four. Now exhale for six. One, two, three, four, five, six."

His chest rises and falls, shallow at first, then deeper. Uneven breaths tremble through his hands. His fingers twitch. His pulse hammers a warning beat while he fights the urge to pull away.

"Tense shoulders," she notes. "Relax your jaw."

Brick's jaw loosens reluctantly, the tightness melting into a dull ache. With his eyes halfway closed, he chews on something unfamiliar curling inside him—a fragile peace. It tastes strange.

"How does that feel?"

"Like... I want to punch something less." His voice is rough, oddly sheepish. "I don't exactly trust it. But it's better than the last million punches I wanted to throw."

Dr. Greene's smile is patient. It doesn't offer easy solutions. "Good. The next step is to close your eyes and focus on where you feel the guilt, or the weight of it. What parts of your body hold it?"

Brick's breath catches as he closes his eyes. His shoulders slump, as if he is lowering his defenses for the first time in a long while. The room blurs at the edges as a dull heat settles low in his chest. His fingers twitch against his ribs, as if trying to hush a whispering storm he can't shake.

"They say guilt is a creature with claws," Brick murmurs, his voice now small. "Mine has sharp barbs right here." His fingers press against his ribs, tracing invisible wounds.

Dr. Greene's voice becomes a steady anchor beneath the storm. "Good. Naming it is the first step to begin owning it."

Brick shifts. The fortress of his posture cracks just enough for something raw and real to slip through. The room feels warmer, less like a cage and more like a place where he might learn to breathe without breaking.

"Have you ever thought you could get past this?" he asks quietly. The admission surprises even him.

Dr. Greene's eyes hold his with steady light. "It's possible. But it's a journey—one breath, one moment at a time."

Brick exhales slowly. The tension in his limbs loosens, if only by a fraction. The urge to run fades beneath something fragile and new—the possibility that maybe, just maybe, he can start rewriting the storm inside.

Dr. Greene's gaze shifts, and her voice lowers, steady and measured. "Tell me about that day on the field—the incident you mentioned."

Brick's throat tightens, and his voice thickens, reluctant but pressing forward. "I was charging, pushing through the offensive line. Everything went slow—like moving through fog—but then it snapped." He pauses, his jaw clenching. "The moment I hit him, I knew right away it was wrong."

His fingers twitch against the armrest, knuckles whitening.

"A split second. Like a blindside whack—too hard, too fast."

The room hums with quiet intensity. Brick inhales sharply, then exhales slowly and heavily. He leans back against the couch, his eyes drifting past the amber lamp's shadows to some unreachable place.

"The sounds," he begins, his voice hoarse. "Helmets slamming—like thunder rolling over wet concrete. The crash... the thud when bodies collide. Solid. Final." His hands clench into fists, trembling. "I remember the weight—his weight on the turf, not bouncing back. And the face. That flash of pure shock staring up at me before everything went dark for him."

His voice trembles, cracking like a fragile thread. A muscle twitches in his jaw; his fingers curl tighter, knuckles whitening beneath the pressure.

"That play nearly ended everything—my career, his life, maybe. I keep replaying it, trying to find the seconds I could have softened or stopped sooner. But it all happened too fast. Too brutally."

Dr. Greene nods gently, inviting yet unobtrusive. "Where do you feel that guilt now? Anywhere in your body?"

Brick shuts his eyes and draws in a slow, ragged breath. A heat blooms in his chest—a tightening coil that presses relentlessly, like hot iron curling around his ribs. "Here." His hand tugs at his shirt near his sternum. "It burns. Constantly. Like fire trying to claw its way out."

He swallows hard, and his voice drops. "Sometimes, when it gets bad, I want to hit something. Smash something. Just so I can stop feeling it... for a minute."

The confession hangs in the air, fragile and raw.

"I hate it," Brick mutters, his voice catching as his eyes dart away. "Losing control. It scares the hell out of me." A muscle quivers along his jaw. "It terrifies me, really. Because when I'm like that..." He trails off, his breath shallow. "I'm dangerous. Not just to myself, but to everyone. To the people I care about."

The sterile walls seem to close in. His hands grip the edge of the sofa, knuckles pale beneath the pressure.

There was the night he had thrown a glass at his apartment wall. The way his roommate had flinched. The apology that felt like nothing against the fear in someone else's eyes. He had promised himself it wouldn't happen again. It always did.

"I don't know how to stop it," he whispers. His jaw trembles. The words barely rise, fragile as smoke. "That feeling... it's like a storm inside me, and I'm the one falling apart."

Dr. Greene leans forward. Her voice remains steady and warm. "Acknowledging that fear—that danger—it's a dangerous kind of bravery. It's the first step toward changing the story you tell yourself."

Brick blinks. The weight of her words settles like slow rain over dry earth. They shroud the edges of his wounds with something unfamiliar.

Hope.

"When's the first time you remember... feeling out of control?" Dr. Greene's voice threads through the quiet room, soft. She lets the question hang for a beat, inviting him in.

Brick's breath catches, a sharp hitch deep in his chest. The muscles in his arms tighten, fists curling involuntarily as an old memory splits through the fog of his defenses.

"I... it was at home." His voice drops, rough and hesitant, like stepping onto thin ice.

"Dad was yelling. Real loud—too loud—and Mom was crying." The words come out strained. "The walls... shit, it felt like the whole house was shaking. Like it was going to crack right open."

Back then, Brick was small enough to fit in the space between the couch and the wall, but not small enough to disappear. That helplessness had burrowed into him, a living thing that never quite left. He learned then that the world didn't care how scared you were—it would shake anyway.

He stares at his hands, knuckles whitening. "I was just a kid, but... the fear? It grabbed me hard. Like a vise."

He swallows past something thick. His jaw flexes under the weight of the memory.

"I smashed a lamp once." The words come out raw. "I threw it across the room... couldn't make the noise stop." He pauses, fingers digging into his palms. "I thought if I could break something, maybe I could break the tension too."

Power drains from his voice. "But after... I felt small. Powerless. Ashamed." His eyes flicker upward, searching Dr. Greene's face for some sign of judgment.

"That anger?" His fists clenched tighter. "It wasn't about being mad. It was the only way I knew to hold on—to control something when everything else was slipping."

Dr. Greene watches him. The slight lift of an eyebrow invites deeper honesty.

"What did you want most," she asks softly, "at that moment?"

That iron mask cracks. Hairline fractures glow faintly beneath the surface.

Brick's gaze drops. His fingers fumble at the cuff of his sleeve. His voice tightens to a whisper, fragile enough to hear a pin drop.

"I just... wanted someone to pick me up. Tell me I was okay. That I wasn't a bad kid."

The air thickens. The soft ticking of the clock suddenly sounds loud against the silence.

Brick has spent years building walls so high that admitting this—admitting he needed someone, that the shame had calcified inside him like scar tissue—feels like standing naked in a room full of strangers. Except this isn't a room full of strangers. It is just him and Dr. Greene, and somehow that makes it harder.

Brick bows his head. The hard edges of his frame dip. His shoulders ease as if releasing a secret too long carried alone.

A single tear escapes, tracing a slow path down his cheek.

Dr. Greene nodded once—quietly. There was no need for more words.

This moment marked something: a turning point, the first soft fissure in Brick's armor where understanding could begin to seep in.

Dr. Greene's voice sliced through the silence, calm and deliberate. "Try this for homework: when you feel yourself spiraling, name the feeling right then, instead of acting on it. Say it out loud or in your head. Naming breaks the chain; it interrupts the impulse loop."

Her eyes locked onto his, patient but firm. Brick felt the weight of that gaze—not judgmental, which somehow made it harder to bear. He was used to anger, to people who flinched or pulled away. This steady attention was different. It stripped something raw inside him.

He folded his arms tighter, skepticism hardening his jaw. The words sat heavy in his throat like an unpalatable pill. But he leaned in just enough to stay tethered. The air felt thick, weighted with the strange exposure of having spoken the truth aloud. Yet the task itself felt almost manageable—small, concrete, like a lifeline tossed into rough water.

"You really think saying it makes a difference?" His voice came out rough and edged, testing the truth beneath her calm.

"It doesn't erase the feeling," Dr. Greene said gently, "but it gives you space to choose your next move. That space is power." She gestured softly, as if offering a key. "You already showed more courage today than most do in months. Coming here and speaking your truth—that's no small feat."

Brick glances away, then back. He weighs this strange currency called honesty. "So you want me to come back?"

She nods, leaning forward just a fraction. "I do. This is a beginning, not an easy fix. Are you willing?"

The room holds its breath. He shifts in the chair, muscles coiled beneath rough skin. Finally, Brick exhales—slow and ragged—and nods. "Yeah. Yeah, I'll come back."

Relief flickers in Dr. Greene's smile, a brief crack in the clinical calm.

Brick rouses himself. The oak floor creaks beneath his boots as he stands. His hands fumble toward the business card she extends. Just a sliver of paper—sterile, impersonal—but he clutches it as if it might save him. He avoids her eyes, rubbing the back of his neck as if shaking off cold doubt.

The unexpected sting of a tear blurs his vision. His palm catches it quickly, trembling fingers pressing the wetness away as if wiping betrayal from his own face. The weight of the moment lands heavy and raw beneath the veneer of controlled anger he has worn for years.

Stepping out of the office, the waiting room swallows him in its muted hues—taupe walls, plastic chairs lined against the far wall, the faint scent of lavender lingering in the stale air like a whispered comfort. He glances upward at the softly ticking clock, a measured metronome marking time forward despite how trapped he feels.

A subtle shift occurs. The tension knotted in his shoulders lessens slightly. The armor feels, somehow, a little lighter.

Brick pauses in the doorway as the afternoon sun filters weakly through the window, scattering fragmented light onto the linoleum floor. He inhales shallowly. The sterile scent of the clinic mingles with something sharper—his own sweat and the faint tang of stress clinging to his skin.

His boots scrape quietly on the floor as he moves toward the exit. Each step is heavier with uncertainty yet edged with that fragile hope.

Just before he crosses the threshold, Dr. Greene's voice catches him once more, softer this time. "You're not alone in this."

He glances back. A flicker of something like gratitude breaks through the storm behind his eyes.

Outside, the world hums on—cars slipping past, distant shouts echoing from the nearby campus, and the faint rustle of leaves in an early spring breeze. The harsh brightness of the afternoon contrasts sharply with the dim interior he is leaving. His pulse thumps steadily as he moves down the corridor, now empty save for a cleaning cart and the soft hum of fluorescent lights.

"Naming it is supposed to stop it. Break the chain..." He mutters the words under his breath, testing them like a new rhythm.

His fingers linger over the smooth edge of the card in his pocket. He lets the memory surface—the terror of losing control, the shattered moments echoing in his mind. But beneath that, something stirs: an ember, fragile but present.

The sun warms his face as he steps onto the street, the city's pulse a distant drumbeat. He walks forward, his shoulders still squared but slightly eased. Uncertain, yes, but no longer entirely alone.

"I'll try," he whispers, his voice rough but sincere.

The resignation letter crackled beneath Natalie's fingertips—the sharp edges of the paper and the faint scratch of typed words pressing into her skin. She stared at it, folded neatly beneath the glass paperweight, unable to look away.

Her eyes drifted over the cluttered desk as she took in the yellowed clippings scattered across the office walls. They were pinned like trophies in a war chest, each headline screaming about the team's crisis, each one a scar she carried in her chest. The box beside her yawned open, its flaps creased and worn. Inside lay the remnants of her professional life here: framed photos of team events, a leather portfolio stuffed with strategy notes, and the accumulated weight of months spent trying to reshape a man's public image and, somehow, his heart.

Outside the tall windows, the city's muted hum seeped into the room, but inside, silence hung thick and suffocating. She pressed her palms flat against the cool wood of the desk. A tremor ran beneath her hands.

Her breath came shallow and uneven, like a candle struggling against a draft in the quiet room.

The phone buzzed. She unlocked it, scrolling back to Brick's last message—raw and jagged, the kind of words that echoed long after they were written: *"Don't expect me to change for some PR girl. I'm not your project."* Each syllable dripped with frustration and dismissal, scratching at the threadbare edges of her resolve. Exhaustion coiled through her chest, dragging doubt behind it like a storm cloud. Maybe he was right. Maybe she had been chasing ghosts all along. Quitting whispered to her—a tempting escape from the chaos she couldn't seem to tame.

Then the phone rang.

Emma's name lit up the screen. Natalie's finger hovered for a moment before she swiped to answer, her voice guarded.

"You okay, Nat?" Emma's warmth cut through the fog like sunlight through cracked blinds. "You sound... off."

Natalie let out a hollow breath. "This whole mess... I don't know if I'm making any difference."

A pause filled the line—the kind thick with empathy and understanding.

"You have made a difference," Emma insisted, her voice firm yet gentle. "Remember last month when Brick flipped out after that scrimmage? You didn't just smooth things over; you got into his head. That media blackout? That was you. You started the shift in this team's culture. You're changing him. Don't forget that."

The words settled around Natalie, softening the hard edges of doubt. "I'm scared I'm running out of time and patience."

"Patience will catch up." Emma's voice became a lifeline. "You're stronger than you give yourself credit for. Don't throw in the towel yet."

The call ended, but fragile warmth lingered. Natalie's fingers remained on the phone, grounding herself in those carefully woven threads of hope.

A firm knock cut through the moment.

Coach Hale's heavy frame filled the doorway, his gaze steady and appraising. The room seemed to hold its breath. His voice rumbled like distant thunder when he spoke, deeper than usual but laced with something rare—softness.

"I heard Emma's pep talk." He stepped inside, closing the door behind him. "She's right."

Natalie shifted, wary but willing to listen.

"Listen, Natalie," he said, folding his hands behind his back. "You're the one who taught that hardhead to care—not just on the field, but about himself and the team. Without you, Brick's a powder keg with no fuse."

Her throat constricted. Her fingers trembled as she pressed a hand over her heart, her eyes blinking rapidly against the swell of tears threatening to spill.

"I'm scared, Coach. I'm scared I'm not enough."

He stepped closer, his eyes steady and unwavering. "You're more than enough. Don't let your fear drown the fire you lit."

Slowly, Natalie reached for the resignation letter. The paper felt fragile now, almost delicate beneath her touch. She folded it and then slipped it back into the drawer without sealing her fate. The drawer clicked softly shut—a muted promise to herself to try once more.

She rose from her chair, an effort that felt both heavy and exhilarating.

The framed headline on the wall leaned askew—a snapshot of past victories and battles fought. She straightened it carefully, the purposeful act grounding her. Aged paper and polished wood mingled in the quiet office, serving as a reminder of battles fought and those yet to come.

The office lights dimmed slightly as she moved toward the door. Beyond the windows, the city glimmered with a million restless lives. But here, in this moment, Natalie steeled herself with a single thought: some fights were worth hanging on for, no matter how hard the war.

She paused once at the threshold, her shoulders squared and her breath steady. Then she stepped out into the layered shadows of the stadium's executive level, the soft echo of her footsteps creating a new rhythm of resolve.

Brick stood just inside Natalie's office. The fluorescent lights cast a pale glow across his face, sharp and unyielding. His fingers squeezed the therapy stress ball until it creaked—a worn, stubborn thing, much like the knot twisting inside him. His heart hammered against his ribs, pounding out a line of apology he had rehearsed a dozen times. But the words still caught in his throat.

The resignation papers lay folded on her desk like a verdict.

Natalie leaned against the wall, her arms crossed tightly. Her eyes were steady but unreadable. The crease between her brows deepened like a storm rolling in, her posture locked as if bracing against another blow. She had seen this before—the apologies wrapped in the aftermath of rage, the promises that dissolved the second his fists clenched. But tonight, something flickered behind his eyes: a buried desperation that clawed at her defenses, even as she fought to keep them up.

The office hummed with tension. Polished wood and cold-brewed coffee hung in the sterile air, mingling with the faint salt smell of his sweat.

"I need help." His voice cracked, raw at the edges. "Not from PR. I need you. I promise I'll work on it. I can't lose you. Not like this."

Natalie's lips pressed flat. "Do you really think words can fix this? Or is this just another meltdown waiting to happen?"

Brick's shoulders sagged, but he didn't retreat.

"No. I'm done with that." He swallowed hard, his grip tightening on the ball. Starting therapy had terrified him—admitting he needed help, that something inside him was fractured. Dr. Greene had pushed him toward truths he'd buried for years. "I started therapy. Dr. Greene told me that real control isn't about being bigger or louder."

His hands squeezed the rubber until it groaned. "I'm scared, Nat. Scared of hurting people. Of being... unlovable."

The words spilled out slowly and heavily, each one a weight he'd carried alone.

Natalie's arms remained crossed, but something shifted behind her eyes. The old defenses cracked at the edges, worn down by the rawness in his voice. She had wanted to protect herself from him so many times. But there was a truth in his fear that matched her own.

Her foot tapped once against the floor, a quiet war between wanting to shield herself and wanting to reach out.

"If I stay," she said carefully, her voice low, "it's because I'm listening. Not because I'm fixing you. I'm not your crutch, Brick. You've got to be honest—all the way—or I walk."

His gaze dropped and then snapped up.

The raw ache behind the defiance was unmistakable. He took a shaky breath and exhaled it slowly. A subtle nod tugged at the corner of his mouth, like the first crack in a frozen lake.

"Okay," he managed, his voice rough but steadier now. "No promises. Just... being here. For now."

A quiet understanding settled between them, fragile but real. Brick exhaled again, a breath held too long finally loosening as he stepped further inside. The door clicked shut behind him with a soft certainty.

Brick parted his lips to speak, but the words stuck, catching in the hollow of his throat. His chest tightened. The air thinned—too sharp, too fast. His breath stuttered, stabbing shallow and quick, like shards of glass sliding beneath his ribs. His fists hammered against his thighs, nails digging crescent moons into his skin, knuckles chalk-white beneath the strain. The color drained from his face in swift bands, his skin paling as if blood were fleeing some invisible flame.

Natalie's eyes snapped sharp, trained and steady. Years of crisis work told her immediately—this was more than nerves. A panic attack. She knew it before he even whispered it to himself.

Her voice dropped low—soft yet resolute. An anchor in the unsteady storm. "Okay, Brick. Listen. Breathe with me. In... one, two, three, four."

She lifts a hand, palm open—a quiet invitation.

Brick's hands tremble in his lap, a subtle quake betraying his effort. He obeys, hesitant and jagged. The air fills his nostrils gradually, cool and sharp against the heat burning under his skin. Six beats to empty it—his exhales come ragged and uncertain. But Natalie's voice never wavers, threading through the chaos like a lifeline.

"Out... one, two, three, four, five, six. Slow. Steady."

The office chair creaks softly. Fluorescent lights hum overhead, casting a sterile glow. Sweat beads on Brick's brow, tiny crystals glinting against damp strands of hair matted to his scalp. His chest heaves in desperate, uneven gasps, muscles trembling beneath his worn jersey.

Outside, the muffled thrum of the campus fades into a quiet backdrop, drowned beneath the pulse of his own rapidly beating heart.

Between uneven breaths, a fragile confession slips free. "I'm scared." His voice cracks, rough and fragile—as if speaking aloud might shatter him completely. "All the damn time. Like... like it's always lurking, waiting for me to snap. It makes me dangerous. To everyone. Especially to you."

Natalie's fingers find his, warm and firm. She curls his trembling hand in her palm, grounding him like a lifeline in the stormy sea ripping through his mind. Her touch is gentle—reassuring without smothering.

"You're safe here," she murmurs. "You're not alone, Brick. I'm right here." Her voice carries the calm groove of certainty, seeping into the edges of his panic. "Listen to me. Keep breathing."

Brick's head tips forward, heavy as if surrendering the battle. It settles softly on her knee, the weight slight but laden with trust. His exhausted eyes flutter closed. The jagged breath smooths, just enough to cradle a tender sliver of calm. The rigid armor cracks, if only for a moment, under her steady presence.

His fingers entwine with hers—fragile but refusing to let go. The tension in his shoulders loosens, a slow release like steam escaping a pressured valve. Natalie stays still, their connection wordless—the quiet kind of intimacy that doesn't burn bright but glows steadily, warm beneath the surface.

Fear, shame, relief—something unspoken threads between them in taut silence.

A long breath, deeper this time, fills Brick's lungs. A whisper slips free, barely audible but charged with raw gratitude. "Thank you."

Natalie offers no answers, no swift solutions. Instead, she holds space—solid and unwavering—as their fingers lace tightly, a silent pact made in the stillness. The glow of the desk lamp casts gentle shadows that cradle them both. The night beyond the window lies cloaked in silent promise.

Time stretches thin and infinite, marked only by the rhythm of steady breaths and the faint pulse beneath intertwined hands.

"I don't know how to do this without you," Brick whispers. "Without losing myself again."

Natalie's gaze softens, a flicker of something unyielding beneath the calm. "You won't have to find out alone."

Brick exhales slowly, the fight ebbing, fear receding enough to open a hesitant door. The tremor in his hand steadies imperceptibly. He shifts, the rough scrape of fabric the only sign of movement. The night's heavy tension lightens, not banished but held—a fragile truce between them.

Words come again, quieter this time, their cadence slow and tentative.

"Maybe real control… isn't about being bigger or louder."

"No," Natalie agrees, her voice firm yet kind. "It's about what you let in."

His eyes meet hers, a raw flicker of vulnerability shining bright. "Not easy."

"Nothing worth having ever is."

They remain locked in the fragile breath of that moment, two worlds colliding but not yet merging—a tension charged with promise. Brick's jaw loosens, a small spark of hope igniting beneath the weight of his confession and her steadfast presence.

The subtle scrape of the leather chair breaks the hush as Natalie shifts, still holding his hand, their fingers weaving together like a quiet lifeline against the storm raging within him.

He presses a palm to his chest, steadying his heartbeat. The fog of panic retreats into a distant shadow. The scent of night air seeping faintly through the cracked window—cool and clean—mixes with the faint pepper of paper and coffee lingering on Natalie's desk.

His breathing has become something he can measure now, something almost controlled. It surprises him. This fragile quiet. The slow, ongoing nature of his healing journey stretches ahead of him, uncertain and winding, but for the first time in weeks, he can imagine walking it without falling apart.

Brick's gaze drifts toward the city lights beyond the clinic's high windows, flickering and distant. The impossible vastness outside contrasts starkly with the intimate stillness cradling them here. In this confined room, with soft light and his heart still fluttering, the fissures in his armor start to widen.

He looks back, his voice barely more than a breath. "Let's keep trying."

Natalie's thumb brushes over the back of his hand, creating a soft, grounding rhythm.

"We're in this together."

Brick's fingers tighten once, then relax. His breathing finally becomes even and measured. The quiet pulse between them speaks louder than any promise made in words.

In that suspended moment, the gulf between Brick's chaos and Natalie's steady calm shrinks to a single touch—the fragile beginning of a new kind of strength.

Brick's breaths lengthen, slower now. The tight cage around his ribs eases just a fraction. The late-evening hum of the stadium corridor filters through the open door—distant yet alive with the pulse of the city beyond. Natalie watches him, her sharp gaze softening where the shadows catch her face. "So, what do you want?" she asks, her voice low but steady.

He swallows, his jaw flexing with the weight of the question. When he finally looks up, there's no armor left—only raw clarity. "I want to get better," he says, the words rough-edged. "Not for the damn cameras or PR crap. For real. I want you to see that I'm trying—actually trying to be someone you can trust."

Her lips flatten into a tight line that barely contains hope, even as caution flutters in her eyes like a shadow reluctant to leave. She crosses her arms, then hesitates, tilting her head ever so slightly—as if weighing a fragile promise. "That's a start," she says finally. "But if you want me around, Brick, you need to understand something. Control isn't about shutting people out or keeping everything bottled inside.

It means being honest about the rage, the fear, all of it. I have to know what's really going on."

He glances away. His fingers twitch against the strap of the therapy stress ball pressed into his palm. The silence stretches thin and brittle.

"Boundaries," she continues, her voice softening at the edges, "aren't walls. They're lines we agree to keep—so no one gets hurt. I'll listen, but I'm not here to fix you. You have to want that. And I will protect myself when I need to."

Something in her words lands differently—not as judgment but as permission—permission for him to fall short, to fail, to try anyway. Brick's voice, when it comes, is steadier, thicker with resolve. "I hear you." He swallows. "And I have boundaries too." He meets her eyes, steady and worn but sincere. "If I screw up, don't just walk away. Tell me straight. Don't let me guess where I stand. I want... honesty. No more ghosting."

A silent beat stretches between them. The tension mingles with something quieter—something like a truce. They both nod, a quiet covenant sealed without fanfare.

Natalie moves to the door and locks the office with deliberate care.

Outside, the twilight deepens. Lantern-like streetlights flicker awake, casting amber pools across the pavement.

Brick exhales—a slow, measured breath. He clenches his jaw and flexes his fingers, fighting the tremor still clinging to his skin. The air tastes faintly of leather and after-rain chill, crisp and sharp against his tongue.

Natalie steps beside him. The scrape of her shoes is steady on the polished floor. Her hand brushes lightly against the small of his back—no heat, no claim. Just a grounding contact that anchors them both in this fragile new reality. Brick stiffens, then sighs, releasing a whispered breath of tension he hadn't realized he was holding.

She feels it too, he realizes: that conflict between self-protection and the dangerous pull toward trust. Her professional caution battles something softer, something that might break if he isn't careful—if she isn't.

"I'm not walking away," he mutters, his voice low enough for only her to hear.

She looks up. The barest curve of a smile breaks her usually poised facade, transforming her entirely. "Good. Because this? It's hard. But maybe it's worth it."

They move together into the darkening corridor. The echo of their footsteps mingles with the distant sounds of the city—a siren, a passing car, the faint whisper of wind through the stadium vents. Brick's thoughts pulse quietly, fragile yet fierce: maybe real strength isn't about what you hold back but about who you let in.

He holds that last thought close, his shoulders squared yet more open than before, as they vanish into the night.

Earned Trust

Polished concrete. Fresh paint. The scents drifted through the stadium's executive hallway as Natalie pushed through just before noon, her heels striking the terrazzo floor with sharp, measured clicks. The sound echoed off charcoal-gray walls lined with framed front pages—headlines that screamed triumph and whispered scandal in equal measure.

The PR office hummed with low murmurs. Phones glowed. Fingers paused mid-keystroke as she passed, her presence drawing the room's breath into a collective stillness. Someone's computer fan whirred softly. Someone else swallowed.

Across the hall, framed by a distant glass wall, Brick stood near the foyer. Sunlight carved sharp angles through towering windows, half of his face shadowed, half illuminated. His broad shoulders were squared but relaxed, hands deep in his jacket pockets. He didn't step forward or retreat; he simply watched her approach with a hard-edged gaze that flickered—just barely—with something like hope before shutting it down again.

Their eyes met. Natalie offered the smallest tilt of her chin.

The tension between them hummed, quiet but undeniable. Like a storm building or breaking.

When she reached him, her voice came steady and clipped. "Brick, I need time before we talk. When I'm ready, we'll have a private conversation on my terms."

His jaw tightened, just barely visible. But then he nodded, slow and certain. "I respect that. No rush." His words were low, almost a promise.

He wanted to say more; she could see it in the way his hands clenched slightly in his pockets before he forced them still again. This was new for him—this waiting, this restraint. The impulse to seize control and force outcomes had always come naturally, but now he was learning to let it go.

"Thank you," Natalie said.

Nothing else. No explanation. No softness. Just the truth of what needed to happen.

Brick turned and disappeared into a cluster of waiting staff, leaving behind an unspoken understanding. The air still carried the faint metallic scent of anticipation, mingled with sunlight spilling through the high windows.

Natalie strode to the glass elevator. The doors slid open smoothly. She stepped inside, her fingers brushing the polished chrome handrail, tracing its cool surface. Shoulders square, back straight, deliberate—always deliberate.

The elevator hummed upward.

Below, Brick's shadow merged with the stadium's angles and lines. His chest rose and fell with a quieter breath. No clenched fists, no flaring nostrils—just a slow, steady calm as he turned to face the day ahead, waiting for the moment when their paths would cross again on terms that were made clear and honored.

The hallway breathed around him. Whispers rose again from the open office nearby—fragments of curious speculation blending with crisp keyboard taps. The buzz settled into a low hum, a living pulse marking the fragile boundary between what had been and what might become.

Natalie stepped out into the spacious PR office, where glass walls gave everything a weightless quality. Everything was sharp-edged and bright. Her gaze settled on the skyline—a vivid patchwork of light and steel—and for a moment, the storm in her chest stilled.

Below, in the foyer, Brick's voice carried upward through the open space. Soft. Certain.

"You're not going to rush me, huh?"

She glanced down, and a faint smile flickered at the corner of her mouth.

"Not a chance," she replied. Warm. Steady.

The space between them held—charged, patient, pregnant with promise. Waiting.

Natalie's fingertips flicked the lock button on the glass door. The soft click sliced through the afternoon hum outside. She straightened her shoulders and turned, her heels striking crisply against the polished floor as Brick stepped inside. Muted sunlight filtered through the tall windows, casting long shadows across the sleek surfaces of the PR office.

She had built her career on control, on knowing exactly what she needed and stating it without apology. This—whatever this was becoming—demanded the same clarity, or it would collapse under its own weight.

"Have a seat," Natalie said, her voice steady and edged. She sank behind the glass desk, the cool surface grounding her palms. "If we're moving forward, it's on my terms: emotional honesty. No games."

Her eyes locked onto his—unblinking, unapologetic.

Brick's jaw tightened. The usual fire that sparked behind his gaze simmered to a steady burn. He eased onto the edge of the chair opposite her, his hands resting on his thighs. "Go on."

Natalie listed the boundaries like a methodical pulse—each one precise and non-negotiable. "I need the ability to ask for time and space when things get heavy, especially during press events. No ambushes. No trying to get under my skin when the cameras are rolling." Her voice cut clean through any possible doubt. "During work hours, my role as PR lead takes priority. That means I can't drop everything because you want to vent or unload. We'll schedule that: private time."

The sharp aroma of dark roast drifted from her mug, mingling with the worn leather scent of the office chair. Beyond the glass, distant footsteps echoed softly down the hallway, swallowed by the gravity of the moment.

Brick sat quietly. His fists unclenched, opening like hands finally willing to let something go. He had spent years controlling every variable and every outcome. Vulnerability felt like standing on the edge of a cliff in the dark. But here, in this glass-walled office, with her words mapping the territory between them, he could almost see the ground below—almost believe he wouldn't fall.

His posture shifted. His shoulders were broad but relaxed, no longer bracing for verbal blows or defensive maneuvers. When she paused, he nodded once, a low sound of assent rumbling from his chest. "If I screw up," Brick said, his voice low and rough around the edges, "you've got to tell me. Don't just... walk away. No silence."

Natalie's jaw tightened. She blinked once, slow and deliberate, before meeting his gaze again. The cost of these rules glittered in the silence between them—emotional barriers, trust on the line, and vulnerability needing careful tending. But something shifted as they exchanged matching nods. A shared understanding blossomed; the agreement was rough around the edges but real.

Brick pushed off from the chair, moving toward the door with steady purpose. There was no attempt to seize control. No dictating terms anymore. The door swung closed behind him with a muted thud, sealing the conversation in soft privacy.

Natalie sank back into her chair. Her eyes drifted past the glass, settling on the cityscape stretched beneath the horizon. The late afternoon sun caught on distant windows, flickering golden reflections like tiny, fractured promises. Her fingers curled lightly around the edge of the desk, grounding herself in the moment.

There was a fragile steadiness now. Fragile, but undeniable.

The pulse of urgency had thinned, replaced by something quieter—the steady beat of progress made, of boundaries respected, and of trust tentatively rebuilt. The city carried on outside, oblivious to the small revolution unfolding in this glass-walled sanctuary. But here, beneath the sharp lines and clinical clarity, something real had shifted.

Brick's promise lingered in the air, mingling with hers—a pact written not in ink but in intention.

They were no longer enemies mapping battle lines; they were two people carving a precarious path forward, one rule at a time.

The late afternoon sun drapes the practice field in a golden haze. The air thickens with the thud of padded bodies smashing into the turf, sharp whistles slicing through the chaos. Players surge through drills, breaths ragged, feet skidding against worn grass grit. Muscle, sweat, and relentless push hum low beneath it all.

Inside the media room, behind cool glass, Natalie leans on the sill. Steam swirls from the mug cupped between her fingers, mingling with the faint tang of turf carried on the breeze. Her eyes trace the field's choreography, finding Logan "Brick" Turner moving with something she hasn't seen before—steadiness instead of volatility. Measured. Watchful. Unusual in its softness.

A rough snap fractures the rhythm. A scramble falters. A missed read. Brick steps away from the fray and moves toward Caleb Monroe, who limps off the field beside the sideline. Caleb's shoulders slump beneath the glare and clatter, frustration flickering across his face.

Brick approaches. His massive shadow falls to calf level, hands resting on bent knees. He is now eye to eye with the younger player. Cleats dig slightly into the grass. The faint scent of leather and sweat clings to his gear.

"Try planting your right foot, not your left," Brick says, his voice low and calm—a rare softness cutting through the field's roar. "It takes the hit better."

He lifts one booted foot and shifts his weight with deliberate grace. The pivot across the leather grip of his cleat unfolds smoothly and measured. Balance instead of reckless force—a secret whispered in a storm.

Caleb's jaw clenches. His eyes sharpen as he absorbs the advice. Then a slow exhale eases his shoulders. He nods once, sharp and sure.

"Right. Got it."

Brick straightens with a quiet grunt. He watches Caleb slope back to the line.

The next snap crackles sharper. Caleb's feet land firmly and surely. The play unfolds more smoothly beneath his renewed footing. He bursts past a would-be blocker with a tighter cut, traction holding steady instead of slipping.

Caleb skids to the sideline, breath wild but triumphant. A wide smile crests his features. He searches Brick's face for approval, his eyes gleaming with something like awe.

"That was cleaner than last time. I didn't think changing a foot would make a difference."

Brick cracks the ghost of a grin. He rubs the stubble along his jaw. "Details, man. It's the little things we miss that get us knocked down."

The familiar drawl of DeShawn Price carries across the field, laced with teasing warmth. "Look at Turner—gone soft on us! Who knew the big bad beast had moves to teach the rookies?"

Laughter crackles among teammates—light, genuine, with no edge of mockery. Nods ripple through the group. The atmosphere shifts, a camaraderie recalibrating, recognizing the strength in patience and guidance instead of brute force alone.

Brick's gaze flickers toward the media room window. There, framed by steel and glass, Natalie holds steady, cup paused mid-air in quiet salute.

His chin lifts slightly, the smallest nod, sharp and discreet—a silent conversation between worlds.

Natalie returns it without hesitation. Her eyes soften, and acknowledgment blooms like dawn between them.

This moment signals something the team feels without speaking it aloud—a subtle but meaningful shift in how strength is measured. Brick's respect is hard-earned, and this teasing camaraderie indicates acceptance of a new leadership style, one threaded with patience instead of fear.

Practice swells onward. Brick melts back into the rhythm of drills, the ground vibrating under synchronized stomps, whistles, and shouted calls. Yet beneath the usual pulse, a new current threads through—one that transforms fear into admiration. The air relaxes subtly, now charged with possibility, marked by the steady beat of a player learning not just to fight, but to lead.

Late afternoon sunlight spills through the tall windows of the PR office, casting long, golden fingers across Natalie's desk. Papers rustle softly. Beyond the glass, the stadium hums—a distant murmur punctuated by the sharp whistle of practice and the occasional thud of a football hitting the turf.

Natalie's fingers hover over her scattered notes, then trace the margins. A slight tremble betrays her calm. Half-formed thoughts from the day's whirlwind scatter across the page like leaves she can't quite gather.

A restless ache coils low in her chest, hope twisted tight with something sharper—the first turn of a knot slowly tightening.

She presses her palm flat against the cool glass surface, then rises. The chair's scrape is muffled by the thick carpet. Her steps carry her quietly down the short hallway to the break room, where Nina's graceful movements cradle a steaming teapot, releasing fragile curls of jasmine steam into the air.

Nina turns. Her eyes read the subtle pull in Natalie's posture like an open book—the defensive hunch of her shoulders and the careful distance maintained.

"So... you still miss him, huh?"

Her voice carries neither judgment nor surprise, just steady understanding.

Natalie exhales. Her shoulders sag, weighed down by something unseen.

"Yeah." The word barely rises above the soft hiss of brewing tea. "I miss Brick." Her gaze shifts away, her fingertips tapping the edge of the counter, hesitant, as if measuring truth against silence. "I want the respect he gives the team—the kind that doesn't waver with every slip. But I also want..." She trails off, searching. "Vulnerability. I want him to let me in. Not just see the soldier, but see the man underneath."

Nina pours the amber liquid into a delicate cup. Her eyes soften as she nods.

"That's a high demand."

Natalie's lips twitch into a half-smile, bittersweet. "It's a contradiction I wear all the time." She folds her arms, her words slipping like water through her fingers. "I want control, but I want to surrender. Professional distance, but emotional closeness. I'm tired of guarding the perimeter, and I'm still getting bruised."

Behind the sharp scent of jasmine, a pause settles between them—quiet, an acknowledgment of the invisible battles that rage beneath professionalism—the cost of keeping composure when your heart fractures underneath.

Natalie lifts the cup, warm in her hands, but she sets it down before the first sip, retreating back toward her office. The door clicks softly behind her.

Seated once more, she pulls her chair close to the desk, fingers poised over the keyboard, frozen.

The faded light paints a soft halo around her, illuminating the faint crease between her brows. She runs through her thoughts like a checklist in a familiar language: What do I want? From him, from us? From my role here?

She writes the unspoken answers in the air.

Trust: unvarnished and raw. The courage to stumble and own it.

Patience: the kind that holds space without judgment.

Clarity: a mutual respect that protects, not confines.

Desire to grow, to heal—not just a polished facade for the crowd.

And beneath it all, shimmering quietly, is hope. Hope she hasn't allowed herself to fully claim; that maybe, just maybe, this fragile thing could bloom.

Her phone buzzes softly, breaking the quiet.

A new message from Brick glows on the screen: *You good?*

Nerves pulse through her stomach, mixed with a warmth she can't quite name. Her thumb flies over the screen, crafting words that bridge the distance between them. She hits send.

The phone rests heavily in her palm. For a heartbeat, she gazes out the window toward the first hint of twilight settling over the stadium—a tender dusk folding the day away. The next chapter waits just beyond the glass.

Somehow, Natalie feels steadier, as if leaning into that uncertain hope—just for a moment—has anchored her to something real.

Brick's thumbs hover over his phone screen. The glow traces the hard planes of his face as dusk seeps into the sky behind him. He types out "You good?" then tucks the phone away, his hands buried deep in the pockets of his battered leather jacket.

The locked glass doors of the facility reflect a slightly distorted version of himself—tall, broad, and purposely still. He fights the impulse to knock on the door and demand entry, held back by a hope that this time, things might be different. The cool snap of evening air curls around him, carrying the scent of cut grass and distant city traffic, sharpening his senses. It's not just the chill; it's the quiet between beats, the unsaid words between him and Natalie that pulls tight inside his chest.

The hallway light hums softly when she appears—a calm figure stepping out from the shadows as if she owns the silence. Years of clashes and fragile truces have carved the shape of this moment, quiet but charged beneath the cool polish. Natalie's presence carries that poised energy, steady and unflinching. Her eyes catch his immediately, and a flicker of acknowledgment passes between them beneath the stadium's steel bones.

"Want to walk?" She gestures toward the concourse, her voice low but firm—the kind that doesn't ask but offers a rare choice anyway.

He nods, setting his jaw with that familiar stubborn edge, then falls into step beside her. Concrete echoes beneath their feet. The stadium lights above cast long shadows, glowing bluish-white against their backs. Around them, the leathered roar of empty seats waits for a crowd that has folded away for the night, the distant hum of city life blending with the sharp tang of grass and sweat still lingering in the air.

Natalie breaks the quiet. "I don't want a perfect version of you. I want a real one." Her voice is soft but resolute; the words hang between them like a challenge wrapped in mercy.

Brick's gaze drops to their feet, fingers tightening instinctively around the cold metal railing. When he looks up, his eyes flicker—unsteady, bare—as if weighing a truth too heavy to hold. "I'm scared." His voice is rough, almost lost in the steady rhythm of their steps. "Scared of screwing it all up. Of disappointing you." He swallows hard. "But I'm trying. Trying to change without grabbing for control like a lifeline."

She glances at him, a half-smile tugging at her lips—a mixture of understanding and something warmer. "Change isn't about control or perfection. It's about being honest when you're scared."

A brief laugh slips out of Brick, sharp and a little bitter. "Restraint feels unnatural to me, like wearing a suit two sizes too small."

Natalie's chuckle joins his—light and genuine. The sound unravels the tension threading through their shared space.

He stops for a breath. The moment swells with possibility. Then he squares his shoulders. "Mind if I...?" His voice hesitates, carrying the weight of permission.

Her answer comes unspoken as her fingers curl around his—cool skin sliding against calloused warmth. They lace together, slow and deliberate, as if testing gravity for the first time.

Their steps resume toward the practice field gate, the chain-link fence cold and solid beside them. Brick stays close, his hand tight in hers, their shoulders brushing. They stand like that—a singular force against the hush of the fading day.

Together, they exhale slowly, shedding months of fought battles.

The city spills lights beyond the gates, but here, beneath the steel skeleton of the stadium, their breath mingles with the sharp autumn air. The soft scrape of shoes is the only soundtrack.

In that quiet orbit, Brick and Natalie share a space that is less guarded and more real. The weight of control finally lifts like the night sky above.

The door clicks shut behind Brick. The city night filters through partially drawn curtains—a low murmur of distant traffic and the occasional horn's bleat.

Natalie's apartment wraps around him like a quiet breath. A soft amber glow pools from her carefully placed lamps, liquid honey spilling across the walls. Long shadows stretch lazily and warmly, punctuated by the gleam of framed photographs and delicate artifacts on deep wooden shelves. Each piece is deliberately chosen, not clutter—stories nailed down in moments: a cracked ceramic bowl, a single book opened face-up on the coffee table, and the faint peppering of rain tapping at the window, mingling with sandalwood and the worn leather scent of the couch beneath him.

She steps back and lets the door close fully. A soft smile crosses her face. "Let me."

The words are calm—an invitation carrying no pressure but all the authority of someone holding the reins. Brick's broad shoulders dip as he nods. The tension in his clenched jaw loosens just enough to let the moment breathe.

His fingers hang loosely at his sides. The usual urge to take control eases, quietly yielding to her lead. It's an unspoken surrender, unfamiliar yet strangely freeing. Part of him has always needed to be the one in charge, the one protecting. Letting that go, even fractionally, feels like stepping off a cliff and trusting that the ground will catch him.

Natalie moves with deliberate grace, reaching for his hand gently before leading him toward the couch. Her touch is featherlight yet insistent, guiding without demanding. When her fingertips trace along his wrist, Brick shifts—his muscles coiling and relaxing in the same breath. He watches her with sharp, curious eyes that now hold something raw, less guarded than before.

"Is this okay?" she asks, her voice hushed, leaning close enough that her breath brushes his skin.

"Yeah." His voice is rough but steady. "I trust you."

Her hand travels slowly higher, pausing and waiting. "Mind if I touch your face?"

His brow lifts for a heartbeat, his eyes widening just enough before thinning into calm acceptance. "Go ahead."

She cups his cheek, warm and sure. Her thumb brushes along the ridge of the scar above his brow—a tender acknowledgment rather than an intrusion. Brick closes his eyes briefly, then opens them, locking his gaze with hers again.

"Tell me if it's too much, alright?"

A short laugh slips from him, unguarded. "Feels like not enough sometimes."

They move together in an unhurried rhythm. Time folds inward on itself. The air hums with barely spoken needs and promises—a delicate dance of asking and receiving. Natalie's voice remains steady and kind, each advance checked with careful questions: the glance, the touch, the whispered word.

Brick answers with honest confessions. His deep tones weave insecurity and willingness, fear and hope together.

"Can I kiss you here?" she asks softly, tilting her head toward his throat.

He exhales, low and raw. "Please."

The kiss is a brush of silk and heat—slow, full of hesitation turned surrender. When their lips part, Brick's hand comes up to rest lightly on Natalie's waist, his fingers curling with cautious reverence. She leans into the touch, her eyes gleaming with fierce tenderness.

Natalie recognizes the rarity of this moment—Brick open like this, unguarded and trembling beneath her hands. She feels the weight of it, the stakes. Hope flickers in her chest, fragile and tentative, mixed with the lingering doubt that she might break something precious.

Whispers trail between them, layering over the quiet sounds of the city night: distant car horns, a soft hum of life beyond these walls. Their voices dip and rise, rich with vulnerability.

"I'm scared," Brick admits, his voice shaky but earnest. "Scared I'll mess it all up."

Natalie's thumb strokes slow circles on his skin. "Trust isn't about not falling; it's about falling and knowing someone's there to catch you."

A tear slips free, tracing a warm line down his cheek. Natalie brushes it away, her fingers trembling just the slightest bit.

Laughter suddenly bubbles from Brick, surprising them both. "You're going to turn me into a sap, you know that?"

"Good," she replies, her eyes shining. "I like sap."

They settle back onto the sofa. The cushions are worn and soft around them—a stark contrast to Brick's usual hardened edges. His arms wrap around Natalie in a careful, protective circle that feels like both a shield and a surrender. Her head rests against his chest, her breath even and slow. Their warmth mingles as the night deepens its hold.

Words tumble quietly between them, reflections on how far they have come to get here. The battles fought and the ones still waiting. The room contracts to this fragile space where power doesn't mean control but presence. Where tenderness is armor shed, not hidden beneath.

"This," Brick breathes into her hair, "is all the proof I need that I can change."

Natalie lifts her face, her eyes meeting his with steady confidence. "And we do it together."

Her smile fades into peaceful sleep, her eyelashes fluttering shut as she lets go completely. Brick remains awake a moment longer, watching the steady rise and fall of her chest beneath his chin.

The gruff mask he wears so often cracks. The storm beneath slips away to reveal something softer—something hopeful.

Outside, the city pulses with unforgiving vibrancy. Inside, two hearts beat in sync, discovering the quiet strength found in trust—and in choosing each other again.

Rivalry Game

The locker room thrums—hearts thudding against locked jaws, sneakers clacking on tile, and music spilling from rickety speakers clinging to a wall scarred with years of sweat and battle. Brick perches on the narrow metal bench, shoulders squared under the harsh glare of fluorescent lights. His earbuds dangle, forgotten. He focuses on the slow, deliberate rhythm of his breath—inhale for four, hold, exhale for six—anchoring himself against the swelling anticipation. These exercises came from Dr. Reeves, his therapist, a lifeline when the rage threatened to consume him. Tonight, they mean everything.

Around him, teammates move with restless energy. Caleb drapes a towel over his neck, stretching a sinewy arm overhead. DeShawn cracks a grin as he ties his cleats, the scent of leather mingling with the cold tang of sweat and liniment. The air hums with a raw, kinetic charge, pressing the room into a fiery crucible. Yet Brick's world narrows. Just breathe. Just the cadence that pushes back the storm of adrenaline threatening to ignite old ghosts.

                    CK FRANCO

Coach Marcus Hale steps onto the small platform before the whiteboard. His presence commands immediate attention.

His deep voice rolls through the locker room like thunder cracking open the sky. "Discipline. Legacy. This isn't just a game—it's a test of who we are. We fight with our heads *and* our hearts. Every play. Every snap. Every moment out there counts."

His eyes scan the room, hard and steady. Then they settle on Brick like a spotlight.

"You—Turner—we're counting on you. You know what's at stake."

That locked gaze carries weight, a silent summons brushing across Brick's skin like electricity. The weight of Marcus's belief in him presses against the weight of expectation. They both know what this game means—for the team, for the season, for Brick's shot at redemption. The coach's authority settles like iron in the belly of the room.

Breaths catch between exhales.

Nearby, by the tunnel entrance, Natalie stands like a calm island amid the turmoil. Her clipboard rests lightly in one hand, fingers tapping faint rhythms against its surface. She watches the team, routine and stress entwined in her gaze. When Brick's eyes flicker toward her, she meets them across the scattered bodies—two silent messages passed in that moment: she believes in this man beneath the storm.

A smile tugs at her lips. Quiet. Just a crescent. But fierce enough to send a spark of warmth through the cold tension between them. Her eyes hold steady, unwavering.

Brick catches it—an ember kindled in the tight knot of resolve.

Caleb's voice slices through the tension, pitched with teasing warmth. "Hey, don't go smashing the locker room, Turner. Save the Hulk act for the field."

DeShawn shook his head with a laugh. "Yeah, man, keep that temper on a leash—we want the sharp edge, not the wrecking ball."

Their grins are wide, but their eyes reflect the quiet control Brick has mastered tonight. They know the guard has been lowered, even if just a wedge.

Brick turns slightly toward them. A half-smile quirks his jawline—wry, unspoken thanks pass between friends who see more than the rage-fueled reputation.

The buzz of voices, the scent of sweat and anticipation, the metallic clang of lockers—all blur around him as Brick sinks his gaze inward again. He closes his eyes.

The world contracts.

Inhale—one, two, three, four.

Hold.

Exhale—six quiet beats, like rain dripping from a dark sky.

One last time.

He rises. The worn leather of his jersey creaks softly as he slings his helmet over his broad shoulder. His movements are measured. Deliberate. Carved from hours of practice and pain.

The room shifts with his movement—a ripple through the brotherhood. Teammates nod. Shoulders brush against his in curt affirmations.

Footsteps echo down the locker room.

The rhythm builds.

Destiny waits.

Brick steps toward the tunnel, breath steady, heart laser-focused. The murmurs dim. The crowd calls from beyond the doors, an ocean roaring just out of sight.

He exhales and walks with the team toward the gate, where chaos waits to be met and conquered.

The air thrums in the narrow concrete tunnel, the pounding of cleats resembling a stampede of steel and sweat. Brick's chest rises and falls unevenly with the sudden surge of adrenaline that crashes over him like hot waves. One mistake tonight—one slip back into the old Brick—and everything crumbles: the sponsorships, the redemption arc, the second chance he's clawed for. Gone. The weight of it settles heavily in his ribs.

Outside, a blaze of stadium lights slices through the dusk, flooding the field with electric white. The roar of the home crowd flames up, a living beast breathing fire and fury just beyond the tunnel's mouth.

Brick's jaw is clenched so tightly that his teeth bruise the edges of his tongue. His hands curl into loose fists at his sides, yet a flicker of softness passes through his eyes as he exhales the mantra—four counts in, hold, six counts out—each breath a cool river cutting through wildfire. Four. Hold. Six. The chaos crashes outside, but he distills it, reshapes it into the rhythm of his own quiet storm.

Ahead, the tunnel opens, the flood of light a sudden blast that bakes his skin. Quick sweat prickles down his spine. Fans erupt—voices thunderously loud and sharp-edged, a tide of sound threatening to swallow him whole. He steps forward, the hard turf beneath his scuffed cleats vibrating with the heartbeat of the crowd.

Across the field, a shadow moved into focus—Derrick "Rhino" Carter crouched like a gargoyle on the far sideline, his wide frame rippling with tension. They had crossed paths since high school, and Rhino had never forgiven Brick for the attention, the escape route that seemed to open before him while Rhino remained tethered to the same grinding streets. Now, every meeting was a chance for Rhino to prove that Brick hadn't changed, to find the fault line and crack it wide open.

Their eyes locked. Rhino's gaze cut sharp, laced with low, unspoken menace—a challenge coiling like rope around a fist. A promise of battle. A warning veiled beneath bravado.

The coin flipped, spinning silver under the floodlight's glare. Rhino smirked, leaning into the moment like a predator tightening its grip. His voice washed over the field, rough and mocking, threaded through cameras and cheers:

"Heard you're clean now, pretty boy. Since when did you start playing by the rules? Bet you're scared of your own shadow."

The crowd shifted, sensing the venom, whispers rippling through the stands. The jab landed like a thrown rock, aimed to shatter steel resolve. But Brick stood statuesque, jaw clenched, eyes steady. The heat of old outrage flickered—that feral thing that used to drive his fists—but he buried it beneath a calm mask, the mantra humming in his chest like a tether.

Jaxon's hand landed squarely on Brick's shoulder, grounding him. "Hey, man—keep that fire where it counts. We need your head in the game, not your fists." His voice was steady but carried an easy grit that lowered the temperature just enough.

Brick nodded, inhaling slowly and deeply. The noise flooded back—the crowd's roar, the scent of fresh-cut grass mixed with ozone from the lights, and the sharp tang of sweat and leather. He let the mantra settle, steadying the wild charge inside.

One step after the next, Brick moved into position on the defensive line. Solid ground beneath fierce, blazing light. The edges blurred—except for the unshakable weight of the present.

"Still riding that PR leash, huh?" Rhino snapped from the opposite line, his voice loud enough to echo in Brick's ribs. "What, scared of yourself?"

Brick met the jab without blinking, his voice low and crisp. "I've learned control. You should try it sometime."

Rhino sneered. "Control is weakness. We all know what you're made of, Turner. Don't think we've forgotten."

"Try me," Brick snapped back, fingers flexing inside his gloves, a flicker of steel in the tempered calm.

Jaxon leaned in, his voice a steady anchor. "Eyes up, Brick. Remember what we're here for."

The growl of the crowd swelled, waves of color blurring in motion and heat. Cameras swiveled in arcs, capturing the raw energy simmering on the field. Brick's gaze flicked to the stands where Natalie watched, binoculars pressed to her face, the faintest smile playing at her lips— a quiet confirmation between them, like a secret promise.

Around him, teammates locked shoulders and locked eyes, forming a fortress born of years on rough fields and shared storms. Brick exhaled, taking a slow breath to calm the storm inside, the mantra a whispered chant beneath the roar.

Four. Hold. Six.

His feet settled, rooted and ready.

The whistle blew sharply.

Brick stepped forward into the blaze of battle, his eyes flicking once more across the field. The stadium's roar surged up, crushing and triumphant, but inside, Brick carried the cool calm of fire restrained.

He was ready.

The stadium hummed like a living beast as the snap cracked through the crisp autumn air. Brick exploded off the line—every muscle coiled like a spring ready to release. His hands flashed with surgical precision as he jammed Rhino's shoulder pads.

The crowd's roar faded into dull noise. Only the snap's sharp pop remained, accompanied by grunts and scrambling cleats.

Each play was a battle honed by years of sweat and discipline. Brick pivoted—sharp and measured, weight balanced. Leveraging every inch, he shoved Rhino backward. No wild swings. No reckless hits. Just pure technique forged through grit and pain. The turf kicked beneath him, synthetic grass whispering against his cleats as he disengaged, already moving to meet the next opponent.

His breath tasted faintly metallic, his heart hammering in sync with the line's cadence.

Then it flickered—harsh lights of a past stadium, snarls of old fights, and the surge of raw fury spilling over.

His jaw clenched until the muscle twitched, a familiar burn flaring at his temple. The old fire stirred, raw and wild, but he pressed it down like a chokehold. Ghosts of old melees crowded his vision—flashes of red and the sting of punishment. But he shook it off, low breath pumping deep into his belly.

The rhythm of his footwork pulled him back, each step a tether to the present. He zoned in, calibrating his mind to the current play. His eyes were sharp, senses razor-edged.

From the press box, Victor Cross scribbled furiously, his hands moving faster than his narrowed eyes could keep up. His camera lens stayed glued on Brick, searching for the chaos he expected.

But all it captured was ironclad restraint—a controlled furnace of power that refused to burst into flame.

Frustration wrinkled Victor's brow as he flipped pages, hoping to find the narrative of a meltdown, an outburst—anything to spin. Instead, Brick's quiet dominance mocked the journalist's designs.

Natalie perched in the stands nearby, binoculars pressed lightly against her face. Her breath hitched with every powerful move Brick made, her gaze flicking between him and the field, sharp as a hawk's, lips faintly parted in awe.

Watching his restraint settled something in her chest. Real progress. She could feel it in the way he moved—controlled, grounded, and present. Not the Brick who had exploded into rage just months ago.

She nudged Emma and Nina, nodding subtly toward the defensive line where Brick stood like a fortress, preventing the enemy's advance. Pride softened the lines around her eyes—a warmth she buried deep, but that radiated all the same.

The scoreboard's floodlights glared overhead, casting elongated shadows that rippled across the turf. The scent of turf mingled with the faint tang of sweat and freshly sliced air. The stadium vibrated with tension and hope, a symphony of shouts and whistles building an electric pulse around Brick's calm core.

"Keep your eyes on the mailman," Brick growled, low enough for only the linemen near him to hear.

Caleb grinned, elbowing DeShawn. "Don't Hulk out on us, Turner."

"Which one?" DeShawn chuckled, hands fixed on his hips but eyes locked forward.

"That one who thinks he's got legs," Brick snapped back, his tone clipped but steady. "Don't get lazy. When he breaks, you break him harder."

DeShawn flicked his wrist, smirking. "Looking sharp today. You actually got your head in the game."

Brick's eyes never left the line. "Try and catch me, boys."

The huddle shifted with breathless energy, the world narrowing until there was only the succession of snaps and the pounding charge of hearts aligned. Brick stepped back, his eyes scanning the formation. Fingers tapped the calls—quick and crisp. Each word was a piece of the defensive puzzle locking into place.

A soft smirk tugged at the corner of his mouth, fleeting but sharp. He caught a glance from a young teammate and nodded, giving silent permission to hold fast and trust the process.

Another snap. Another clean shed.

Rhino met the ground a fraction too late. Brick's calculated push sent him stumbling out of the play, his frustration blooming in silent defeat. The lineman snarled, his eyes burning with intent, but Brick didn't flinch. He didn't respond beyond the next snap.

"Technique beats temper every time," Brick snapped under his breath, his voice gravelly with effort.

The crowd's roar swelled again, waves of sound crashing around the gridiron. Brick's chest heaved, sweat slick along his scalp beneath the helmet, but his mind remained a fortress of focus.

Step by step.

Snap by snap.

He carved order from chaos.

He strode back to the huddle, shoulders square and breath steady. His voice cut through the noise: "Gap left. Mike linebacker blitz. Watch the counter. Respect the carry. Eyes on the ball."

His teammates shifted, their faces tightening with renewed resolve. The defense breathed as one, tightrope walking between aggression and discipline.

On the sidelines, the tension rippled. But Brick's control calmed the currents, a beacon burning steadily against the storm.

The stadium pulsed with raw anticipation as the next play awaited; the battle was far from over. In this moment, Brick stood unshaken, the embodiment of controlled ferocity.

The whistle's sharp blast faded, and the tension hung thick in the humid air.

The concrete beneath Brick's cleats still hummed with residual vibrations from the roaring crowd, but his focus narrowed to a single figure—Derrick "Rhino" Carter, the opposing offensive lineman with eyes like a predator sizing up its prey. Rhino shifted closer, his shoulder driving into Brick's with deliberate force—late and unnecessary.

The contact twisted the familiar scent of fresh turf and sweat into something edgier: a challenge, a poison seed.

"Still got that leash yanking you back, Turner?" Rhino's voice cut low and venomous through the noise. "Heard you're soft now, playing nice for the PR cameras." He leaned closer, his breath hot against Brick's face mask. "Where's the rage? Where's the fighter we used to know?"

Brick's jaw clenched until the taste of iron filled his mouth. His fists curled slowly at his sides, fingers twitching like restrained fire. His vision dimmed, and the crowd's roar receded as red flashed behind his eyes—instinct clawing toward the surface, demanding release.

Then he closed his eyes.

The world contracted into a pinprick of breath. Deep. Measured. Inhale for four. Hold. Exhale for six. The mantra steadied the pulse hammering through his veins. Each breath dragged him down into his core, where the rage couldn't touch him.

When he opened his eyes, the harshness had faded.

Instead of the storm Rhino wanted, Brick's hand reached down. His fingers clasped around the player's forearm—the one he had knocked sprawling just moments before—and hauled him up with quiet authority. No words. No aggression. Just the steady grip of a man choosing his own path.

From the sideline, Caleb's voice cracked through the tension. "That's the calm before the storm, Brick. Keep the heat low."

DeShawn chuckled, warm and admiring. "Quiet strength, man. That's what wins games."

Eli, perched on the bench, flashed a thumbs-up—a small beacon demanding the discipline Brick battled to uphold.

The defensive line responded like a single, breathing organism. Brick's steady presence sent ripples through the group, transforming restraint into razor-sharp cohesion.

Conversations tightened into concise bursts. Calls were clipped. Movements synced. The sharp tang of pine-scented sweat mingled with the electric buzz of resolve.

The stadium's cacophony folded inward. Fragmented chants and jeers blended into a distant hum. Brick moved with purpose, sliding a heavy hand across his helmet's protective bars before dragging his gaze over his teammates' flushed faces. He caught silent nods, clenched fists, and small confirmations that the fight on the field was sharper now—not fueled by rage, but by clear-headed strategy and shared will.

The team's unity tightened because they had seen what Brick used to be: raw, volatile, and out of control. Now, they watched him choose discipline over instinct, and that choice inspired something deeper than fear; it inspired trust. They moved with precision because Brick moved with purpose. They covered their gaps because he covered his.

Grass stains smeared his jersey in patchwork patterns, and cheap bruises were worn without losing his cool.

One snap followed another, each controlled and deliberate, like a heartbeat keeping perfect time to the rhythm of the game.

Brick's breath tasted faintly metallic, and grit from the turf stuck in the back of his throat. Salt stung as sweat ran down his face.

The quarter wore on.

Rhino prowled nearby, still seething and seeking an opening. But Brick's unyielding calm blunted every attempt at provocation. The sun's fading rays cast long shadows across the field, while a cool breeze crawled past the stands, carrying the crowd's restless energy and turning it into a tangible pulse that the team rode like a wave.

During a brief lull, two teammates brushed past him. Their pads slapped against Brick's shoulders—firm, grounding gestures that carried more weight than words. The murmurs of encouragement rippled through the pack like wildfire.

His shoulders didn't buckle; they pressed back, broad and unyielding under the weight of expectation.

Nearby, Caleb's voice cut through again, steady and sure. "Keep it locked, Brick. Eyes on the prize."

The defensive unit locked into place. Early stumbles gave way to fluid synchronization. Zones were covered with precision. Gaps closed like seams stitched with iron thread. Brick's commands sliced through the field noise—clear, steady, a pulse to follow.

The quarter's final seconds ticked away under the floodlights' halo. Brick's helmet bounced lightly as he strode toward the sideline, every step a deliberate claim of control.

Teammates' hands found him in passing. Shoulders clapped, and backs were patted—small affirmations of solidarity and strength.

His breath, steady now, mingled with the cooling air. The faint musk of grass and sweat pressed against his skin.

The final whistle shrieked.

Brick didn't linger to savor the moment. There was no bragging, no loud triumph—just steady steps back toward the sanctuary of the locker room, where battles of a different kind awaited, carried in the quiet strength of a man who was fighting harder than any of them could see.

The stadium rumbled—a roar thick with adrenaline and anticipation—but it snapped undone. A sharp, sickening crack of collision fractured the noise. Eli's body hit the turf with a hollow thud, limbs splaying like a marionette cut loose.

The crowd's thunder dissolved into stunned silence, pierced by urgent whistles slicing through the charged air. Shouts morphed from play calls to desperate cries: "Hold! Hold!"

Brick's instincts ignited. He was the first defender through the swirling chaos.

With muscles coiled and breath tightening, he forced back those crowding around Eli's prone form. Arms swinging and shoulders driving, he fended off the press like a living barrier. His jaw clenched as he dropped to one knee beside Eli, the world narrowing to the cracked helmet and the shallow rise and fall of a chest.

His fingers found Eli's jaw—careful, cradling the neck with steady hands.

A cold pulse hummed beneath Brick's palm—steady, fragile.

He checked, sensed, and listened. The distant roar faded behind the sharp clip of medics closing in, their footfalls quickening across the turf.

"Give them space!" Brick's voice cut through the rising tension—quiet but firm. His eyes blazed with authority as he shepherded teammates away, snapping instructions: "Back! Give room!"

In that moment, something shifted behind his sternum—a resignation settling like concrete. This was no longer about the play; this was about holding together what threatened to splinter.

Young players shuffled reluctantly but respected the order. The swarm recoiled before the thin line of his control.

The medics descended—efficient shadows weaving around Eli's still frame. Tubes. Hands steadied. Silent exchanges flashed between experienced eyes. The acrid scent of turf mingled with sweat and antiseptic under the stadium lights.

In the stands, Natalie's jaw clenched like steel. Her fingers dug into Emma's palm until her knuckles blanched. Her breath caught, a hollow tightness plugging her chest.

Emma's eyes never left the field, her pupils fixed on that fragile form below. The grass lay starkly green against the artificial lights—a brutal contrast that made everything feel sharper, more real, and more terrifying.

Nearby, Nina's eyes tracked every medic's movement, her lips parting in silent encouragement. The stadium held its breath, a pulsing beast watching a stage far beyond sport.

Then—a faint movement. A weak thumbs-up. Barely more than a twitch of determination.

Relief trickled through Natalie like rain, and she exhaled, releasing burdens she scarcely realized she was carrying. Emma's grip loosened, just slightly.

The hush broke suddenly. The crowd erupted in a wave of supportive noise, crashing over the stunned spaces between adrenaline and fear. Chanting rose—muted but fierce—"Eli! Eli! Eli!"—a chant weaving strength into vulnerability.

From the sideline, DeShawn muttered low, "Man, he just took that hit like a freight train."

Caleb's eyes narrowed, and his fists unclenched slowly. "Brick, don't just stand there. He's got Eli's six. Always."

Brick rose slowly, his shoulders squared. His expression tightened into calm control as he moved around Eli like a living shield, each footfall deliberate and measured. The cameras whirled, capturing every agonizing second, but Brick's gaze stayed locked forward, unwavering and defiant against the glare of scrutiny.

"Let them work," Brick commanded, his voice low but firm as he rallied the closest players away from the stretcher. "Watch the space. Keep it clean."

"You're telling me we're supposed to just stand here and watch?" one younger player snapped, his eyes wide with desperate energy.

Brick's glare hardened. "Yeah. Because if we don't, Eli's the one who loses."

The players stepped back, and the tension eased just enough to let calm thread through their ragged nerves.

The stretcher descended with quiet solemnity as hands lifted Eli gently. Brick fell into step beside the stretcher, his fingers curling around Eli's grip. A silent promise passed in the squeeze—a tether forged in fragile trust.

The journey off the field slowed to a crawl, the weight of every silent prayer trailing behind them as the crowd's cheers surged and faltered. Brick's eyes flicked once to his teammates, scanning their faces—young, tense, and wide-eyed with unspoken fears. His jaw clenched, a steel knot of resolve settling beneath his skin.

He turned to them then, the set of his expression carved from battle-ready stone. This was no time for fractures. Not now. Not when a fractured team needed steady hands and steady hearts.

A medic signaled. Time.

The stretcher wheels began to roll. Brick matched every step, then stopped—an anchor as Eli's hand tightened briefly around his fingers. The grip was weak, but the message was clear: Don't let go.

Brick squeezed once. Twice. Then released, watching as the tunnel doors swallowed Eli's figure beneath the stadium's bulk.

He turned slowly toward his team.

The silence hung thick. Charged.

The game waited.

So did the weight of leadership.

The locker room door thudded shut behind the last of the players filing in, turning the space into a furnace of heavy breaths and ragged adrenaline. Dark, sticky blood smeared across Brick's sleeve, clinging to the sweat-slick fabric—a raw reminder of the tackle that had nearly broken Eli. The iron scent mixed with sharp leather and damp linoleum. Around him, teammates dropped onto benches, their faces taut with a mixture of jitters and simmering frustration. The silence crackled more electrically than it did when empty.

Coach Hale rose from the front, his eyes flickering around the room as he opened his mouth. But Brick moved first. His boots scraped against the cracked tile—a sharp punctuation to the rising tension. He stepped off the bench, muscles coiling visibly beneath his bruised jersey as he took a deep breath. When he spoke, his voice was steady, low—like gravel meeting resolve.

"We don't win this with fists." He paused, letting the words settle. "We win it with our heads. And our hearts. For Eli."

His gaze swept the group like a spotlight, pinpointing nods and flickers of attention.

"Eli doesn't want to see us breaking down right now. He wants us focused, running hard, and playing smart." Brick stepped forward, the space between man and team narrowing. His tone sharpened, cutting through the charged air. "Every snap, every block, every tackle—that's for him. That's for each other. We carry him through this second half. Through every damn play."

The room stilled. Shadows shifted beneath the harsh fluorescent glare. Brick's words ricocheted—no longer just echoes of Coach Hale's lectures, but his own: tough, raw, fiercely loyal.

He didn't raise his voice; he didn't need to. The players leaned in, the weight of the moment folding around them like a second skin.

Natalie pressed her palm against the cool glass of the hallway window, the faint buzz of nearby voices muted behind the barrier. Her breath caught as she watched the tight set of Brick's jaw and the resolute tilt of his chin. A slow heat pooled behind her eyes, a swell of pride that stung sharper than she had expected.

Caleb, leaning back on a bench with his arms crossed, shifted. He exhaled the tightness from his chest, something settling within him. A rare softness flickered across his grin. "Man, you got this," he said, his voice low but steady, the weight of respect clear beneath the words.

DeShawn spat out a rough laugh, then nodded as if Brick's words had planted something steady beneath the chaos. "Brick's speaking facts," he added with a smirk, wrapping an arm around Caleb's shoulder.

The usual clatter of locker doors and hushed curses faded into a shared stillness: thick, charged.

Coach Hale nodded, stepping back. The weight of leadership gently passed as Brick claimed it. "That's the fire we need," he said.

Brick glanced toward the empty locker where Eli had sat, then back at the team. "We're done with the bullshit. Heads clear. Hearts full."

The room exhaled and then rose—a low, united yell that burst from chests like a battle cry. Fingers clapped hard against padded backs and shoulders. The sound grew from a murmur into a roar that shook the lockers.

A weathered hand landed on Brick's biceps—firm and warm. Nina's presence grounded him further. He nodded once, sharp and sure, before stepping back into the rhythm of strategy and focus.

"We know the plan for the second half," Brick said, his voice even but edged with urgency. "Stick to it. Protect each other. Show them what this team really is."

As movement hummed back to life, players shifted. Tape crunched, and boots hit the floor in slow, charged preparation. The locker room crackled with something new—not just adrenaline, but purpose.

Brick's eyes scanned their faces—grit tempered by loyalty. The rage that had once threatened to drown him now seemed braided with control and clarity. Something earned. Something hard-won. These players had doubted him before, when his aggression had threatened to crack him open. Now they watched him as if he were the steadiness they needed, the proof that control was stronger than fury.

A teammate clapped him hard on the shoulder. It was not a token gesture; it was a shared vow.

Brick swallowed, tugging off his bloodied sleeve. He wiped a flicker of crimson from his brow and met their gazes again—steady, real.

With his voice dropping even lower, he said, "Let's bring it home."

No promises were needed here. No fiery bluster. This was leadership pulled from the rawest parts of himself—earned, heavy, and unbreakable.

The air snaps sharply with tension as the defense charges back onto the turf. Brick's eyes skim the offensive line like a hawk spotting movement below. He plants himself just off the ball, his finger stabbing toward the formation. "Watch the sweep!" he barks, his voice gravelly but steady. Around him, bodies shift and pivot, teammates catching that single phrase like a spark thrown to dry grass. Brick's gaze locks onto Caleb near the edge, his fingers pointing at the gap that needs to be sealed. The kid responds without hesitation—a small nod that carries the weight of trust earned through brutal practice and harder moments. The play's rhythm snaps into sharper focus; discipline over chaos.

Sunlight slices through the stadium, burning a trail past the scaffolding above. Sweat beads on Brick's brow, stinging his eyelids before tracing itchy rivers down his hardened cheek. The sharp, earthy scent of grass and pine tar clings to the air, thick and familiar under his nose. Beneath his cleats, the turf yields just enough to remind him he's locked in, every muscle coiled and ready. Every breath is loud in his ears, but the hum of the crowd fades beneath the steel clatter of cleats hitting the earth. He feels the weight of the moment—less a burden than a challenge met head-on, a physical presence pressing in that sharpens rather than dulls his focus.

The snap cracks sharply. Brick explodes off the line, a coil spring released with purpose. He moves with calculated precision, a machine tempered by muscle and instinct. His shoulder hammers into the blocker's midsection, leverage perfect, feet planted with iron will. The guy doesn't budge an inch. Brick's cleats rasp against the turf as he shuffles, adjusting and finding the angle. He pivots, hooks a second blocker's knee, and flips the momentum. The runner stumbles sideways, swallowed by the swarm of defenders closing in.

Brick hits the turf hard but pops up instantly.

"Blue thirty-two, pick it up!" he growls, snapping the call to the line.

His voice cuts through the din like a blade. Each movement is calculated—there's no flash, no showboating—just the raw, relentless efficiency of a man waging war in measured strikes. The defense tightens, shifting like a living thing responding to Brick's command.

From the far sideline, Rhino's shadow lunges again, his jabs sharper and more personal now. His smirk twists as he tries to provoke, throwing an elbow just below the ribs. Brick ducks, barely sidestepping the cheap shot with balletic grace that belies the tension coiling beneath his skin. Instead of retaliating, Brick catches Rhino's momentum, twisting the man's arm and steering him off balance. Rhino stumbles, swallowing a harsh grunt, his eyes flashing with fury.

"Keep it clean," Brick snaps under his breath, glancing at the officials who hover nearby, their whistles tucked like swords ready to strike. Rhino clenches his jaw but can't throw the punch. Frustration snarls across the opponent's face; he has nothing to wrest from Brick's calm fortress.

Up in the press box, Victor Cross's eyes narrow behind thick glasses. His pen hovers impatiently, twitching for the spectacle he had counted on. Every twitch pulls tighter in his jaw as Brick methodically dismantles the chaos Victor craves: no explosion, no drama—just steel discipline. The realization twists in Victor's gut like a knife turning. The story he had prepared, the redemption arc shadowed by violence and volatility, slips away with each calculated movement below. Victor's fingers curl slightly, clenching the notes he had scribbled but unwilling to cross the line Brick refuses to offer.

On the sidelines, Natalie's gaze tracks Brick, binoculars pressed lightly against her face. Her breath catches behind her teeth; she presses her fingers harder against the lenses, the tight knot in her chest refusing to loosen. Emma and Nina lean in beside her, tension coiling between them as they share silent nods that speak volumes. This is the new Brick—unshackled from the past but still burning with purpose.

Brick gritted his teeth, muscles taut as he read the offense again—twice over, three times if it swayed his judgment. A second ago, the runner feinted right. Now the quarterback shifted left. "Blue fifty-one!" Brick shouted, snapping the change through the line. A ripple of movement followed his command, flowing like elements responding to a lightning strike.

The block broke just short. Brick lunged forward, sweeping the runner off balance with a textbook tackle that emphasized technique over fury. The hit echoed, a crisp slap of impact muffled briefly by the rising roar of the crowd. His boots scuffed the dirt as he rose, eyes scanning for the next threat, his voice already carving new orders in the thickening air.

"Blue sixty-four, hold the point! Reset!"

His voice hummed with authority and calm precision.

The quarter ticked toward its close. Brick crouched, signaling a substitution with a slow, deliberate hand raise. His breath came measured and controlled—no ragged edges to his calm. The team surged forward, feeding off the shift. The defense morphed into a well-oiled machine, shifting, tightening, coiling like a serpent about to strike.

On the sideline, Caleb caught Brick's gaze and offered a brief nod, the kind that carried unspoken respect. DeShawn exhaled a low whistle, cracking a smile that was all teeth and calm admiration.

The stadium lights flickered, casting long shadows as the third quarter bled into the next. Brick stood tall, the fulcrum holding the team steady. His voice cut through once more, clear and fatal.

"Keep the lane tight! Eyes up, hands ready. Let's end this quarter clean."

The defense moved as one under his leadership, every sinew coiled with purpose, every player reshaped by the smooth discipline Brick commanded—turning the tide, step by step, breath by breath.

###

The pileup unraveled with a sudden, jagged snap. Rhino's hand shot out like a viper, fingers clamping hard onto Brick's facemask. The plastic helmet groaned under the grip—sharp and cruel amidst the roar. Brick's pulse thundered in his ears, old fire sparking raw beneath his skin, ready to ignite like a match in a wind tunnel.

But the rage, hot and familiar, met a steel barrier inside him—a choice he had made a hundred times before, a rewiring of the man he used to be.

Instead of paving the way with punches, Brick clamped his large hand over Rhino's wrist, fingers crushing with deliberate calm. He twisted it down—slow, controlled, precise—and stepped back, palms raised.

Peace. Clear as language.

The officials converged like wolves on a scent. Flags fluttered—crisp and bright against the emerald field. The whistle pierced the chaos. Shrill. Final.

"Unnecessary roughness," the referee's voice cut through the charged air, delivering a harsh judgment that found Rhino's name. Brick watched as Rhino's face twisted in fury and disappointment; the man pointed toward the sidelines. Cameras flashed, capturing every scowl and shove as he was escorted off the field, ejected and silenced.

Around Brick, the locker room's brotherhood surged forward. Hands battered his pads with thudding applause, and voices rose in unison. "Brick! Brick! Brick!" The chant thrummed through the turf, an echo of respect. His teammates' breath mingled with the scent of sweat and turf dust, their eyes bright with the fire of battle and relief.

Brick didn't break into a grin. His jaw tensed, lips thinning as he scanned the crowd. Without a word, he stepped forward, pulling the nearest defenders into a tight huddle, their armor scraping together in a familiar rhythm.

"No distractions," he said, his voice low but unmistakable, cutting through the lingering haze. He locked eyes with each man. "Fight with our minds. Eyes sharp, hearts steady."

The stadium's stands shifted above, and Natalie's sharp whoop sliced through the clamor. Her hands clapped, loud and proud. Emma's laughter bubbled up like cool water, a bright contrast to the tension, and Nina's voice joined—a clear, ringing note that lifted the chant higher.

"BRICK! BRICK! BRICK!"

Their voices rippled like thunder, electrifying the sweat-slicked bodies poised for battle.

Brick nodded once, a brief tilt of his head. No swagger, no bravado—just a warrior ready. He stepped back, his voice tightening into sharp focus.

"Zone seven, flip left. Tight coverage on three. Let's keep the heat on 'em."

Pads clattered, and helmets shimmered under the floodlights. The team broke from the huddle with new purpose. The air tasted metallic and was taut with anticipation, every breath charged with the promise of a fight won without losing oneself.

Brick led the charge, his eyes sweeping the line, his heart steady beneath the bruising weight. The field awaited, a battleground illuminated by the ceaseless glare of stadium lights and the piercing eyes of thousands. But inside him, a different fire burned—a controlled blaze, steady and fierce, the strength of restraint made manifest.

The scoreboard's glow blinked a frame-by-frame warning: two minutes left. The lead thinned like smoke.

The huddle tightened around Brick—a coil of muscle and breath. His eyes flicked to Caleb, then to DeShawn. Both were jittery, their shoulders trembling with adrenaline. His gloved fingers jabbed the air, swift and sharp. Each movement was a wordless decree.

"Watch the sweep here." His voice cut low through the crowd's static hum. "Three rush. DeShawn, close the edge. Caleb, press tight on number eighty-seven. Reset on my call."

The play unfolds inside his head. There is no room for hesitation. Caleb's eyes clear, and he nods sharply.

DeShawn exhales, steady—a silent promise between comrades, nerves stretched taut. Brick's clipped commands land with surgical precision, slicing through the chaos that threatens to engulf them.

At the snap, Brick's stance is a tempest barely contained. He scans the offense's web like a reader puzzling over a sentence. His eyes narrow on the quarterback's subtle shuffles—shoulders tensing, fingers flexing over the ball.

The gap appears: a narrow alley between two linemen, an unlit path in a dark forest.

Desperation teaches boldness. The stunt Coach Hale drilled into them—the one Brick had held back from calling—surges forward now. Legs coil and spring. Muscles scream in sweet, controlled agony as he bursts through, a steel-hardened force displacing air and sense.

The quarterback pivots. It is too late.

Brick's outstretched arm grazes the QB's ribs, shoving him sideways into a frantic scramble. The ball escapes in a hurried spiral, floating like a wounded bird toward its receiver.

Caleb's eyes lock on the prize. His feet slide smoothly over the turf, every step a whisper of focused intent. Outstretched fingers meet the ball's ragged arc. Leather crackles against his palms—the pass stolen from the air.

The stadium erupts.

Cheers crash against concrete walls, heat and roar rising from thousands of voices. Jubilation spills like wildfire. The turnover is sealed—Brick's tackle moments before, a linchpin, an unyielding anchor in the storm.

Teammates flooded toward him, their voices rough and wild. Pads thundered against his chest, and helmets bobbed in a frantic dance of victory. Hands tugged him upward—the weight of sweat and triumph lifting him above the earth.

Chants rolled across the field: "BRICK! BRICK! BRICK!"

From the sideline, Coach Hale's voice disappeared beneath the chorus, but his eyes caught Brick's. The nod—subtle and deliberate—spoke volumes: recognition and respect forged in fire, earned like the blood and breath spent across relentless yards.

Brick sank to one knee on the turf's worn grass.

Breath came in ragged bursts, and his heart hammered an erratic rhythm beneath ribs tight with effort. The air tasted thick—salt, metal, and the smoky burn of exertion. The distant hum of the crowd electrified him, the roar of a conquered beast.

His fingers pressed into the cool earth, grounding him and anchoring his racing mind.

Eyes lifted slowly to the stadium's fleeting lights, catching flashes of fans waving. Faces blurred into a sea of hope and triumph.

The weight of the moment settled—a tidal pull beneath the storm. It was the moment he'd fought for: fragile victory, hard-won not just out there on the field but inside himself.

"Head and heart," Brick breathed—a quiet anchor beneath the roar, his breath steady as the crowd lifted in thunderous approval. He is more than the fury of the past, more than the scars. This—the calm before the next fight—is his redemption.

"Let's close this out," he muttered, his voice rough but certain.

From behind, Caleb's grin cut through the tension. "Man, you owned that last play."

DeShawn slapped Brick's back, laughter rattling his chest plate. "Did you catch that? They're already calling you a god or something. Don't go getting big-headed on me now."

Brick's chuckle was dry, edged with exhaustion. "I ain't no god. Just a man who knows when to hold his fire."

"Tomorrow, they'll be writing about how Brick brought down the house without throwing a single punch," Caleb said, shaking his head in disbelief.

"Maybe," Brick replied, his voice low, "or how the calmest storm breaks the nastiest tide."

The crowd's roar swelled again, a living beast carried on the breath of thousands. Brick pulled his helmet low. Weight and warmth settled over his skin, senses sharpening—the creak of cleats, the sharp tang of sweat, the faint pulse of adrenaline riding beneath like a whispered promise.

His teammates clustered close, breathing heavily. Voices rose and fell in a chaotic chorus of relief and hope. In this charge, Brick found a strange serenity—a fragile, fierce moment where the shadows of the past couldn't reach him.

He lifted his head, his eyes scanning the sea of faces: fans, coaches, friends, rivals—all thrown into the crucible of a single, sizzling instant.

This moment, sealed in breath, bone, and fire, stood between the past and the future.

Brick stayed low, his chest heaving. A warrior, bowed but unbroken, as the stadium thundered its wild verdict. The game was far from over, but this stand—his stand—had already spoken.

With distant eyes and tight lips, Brick nodded once, savoring the quiet storm beneath the triumph.

Victory spread like wildfire in the air—sharp, raw, and breathtaking.

And Brick was at its heart.

The turf shuddered beneath a roar. Pads and helmets clanged sharply in the electric air. Brick's teammates crashed into each other, their breaths ragged but victorious. The floodlights cast long shadows across the emerald field, sweat-slicked and gleaming. Cameras whirled, lenses snapping tight-focus shots of the chaos.

Nearby, Victor Cross crouched. His pen flicked across notebook pages with clinical precision, his face unreadable. But his eyes sharpened, recalibrating. Redemption, not scandal—his angle began to morph. For once, the story might feel less hostile.

From the sidelines, Natalie pushed through the crowded aisles. Her heels barely clicked in the cacophony as she raced toward the field's edge. The sharp scent of grass, sweat, and victory mingled with faint ozone from nearly depleted energy drinks. She caught Brick's eye across the distance—intense, weathered, and undeniably present.

Her smile flickered—small but electric. A silent vow. Pride, relief, and something softer lay hidden beneath. The world contracted into that moment between them.

Eli lay on a stretcher just beyond the boundary. His jaw clenched, muscles taut under the floodlights, but his eyes caught Brick's with a faint spark of defiance. Brick was there in an instant, weaving through the crowd with focused urgency. He knelt beside the stretcher, his fingertips grazing Eli's slick, sweat-soaked hand beneath the rail. Their grips locked.

"We've got you, man." Brick's voice dropped, rough from the field's grind. His eyes didn't waver. "You're holding us all up."

Eli's smile tightened with effort. Grateful. Wordless. Whole.

Natalie intercepted Victor as he attempted to push forward. Her presence was a low wall—calm and resolute. His eyebrows drew together, frustration flickering across his sharp features. He adjusted, pulling out a fresh page. His pen scratched anew, shifting gears seamlessly. The whispered undercurrent between them crackled—tense. Nate's cool authority met Victor's dogged persistence, both fighting for their version of the truth.

Coach Hale strode alongside the team, a tower of taut strength and measured calm. His voice wove through the postgame chaos like a steady drumbeat, directing the flow with practiced ease. Brick stepped into the circle of reporters, and rapid-fire questions pelted him like hail.

"Caleb and DeShawn—those guys made every tackle count today," Brick said. His eyes remained bright yet grounded. "It's a team win. Nobody is doing this alone."

A stadium drone hummed low overhead. Brick peppered in brief assessments, deflecting the spectacle and redirecting attention to the collective effort. The reporters pressed, but his controlled cadence undercut any hint of simmering fury from prior games. His words exuded quiet confidence—the calm eye in the storm.

Natalie slid back a step, clipboard in hand. She issued a signal to the media handlers with a sharp nod, already orchestrating the postgame narrative, her fingers poised to smooth over potential cracks. The tension sparking between her and Brick did not dissipate; it thickened—a current humming just beneath the surface.

Their eyes locked again, like the final plays in an unfinished game—a conversation held in silence, fierce and unspoken.

"Feels different today, huh?" Natalie murmured, her voice low. The crowd's distant roar served as a backdrop to their private charge.

Brick's gaze tightened. Respect and something more flickered unguarded for a heartbeat. "Yeah. Like I'm exactly where I'm supposed to be."

A faint, almost imperceptible smile cracked her usual composure. "Keep that feeling."

Around them, the stadium pulsed with life, voices rising. The tang of turf and sweat mingled with the city's distant hum. The night sky stretched vast and unyielding above, stars scattered like pinpricks through the darkness.

Victor scribbled again. The redemption story was inked in sharp strokes. Brick let the applause swell, each beat folding into the next like a slow wave breaking against the shore. This victory wasn't just for the crowd; it was a reclamation.

The silence between Brick and Natalie held weight as she stepped back. Her posture reclaimed its professional poise. The media swarm tightened, questions volleying faster than answers. But Brick basked in the moment's residue—the roaring crowd's echo filling his chest, a rhythm steady and real.

For all the noise and chaos, underneath it all, Brick stood still—a man remade by restraint, by trust, and by unspoken promises breathed into the postgame air.

The Final Drive

The air hums with tension inside the cavernous locker room. Stark fluorescent lights cast sharp shadows across rows of battered lockers. Brick's footsteps thud against the tiled floor as he paces beside the polished wooden bench, fingers tugging and kneading at the rough tape wrapped tightly around his wrists. The adhesive bites into his skin—a small, stinging reminder of the rawness beneath his grip.

Around him, teammates murmur low, habitual rituals threading through the space like an unseen current: fingers snapping, quiet chants, and the steady tap of cleats against concrete.

Coach Hale strides in, his imposing frame a calm pillar amid the swirling storm of nerves. His voice cuts through the hum, clear and commanding. As he moves, players straighten their backs, their eyes glinting with focus sharpened by the weight of expectation. When he pauses before Brick, those deep-set eyes lock onto his, steady and unflinching, searching for something unspoken.

A nod—subtle but firm—ripples across Brick's jaw; it is not just a gesture, but a challenge and a promise he isn't sure he is ready to keep. Yet the weight settles differently this time, steadier, like the first step out of a storm.

At the far end, Caleb twists his gloves between calloused fingers, a nervous tick he seldom sheds before a game. His breath comes quick, the fabric slipping beneath his thumbs as he tries to anchor himself. Nearby, DeShawn breaks the suffocating quiet with a grin that tilts sharply.

"So, Brick—counting the seconds until we demolish those guys? Or just tapping your wrists to keep from throwing fists?"

The words bounced off the walls. Some men cracked brief smiles, while others masked their annoyance behind stoic expressions.

Brick settled onto the cold bench, the slick leather briefly sticking to his sweat-darkened skin. His breath caught for a second, his chest tight, before he pressed his palms flat against the wood. The surface was smooth and grounding, as if it absorbed some of the fire smoldering in his chest. He focused on slow, steady inhales. Exhale. The rhythm that therapy had etched into his muscle memory pressed down his pulse and quieted the storm beneath his ribs.

His eyelids fluttered shut. The echo of roaring crowds muted beneath the darkness. When he exhaled, it felt like letting go of a weight he had carried for too long.

"Brick," Coach Hale's voice sliced through the quiet. "Keep this calm. Lead them."

Brick's fingers tightened around the edge of the bench. He nodded, more to himself than to anyone else, the motion anchoring him deeper into the moment.

Caleb shifted his weight, catching Brick's eye and offering a small, tentative smile. Brick responded with an almost imperceptible lift at the corner of his mouth—a crack in the armor that few ever saw.

DeShawn's voice cut in again, rough and teasing. "Are you always this straightforward?" Caleb shifted, his gloves twisting tighter in his hands. "Or are you just messing with us?"

DeShawn shrugged, his shoulders loose but his eyes sharp. "Gotta get some humor in this cage before it's kill or be killed."

The locker room smelled of sweat, leather mingling with the faint trace of liniment cream—a pungent reminder of bruised bodies and the battle ahead. That scent triggered something in Brick, a flash of memory: the sting of past injuries and the weight of near losses. It settled into his chest like an old wound. The distant murmur from the stadium seeped in from somewhere beyond the concrete walls, a metallic clang ringing out as the last equipment bags slammed shut.

Coach Hale's voice rose again—final and unyielding.

"Tonight's not just any game. It's a test. We hold the line—not just on the field, but here." His gaze swept the room, fire igniting behind his calm eyes. "You're warriors, but more than that—you're brothers. Brick, you set the tone. Lead them steady. Hold the line."

The team shifted like a living thing, rising together. Pads slapped against chests in practiced rhythm, a wave of sound that built and swelled. The men lined up, a force poised to storm into the brutal arena, chanting the team's battle cry.

Brick's legs straightened beneath him. A new, quiet power threaded through his stance. His shoulders squared, and his chest rose steadily, every inch a man forging control where before there had been wildfire.

He lifted the helmet, his fingers finding familiar scratches and worn edges. The padding pressed cold against his skin as he settled it over his head, muffling the distant roar of the stadium outside. From the corner of his eye, he caught Jaxon's glance—a flicker of approval, sharp and quick like a well-timed pass. No words passed between them; the unspoken accord was electric.

Brick stepped toward the tunnel, the collective pulse of the team thundering beneath the helmet, steady now, bound by more than just muscle and sweat. The roar of tens of thousands surged forward, a tidal wave of sound beckoning them into the impossible dance. This time, Brick walked into it not with volatile fire, but with the quiet flame of resolve burning deep inside.

Natalie settled into the stiff-backed chair of the media row, the crisp headset pressing against her ears, the wires humming faintly beneath layers of sound from the stadium below. Her fingers wrapped around the clipboard—a fortress of laminated crisis scripts, social media blurbs, and preseason notes inked in sharp, deliberate handwriting. The glow from the glass wall beside her revealed the vast green field below, patchworked with the golden slant of late afternoon light and the subtle scent of cut grass wafting upward, mingling with the distant hum of player warm-ups.

Around her, reporters shuffled uneasily, their eyes flickering toward the woman everyone knows is the team's public firewall. Some held notepads, while others had cameras half-raised; they carried the electric tension of impending kickoff and unspoken questions, their gazes darting between the field and Natalie like moths circling a flame.

Near the edge of the cluster, Victor Cross stood apart. His lean frame pressed casually against the railing, but his piercing eyes never wavered—the way they locked onto her made a chill crawl beneath Natalie's skin. He watched her the way a hawk eyes a fox: calculating, waiting for a single misstep.

A freelance cameraman edged closer, his voice low and intrusive. "Ms. Brooks, about Turner's suspension last season—do you really think the team can trust him to keep his cool tonight? The fans aren't exactly forgiving."

Natalie's jaw clenched just enough to remind her of the nerves beneath her calm surface. Her voice slipped out smooth and measured. "Look, our focus is on the whole team's performance tonight. Logan is committed to playing with discipline and heart, just like everyone else. We trust our players to hold each other accountable."

The cameraman leaned in, lowering his voice conspiratorially. "But public pressure is mounting. Aren't you concerned this won't be enough to prevent the narrative from spiraling?"

She offered a slight tilt of her chin—a gesture both polite and firm. "Our message is consistent: we're here to win as a team, both on and off the field. We'll address every concern with transparency and focus."

Her eyes flicked back to the notes. Her fingers traced a fresh line across the page where detailed rebuttals to the hardest-hitting potential questions were scribed. She added a brief margin note in abbreviated script, a quiet preparation against Victor's likely escalation: *Recall good behavior. Emphasize team growth. No distractions.*

Victor shifted his weight. His voice rippled through the background. "I'm looking forward to seeing if your narrative holds up once the cameras stop rolling."

Natalie didn't flinch. Instead, she allowed a measured inhale, the faint hum of the stadium's PA system filtering in—announcements, the distant clink of cleats against turf, and the chorus of warm-up chatter—sensory anchors amid the tension.

She stood and stretched for a moment. Her eyes drifted along the neat rows of empty press seats that caught the gleam of floodlight reflections yet to be switched on. She noted the optimal spot near field level where she would station herself postgame—a vantage point clear of the swirling press pack but close enough to maintain control of the narrative.

Pen in hand, she quickly marked the seat on the overhead diagram. Then, glancing at the clipboard's cover, she clipped a tiny, discreet sticky note: "Do not let Victor near Brick." It was a protective shield in paper form, a silent vow to guard the fragile edges of redemption that Brick was clawing toward.

Her breath caught as the locker room doors thundered open below. The team burst forth—a tidal wave of movement and energy. Helmets gleamed, and pads creaked. The sound of feet pounding the turf cut sharply and immediately through the air, mixing with the sharp cadence of coaching shouts. A low roar swelled from the gathered crowd, building into something alive and hungry.

For a moment, Natalie felt it—the weight of what came next pressing against her ribs. The pressure of spinning narratives, controlling the uncontrollable, and guarding people who didn't always want guarding. Her stomach tightened, and her fingers gripped the clipboard's edge.

Then she breathed—once, twice.

Her fist clenched, then unfolded with slow, deliberate grace. Eyes narrowing just a fraction, she locked onto the players' surge—her team. Any doubt was smothered beneath layers of measured control.

Breathing steadily, her heart a quiet drum beneath her ribs, Natalie readied herself to command the storm of words and spin that would follow.

The team's silhouettes blurred as they spilled onto the field, swallowed by the cavernous roar that rose, folding the stadium into a living beast hungry for victory.

Natalie watched—still, rooted. Every sense primed, every nerve taut like a drawn bowstring, ready to fire.

The narrative would be hers to wield tonight, and she would not let it slip.

The air hung thick with tension, the stadium's roar dulled beneath the pounding of leather-heavy cleats on artificial turf. Brick strides into the defensive huddle. The game clock ticks relentlessly—two minutes and twenty-two seconds. Barely ahead, the narrow margin sits heavy on every shoulder.

His eyes sweep the circle, landing first on Caleb. Sweat beads trace rivulets down the wide receiver's face; his chest heaves, each breath sharp and shallow. Nearby, DeShawn's hands twitch as they flex and crack, fingers stretched out like coiled springs ready to release. The bitter tang of turf dust lodges under Brick's nails, the sharp bite of cold metal from his helmet straps, and the salty sweat clinging to his skin—all of it mingles into a familiar cocktail of pregame grit. Inside this tight circle, the world narrows to the murmurs of men poised on the edge.

Brick's voice snaps over the chatter, low and clipped. "Left side moves. Caleb, eyes sharp. Cover tight." There's no room for doubt; his command slices through the tension like a blade. The call isn't new; it's drilled and rehearsed, but the urgency infuses it with a raw edge. His teammates exchange fleeting glances, and then their bodies respond—a choreography refined through sweat and battle.

Without missing a beat, Brick lifts his hand, fingers twisting into the signal Coach Hale has forced into muscle memory: a sharp down-and-left jab followed by two fingers bent like a compass needle pointing seaward. Caleb locks onto the sign instantly. His nod is just a flicker—a subtle promise that the message has landed and will be executed without hesitation.

DeShawn catches Brick's eye and slaps a firm, grounding hand against the defensive lineman's shoulder pad. It's a silent pact, rooted in trust that runs deeper than words. The two of them had clashed a season ago when Brick's volatility threatened to splinter the line. Now, DeShawn's grip conveys something different: *I know who you're becoming. I'm with you.* It vibrates beneath the bright floodlights—the shared weight of expectation that matters.

The huddle tightens. Brick's eyes narrow with focus. His chest rises and falls in a measured rhythm, slower than the pounding of his heartbeat but steady and deliberate. The scar above his right brow twitches like a muscle fighting to stay loose. He sucks in a breath, steadying the tight coil of nerves beneath his skin. The weight in the pit of his stomach eases a fraction—discipline silencing the chaos inside.

"Lock it in," he says, his voice firmer now, with an edge that brooks no argument.

The circle shifts, men sliding into place with fluid precision. Brick steps out last, shouldering into his stance. The turf is rough and familiar beneath his cleats. The air vibrates with anticipation—a silent drumbeat in the charged stillness before the storm of contact and fury. The play change is etched into muscle memory now, a brittle thread connecting everyone in this moment.

The defense aligns around him. Tension coils like drawn bows. Brick's jaw clenches. Around him, breaths fog in the cool evening air, mingling with the distant clang of metal from the stands—faint but persistent. The coarse fabric of his jersey chafes against his skin.

The world is quiet enough here that every whisper, every subtle adjustment, echoes with significance. His mind sharpens; the din of the crowd fades, replaced by a singular clarity: this stand, this moment—everything hinges on what happens next. He's learning to channel the old fury into something sharper—not blind rage, but focused precision. A skill forged through countless moments like this, where anger becomes discipline, and volatility transforms into control.

From the corner of his eye, Brick catches Caleb's steady gaze and DeShawn's taut readiness. No fear. No doubt. Just unity—a fractured team forged into a blade.

"On three," Brick's voice resounds, nearly a growl. "One... two... three... shark."

Metallic clanks underscore the chant as plates of armor collide, cleats dig deep, and the line surges forward, the huddle's last chords still humming in Brick's veins.

The defense bends and flexes under the floodlights, each man a blade honed for control, restraint, and victory. Brick moves into place, shoulders squared, muscles coiled—ready to meet the oncoming storm with something sharper than raw fury: focus.

Here, with the game slipping into its final, decisive moments, he is not a man ruled by anger but a leader carved from it, tempered and resolute. The play change is locked in. The challenge is accepted. The battle resumes.

The snap cracked through the thickening evening air—a precise cut in the frenzy.

The ball zipped forward on a perfect arc, spiraling toward the receiver slipping past Brick's peripheral vision. Seven yards. The grass hummed beneath the cleats as Brick's eyes narrowed. His jaw clenched.

"Shift left! DeShawn, run coverage—now!"

The words hissed between his teeth, sharp and urgent. His hand jabbed toward the sideline, fingers rigid with command. Caleb caught the flicker of Brick's gaze from his slot position and locked in without hesitation.

Caleb's fingers squeezed his worn leather gloves, slick with sweat and turf dust. He crouched low, his eyes glued to his assigned receiver. There was no room for error now. The weight of the moment pressed down—familiar, drilling-ground pressure that his body knew by heart, even if his mind wanted to second-guess.

DeShawn pivoted, his muscles fluid and taut. He slid toward the run path that Brick had marked moments ago. The defense rippled, bending like a living organism under Brick's control.

A hand signal cut through the tension: the slash of his forearm across his chest, the palm flick. Each movement was etched into muscle memory by Coach Hale's endless drills. As if the air itself answered, teammates adjusted, shifted their weight, and repositioned like cogs meshing in a machine built for this.

The offense readied itself. The receiver sprinted deeper, his eyes alive with daylight.

Seconds stretched taut. The receiver fell out of bounds. The crowd's energy dipped, suspended in suspense. Brick could taste the cut grass mixed with sweat and smell the metallic edge of the moment hanging thick in the stadium air.

He exhaled slowly.

His chest rose and fell beneath damp fabric.

His pulse remained steady beneath the storm.

"Hold the line. Don't let them breathe."

The roar swelled again. It was second down. The ball snapped into a blur, and Brick's world narrowed to cleats pounding and breath rasping. The runner charged forward—a living force barreling through the mass of bodies.

Brick's blocker surged, forearms locked around his like a vise. But Brick's hands were callused and sure. He slid them down, prying with slow, brutal patience. Iron and blood filled his mouth. Damp earth. Sweat. The world tightened to bone and will.

Then he broke free, muscle snapping like drawn wire.

He lunged squarely into the gap.

The collision rocked the field, impact detonating through his chest—cold fire igniting as his thighs coiled and snapped. The runner's knees buckled. The crowd's collective inhale crashed into a frustrated groan as the gain halted inches shy of the marker.

Pulverized grass beneath them marked the struggle.

Brick rose, breath ragged, eyes alight.

The sideline erupted, sticks tapping helmets, voices lifting. Teammates pounded backs and shoulders—a chorus of raw energy and unspoken respect.

DeShawn grinned, slapping Brick's broad shoulder pads. "Did you catch that? We're rolling now."

Brick snorted low. "Focus. Keep your head clear."

The smirk that crossed his face tasted of battle and brotherhood.

He stepped toward the huddle, the game's rhythm pulsing through his veins. Caleb joined the gathering mass, his cadence calm but charged. The weight of the moment pressed but didn't break them. Each breath shared and every glance cast spoke in a language forged in pressure and trust.

"Third down is coming. Let's pin them back," Brick growled, his hand carving the air with precise signals.

DeShawn kept his voice low, the tension thick. "Do you really think we'll stop this drive cleanly?"

"Confidence is a weapon," Brick answered, cutting through the doubt. "And right now, I'm loaded."

Caleb's tight smile returned.

As they locked in, the sideline noise receded. Only the raw hum of focus remained—only shared will. The earth beneath them felt alive, humming with possibility. The defense reset, their breaths syncing like the deep pulse of the night itself.

The moment lingered—fragile and fierce.

Eyes aflame with the fight ahead.

The stadium's breath catches. A collective pulse is held tight as the opponent lines up for third down.

Time compresses—measured in heartbeats and the sharp slap of cleats against turf rather than in seconds. Logan "Brick" Turner's eyes sharpen, his muscles coiled like springs beneath his sweat-blackened jersey.

The quarterback waits, a flash of doubt crossing his face. Then he fakes the handoff.

A heartbeat later, he heaves the ball deep downfield, slicing through the electric dusk.

Brick pivots. His body moves on instinct honed through seasons of bone-cracking hits and impossible plays. The secondary tightens—Caleb Monroe's lean form shifts at the receiver's hip, his pulse thudding in the air charged by roaring fans and the jagged crackle of stadium lights.

Brick and the others compress space, their motions synchronous, hearts syncing with the chill tension coiling through the stands.

Time fractures. Caleb leaps, flesh and sinew soaring amidst the roar.

Fingers brush the spinning oblong missile. The ball's skin kisses his hands but slips through, tumbling incomplete.

The margin between victory and chaos shrinks to breathless whispers.

Brick crops the moment, his voice slicing through the roar as the offense scrambles back to the line. "This is ours. Stay locked."

No more slipping. Not tonight.

His tone is dry steel forged in countless battles, confidence wrapping every syllable. The huddle snaps tight, a sanctuary of heat and focus under the bleeding floodlights. He casts swift glances: Caleb's sharp nod, DeShawn's pounding fist, bodies forming an unyielding wall ready to swallow all pressure whole.

"These splits change," Brick directs, tracing a tactical map with his fingers. "Caleb, shadow two-step—don't lose sight. DeShawn, scrape the edge—no lanes open. Secondary, tighten zones. No gifts."

Caleb's jaw tightens, vigilance sparking behind his eyes. DeShawn flexes his fingers, his grin a silent promise of fire and grit.

Across the line, Brick's command hums with unspoken urgency, the raw heartbeat of a defense clinging to the thinnest thread of a lead.

From the sideline, Natalie Brooks watches, her fists curled tight and knuckles paling. Beneath her calm mask, nerves prickled like static under her skin.

Her breath is measured but taut, a slow current of controlled tension running beneath her poised exterior. The crisp rustle of her notes scratches faintly as she adjusts, her eyes flicking from the gathered reporters to the press box, noting the skeptics rising from their seats, cameras poised and pens ready to seize any crack.

She catches the subtle shift in the atmosphere—the murmurs of doubt playing at the edges of the roaring crowd. But tonight, this defense, this fragile fortress of men, holds fast.

Natalie's gaze hardens. They need this narrative; Brick needs this redemption. She needs him to prove that redemption is still possible—for him, and perhaps for herself.

Her mind sharpens, running through every prepared line and every crisis phrase rehearsed until exhaustion. The chill of the evening air tastes faintly metallic—almost like the spark before a storm breaks. Her fingers wrap tighter around her clipboard.

The offense snaps again. The world narrows to green turf under blazing lights. The hum of thousands fades beneath the scream of the moment.

The defense stiffens, eyes locked on the target.

Brick's presence swells, a tidal force anchoring murmuring nerves. His voice cuts through the charged silence as the defense breaks the huddle. "Listen up—we breathe together now. One stop. Just one."

DeShawn shifts, sliding into position like a shadow molding itself around the edge of light. Caleb mirrors the receiver's twitch, muscles taut, eyes flickering with controlled fire.

The countdown thins. The clock bleeds forward like a slow wound.

Around them, the team's breathing deepens, synchronized with the roar that tickles the edges of fractured nerves. Coaches lean forward, hands on hips, voices low but sharp.

Natalie's pulse beats against the taut fabric of her calm—every second a thread unraveling toward the unknown.

A defiant chant pulses faintly from the distant stands, a mantra folded beneath the clamor. Brick's words still thrum in the bones of every man: "Stay locked. This is ours."

The defense settles into formation—a wall sculpted by sweat and resolve.

Brick's eyes blaze, the fire tempered now by a quiet steel—the kind shaped only by pain, guilt, and the unyielding will to rise from the ashes. He has carried the weight of his failures into this moment. Tonight, they will answer for something.

They lock in. Ready.

The game clock ticks mercilessly. Every second is a sacrament in this high-stakes rite.

The silence before the storm is palpable. Tangy. Like ozone before lightning strikes.

And they wait.

The clock's harsh glow reads 1:01. Fourth and short. The stadium hums with low electric tension as the offense lines up, huddling tight against the roaring sea of blue and silver fans. Brick's eyes zero in on the quarterback, fingers twitching at the tape wrapped around his wrists. Every muscle sharpens, alert to the flicker of movement, the subtle twitch of a shoulder, the tell in a stance that screams the play before it unfolds.

He catches the shift in the opponent's formation—an alignment that whispers danger, something their game plans never anticipated. A stunt surfaces in his mind: dangerous, complex, and never tested in live moments like this. He knows the risk, but it could turn the tide if executed correctly. The air hangs thick around him, charged and heavy with expectation.

With a voice raw and fierce, Brick barks the change to his front seven. "Shift right, loop left. Roll on my count."

His teammates snap instantly to the signal, feet skidding on the turf as DeShawn glides over with smooth precision, sliding into the gap Brick carved out.

The stadium noise dims to distant thunder in his ears. Brick crouches—coiled like a spring wound tight. The snap cracks sharp and sudden. He's off.

He explodes off the line, a blur of power and grace—a kinetic force spiraling with deliberate fury. Fluid and brutal, his barrel roll spins past surprised blockers with the agility of a predator. Arms reach, desperate to contain him, but his momentum tears through their defenses. He barrels forward, closing the space between himself and the quarterback in a heartbeat, breath sharp against the cool night air.

The quarterback pivots, his eyes wild, seeking salvation. Brick's presence forces him sideways, scrambling for footing and a passing lane that tightens with every heartbeat. In years past, his rage would have cost him the moment; tonight, there is calm calculation behind the aggression. On the sidelines, the team holds its breath, the collective pulse of the stadium syncing with that desperate dash.

Downfield, Caleb mirrors the chaos, his eyes locked on the receiver streaking toward the end zone. The receiver stretches for the pass, his hand outstretched like a lifeline. Caleb matches every inch, his limbs coiling and leaping with the clarity of purpose honed by months of quiet training and whispered encouragement from Coach Hale.

His dive is a symphony of power and timing—his fingertips brushing the spiraling football with a white-knuckled tip. The ball dances in fragile suspension before dropping. Incomplete.

The stadium detonates. An explosion of sound rips through the night, fans erupting like a storm unleashed. The crowd surges, a wave crashing against the confines of the arena, chanting Brick's name with unbridled joy and reverence.

His knees fold beneath him. Grass presses cool against his palms. Each breath feels heavy and slow—no fire this time, just a raw, aching relief that settles into his bones. The taste of adrenaline still burns sharp on his tongue, but beneath it lies something softer, almost foreign: gratitude. Fragile and fierce.

Teammates rush forward, hands gripping his shoulders, voices loud with raw celebration. DeShawn slaps a heavy hand on his back, breath ragged but voice steady. "Hell yeah, that's our man," he huffs, grinning widely.

Caleb folds Brick into a fierce hug, their breaths mingling in a charged, unspoken exchange. Coach Hale's steps crunch across the turf, slow and deliberate, eyes narrowing with approval. The nod he offers Brick speaks louder than any cheer—respect forged not from flawless plays but from hard-won grit and unwavering heart.

Brick's fingers loosen their grip on the turf, trembling almost imperceptibly as the crowd's thunder settles like a rumble through his veins. The roar swells again, echoing off the distant cityscape and steel stands, carrying with it the weight of redemption and promise.

The roar cascades from the stands like a tidal wave, crashing over Brick's skin with the raw heat of a battle won.

His teammates explode around him—hands grabbing, clapping, and hauling him off the ground before he even fully registers the shift. Caleb's arms wrap tightly around his waist, pulling him into a grip brimming with fierce relief. The boy's breath comes ragged against Brick's neck, hot and wild.

"That's our man!" DeShawn's voice cuts through the noise, heavy with pride. His palm slaps firmly across Brick's back—a thunderclap of approval that echoes the pounding in Brick's chest.

The grass beneath them is damp with sweat and clinging dust. The musk of turf and adrenaline swirls thick in the floodlights' glare.

Coach Hale's long strides close the distance. Gravel crunches underfoot. His broad frame seems to grow as he nears. His eyes fix on Brick, steady and unyielding under the brim of his cap.

The nod Hale offers isn't just an acknowledgment; it's a passing of trust, a silent decree. Brick catches it like a lifeline. His jaw tightens. Years of struggle press down—and then lift—in an instant. This nod means everything. It signifies that Coach finally sees him as the player he has fought to become, not the liability he once was.

The jumbotron pulses to life above—a giant eye capturing every flicker across Brick's face. Grim determination melts into stunned triumph. The instant replay rolls: that stunt call barked to his line, that near-mad dash that crushed the quarterback's rhythm. Social feeds explode in real time. Fingers tap out celebrations from thousands of miles away. Each glowing screen becomes a beacon of Brick's redemption, shining through the storm. This moment isn't just his anymore; it belongs to everyone watching, everyone who doubted him and now can't look away.

The crowd surges together. Thousands of souls tethered by hope and electric suspense rise in a synchronized wave. The stadium quakes with their chant.

"Brick! Brick! Brick!"

His name thunders through the air like a battering ram. It echoes from the metal and concrete bones of the coliseum. Faces blur in the floodlight haze. Fists pump. Scarves wave like flags of war.

Brick's breath hitches, his ribs rising and falling like restless waves beneath a tightening chest—weighted not just by weariness, but by a fragile hope trembling just beneath the surface. Astonishment flickers in his eyes, a storm of disbelief swirling beneath the surface calm he has fought so hard to claim.

Hands reach for him—countless and insistent. Fellow warriors surround him in a circle etched by sweat and shared struggle. Staff and players press forward, their voices braiding together—congratulations, relief, welcome. Each word is a brick laid in softer foundations; each pat on his shoulder is a chisel cutting away old scars.

The helmet slips from Brick's head and thuds softly onto the grass.

Cool night air brushes across his damp skin, carrying the faint, bitter tang of grass, sweat, and triumph. He stands rooted in the center of this tempest of sound and motion, unguarded in a way that is only possible here, in this tower of strength forged through pain and persistence.

Caleb's grip tightens for a fleeting moment, his voice threading low against the rising chaos.

"You nailed it, man. Hell, we all did—because you held us up."

DeShawn grins wider, shaking his head as they all lock eyes in this rare sanctuary forged from battlefield victories.

"I didn't think we'd see it, Brick. But damn. You're the heart tonight."

For a split second, the helmet cracks the silence—a hard emblem of battles past and those still to come.

Brick tilts his head back, eyes closed against the unwieldy surge of feeling. His muscles tremble with the tremors of release. Around him, laughter and cheers ripple like storm currents. But beneath it all, threads of unspoken truths and fragile hopes weave through the gathering.

A deep breath swells in the night air, his spirit caught between the relentless pressure that built this moment and the quiet promise embedded in every resounding cheer. This is more than just a win; it's a fragile reclaiming of something thought lost in the shadows: control, respect, redemption.

And for those few endless heartbeats flooding the field, Brick lets the noise envelop him—close, fierce, and warm. A fire tempered not by rage, but by the steady burn of solidarity.

"Ready for the next one?" Caleb asks softly, his voice threading through the hum.

Brick opens his eyes. A flicker of a smile ghosts across his lips. The battle isn't over, but tonight, in this charged circle of friends and fighters, he has found the quiet epicenter of his own power.

"Let's keep moving," Brick says, his voice low but resolute. "We've got a season to win."

Around him, the crowd's chorus throbs again. The rhythm of hope echoes beneath the endless floodlights as the teammates close in tighter. Here, amid sweat, grass, and roaring victory, Brick stands no longer alone. He stands at the heart of a tempest that refuses to break.

Victor Cross weaves through the press. His sharp eyes glint from beneath the brim of his hat, hunting for an opening. The cluster tightens around Brick. Victor's elbow nudges forward, already shaping the question on his tongue—something with teeth, meant to cut beneath the surface.

But Natalie steps in first.

Her smile doesn't waver as she angles herself between Victor and his prey. "Victor, thanks for waiting." Her voice is smooth and even, the kind that acknowledges conflict without breaking stride. "Let's save the tough ones for later, yeah? The team deserves space to breathe right now."

He flicks a glance her way. Challenge flickers across his face before something like measured retreat settles in. She steers his arm aside, her grip light but firm—redirecting restless energy the way one would guide a current. Victor's jaw tightens. He doesn't argue. Not yet.

Natalie turned back to the assembled chaos. Her clipboard was tucked under one arm, and her headset was snug over her ears. The stadium hummed beneath the floodlights—a low, thrumming pulse accompanied by the faint smell of cut grass and sweat, along with the chatter of reporters jockeying for angles.

Her gaze sharpened as she assessed the cluster of players.

Brick stood at the center, still wearing the battle grime that clung to his jersey like a second skin. He looked solid and unmoved. But beneath that stillness, Natalie caught the slight tension in his shoulders—the exhaustion of holding so much together, game after game, conversation after conversation. The weight of being the one people wanted a piece of.

Jaxon occupied the space to Brick's right, his shoulders back and confidence radiating. Caleb lingered close, his fingers working the edge of his glove with nervous energy.

"Alright, team." Natalie's voice barely carried above the crowd noise, but it cut through. They leaned in. "Leadership. Team unity. We lead with strength, not solo heroes. Keep the message tight."

Jaxon nodded. He stepped forward and pulled the reporters in with words that sounded effortless, his voice warm but measured—the kind of controlled charisma that came from rallying eighteen other men on a field every Sunday.

"This win belongs to every one of us," he said, his eyes scanning the cameras. "Brick laid the foundation. But without Caleb's quick reads and DeShawn's grit, none of this happens."

Caleb swallowed hard, his throat knotted with nerves. When a reporter's question swung toward him, he leaned forward slightly, his words spilling out soft but raw.

"Brick's the heart," he said, his voice thick with something between reverence and humility. "He's been holding us together all season. Those late nights, the way he shows up—everyone sees it."

Brick listened, his jaw clenched and unclenched. When the microphone finally swung toward him, he stepped forward.

Calm settled over him, like armor worn thin but steady.

"We win as a unit," he said, his voice low and clear. "Caleb's the eyes in the backfield. DeShawn's grit on every run—that's what flips momentum. Those are the plays that count."

He paused and scanned the hungry faces.

"This isn't about me. It's about commitment and discipline, from the line to the rookies. We built that together."

Cameras clicked and flashed. The man who had once burned with unchecked rage now spoke with the cool precision of someone forged in fire and restraint.

Questions rippled onward. Natalie stepped ahead, intercepting anything that drifted into territory too personal or too raw. Her gestures were subtle yet firm. She stood between Brick and the chaos of scrutiny like a moat—gently but unyieldingly redirecting.

Reporters pressed in. Some were gentle, while others sharpened their focus, hunting for a crack. She deflected each one, her eyes locking briefly with Victor's across the crowd. His glare flickered, and frustration etched itself into the tightening of his lips. He held back.

"Let's remember this," Natalie said, her voice cutting across the din. "Tonight's victory is a result of effort and sportsmanship. The story stays here—on the group's grit and unity."

She raised a hand and signaled the close.

"Thanks, everyone. The team appreciates your respect tonight. Let's keep the focus where it belongs—on what they built together."

Her voice carried across the field, crisp and unyielding. The flood-lights caught her steady gaze as Victor stepped back. The moment slipped from his grasp.

The media swarm began to loosen, and players relaxed into the afterglow. Natalie exhaled quietly, already scheming the next moves in this delicate dance between control and truth.

The buzz of celebration thinned as Natalie slipped through the maze of cables and scattered equipment near the tunnel edge. Flood-lights cast long shadows across the damp concrete—fingers stretching, grasping. Beneath the sharp scent of cut grass and sweat, ozone from the cooling field machinery hung faintly in the air.

She found him there—Brick—seated on a scuffed maintenance crate, his helmet resting at his feet like a loyal sentinel. His jersey clung to him, sodden with sweat and smeared with streaks of green from the turf. The jagged scar above his brow caught the light, tracing battles both won and still raging beneath the surface—a map of grind earned through seasons of grueling games, each one stripping away more of who he thought he was.

He doesn't look up when she approaches. His shoulders tense any-way, bracing himself.

Natalie crouches slowly in front of him, careful not to crowd his space. Her voice cuts through the fading roar—soft but steady. "That's the narrative I want them to remember."

Brick's gaze flickers to her, and his eyes narrow. Something unspo-ken settles in their depths.

She holds up the folder from the media session, her thumb brush-ing the edge where she pinned a note earlier. "I controlled the questions. Steered the story." She taps the damp fabric over his heart. "You showed them what you're really made of."

A heavy pause hangs in the air, thick with unsaid words.

Then, from his throat, a quiet rasp escapes: "Thanks. Not just for the spin." The corner of his mouth quivers briefly, betraying an emotion he doesn't name. "For... seeing the change."

Natalie's hand moves without hesitation, reaching across to cover his own, which rests on the crate. His skin is warm, rough from hours of grind and grit, with lines worn deep by pain and resolve. He doesn't withdraw. Instead, his fingers twitch, curling slightly around hers in a silent pact.

"The weight's still there, huh?" she says gently, her voice dipping low.

Brick inhales shallowly, his usual fire dimmed but not quenched. "It's like this," he begins, his voice cracking. "Every step forward... I feel it clawing back. The past I thought I left behind. It's as if no matter what I do, that shadow is going to stretch over me forever."

He's lived with this weight for so long that it has become part of his skeleton—the fear that one mistake erases everything, that redemption is just a word people use when they haven't seen the real damage yet.

She nods, her eyes fixed on the subtle tremor in his jaw, the way his knuckles whiten against the crate's rough wood. "People change. Not because the past disappears, but because we learn to hold it differently."

He scoffs, a bitter edge to the sound. "Easy for you to say. You don't carry the mess, the broken ones, the ones who almost never get a second chance."

Natalie's gaze lifts, steady and unwavering. "I don't carry your past, but I do carry belief in who you are now."

For a heartbeat, Brick's defiance falters. Something raw and unguarded takes its place. His voice lowers further. "I'm tired of fighting to prove I'm not the man they think I am. You think this"—he gestures vaguely toward the distant hum of the stadium settling into night—"this game, this win, changes that?"

She squeezes his hand softly, grounding them both. "It's a start. Your story—our story—it's still being written. And I'll be here every damn step, making sure it's told right."

The cavernous tunnel muffles the lingering cheers. Now, only distant rumbles remain. It's as if the world shrinks to the narrow space between them.

Natalie shifts closer. The rough scrape of cracked concrete underfoot grounds the moment in stark reality. The faint aroma of leather and grass mingles with the subtle scent of her lavender hand lotion—a quiet reminder of the everyday beneath the storm.

Brick's eyes catch hers. The storm behind them is momentarily stilled, replaced by a fragile clarity that makes his shoulders sag, tension draining like air from a punctured tire. The armor worn for so long feels lighter, less like a cage.

Neither rushes to fill the quiet that settles between them. An unspoken weight hangs there—battles won and those still ahead. The night's pulse thrums hazily beyond the tunnel mouth, a soft glow promising redemption, hard-won and still unfolding.

He shifts slightly, the hard edge of exhaustion mingling with relief. His fingers tighten around hers, anchoring himself to something solid. Natalie's thumb traces lazy circles on his skin, a steady beacon amid the shadows.

From somewhere beyond, faint echoes rise and fade, the last remnants of celebration bleeding into the steady rhythm of cooling machinery. The stadium breathes around them—vast, indifferent. But here, just off the field, near the hushed sanctuary of the tunnel, they exist in a fragile bubble, suspended between past mistakes and future hope.

Brick's voice breaks the stillness, quieter than before but resolute. "Maybe... this time, it's different."

Natalie meets him halfway, a small, knowing smile playing at her lips. "It is."

Their hands remain locked in that fleeting clasp—silent, steady, unyielding. The night wraps its dark velvet around the edges of the stadium. Beyond the tunnel, the championship lights spill outward, pulsating softly like a heartbeat shared and promised.

They sit, shadows entwined. The cacophony recedes, and a gentle, hopeful quiet swells in its place.

###

The locker room hums with restless energy. Sweat and liniment hang thick in the air—sharp, acrid, and clinging. Caleb leans against a locker, tugging at his gloves. His breath comes unevenly, and his shoulders rise and fall like slow waves.

He's come a long way. Once, he had flinched at attention; now, he just trembles.

Emma steps in—calm and steady. Her eyes hold quiet pride as she pulls him into a brief hug without hesitation.

"Get ready, kid," she murmurs, her voice low but teasing. "Tonight's gonna put you right under the damn spotlight."

Caleb's smile flickers—delicate and uncertain. Nerves mingle with a spark of triumph. His fingers tremble as they settle at his sides. "Guess I better learn how to look like I belong up there."

Emma chuckles. The sound bounces off metal and concrete. "You've earned it. Don't let them rattle you."

He nods. His jaw tightens, then relaxes. Around them, celebration swells—voices rising, laughter sharp and bright. But Caleb lingers in the quiet space between the chaos and the strange stillness of new expectations pressing in.

Not far off, DeShawn's booming laughter cuts through the noise. A cluster of reporters huddles at the sideline edge, leaning in. His voice carries the weight of inside knowledge, playful and sly.

"So the big guy's all soft now, huh?" DeShawn drawls. He shoots a glance toward Natalie—sharp enough to slice through the jocularity. His eyes flash with the hint of a secret, something simmering beneath the bravado.

A reporter chuckles, stepping closer. "Really? You're saying Brick's changed?"

"Turned into a damn marshmallow overnight." DeShawn smirks, tilting his head. "But don't get comfortable. That backbone's still buried in there somewhere. You'll see."

Natalie stands a few feet away. She catches the look. Her jaw tightens for a fraction of a second. Something flickers across her eyes—warning, maybe resolve—but her smile remains steady, carefully measured.

"That's the story we want," she says crisply. "Brick's growth. It's the season's headline."

Beneath the surface chatter, tension plays out in glances and clipped words—a silent game.

High above the field, the press box breathes with pale light and humming machinery. Victor Cross slides through the narrow door, notebook in hand. His face tightens with concentration.

He has built his reputation on finding what others miss, on the contradictions beneath the shine. This story—Brick's redemption arc—feels too clean, too convenient. Victor learned long ago that when narratives feel perfect, something is always rotting underneath.

The stale scent of recycled air mingles with cold metal. Below, the crowd's distant thrum pulses like a heartbeat in the building's veins.

He flips through pages of scribbled notes, his eyes sharp, searching for cracks in the polished story. Each line he writes binds the threads tighter: angles of past controversies, subtle contradictions, whispers from unnamed sources tucked between facts like landmines.

His fingers tap on the table's edge—nervous, deliberate. He pauses, then scrawls another note in the margin. A small spark of anticipation lights the corners of his eyes.

Whatever celebration unfolds below, he is already drafting the next headline, the next challenge.

His gaze drifts to the window overlooking the floodlit field. The team's triumph rises like a wave breaking on distant shores, but Victor's eyes carry a shadow beneath the glow. He is already charting the course that might undo this moment.

Back near the locker room, Emma glances toward the field and catches Caleb's eye. He offers a shy nod, still wrapped in the tension between pride and apprehension. Voices rise and fall around them, laughter mingling with quickened breaths. Fresh grass and adrenaline swirl in the air.

DeShawn's laughter rings out again, louder. It cuts through the murmurs like whiskey—warm, sharp, and charged with meaning.

"Tell me something," a reporter calls out, curiosity edging their voice. "What's really going on with Natalie and Brick? You're hinting at something bigger."

DeShawn grins and tilts his head conspiratorially. "Oh, you know how it goes. Fire meets ice. Sparks fly. But don't expect me to spill all the beans just yet."

Natalie steps closer, her presence falling like a cool breeze over heated embers. "Focus on the team," she says, her voice firm but not unkind. "That's the narrative that matters tonight."

DeShawn's eyes flicker in acknowledgment, and a silent truce passes between them beneath the surface of the game.

In the press box, Victor taps furiously at his pen. His notebook is filled with ink and intent. The stark fluorescent lights hum overhead as he leans into the story. Each word becomes a tactical move in a larger game. His expression tightens; there's no room for compromise here.

The stadium's roar ebbs and flows below, a tide of celebration washing through steel and concrete corridors. Cheers echo, and drinks are raised. However, Victor's retreat from the field leaves behind something cold and quiet—a whisper that beneath the victory lies a thread of reckoning waiting to unravel.

The night crackles with triumph and tension, the air thick with promise and the unspoken knowledge that some battles are fought long after the final whistle blows..

Aftermath

Brick wakes with a dull ache thudding behind his eyes, curled awkwardly on the couch as if he had fallen asleep mid-fight. Morning light stains the edges of the curtains, pale and hesitant, as if unsure whether to invade the quiet sanctuary of his messy apartment. He cracks his fingers. The familiar ache in his knuckles pulses—a stubborn reminder that another day has begun.

His palm brushes past the worn fabric of the throw pillow and curls tightly around his phone. A cascade of notifications flashes across the screen: red dots from news apps, alerts from social feeds. Blue banners shout out headlines—championship glory, the team's triumphant night—but one claws its way in: Victor Cross has dropped a new exposé. The city's media pulse thrums under the weight of scrutiny as the glow from the screen paints Brick's face a harsh blue.

His thumb hesitates, then taps the article.

The words crawl into his consciousness with slow venom. Brick's suspension. The fight from last season—a blur until Cross etches it sharply: the name, the date, the fallout in bullet points. Therapy sessions framed through a lens smeared with suspicion, as if healing itself demands public skepticism. Cross's voice sneers between the lines, questioning progress and implying a lurking relapse behind the veneer of redemption.

He knows what it cost him: six months of his life, gone. The other guy's face—Matteson—swollen and bleeding. The locker room silence afterward. The contract negotiations that nearly fell through. All of it waits in these paragraphs to be weaponized.

The metallic taste floods his mouth: cold and bitter.

He scrolls further. The article's social life ignites—threads sprawling beneath the main story flicker with voices. "Redemption story of the year," one fan praises, their words filled with cautious hope. Another reposts with biting ridicule, spitting venom about "can't escape the past." Old criticisms resurface like ghosts, calls for sanctions, and doubts about his temperament. The sharp stings of condemnation and the hesitant warmth of support tangle in a cruel dance.

His fingers are clenched, knuckles white.

His chest tightens; breaths are shallow and trembling. The screen flickers to a clip—the final defensive play from last night's game. He watches himself, muscles coiled and unleashed, every move precise and measured. The roar of the crowd is muted, replaced by the steady pounding in his ears. His heart wrenches. Pride and dread twist together, impossible to separate.

Should he reach out to Natalie? Draft a response? Sound controlled and resolute, or let the frustration bleed through his words? Message her? Yeah, right. What would he even say? "Hey, my past is back. Again." No thanks.

His thumb hovers over her name, then pulls away.

A tension coils in his gut, the familiar war between fight and retreat sparking beneath his skin.

Voices murmur from the street below, distant but insistent—a city waking, oblivious to the storm gathering in this room. The scent of cold coffee from an abandoned cup mingles with the faint trace of sweat and leather from the night before. Brick exhales sharply, pushing the phone away.

The screen clicks, faces down against the battered wood of the coffee table. The cold surface grounds him, offering nothing.

He shifts and drags a rough hand through his thick hair. His gaze drifts through the wide window. Above the city's soft hum, the early haze cloaks skyscrapers in muted grays, their glass facades ghostly and untouchable. In the daylight, they seem quieter, less imposing, but no less indifferent.

The watchful eyes he feels don't belong to strangers anymore. They are baked into the walls of this city, into every headline, every frame of footage. Every second he tries to rebuild, someone is watching for the crack, waiting for him to break again.

Silence presses in, broken only by distant horns and the stirrings of morning life beneath the pale light.

He doesn't speak. He doesn't move.

The future still hangs, fragile and unresolved, beyond the muted skyline.

The sliding glass doors sighed shut behind Natalie as she stepped into the PR office. Eucalyptus and stale coffee hung in the air—more soothing than the chaos already unfolding elsewhere. Morning light filtered through floor-to-ceiling windows, casting sharp patterns across the sleek conference table where Nina sat, brows knit, scanning a tablet. The hum of muted screens and the low murmur of distant voices created a quiet tension threaded through it all.

Nina looked up, her voice steady but edged with urgency. "Here are the main points from Cross's latest. He leads with the suspension, drags up that altercation from two years back, and then slaps on the therapy like it's some kind of warning flag." She scrolled down. "He calls Brick's 'comeback' a gamble at best and highlights the possibility of relapse, questioning whether this is real change or just temporary damage control."

Victor Cross had always favored the blade over the scalpel—sensationalism dressed as journalism. Natalie had learned that the hard way three years ago when his piece on another client had nearly derailed a career. This was personal now, and Cross knew it.

Natalie slid her chair closer, her jaw tightening.

Her finger hovered over the tablet, tracing jagged lines of text. The stylus danced over phrases like "volatile history," "public patience waning," and "team's gamble on redemption." Each word landed like a calculated jab, meant to crack her carefully built armor.

"This piece pushes fear rather than facts," she murmured, cold logic slicing through the room's stillness.

Nina tapped entries into her tablet, her eyes flicking upward. "I've already flagged the interview clips where Brick openly addressed his anger management issues, along with transcripts from the wellness staff noting his consistent progress."

Natalie nodded sharply. "Good. Pull every document that provides context for his journey—anything showing accountability, therapy milestones, and team-led initiatives that contradict this narrative." She tapped keys, opening folders stamped with official seals and careful signatures. "We need indisputable facts, not spin."

The corner office suddenly thrummed with methodical energy. Their voices remained low but charged.

Natalie leaned forward, her fingers racing across the keyboard to draft the statement that would shift the battlefield. Every word was carefully chosen, with metaphors stripped away for clarity and strength.

"The team stands firmly behind Logan Turner's commitment to growth and accountability," she typed, then rewrote the line twice. The final version balanced resolve with measured optimism. The cursor blinked on the screen, ready to carry a message of redemption and resolve.

A click summoned the conference call. Marcus Hale's unmistakable drawl answered—calm and authoritative.

"Morning, Natalie. What's the game plan?"

"Emergency press conference," she replied, her eyes flicking between the statement draft and the schedule. "We need Jaxon to prepare a brief teammate testimony—something personal about Brick's leadership. Emma's on board for support if questions turn technical. We will emphasize accountability, team values, and real progress—not sensationalism."

Coach Hale's gruff chuckle rumbled through the speaker. "Solid move. Keep it tight and honest. Nobody likes a cover-up."

"I'll map out potential questions and responses," Natalie said, mentally replaying the barbed attacks Victor Cross was sure to launch. "Control the narrative before it spirals."

Minutes later, the statement gleamed with cold polish. Natalie's finger hovered over the "send" button. Her heart thudded—part adrenaline, part dread. She exhaled and clicked.

The statement zipped through internal channels, landing instantly in inboxes and calendars. A digital alert pinged, and the press conference time was locked in place.

She stood abruptly, stretching her legs after hours bent over the keyboard's glare. She turned to Nina without looking back. "Assemble those teammate statements. We need voices backing what the stats and reports already prove."

Nina gave a curt nod, already gathering files. "On it," she said, her fingers flying over her tablet as she moved.

Natalie turned to the expansive windows. The city's early hum cast long reflections on the glass. Somewhere beneath the distant traffic and faint footsteps, a battle was underway—not just in headlines, but in hearts and minds. The war for Brick's future had shifted to this polished tower high above the gridiron. Every move was calculated, like chess.

Light spilled wider across the office as schedules filled. Phones pinged relentlessly. The clock edged toward midday—the crucible.

Outside, the stadium waited in silence, an empty coliseum poised to explode with flashing cameras and urgent questions.

Inside, Natalie squared her shoulders and drew a slow breath. The media war was only just beginning. For the first time that morning, the tremors of uncertainty were leveling into something sharper and clearer—a controlled fire the team was ready to face head-on.

She glanced at Nina, who was already moving through the organized chaos. Her lips twitched at the corners, just enough to crack the room's tension. She leaned back, fingers steepled, the rush of small victories warming her chest amid the morning's weight.

"Nina, make those statements cut clean," Natalie said, her voice tight. "Facts first—no theatrics."

Nina kept pace, her fingers still flying. "Got it. Precision over passion."

Natalie settled back behind the desk, her fingertips resting lightly on the glass. Her eyes were sharp, and her mind relentless. The remote hum of servers and distant newsroom chatter seeped through the walls—a constant reminder that every sentence would be scrutinized and every pause weaponized.

The storm outside roared, but inside, steel was being forged—words shaped into armor.

Before the feed launched and the world tuned in, Natalie's voice barely left her lips, steady and sure:

"We've got this."

The fluorescent lights hummed overhead as Natalie stepped up to the podium. The room fell silent—sterile white walls, rigid rows of journalists clutching notebooks and cameras—all crystallizing into that sharp, brittle quiet that precedes a storm. She breathed in the scent of polished wood and stale coffee, anchoring herself in the familiar. Her navy blazer fit like armor, tailored and precise. When she lifted her gaze across the crowd, her eyes cut through the noise with steady resolve.

"Good afternoon." Her voice was even, firm enough to hold the room without demanding attention. "We're here to address narratives that threaten to distract from the remarkable season our team just completed. Our commitment is unwavering: growth, accountability, and a relentless pursuit of excellence—on the field and off." She paused, allowing the words to settle. "This isn't about past mistakes; it's about the standards we uphold today."

The shift was immediate. Cameras began their muted flashing, and heads leaned forward, caught by her composed authority as the story pivoted—away from shadows and toward transformation.

Nina threaded her way through the dense sea of reporters, her arms laden with clipboards and printed statements. Papers rustled softly. Whispered thanks followed her as she distributed the vetted testimonials—each one a carefully sculpted testament to Brick's evolution.

Behind Natalie, Jaxon moved into position. His height gave him an effortless presence. Heat flushed his skin from the day's intensity, but his eyes remained sharp and clear beneath a furrowed brow. He leaned into the microphone, his voice steady with conviction.

"Brick isn't just some defensive lineman who flipped the script this season." His cadence was measured and intimate—a teammate's truth rather than a prepared statement. "He's the guy who held us up when it counted. He held the line during that final drive when everything hung in the balance. I've seen his leadership. It's not just the tackles—it's the locker room. It's him." He paused and straightened slightly. "That's the Logan Turner we know this year."

Murmurs rippled through the crowd. Approval mingled with genuine recognition.

Then a hand shot up. Victor Cross rose with calculated sharpness etched into every line of his face, his brow drawn tight as his voice cut through the composed atmosphere like a blade. "Ms. Brooks, given Brick's history and his recent acknowledgment of therapy, how can you assure the public that his mental health challenges aren't a liability on the field or a risk to team culture?"

A flash of tightness crossed Natalie's jaw. Her fingers curled briefly around the edge of the podium before she squared her shoulders and met Cross's gaze without blinking. When she spoke, her tone remained measured but unyielding.

"Our organization has implemented rigorous accountability and support measures at every level. Therapy isn't a sign of weakness; it's critical for maintaining peak performance and resilience." She shifted her weight slightly, commanding the space. "Brick and our team engage with in-house programs designed specifically to support players' mental health, alongside professional standards for rehabilitation and discipline. We stand behind evidence-based approaches, not stigmas."

Her eyes scanned the room as reporters absorbed the pivot. The air pulsed with reassessment.

Cross pressed harder, his voice edged with challenge. "But doesn't this history suggest instability? Could this jeopardize future commitments?"

Natalie's next strike was measured but unyielding. A pause. Long enough to feel deliberate. "I'd remind this room that past articles have sometimes relied on selective, out-of-context quotes to cast doubt without merit." Her voice lowered for impact. "We need to ask ourselves—does such coverage serve the public interest, or does it feed a narrative sustained by vendetta?" Another pause. "Our focus should remain on facts, on growth, and on supporting those who choose progress over perpetuating stigma."

Whispers swelled as cameras recorded every syllable. Reporters exchanged glances, some nodding subtly. Behind the lenses, phones buzzed, and fingertips scrolled to capture soundbites already rippling across social feeds.

The digital tide began to turn. Clips of Natalie's words spread online, and hashtags questioning Cross's credibility trended. Voices emerged—not just defending Brick but critiquing sensationalism itself. The conference's impact extended far beyond these walls.

Natalie surveyed the shifting energy. She drew the room back in with a closing statement that resonated beneath the buzz of cameras.

"This is a story of what happens when someone chooses growth over avoidance, when a team chooses support over abandonment." Her voice softened, no longer demanding but inviting—a quiet challenge for belief. "That's what matters."

She stepped away from the podium as flashes erupted. Phones vibrated against tables, and reporters picked apart every moment, their voices swelling around her. The room, once taut with anticipation, now pulsed with a new narrative—one of resilience, leadership, and the quiet power of unwavering conviction.

The narrow corridor behind the press room smelled faintly of recycled air and stale coffee. Beyond the thin walls, distant murmurs and clicking cameras drifted through like ghosts of the storm that had not yet passed. Natalie stepped carefully in her sneakers—heels abandoned hours ago—beside Nina, whose steady footsteps echoed with quiet confidence in the dim light. Ahead, a lean man in a tailored suit waited. His dark eyes scanned the glossy walls, absorbing the tension that clung to the air like humidity before rain.

The league's media oversight representative has been summoned to sift through the dirt Victor Cross pitched like stones in his latest exposé. His department polices ethical standards in sports journalism, serving as a gatekeeper tasked with preserving league reputations through rigorous reviews of contested coverage. Past controversies involving Cross's selective reporting have made the league wary. They take these complaints seriously now.

Natalie lays a slim but weighty binder on the conference table. The pages fan open like evidence against a history rewritten with malice: time-stamped interviews, original transcripts of press appearances, and video clips exposing selective editing, along with marked pages showing Cross's twisted quote mining.

Nina watches the representative's face closely. His fingers skim the pages like a warning, as if daring the truth to slip away. She recognizes the shift in his expression—the slight narrowing of his eyes and the careful way he turns each sheet.

"I've flagged several instances here," the representative murmurs, his voice low but firm. "Quotes taken out of context, timeline discrepancies, and at least two interviews altered in headline summaries. Your annotations are thorough."

Natalie meets his gaze, her eyes sharp beneath the dim overhead glow. "Victor's angle thrives on distortion. We wanted to provide unfiltered sources so the league can see the full picture."

Nina's jaw tightened. *This isn't just spin; it's a slow swing at everything Brick has tried to build.* She leaned forward slightly. "He's weaponizing Brick's past, framing rehabilitation as weakness. The intent is clear—damage control disguised as journalism."

The representative nodded, flipping through the packets with deliberate care. "This requires a formal review. We'll need to verify these documents and interview your witnesses. If misconduct is proven, it could affect Cross's standing and future access to league events."

Relief nudged at Natalie's ribs, lightening the tight knot she had carried since dawn. Her eyes flicked to Nina's, catching the faint rise of an eyebrow and a quick, satisfied smile shared in silence. They had delivered something solid—something that might actually matter.

But when Natalie pulled out her phone, her thumb hovered over the messaging app. There were no new texts from Brick. The absence hummed louder than she had expected. She stowed the device and inhaled deeply, taking in the sterile air mixed with a trace of her own coffee breath.

"I'll step outside for a moment," she said quietly, straightening her shoulders.

Nina nodded, folding her arms, her eyes fixed on the stack of papers. The weight of battles fought on invisible fronts settled over them—neither triumphant nor defeated, but determined.

The league representative gathers the documents with meticulous care, sliding the binder into a leather satchel. "We'll follow up with both of you soon. Expect formal notices within the week."

"Thank you," Natalie replies, her voice steady but edged with something urgent that she can't quite name.

The representative's footsteps fade toward the stairwell. The door clicks softly behind him. Outside, the distant shouts and footsteps of game day recede like a storm moving inland. Here, in this quiet battlefront, they have moved something. Shifted something.

Natalie leans against the edge of the table, her eyes closing for just a moment. The adrenaline drains slowly, replaced by something more fragile. Something that feels like determination but tastes like waiting. She doesn't yet know how Brick is holding up—whether the walls he has built around his past are cracking under public scrutiny—but she knows their fight is far from over.

Nina breaks the silence with a wry smile. "We've moved the scales a little, haven't we?"

Natalie quirks a half-smile, blinking away the tension in her jaw. "More than a little."

The air holds the faint hum of shifting power, a murmur of quiet resistance blooming in the shadows. Together, they step out into the corridor, their footsteps soft but unyielding. The afternoon sun spills pale light through distant windows, casting long lines that point toward the door. Toward whatever comes next.

Here, backstage behind the flashbulbs and headlines, a line is drawn. The institutional machine has been nudged, perhaps unsettled, by two women armed not with loud defiance but with sharp intellect and unyielding resolve.

They stand shoulder to shoulder in the quiet, waiting for the next move, acutely aware that beyond these walls, the story still breathes and shifts. Their work has only just begun.

The locker room yawned empty. Its cavernous silence pressed down, broken only by the persistent hum of fluorescent lights overhead. Brick sat alone on the cold metal bench, the hard surface biting into his thighs. His fingers curled loosely between his knees.

His eyes settled on the scuffed leather of his cleats—worn and cracked, like the narrative the media wanted to rewrite for him.

From somewhere beyond the concrete walls, faint echoes drifted in: the murmur of reporters, the rustle of equipment, and the distant swell of voices crowding the stadium. The noise felt like a tide he couldn't escape, pressing in with its relentlessness.

His thumb dragged along the jagged scar arching above his right eyebrow—a souvenir from that moment, the one that had nearly ended everything. Four years ago, a bad hit during practice resulted in a concussion, stitches, and the kind of silence that follows when a career hangs by a thread. Now, every time he touched it, he remembered the rehab, the doubt, and the whispers that maybe he was done. The skin there ached slightly, tender beneath his calloused fingertips.

Thoughts swarmed. The media painted him as a "charity case," a cautionary tale thrown across headlines like a spectator's jeer. Victor Cross's latest hit piece was already weaving shadows over what should have been the light of victory. The piece called it a "comeback story," but the subtext was clear: *When will he break again?*

A tightness knotted in Brick's chest. His thumb lingered on the scar, now more raw than he remembered—exposed like the worn leather of his cleats. He imagined the whispers flowing through the stands and social feeds: *Wasn't he suspended last season? How long before he blows up again? Therapy? That's just an excuse.*

The locker room's stale air pressed against him—sweat and cedarwood mingling with antiseptic from yesterday's cleaning. Heavy. Suffocating. As if the walls themselves knew what he was afraid to admit: that one wrong move, one relapse, one bad article could unravel everything he had fought to rebuild.

His breath came shallow. His jaw clenched. What would happen if he couldn't hold it together? What would happen when the cameras caught him on a bad day? The fear coiled beneath his ribs, a living thing with teeth.

The slow scrape of the door against the linoleum cut through the silence.

Jaxon strode in, his breath steady and his eyes bright with the kind of energy that Brick envied at that moment. He crossed to Brick swiftly, a hand landing solidly on his shoulder—the brief warmth serving as a tether to something solid.

"You didn't just win that game, Brick," Jaxon said, his voice low but firm. "Nah, you flipped the whole season on its head."

Brick didn't look up, but the words landed—a weight settled deep in his ribs. Jaxon didn't linger; he turned and slipped back toward the hallway, the shuffle of his sneakers fading into the murmur beyond.

Left alone again, the solitude pressed in, squeezing the last remnants of pride from his chest. Brick brought his palms to his face, rubbing over tight skin and feeling the scrape of his short, rough beard. His breath caught, and a knot tightened in his throat. He swallowed hard.

He ran through potential responses—calm, controlled, defiant—knowing the media's knives would be sharpened and waiting. But beneath that calculated composure, something else stirred: a rising panic. The sense that no matter what he said, no matter how well he performed, the narrative was already written. They wanted the cautionary tale. They wanted the fall. Give them the triumph, and they'd spend the next week hunting for cracks.

What do you say when they ask if you're broken?

What do you say when they want your apology for things you can't undo?

He reached toward the handle of his locker. The cool metal bit into his fingers as he pulled it open, revealing the neatly arranged contents inside: a battered football, his old roll of tape, and a faded photograph peeking from beneath a folded practice jersey—his family at his first college game, before any of this.

He closed the door. A soft thud signaled finality.

He sank back onto the bench, his muscles slackening. Every nerve was raw with expectancy. Beyond the door, muffled noise pulsed with life. But here—in this temporary sanctuary—time seemed to slow.

The hollow electronics buzzed outside. Filtered sunlight from the high windows cast long, sterile beams across the tile. This room held echoes of battle and brotherhood. But in the quiet now, it felt like a cold gallery of mistakes and uncertain hope.

His jaw flexed, wrestling with the fragility beneath the surface.

He waited.

He waited for Natalie to find him, to bring steadiness to this storm of doubt. He waited for something—a line, a sign—that would keep him from slipping.

The weight of victory and the shadow of yesterday's headline collided inside him, the two forces threatening to tear him in half.

But he stayed seated, anchored by the silence and the anticipation of what was to come.

\#\#\#

The locker room hung in a tangible silence, shadows pooling beneath harsh fluorescent lights that hummed faintly overhead. Brick sat on the metal bench, his broad shoulders hunched as if carrying the entire weight of the day. The pale blue locker doors stood sentinel around him, their cold steel a stark contrast to the lingering heat from last night's game still pulsing in his muscles.

Natalie steps inside, the faint click of her heels muffled by the thick air. She spots him instantly, staring at the scuffed cleats resting on a cracked tile floor. She closes the gap with calm ease, palms open and voice steady.

"I handled Cross at the conference," she says quietly, settling beside him. "The league is reviewing his sources and methods. It won't be easy for him to spin this; they're looking into journalistic misconduct."

The weight of managing that fallout settles across her shoulders, a responsibility that extends far beyond the facts she has stated. She carries it silently, her composure a mask for the pressure underneath.

Brick shifts, the tension in his body like a coiled wire ready to snap. His lips twitch, attempting a joke that falters halfway.

"So... this is what it's come to? A full-on PR battle royale?"

He exhales, his voice breaking as the bravado folds. "The truth is, Nat... I'm terrified. No matter what I do, my past is going to tattoo itself on every headline, like I'm stuck in the reruns of my worst screw-ups." His fingers brush the scar above his brow, seeking something—courage, maybe, or forgiveness from himself. "People don't forget, do they? They don't let me forget."

Natalie's eyes soften, the tension around them easing, but her steady stare never wavers. She doesn't speak right away; she just lets him unload into the hollow room. The faint metallic scent of lockers mingles with musky sweat. There is also something antiseptic—clean, sterile, yet somehow cold. The quiet feels vast, swallowing the weight of his unspoken fears.

Finally, she leans in just enough to be heard without breaking the fragile calm. "What I saw on that field—what I saw in you during the final drive..." Her voice drops, thoughtful. "You weren't just playing defense. You were leading, keeping your cool when everything could have exploded. The discipline you showed, the focus—you chose to control your rage and protect the team. And it worked. You carried the entire defense on those last snaps."

His fingers twitch near the scar, tracing an invisible line over old wounds. His eyes glisten with a mixture of relief and vulnerability. He swallows hard, his gaze fixed downward as if the confession might slip away if he looks up. "Sometimes I wonder if someone will ever look at the whole of me, not flinch, not shrink back at the storm beneath the surface."

There's a tremor in his voice when he finally confesses, "Maybe... maybe with you, I could have that. Be seen without the blade waiting to cut."

Natalie's hand finds his, cool and sure against his rough skin. She entwines her fingers with his, grounding the moment. Her voice is quiet but unwavering. "I believe it. I've seen the truth in how you play and how you carry yourself after the game when no one's watching. You've changed, Brick, not because you have to—but because you want to."

His breath catches. The world between them shrinks. No words rush to fill the space.

Their bodies shift instinctively. Brick pulls Natalie into a close, tender hug—no heat, no tension, just quiet strength and the relief of being known.

The distant echo of footsteps fades as the midday light casts long, soft shadows across their intertwined hands. They remain there, side by side on the cold bench, a fragile sanctuary amid the storm outside. Each heartbeat is a quiet testament to trust finally taking root, a whispered truce between past and present.

Natalie's breath warms Brick's temple as they lean into each other, fingers locked like anchors. Outside, headlines scream and chatter rises—inside, a fragile peace blooms.

No promises are made, no future is guaranteed. Only the here and now, two sides of a battle-worn soul resting, momentarily whole.

###

The sharp buzz vibrates against Brick's thigh. His phone slides across the cold metal bench. He snags it with a rough tug, eyes narrowing at the screen.

"Congrats on how you handled today. Natalie's fire took the heat off you—well done. Keep that up."

The owner's message sits there, crisp and unmistakably sincere. Brick's jaw tightens. He swipes to dismiss it. The words linger anyway, pulsing steadily in his mind like a second heartbeat.

His thumb hovered over the keyboard. For a long moment, he stared at the response forming in his head—something sharp, something that pushed back. Then his fingers clenched into a fist. Not yet.

On both screens, a cascade of headlines spilled down: "Team Unites Behind Defensive Titan," "Leadership Off Field Shines Amid Pressure," and "Skepticism Grows Over Victor Cross's Tactics." The venom from this morning's coverage had thinned, diluted by the team's unyielding front and Natalie's cool command. The tide was shifting. Not gone, just shifting.

The locker room air stirred imperceptibly—as if the walls themselves exhaled relief. Brick's shoulders, tense all morning, finally slackened an inch. The weight that had pressed down since dawn loosened its grip, just enough to allow him to breathe.

He sat on the bench, scrolling through the threads. The smell of damp sweat and worn leather wrapped around him. Natalie's phone lit up beside his. She scrolled too, silently. Their shoulders nearly touched—close enough to catch the heat radiating through the fabric, far enough to maintain the boundary between them.

The stadium hummed beyond the vents, distant and muffled.

Natalie tapped her screen, highlighting shifts in the conversation: support threading through doubt. Her gaze flicked toward Brick's profile, tracing the set of his jaw and the stubborn line of his mouth. No flinching. No retreat.

"You ever get used to this?" Brick's voice broke the quiet, low and rough, like gravel shifting underfoot.

She glanced sideways, a quick smile tugging at one corner of her mouth. "Never. But I learned how to ride it." She paused, her fingers stilling on her screen. "You learn to see the shapes the storm makes, where the light leaks through."

He let out a short, dry laugh and shook his head.

"It's the scars you don't see that teach the best lessons," she said, her tone steady but soft, the unspoken weight hanging between them like something solid.

Their eyes met for just a slice of seconds. Something unguarded flickered across his face before she looked back down at the screen.

Brick knew what came next: the follow-ups Nikki was already lining up, Coach Hale and Emma holding the team steady in their own quiet ways. He knew what he had to do—show up every damn day: to practice, to therapy, to the hard work of rewriting his story.

"I'm not going anywhere," he murmured, his fingers tightening on the phone like it was a lifeline.

Natalie's hand slid over, her fingers curling around his with a gentle certainty that grounded them both.

"Good."

They sat like that for another moment. The stadium's noise ebbed and flowed beyond the walls. Inside this concrete space, in this small pocket of time, something had shifted. Not victory. Not absolution. Just a tentative foothold on solid ground after weeks of sliding backward.

Brick shifted, pushing off the bench, muscles coiling as he stood. Natalie rose with him, shoulders squared in tandem, steps measured and resolute.

The locker room felt colder now, but it wasn't oppressive. It felt like the air before a storm breaks—heavy with potential, electric with what comes next.

They walked into the waiting expanse beyond the lockers, side by side. The future was uncertain, the narratives still spinning, still hungry. But in this moment, the air hummed with something steady: not rage. Not relief.

Resolve.

Choosing Each Other

B rick's apartment door thuds softly behind them. The sharp clatter swallows into the thick walls. Outside, the city's pulse dims to a distant hum—sirens and honking filtered through glass and shadow.

Muted street lamps cast patterns across the hardwood. Dust motes swirl lazily in the fading light. Nothing like the morning's chaos. Those sharp voices. Flashing cameras. The heavy thrum of reputations hanging by threads. That feels miles away now.

Here, it's quieter. Too quiet.

Natalie drops her bag on the couch. The leather yields with a hollow thud. She sinks down, her heels tapping briefly against the polished wood. Her shoulders are taut. The tight line of her jaw softens just enough to betray the exhaustion beneath her usual calm.

She thinks of the cameras and the hostile questions. The way she'd stood beside Brick without flinching, even as doubt gnawed at her own armor.

Across the room, Brick stands frozen near the entryway. His hands curl around a battered team cap on the coffee table—deep blue fabric fraying at the brim. A mute witness to every fight he's fought today and the ones still to come.

His fingers brush the embroidered logo, tracing the raised stitching like a mantra. Like an anchor.

The room carries the scent of late-night cold brew: sharp and bitter, with faint ozone from the rain that fell hours before. Brick's eyes do not meet Natalie's; they flicker with something raw and unguarded, as if the weight of the day has finally cracked the armor he drapes so carefully around himself.

A silence stretches between them—taut and charged. It is not emptiness; it is more like the sharp intake of breath before a plunge.

Natalie watches him and feels the strain in his frame, the flicker of pain in his dark gaze. She wants to fill the quiet with words, but she knows this moment is sacred. The storm outside has passed, but the internal thunder is only gathering.

Neither moves; neither speaks.

Brick shifts, the cap heavy in his hands. His body leans forward, hesitating—anchored by storms he has kept locked away.

Is he ready to settle? To sit down? To let the burden show beneath the surface?

Around him, the muted city breathes through the windows. The apartment bathes in gentle darkness, both refuge and reckoning.

Natalie breaks the silence first, her voice steady but soft, threading through the tension without breaking it.

"You handled yourself well today."

Brick's head shakes slowly, his voice rough as gravel dragged across stone.

"That's not what I want to fix right now."

He steps away from the couch, the cap clutched like a lifeline. His movements are restless, pacing just enough to crack the quiet, but not enough to escape the gravity pulling at him.

The tension coils in the room, thickening like smoke, as if the air itself waits for him to breach the dam.

He settles onto the edge of the couch, leaving a deliberate space between them. His posture stiffens, fists clenched against his knees, his body bracing for something heavy.

Natalie leans forward slightly, matching his guarded stance and giving no sign of retreat.

The unspoken words lodge between them, dull and insistent.

Brick's gaze falls to his hands, fingers twitching with nervous energy. He inhales deeply, preparing himself.

"I'm not good at this," he says, his jaw tightening. "Talking. Feeling this much."

He swallows; each word costs him something.

The cap slips through his fingers, resting forgotten on the couch between them.

His eyes narrow as memory claws forward.

"That incident," he begins haltingly, "it's like a ghost. It won't let me forget. I walk into every room dragging the echo of someone's disappointment—mine most of all."

A pause, heavy and aching.

The apartment seems to hold its breath with him.

Past mistakes. Glares. Whispers. Each one is a fresh burn on his skin.

He looks up briefly. His throat clenches, his voice faltering like a worn wire snapping under strain.

"Discipline. Public wins. They feel hollow if no one sees the mess behind these walls." He swallows hard. "I want you to stay. Not because I need fixing, but because I want to be chosen for exactly who I am."

His voice fractures on the last words. Terror threads through it—the fear that she might recoil from the imperfect whole he dares to show.

He drops his head, fingers creasing the cap's edge, waiting—raw and bare.

Natalie's eyes soften. Understanding flickers across her face. She shifts closer, her hand trembling as it finds his arm. Light contact, charged and deliberate.

"What if," she breathes, "we both take the chance that we're enough for each other?"

The room hums with shared risk. Her fingers warm against his cold skin. Two fractured shields lowered to breathe in a fragile truce of trust.

The city's distant chatter fades further into the night, creating a quiet sanctuary where fears can finally be named.

Brick remains still, the cap held close—a silent promise, an unspoken question hanging in the air as the apartment settles around them, bathed in the quiet after the storm.

Natalie settles onto the couch with practiced ease. Her bag drops to the floor—leather thudding against the rug. Punctuation to the quiet.

"You handled yourself well today."

The words hang safe. Professional. Like a lifeline tossed after the chaos of flashing cameras and barbed questions. Her eyes search Brick's face, hoping this might bridge whatever chasm lies between them.

Brick's jaw tightens. His fingers twist the brim of the team cap, knuckles whitening. No grin appears. Instead, a sharp shake of his head cuts through the silence.

"That's not what I want to talk about." His voice is rough and gravelly, catching in the dim light.

He stands. The worn wooden floor creaks under his weight. The cap cradles in his hands like a fragile shield as he paces in restless strides—a predator in a cage. His shoulders are heavy, fatigue etched deep.

Natalie leans forward slightly, her gaze steady and undeterred. She waits. The silence thickens like smoke, each breath measured.

Brick stops. His eyes flick to the faded gray couch where she sits. He lowers himself onto the edge, deliberately leaving space between them—a gulf of unsaid words and mounting nerves. His hands clutch the cap as if it anchors him, but his fingers betray him. They fidget, tracing invisible patterns on the fabric.

The apartment holds its breath.

Shadows pool in the corners, thickening like ink. Outside, the city hums—a dull pulse behind cracked blinds. Cold takeout lingers faintly in the air, mingling with the sharp tang of sweat on his skin. The harsh buzz of fluorescent lights filters through thick curtains.

Every muscle in Brick's back coils tight. He searches his hands as if looking for something lost long ago. The silence presses in from all sides, tightening like a noose around his chest.

Natalie's breath catches—a quick hitch she fights to steady. Her fingers tighten briefly around the couch's armrest, but her posture remains calm and grounded. She knows this moment is the thin edge of a fragile razor—ready to split everything open or carve a new path forward.

"Talk to me," she says quietly, steady—a lifeline offered without push or demand.

Brick's head dips, shadowed beneath the streetlights seeping through the window. When his voice comes, it cracks.

"It's not the headlines. Not the interviews." His words stumble over themselves, raw and brittle. "It's what's underneath. What no one sees."

The gap between them thins, charged. He doesn't look up. His hands clutch the cap tighter—knuckles pale against dark fabric.

Natalie moves a fraction closer. She doesn't reach out yet. Her eyes hold steady, like a heartbeat in the quiet.

"This isn't easy," Brick admits. His voice, barely more than a rasp, scrapes the stillness. "I'm not good at this—talking, feeling this much."

He swallows hard.

Natalie nods. "You don't have to do it alone."

"Alone is all I know." His laugh is humorless and jagged.

Tension crackles—electric, fragile. The gap stretches, filled with ghosts and fears neither is bold enough to name yet.

He shifts, his jaw tight, preparing to pull apart the walls he's built, brick by brick.

"You don't get to manage me," he says in a low voice. A fight flickers behind his dark eyes. "Not with rules, smiles, or bullshit platitudes."

"I'm not here to control you." Natalie's voice is soft but unyielding. "I'm here to stand with you."

The air thickens. Breath catches. They lean into the space that's both a battlefield and a sanctuary.

Brick's fingers twitch over the cap, then go still.

His gaze drops to the worn fabric, shadowed and folded like armor he's reluctantly ready to shed.

Natalie waits—just waits.

The room presses closer, expectant, electric.

Brick looks up slowly. His eyes meet hers for the barest moment. He steels himself.

The silence tightens, a coiled promise. The night holds its breath as Brick prepares to speak what has been locked inside—tough edges ready to crack open under the weight of trust yet to be given.

The cap shifts between Brick's fingers, rough and familiar, a worn shield beneath his touch. His eyes do not lift; they map the braiding of the fabric, tracing invisible lines that catch threads of light from the streetlamp's glow slipping through the blinds.

"I'm not good at this." His voice cracks, sharp and uneven, like ice breaking beneath a winter's step. He hesitates, then adds quietly, "Talking. Feeling this much." The words come out in short bursts, each one heavier than the last, as if letting air back into a sealed chest.

Natalie's breath catches. Her fingers grip the edge of the couch as she leans slightly forward. Outside, the city's roar fades, replaced by the muffled tick of a clock and the faint scent of fresh coffee lingering from earlier. The space between them hums with unspoken truths—heavy, fragile, and impossible to ignore.

Brick's gaze drifts to the floor and then back to his hands. His fingers tighten on the cap as if it is an anchor to something solid, something safe. "There's this... weight," he says slowly, the edge of pain threading through his voice. "From before—the accident."

He swallows hard, his jaw clenched. The memory folds over him like a shadow stretching longer in twilight. That split-second fumble during regionals—a kid rushing at him, the ball spiraling loose, his career nearly ending on that play. The fallout came swiftly: whispers in locker rooms, coaches questioning his reliability, and his own family looking at him as if he had shattered something irreplaceable.

"That moment almost ended everything: my career, my trust. They looked at me like I was broken... like I was the danger." His breath hitches. "Disappointment doesn't just stay in the past; it follows. It sits heavy in a room, like a scar nobody talks about but everyone sees."

The quiet bends around his confession, the room holding its breath with him. Natalie's chest tightens, the weight of his pain slipping beneath her skin.

"I can scrimmage, train, and win every damn game," Brick continues, his voice rougher now, raw edges showing. "I put on the mask, play the part—controlled, disciplined, unbreakable." He finally lifts his eyes, shadowed and searching. "But none of it means anything if nobody sees the rest—the mess behind all this." He taps the cap as if it's the lid on his secrets. "The storm I'm always trying to quiet."

His shoulders crease forward, as if the act of speaking has loosened some invisible chains. His next words come slowly, weighted with a hope he's terrified to admit. "I want you to stick around. Not because I'm some broken thing that needs mending."

He stops. A flicker of something crosses his face—the instinct to guard himself, to pull back before the rejection can come. But he pushes through it.

"I want to be chosen for exactly who I am." His voice breaks, the barbed edges of vulnerability now exposed. "The mess and all."

The admission hangs between them like fragile glass—beautiful, trembling, and easily shattered.

"I'm terrified," he whispers, his voice barely above a breath. His hands clench tighter, bones pressing through the fabric of the cap. "That if you step past this wall, you'll see the parts I keep hidden. The parts that aren't enough."

The air grows thick, the scent of leather, worn cotton, and the faint musk of sweat wrapping around them like a fragile cloak. Brick lowers his head, shadows folding over his face like a drawn veil.

He waits. Not for judgment. Not for answers.

Just for the quiet grace of understanding.

Natalie's heart hammers in the dim room, its rhythm syncing with the charged silence between them.

The room feels smaller now, the low hum of the city tucked outside the windows, muted by thick glass and the closing door. It is a world away from the chaos that had spilled from the press conference hours ago.

Natalie's breath caught, hitched in her chest as Brick's words settled between them—raw, trembling, like something fragile about to shatter.

She swallowed, her throat tight. She steadied herself against the sudden swell of something unspoken, her gaze flickering to his hands. He clutched that worn team cap, his knuckles pale as bone.

"I..." Her voice emerged cautiously at first, the edges brittle. Then it found a firmer hold. "This armor I wear, the rules I set—that's not just some corporate shell. It's the only way I've kept from falling apart."

Her eyes met his, searching, quietly inviting him into a place she had guarded for years.

"I grew up knowing that chaos was waiting to swallow me whole. Abandonment wasn't some distant fear—it was the soundtrack of my childhood."

She shifted, and the couch creaked softly beneath her. Her fingers tightened around the seam of the cushion, her knuckles whitening.

The scent of leather and faint musk grounded her as she inhaled deeply. When she spoke again, her voice fell to a whisper—steady but tender.

"When I was a teenager, Mom left me alone for hours after school. I remember sitting by the window, waiting."

She paused, letting the silence hang.

"Waiting for her to come back. For someone to come back. But no one did."

Her words hovered, threadbare and unshielded. Cracks showed beneath her composure.

"In that quiet, I learned something: love wasn't something you were given; it was something you earned. By being perfect. By never making a mistake."

She shifted forward, fingers still gripping the cushion.

"So I built my walls—high, tight. Rules, professionalism—control. They're not just lines on a contract; they're the chains that kept me safe from being too much. From being the storm no one could weather."

A tremor ran through her. Her eyes flickered away, then back—bare and pleading.

"My biggest fear?" She breathed the confession, raw in the dim light. "That if someone sees beneath this calm, if they truly see *me*, I'll break. I'll be too much—too much chaos, too much emotion. And they'll run."

Her fingertips brushed her sleeve, betraying the tension twisting inside her body.

She leaned forward, hesitant. Then her hand rose with a tremor, reaching out to rest on Brick's forearm. The skin beneath her palm was warm, alive. His heartbeat thrummed beneath her shaky touch.

"What if..." Her voice wavered on the edge of hope and fear. "What if we just take the chance? That we're enough for each other?"

The question hung between them like a fragile promise.

Brick's breath stuttered in the silence that followed. Their shared risk was palpable in the air. Natalie's fingers lingered—a quiet anchor amid the storm they had unearthed together.

They breathed almost in sync, the weight of vulnerability threading a cautious bridge between bruised hearts.

Quiet settled around them like smoke over a still battlefield, thick with words unsaid. Fears laid bare hung fragile in the air between them.

The television hummed softly, its glow pooling across the carpet in weak tributaries, barely reaching the sharp angles of Brick's clenched jaw or the glimmer of moisture brimming in Natalie's eyes. Outside, the city never really slept—its steady pulse a reminder that the crowd's eyes never fully left him. Here, in this cramped sanctuary, time suspended between dread and something dangerously close to hope.

Brick's fingers twitched, tracing invisible patterns on the worn fabric of his jeans. He glanced away, his jaw tightening, before slowly reaching for her hand. The movement was deliberate and slow. When his palm finally closed over hers, there was no flourish—no grand gesture. Just the steady, unshakable weight of connection that neither of them was yet ready to trust but both desperately needed.

Her skin was warm beneath his calloused hand, like a quiet promise.

"I'm going to try," he said. His voice was low, rough from the day's strain—like gravel shifting underfoot. "For real this time."

He didn't elaborate. The sincerity in those words spoke volumes.

"No more hiding behind whatever the hell I used to pretend was armor. Not around you." His eyes lifted to meet hers, heavy with everything he was still learning to say. "I want you to see me—all the messed-up bits, the cracks, the stuff I wish I could smash flat."

Natalie's breath hitched. A shaky laugh trembled against the wet glint gathering in her eyes. The sound was raw and warm—a tiny burst of light in the tension that had been building like the slow rise before a thunderstorm. Her fingers tightened around his.

"You don't have to be perfect with me, Brick," she said carefully. "If perfect meant not falling apart sometimes, then that's not for me." She paused, choosing each word with precision. "I'm willing to bet that safety doesn't come from foolproof defenses or perfect control. It comes from being seen—to the bone—without running away."

Her words hung in the air, trembling like the first notes of a song just starting.

She leaned forward, her eyes shining. Her voice dropped to a quieter tone but steadied. "What if we both accept that maybe we're enough? For each other?"

Her hand edged up his arm—tentative yet determined. The contact was a lifeline, a soft dare wrapped in vulnerability.

Every time he had tried before, the walls went back up. But tonight, the weight of hiding felt heavier than the risk of letting go.

Brick exhaled, and the tension loosened fractionally.

"I want that," he said simply. The words carried weight—not just a want, but a need carved from years of running from shadows. "I'm scared as hell. But what else can I do? We can't keep pretending we're alright when everything's on fire inside."

Natalie nodded. A flicker of a smile broke through her tears. "No pretending anymore," she agreed. Her voice was steady now, fortified by the courage it takes to admit that fear isn't weakness but a call to stay open. "Not with you. I promise to try. To really trust that being known, mess and all, can be the safest place we find."

The apartment seemed to breathe around them. The silence was no longer empty but full of fragile possibility.

Brick shifted closer, sliding into the space beside her on the worn couch with care. Close enough. He left room but closed the unseen distance that had haunted every conversation until now. The faint scent of his cologne—musk and something faintly woodsy—mingled with the soft cotton of their clothes. Cool air brushed over bare skin where their fingers intertwined.

He reached out again. This time, he gently caught her palm and pulled it to rest securely in his own, fingers threading between hers.

"I can't promise I won't screw up." His voice cracked a little. Raw honesty spilled between them. "But I'll try not to run. Not from you. Not from this."

He let out a slow breath.

"I want to be real. For once."

Natalie chuckled—shaky but genuine. The sound wrapped around him like a healing balm. She squeezed his hand, her fingers curling over his knuckles with intention. "Then I'll hold you to that," she whispered. "Being truly seen isn't about comfort zones; it's about trust. That leap where you let go, knowing you might fall, but hoping we'll catch each other."

"We'll catch each other," Brick affirmed quietly, his voice layered with newfound resolve. "Even when it scares the hell out of us. Even on the days it hurts or feels like too much."

He paused. The hush between them was thick but filled with the steady beat of two hearts daring to match pace.

"We choose each other. That's the real start. Every damn day."

Natalie's eyes shone with tears and fierce hope. "Every day," she said. "Even when fear tries to claw back."

Her voice dropped to a whisper. "I choose *you*. All in."

Their bodies shifted closer. The space between them shrank until she leaned in, her head resting lightly against his shoulder. The tension in him eased—a slow release, like air escaping a taut balloon. Brick wrapped his long arms around her, pulling her near, his hands resting securely on her back as if to say, *You're safe here. No masks. No pretenses.*

The television murmured quietly in the background—a distant soundtrack to this fragile sanctuary. The city outside glowed faintly through the windows, indifferent and vast. But inside, in this dimly lit room filled with their tangled breaths and quiet promises, two damaged souls chose to stay.

Caught not by fear,

but by the fierce, trembling hope of vulnerability shared.

Quiet Strength

The darkness outside the windows held the last vestiges of night—a slow bleed of pale rose and lavender seeping into the sky. Inside Natalie's apartment, Brick's breath came slow and steady as his eyes flickered open. The world was still. No blaring alarms, no distant sirens—just the faint hum of the city waking.

He slipped his feet out of bed, socked and silent on the cool hardwood floor. A soft creak escaped the floorboard beneath the kitchen door as he pushed it open.

The apartment still wore its night skin, curtains drawn tight, shadows pooling in corners. Brick moved with the grace of a man who had been here enough times to know the layout blindfolded. His fingers tapped the coffee maker, coaxing it to life. The quiet sputter and hiss of brewing filled the cool air, carrying the rich, earthy scent that nudged awake more than just the mind.

From the bedroom, a rustle stirred. Natalie emerged, wrapped in the soft crumple of sleep's aftershocks, her body still heavy with the weight of dreams. Her hair was tousled like a wild brushstroke across her pillow, and her bare feet skimmed the floor as she followed the scent, drawn instinctively toward the kitchen. She leaned against the doorway—half-shielded by shadows—her tired eyes tracking Brick's easy rhythm as he navigated the confined space. A quiet smile teased the edges of her lips.

He caught sight of her. His mouth lifted slightly, as if to say, *You're finally up.*

Without turning, Brick grabbed two mugs from the shelf; the cool ceramic felt smooth against his palms. The coffee poured dark and aromatic, and steam curled up in lazy spirals.

He set one mug down on the counter and turned, his brow arching under the low light. A small grin broke his usually guarded expression.

"You know," Brick said, his voice rough but amused, "you might actually miss your favorite stuff if you ever tried waking up before noon."

Natalie took the mug, her fingers curling around it like a lifeline as warmth spread through her. She quirked a brow, a smirk flickering. "And depriving you of this quiet is cruel. I enjoy my beauty sleep."

"It isn't the beauty sleep I'm worried about," Brick said, grinning wider. "More like you missing your shot at world domination." He lifted his mug in mock salute.

She chuckled softly, the sound filling the space between them—gentle and real.

"Today's just—simple, huh?" Natalie murmured, her eyes never leaving his. "No deadlines breathing down our necks. No crises exploding."

Brick nodded, his shoulders relaxing. Tension seeped out like air from a punctured tire. "Feels strange. Good strange."

Their voices dropped to a murmur, weaving between minutes and memories like two dancers finding their rhythm. The city outside remained quiet. Light shifted, casting gold across the edges of the room, softening the brick walls and their silhouettes.

Natalie shifted closer, warmth from their mugs rippling through her hands. Brick's gaze dropped to the curve of her fingers, which tightened around the mug's handle. The small distance between them shrank, unspoken understanding settling in the tightness of their shared breath and quiet presence.

She raised her mug in invitation, and he met it. The thrum of the moment hung heavier than words.

"You think Coach will be all over your ass today?" Natalie's voice was teasing but gentle.

Brick's smile faltered just a touch, shadowed. "S'pose he will. Can't win 'em all, right?"

"Maybe today you don't have to." Her gaze lingered, steady and sure.

He reached out, his thumb tracing small circles over her knuckles. A warm electricity hummed beneath that simple touch, steadying the quick beat of his chest.

"Coffee first," he said, his voice thick with something softer than usual. "Then we deal with the rest."

Their smiles exchanged without fanfare—an intimate understanding folded in warmth and trust. The apartment held them in its hush, the usual chaos reduced to the softness of early morning light creeping past the curtains drawn against the night.

Together, shoulder to shoulder in the narrow kitchen, they stood—mugs clasped between steady palms. Here, in this pocket of peace before the day demanded its toll, they breathed in the simple luxury of unhurried time. Before long, the world would intrude. The coach would call. Obligations would pile up. But for now, there was only the slow, sweet rhythm of morning beginning and each other.

Brick stood before the stove, sunlight spilling faintly through half-drawn curtains. Soft golden patterns pooled across the tiled floor. He cracked eggs into a chipped ceramic bowl with the focus of a mechanic rebuilding an engine—rhythmic, imperfect, more beat-up than trained. Beneath his breath, he hummed something tuneless.

"Look, the secret to scrambling?" His voice dropped low and gravelly. "You gotta pretend it's war. Whisk like your life depends on it—'cause if you don't, you're stuck with some sad, soggy mess."

Natalie stood by the counter, a blade gleaming in her hand as she sliced a ripe mango. The sticky, sun-warmed scent curled through the air—honeyed and tropical—then mingled with the sharp tang of fresh citrus. She leaned against the counter, her eyes tracing Brick's awkward dance with the eggs. Her lips twitched into an amused half-smile, the kind that softens frustration and finds humor in brute force tackling a tender task.

"Given the state of your sneakers by the door," she says, arching an eyebrow toward the mangled pair lined up haphazardly like casualties of war, "I'm guessing battle tactics aren't exactly your strong suit."

Brick snorts—the sound rumbles deep in his chest. "These old things? I've earned every single scuff. Trophy cases don't lie. These kicks have seen more fights than my chessboard."

He flips the eggs with slow precision. The sizzle cuts sharply against the copper skillet. Warmth unfolds—the aroma curls up like smoke from a quiet campfire, settling into the room's corners.

They move toward the small kitchen table, battered wood scratched by years of hurried mornings and lingered evenings. Brick sets the plates down with a practiced clink while Natalie lays out the fruit—chunks of mango, orange wedges, and crimson strawberries—colors bleeding into white like a fresh painting.

Their hands reach over the same space. Fingers brush. Neither flinches.

Bodies fit together in the tight quarters without crowding.

Under the table, their feet seek one another. Natalie's toes catch the top of Brick's sneaker. He responds with a gentle nudge—a small private signal carved out from shared space. Their usual defenses soften, replaced by habitual contact. A finger traces the edge of a plate. A knuckle brushes lightly against her cheek as Brick reaches across to tuck a stray strand behind her ear.

The gesture feels unscripted. Ordinary. Like a secret too precious to name.

They chew slowly, savoring the contrast between creamy eggs and bright, tangy fruit. Light laughter breaks between them—warm and easy, like sunlight spilling through a cracked window. Brick's laugh is rougher now, less guarded, the sharp edges rounded by comfort and presence.

"Honestly," he says, his voice softer, "I never thought I'd look forward to mornings like this. No screaming crowds. No flashing lights. Just... eggs and fruit."

Natalie meets his gaze. Quiet amusement lingers in her eyes. "This is strength, too. Not always the loud kind."

Their shared smile anchors them to this uncomplicated moment. The world outside is hushed to a murmur. Time bends. Clock hands slow. Neither moves to break the spell.

Between bites, Brick shifts in his chair. A knuckle brushes her cheek again—a silent question, an offering. She leans into the touch, her eyes closing briefly as if memorizing the feel of him.

"You're getting soft," she teases under her breath. Her lips curve into that slow, teasing smile—no malice, only fondness.

He rolls his eyes, a faint twitch at the corner of his mouth. "Only because you keep poking at me. Like some persistent needle."

"Good," she whispers it close. "Needles keep you sharp."

The kitchen hums with ordinary sounds—silverware against plates, the scrape of chair legs, and the faint flicker of the ceiling fan twisting overhead. The scent of citrus and eggs lingers, wrapping around them like a warm, unspoken promise.

Their conversation drifts without urgency. Plans for the day are murmured quietly. Hopes are unspoken yet understood. Neither presses.

Brick reaches across the table to nudge her hand. Her fingers curl around his briefly—a wordless exchange loaded with hard-won trust.

The plates empty slowly. The last strawberry disappears beneath thoughtful smiles and gentle sighs. Neither moves to leave the table.

Their shared silence feels richer than any spoken declaration. This morning, this simplicity—it feels like balm.

Outside, the city stirs with a slow awakening beneath soft clouds. Inside, light pools in the corners of the kitchen. Two people sit close, savoring the small victories of a morning well kept.

###

Natalie stacks the last plate into the sink. A stubborn smear of scrambled egg clings to the edge, and she winces. "This printer has been a nightmare," she says, her voice low enough to flutter between the quiet hum of the apartment and the glassy stillness of the late morning light. "It has a blinking red error light. The paper is jammed somewhere on the office shelf. Every time I try to print a release statement, it just freezes up."

She pauses, her fingers pressing against her temple. A slow breath escapes her lips in a weary sigh, and her eyes flicker briefly toward the offending plate.

Brick leans against the doorway, arms crossed, a slow smirk pulling at the corner of his mouth. "Hold up, I've got this." Without waiting for a real invitation, he strides over and grabs the chunky machine as if it were a stubborn opponent on the line. His socked feet pad softly across the wooden floor as he sets the printer beside the small desk near the window.

He squats down and grumbles under his breath—a string of colorful curses that neither betray his frustration nor disturb the stillness.

He jabs at the paper tray, his fingers digging into the grooves and edges as he wrestles with the stubborn beast. Plastic creaks under his grip as panels shift slightly beneath his knuckles. His brows knit together, and his forehead tightens as he claws at a stuck corner, pulling with a mix of determination and lingering irritation.

"Hand me the manual," he mutters without looking up, his voice rough with concentration and tinged with theatrical exasperation that makes Natalie's lips twitch.

She reaches for the nearby shelf and pulls the crisp booklet free from a binder. She lingers there with a soft smile, watching him squint at the tiny print. Brick slouches back slightly, the weight of the printer balanced awkwardly on his thighs as he scans the troubleshooting list aloud.

"Okay... step one: open the cartridge access door..." His fingers trace the instructions before moving to flick a small latch. "Step two: reseat the cartridge if it's loose..." He hums, a low, contemplative sound, before popping the compartment open.

A whiff of heating plastic mingles with the faint scent of toner as he lifts out the ink pack. He holds it up like a strange relic, inspecting its edges with the focus of an archaeologist. Then he carefully aligns it again, pushing firmly until it clicks into place. His tongue peeks between his teeth—pure concentration.

"Step three: press and hold reset for five seconds." His finger searches the side panel until it lands on a small, slightly recessed button. He presses down, counting softly. "One. Two. Three. Four. Five."

A sudden mechanical whirr breaks the silence. The printer hums back to life like a beast roused from slumber. The paper tray slides open and shut with a satisfying thunk.

Brick straightens. A triumphant grin spreads across his face as his fist shoots up in a victorious jab. For a moment, the small win feels like something bigger—a rare moment when control was his, where things bent to his will instead of the other way around.

Natalie crosses the room in two strides. Her hand rises to press a kiss against his cheek. The touch is warm and affectionate—a quiet thank you without expectation, carrying more comfort than any words could convey.

He chuckles, rubbing the spot where her lips met, shaking his head with a mock groan. "For what it's worth, I could probably take on an entire motherboard after this."

"Guess you're the knight of the jammed paper now," Natalie says, her eyes gleaming with amusement. "I didn't see that coming."

Brick grabs a fresh sheet of paper and slides it into the tray, then hits 'Print.' After a moment, a crisp page shoots out. The black text of the test print is bold and unblemished.

He holds the paper out, presenting it like a trophy at a press conference. "And here you go, ma'am. The printer, impressively tamed." He drops into a slow, exaggerated bow, one hand stretched forward to deliver the paper like an award.

Natalie laughs. The sound spills softly between them, light and unburdened.

"Well done, Mr. Fix-It."

"Is there anything else broken that I can patch up before you lose your mind?"

She shakes her head, her eyes warm and steady. "Just keep making coffee like that, and we'll be fine."

Brick's smirk deepens as he turns back to the kitchen. The hum of the printer—no longer menacing but cooperative—fills the room alongside their shared laughter. The faint aroma of coffee lingers beneath it all, mingling with the warmth of the morning light spilling across the desk.

In this tiny orbit of domesticity, the world outside feels like a mere echo: distant and quiet.

Natalie unplugs the printer, now tamed and docile. Brick watches with a grin that holds a quiet promise: whatever comes next, they can figure it out together.

Late afternoon light slants through the half-open blinds, casting long stripes across Natalie's kitchen. She pulls a heavy pot from the cabinet. The metal feels cool and reassuring in her hands. "I thought I'd make your mom's chili," she announces, her eyes alight with quiet determination.

The sharp scent of cumin dances in the air as onions hiss under the blade, their thin, translucent layers scattering across the worn wooden board. The rich tang of simmering tomatoes soon follows, mingling with the earthy spice and wrapping the apartment in a warm, promising aroma.

At the doorway, Brick leans against the frame, arms folded but grinning. "Do you really want to risk setting off the fire alarm again? I'm not sure the team's ready for that kind of chaos."

Natalie shoots him a look, dry and amused. "Once and never again. Trust me on this—consider it my gift to you." She waves him away with a mock-serious flick of her fingers, but there's a softness in her tone that belies the playfulness.

Brick steps closer, rubbing the back of his neck. "C'mon, let me help. I can chop—well, I'm not great, but—"

"Nope." She cuts him off with a flourish, a chef's smile tugging at her lips. "Sit down, Mr. Grumpy. This chili is all me."

Grumbling good-naturedly, Brick retreats to the living room, though the muted scent of spices trails after him like a promise.

By the time the chili bubbles softly on the stove, Brick is back, stealing mismatched bowls from his apartment stash and carrying cloth napkins over his forearm. He sets the small table with deliberate care—the worn bowls, a single candle nestled between them, and two spoons aligned like soldiers ready for duty.

Natalie joins him, wiping her hands on a flour-dusted towel. She stirs the pot slowly, her fingers tracing lazy circles on the worn handle. "College was madness. Late nights, too much coffee, and way too many ramen packets." She had been the type to study alone, to disappear into libraries when everything felt chaotic—building order from disorder, control from uncertainty. "But I learned something about patience back then. About slowing down."

Brick watches her, the low hum of the simmering chili filling the quiet moments between stories. His gaze lingers on her, a faint smile tugging at his lips as she moves with quiet confidence through the kitchen.

"I used to sneak out to the creek behind my mom's place," he says after a moment. "It was a quiet spot... where things didn't feel so heavy."

She looks up, her eyes meeting his. The vulnerability in that glance isn't forced—it's earned.

"Your mom's chili sounds like a whole lot more than just food," Brick murmurs.

A memory flickers across his face—his mother's kitchen, the same one where she taught him that cooking was about more than just ingredients. It was about showing up. It was about care.

Natalie chuckles softly, warmth threading through her voice. "It's a kind of comfort. Like carrying a piece of home wherever you go."

"Yeah." Brick leans back, the stiffness in his shoulders melting into something softer. "My mom has this recipe too—she always stirred in a dash of patience, even when I was livid about everything."

The smell of garlic and cumin slides into the space between them, grounding and familiar.

They sit with steaming bowls. Their hands occasionally brush across the table's surface—a fleeting touch, but heavy with the ease of shared history. Brick presses his knuckles lightly to Natalie's cheek, a gesture so ordinary that it feels profound.

"You ever think much about how recipes get passed down?" His voice is quieter now. "How a pinch here, a splash there, ends up being more than the sum of its parts?"

"Yeah. Like people, I guess." Natalie's eyes crinkle into a smile. "A little messy, a little unpredictable, and somehow essential."

Between bites, laughter bubbles up—Brick's laughter is softer now, less guarded, as his mouth curves into genuine amusement at a story Natalie tells about a chaotic campus party involving a rogue fire extinguisher.

"See?" She nudges him with her elbow. "You can laugh without throwing someone through a window."

"Only if you're stirring chili, not my patience," he fires back with a smirk.

When the last spoonful disappears, they clear their dishes together. The comfortable choreography of domesticity is fluent and unspoken. Dessert is simple—warm cinnamon apples, their fragrance weaving through the apartment like a sigh.

They linger at the table, fingers intertwined over empty bowls, savoring the quiet after the meal. The world beyond feels distant, softened by the flickering candlelight and the steady beat of two heartbeats learning to sync.

Brick's gaze drifts to Natalie. The weight behind his usual storm has quieted to a gentle pulse. This—this hum of shared spaces, easy warmth, and unspoken promises—is a kind of victory all its own.

The couch cushions dip gently beneath them, a quiet harbor from the buzzing world outside. A low-stakes movie murmurs from the television, flickering shadows that paint the warm walls with soft hues.

Natalie leans her head against Brick's chest. His heartbeat is steady beneath her ear—a rhythm she has learned to trust. His arm snakes around her shoulders, fingers finding the back of her neck and curling into the soft curls there like a tether. The worn couch fabric ruffles beneath their shifting weight as the room settles into a gentle cocoon, the only sound being the whisper of dialogue fading into the night.

Brick's thumb moves in slow circles through Natalie's hair—absent, effortless. The soft strands slip between his fingers, warm and silky, anchoring him in the moment. His voice slips out, low and almost swallowed by the room's quiet. "Never thought I'd want this... normal, I guess."

The confession hangs suspended, delicate and unexpected. His brow furrows slightly, eyes narrowing as if trying to hold onto a fragile thought, the edges softening with surprise.

Natalie lifts her gaze. The flickering light catches in her eyes, luminous and steady. She blinks slowly, choosing her words with care. "This is strength, too."

Her words fold around the moment, anchoring it—not flashy or loud, but profoundly real. He lets out a slow smile, the corners of his mouth pulling up in a way that reaches his eyes, lighting them with something softer and unguarded. The admission settles, a weight lifted without effort.

They speak in whispers then, their voices low, words wrapping the space like a shared secret.

"Feels like I've been chasing a storm my whole life," Brick says, his breathing steady. "Never thought the running would stop."

Natalie's hand slips into his, their fingers lacing like puzzle pieces fitting together. "Maybe this—this calm—is the real victory."

Their exchange drifts into silence, punctuated only by the murmuring film, a distant current beneath their quiet. The air holds a faint scent of cinnamon from the chili Natalie had simmered earlier, mingling with the warmth of their shared breath and the faint hum of distant traffic bleeding through the walls.

Brick's cheek rests lightly atop Natalie's head as their bodies curve into one another. Their feet touch beneath the worn throw covering the couch, a subtle tether teasing warmth through the fabric. Around them, the apartment sinks further into night—undisturbed and safe.

Their breathing slows and matches, the rise and fall of their chests creating a tender harmony. The television's glow casts ghostly shapes that dance softly across the ceiling and walls, draping the room in a twilight calm. The ordinary magic of the moment lingers, fleeting and fragile.

Natalie's lashes flutter closed. Even as her breath deepens into sleep, her fingers press once more into Brick's palm. His eyes close reluctantly, the quiet peace seeping into bones weary from battles past.

The movie's voice trails into silence. The apartment holds its breath along with them. Outside, the city hums faintly—a distant lullaby to a night that knows this rare stillness.

Together, they drift into sleep.

The sharp thud of cleats striking turf cuts through the murmur of morning practice. The stadium, bathed in raw glare where sunlight slices between shattered clouds, vibrates with the rhythmic grind of bodies colliding. A rookie linebacker—face flushed, eyes wild with frustration—shoves a teammate hard near the defensive line.

The jolt ripples through the gathered players. Voices spike into sharp shouts. Hands push and pull. Chests heave with aggression and adrenaline.

A tight knot forms where the two players collide, their breaths ragged and sharp as tension tightens.

On the sideline, Brick freezes. Fingers curl into tight fists at his sides. The usual fire that crackles along his skin flares briefly in his eyes—old anger rising, quickening his pulse—before something deeper takes hold. Conscious effort. A choice made and held. His muscles coil, then ease into a measured stride forward. His great frame moves with the quiet authority of a predator who has chosen restraint over attack.

The scuffle drew his full attention. He stepped between the two young players, his presence swallowing the chaos. His hands lifted, deliberate and steady, the rough leather of his practice gloves pressing into the cool morning air—a silent command no one dared challenge.

His voice slid low and steady, a deep current beneath the roaring tension.

"Enough. Back off. This isn't how we handle business."

The words didn't just chase the immediate fire from the air; they stripped away the noise, leaving space for reason. Brick's gaze met each player's, steady and unyielding. His hands guided them apart, careful but insistent, the simple touch a reminder of his command—not just physical, but emotional.

"Keep it cool. Control is the real strength here," he said, his voice gravelly but even, the echo of hard-earned lessons laced through every syllable. "You want respect? You earn it with discipline—not fists."

From the far sideline, Coach Hale's eyes narrowed, then softened with approval. His nod was slight, but it carried the weight of years—a signal that Brick was shifting something deep, something vital. A tacit trust earned through relentless mentorship, reinforced in this single moment of choice.

Teammates exchanged wide-eyed looks, whispers brushing past like the wind. Some glanced at Brick with fresh recognition, a flicker of something like awe or disbelief.

"Was that Brick?" murmured Caleb, arms crossed and voice low.

"Controlled," Jaxon replied, a slow grin tugging at his lips. "I did not see that coming."

The two players, chastened, eased away. Tension folded into reluctant respect.

Brick lingered, muscles still taut beneath his sweat-damp practice gear, his eyes sweeping the field before he turned back toward the benches where Natalie waited. Her gaze met his—calm and sharp, searching for the undercurrent beneath his cool exterior. She stepped forward into the grassy haze.

"Are you doing all right?" Her voice threaded quietly through the bustle.

Brick's lips twitched—a slow, reluctant smile that barely touched his eyes, as if disbelief itself needed coaxing. His voice dropped, rougher than usual but steady with quiet pride.

"Yeah. Hell, better than okay. It felt... right. Holding it back instead of letting it blow."

He reached for her hand with a softness that surprised him, contrasting with his usual intensity, his thumb brushing the back of her fingers in a brief tether. Together, they turned toward the locker room corridor, the din of the stadium swelling around them like the noise of a world in motion—one he was learning to face without losing himself.

"Feels like progress," he said, his voice low enough for only her to hear.

She nodded, a flicker of warmth blooming in her eyes.

They walked side by side, the touch lingering a heartbeat longer than necessary—an affirmation of their quiet connection amid the chaos of their worlds. The doorway loomed ahead: harsh lights, booming voices, and endless demands waiting beyond. But for this moment, they moved through it steadily and together, a silent promise carried in the squeeze of a hand.

The hum of the crowd faded in tempo. The weight of what had just passed settled deep—a slow, steady beat beneath the roar. Brick's restraint didn't erase the storm inside, but it shaped it. He carried the fire differently now, less a blaze out of control and more a forge being carefully tended.

Around them, the field held its breath, waiting for the next play, the next challenge. But right now, the biggest victory belonged not to the boldest tackle or the fastest sprint—but to the man learning to master the storm within.

A soft, deliberate knock at the door followed by footsteps—rhythmic taps on hardwood that pulled the evening taut.

Brick didn't look up from the laundry heaped across his lap, the creases in his brow deep as canyons. However, his shoulders shifted slightly, as if he had been waiting. The scent of brownies—rich, dark chocolate warming from the kitchen—drifted through the cracked doorway, mingling with something vanilla-sweet beneath it.

"Hey, y'all! Dessert delivery!" Nina's voice cut through the quiet like brightness itself, playful and warm.

Emma followed, her smile easy, her eyes catching the lamplight with something softer underneath. Relief, maybe. The kind only close friends understood after battles fought and slowly, carefully won. She balanced brownies in one hand, cookies tucked into the crook of her arm like trophies. "We come bearing sweetness and questionable humor."

The door swung open wider. Brick's socked feet shifted against the hardwood as he stood, and the city lights outside cast shadows that stretched long and thin across the worn rug. Natalie marked the threshold with a small smile, her book folding shut—a quiet gesture of truce.

Emma's gaze landed on Brick, and her grin unfurled. "Well, if it isn't Mr. Grumpy Househusband."

Brick shot her a look sharp enough to draw blood, but his jaw twitched with the hint of a smile. He didn't set down the laundry. "I'm less 'grumpy' and more 'getting stuff done'—deal with it."

Nina laughed, her eyes flicking to Natalie. "And you, Natalie Brooks—snagging the gentle giant. I didn't see that one coming when you took this gig."

Natalie's cheeks warmed under the teasing. She kept her voice steady, though something softer crept in. "He has his moments. Mostly when people touch my coffee."

They settled around the small, battered coffee table squatting in the center of the living room. Late blue dusk had settled outside, turning the corners indigo and soft. A bottle of sparkling cider hissed open—a small, intimate sound. Bubbles rose through the glasses like tiny promises. Plastic plates held brownies and cookies, their sweetness stark against the crisp bite of the cider.

Emma raised her glass. "Here's to change. And to small victories that taste like chocolate."

"Speak for yourself," Nina grinned. "I'm just here for the cookies."

They clinked glasses. The sound hung in the quiet room—small, clear, a bell ringing in still air. Stories drifted between them like smoke: practice frustrations, the weight of eyes always watching, laughter shared in glances, and half-joking confessions that meant everything.

At one point, Emma raised an eyebrow at Brick. "So what's it like being in charge of laundry now? You're making a good case for life off the field."

Brick's grin broke through, broad and slow. He held up a frayed, dark sock as if it were an opponent in a match. "Rough gig. Constant deadlines. Rivalries with these bad boys. You try finding a match."

Natalie's laugh was soft and genuine. She tugged at her sleeve and watched Brick—his shoulders less stiff than usual, his eyes crinkling at the corners—and felt something heavy finally settle low in her chest. Emma noticed. When Nina pointed out that Brick was leaning closer than ever before, Emma's hand found Natalie's elbow, gentle but deliberate.

They stepped into the kitchen doorway, away from the others gathering plates.

"I'm serious, Nat." Emma's words were a breath, barely audible. "It's been so long since I saw you look like this. Not just surviving the storm but breathing through it. It suits you."

Natalie's breath caught. For a moment, the constant pressure—the fluorescent lights, the battles fought and refought—scattered like dust in the late afternoon sun. She looked away, then back, and nodded once. The smile that touched her lips was fragile yet real. "It feels... real."

Emma squeezed her arm, and they rejoined the group just as Brick scoffed softly, nudging Emma with his elbow. "Alright, alright. I'm officially the luckiest guy with friends like these making me look good."

The four of them drew close. Laughter bubbled free and easy, filling the space with warmth that pushed back against the chill pressing at the windows. Plates clinked, and hands brushed while reaching for more treats. The silence between words spoke of something deeper than speeches or promises—of belonging, simple and true.

Nina reached out without hesitation, pulling Brick into a hug. Emma closed the circle. Brick leaned in, sturdy and present, no longer the guarded fortress he had been. Natalie's hands threaded into his, anchoring the moment in quiet strength.

They lingered in the kitchen doorway when it came time to leave, reluctant to break what had formed between them. They shared smiles that didn't need translation, an unspoken understanding that Natalie and Brick had become something larger than themselves—something that belonged to all of them now. The air held softness, a tether to tonight's warmth, and a promise that whatever battles came wouldn't overshadow this.

The Future Season

L ight slips across Brick's face. Thin fingers of sunlight sneak beneath the edge of the curtain. He lies still, the pale warmth coaxing him from the edge of sleep. His muscles slacken, but beneath, a quiet alertness holds steady.

The room hums with the scent of vanilla and linen—Natalie's signature, woven into the fabric of the rug and the worn cotton sheets tangled around him.

A rustle beside him. Natalie's breath catches. She stirs, her eyes fluttering open, and reaches blindly for the phone on the nightstand. Her fingers brush against the cold glass, tapping it awake. The screen blazes to life.

A solitary new message.

She goes still. Her chest tightens.

Brick's half-closed eyes catch the sudden stiffness of her spine—the sharp intake of breath. He props himself up on an elbow and shifts closer, the mattress sighing beneath his weight. The subject line blazes across the screen: "POSITION OFFER—Head of PR, Dallas Lightning." Below it, a sender's name. Familiar. Unyielding.

Her lips quiver. Words spill out in a fragile breath: "From Dallas... Executive Director..."

"What's going on?" Brick's voice is quiet but tense, his eyes locked on her face as if he is bracing for a hit.

Natalie hesitates. Her thumb hovers over the screen. She swipes down slowly, skimming paragraphs bathed in official tones—salary figures, relocation clauses, start dates. Her fingers slow at the mention of a six-figure package. Texas. The words settle into her chest, neither closing the email nor pushing it away.

"It's an offer," she murmurs, her voice measured and controlled. "From Dallas."

But something anchors her gaze to the words still glowing on the screen like a bruised truth.

Brick doesn't let it go. His hand slides across the space between them, warm and steady, brushing against hers. "Read it to me," he says softly. "All of it. I'm here."

Her fingers tighten slightly around his. She breathes in, her eyes flickering with the weight of the moment.

"'We're pleased to offer you the position of Head of Public Relations with the Dallas Lightning. This includes a competitive salary package of $185,000 annually, with a relocation to Dallas required...'"

Her voice trails off, steady but soft.

The sun presses fully into the room now, heating the air and muting the softness that had wrapped the night. The quiet intensity between them suddenly hums with something heavier than light—possibility and restraint knitted together, the shape of their morning shifting beneath the weight of future paths stretching wide open.

Brick watches her, every breath a silent question hanging between muscle and skin.

The coffee machine clicks off with a low whirr. Steam curls from the spout like a whisper fading into the morning stillness. Natalie sets two mugs on the granite counter. The deep aroma of fresh coffee folds into the quiet kitchen air, rich and bitter. Her movements are deliberate and slow, as if afraid to break the fragile calm that exists between them only in these early hours.

Her eyes tracked Brick across the room, where he leaned into the mirror, tugging the belt of his robe tight with practiced ease. Soft morning light filtered through half-closed blinds, casting striped shadows across the hardwood floor.

He glanced over and caught her watching. A brow quirked. His lips twitched into a smirk that didn't quite reach the tension knotted in his jaw. The room felt smaller somehow, as if the space between them had shrunk to the width of unsaid words.

Brick poured cream into his coffee, watching the liquid swirl in gentle eddies. "So, Boss Lady," he murmured, the teasing note careful and deliberate, "are you brewing up something stronger than coffee this morning?"

Natalie arched an eyebrow and set down her mug. Her fingers tightened around its rim as a flicker of unease shadowed her gaze. The teasing hummed in the background, but beneath it, something taut and raw quivered—unspoken, waiting.

"You're dangerously close to losing that sharp PR edge and turning into a morning talk show host," she shot back. However, her voice wavered just enough to betray the calculated steadiness on which she'd built her career.

Brick chuckled, but there was hesitation in the sound—a brittle edge. "I guess that means you're the star of the day, and I'm just the guy who waits for the applause."

Natalie breathed out, forcing herself past the dance of humor. She wrapped her hands around her mug, warmth seeping through her fingers. The apartment around them felt suspended, caught between the ordinary and the inevitable.

"The offer isn't just a raise, Brick. It's a step up—a head position, a national profile, a bigger budget, and more…" She paused, searching for the word. "Control."

Her eyes flicked to his face, searching, then back down to the swirl of coffee. "But it also means Dallas—moving halfway across the country and leaving everything we've built here."

Brick's smirk faded. Something softer replaced it—more vulnerable. He folded his arms against the counter, his voice low and steady. "I'm proud of you, Nat. You've got that fire, that skill nobody around here matches." He exhaled slowly. "But this… damn. We fought hard for this balance, for the peace, for us to breathe the same air without work swallowing us whole."

Natalie's gaze sharpened, her voice a whisper edged with raw honesty. "I don't want to leave you. I don't want to ask you to give up your dreams either."

She watched him as if waiting for the ground beneath them to shift—to crack open and spill the truth.

Brick lingered in the pause. His jaw worked beneath the shadow of stubble, and his eyes darkened with thought. He weighed countless unseen scales: pride versus fear, ambition versus loyalty, the life they had carved out against the one calling her away.

The room breathed around them, filled with the faint hiss of the coffee maker cooling, the muted clink of a spoon resting in a saucer, and the thrum of traffic beginning beyond the windows as the city stirred to life.

But he said nothing.

The silence pressed in—charged and electric—a promise and a question hanging between them like thick honey.

At last, Brick pushed back from the counter with slow grace. His fingers brushed the edge before he stepped away, his mouth tight and his eyes unreadable. The quiet stretched, their breaths mismatched in the stillness.

There was no answer yet, only the weight of possibility settling heavy and thick as the morning light pooled at their feet.

Brick's boots thudded against the concrete, creating a steady percussion. The stadium's long corridors stretched ahead, shadowed and hollow, while his duffel swung tight at his side—a familiar weight that settled solidly in his grip.

The air hummed with mingled scents: turf and leather, a sharp green bite tangling with musk, the echoes of past battles imprinted fresh on the fibers of this place. His steps measured out a rhythm that matched the pulse fluttering just under his ribs.

Everything was shifting. He couldn't slow down now.

Coach Hale's voice cut through the quiet—low and precise. "Brick, can I get a minute? A private word." The tone carried weight that did not invite refusal.

Brick nodded, muscles taut but obedient, and followed the coach along the corridor. Decades of frozen glory stared down from the walls: glossy photographs of roaring crowds, triumphant poses, and helmets gleaming under fluorescent lights. Framed jerseys hung like silent judges, reminders of legacy and expectation.

The team's history pressed against him—not just his own burden, but the weight of every man who had worn this uniform before.

The door clicked shut behind them. It was a small office, with walls cramped with whiteboards scrawled with play diagrams and old game tape reels stacked like relics.

The sterile light above flickered briefly, casting quicksilver shadows that cut across the coach's face.

Marcus Hale leaned forward, his eyes steady and his voice calm. "We've been watching you, Brick. Not just your moves on the field. You've grown into a leader—the kind of man this team needs. Not perfect, but real. Someone who has learned from his mistakes."

His hand dropped onto Brick's shoulder, firm enough to anchor but not to squeeze.

Brick's breath caught deep inside. His jaw tightened. Silence crashed between them like thunder. His eyes dropped to his hands, resting heavily on his thighs, fingers curling as if bracing against the weight ahead.

The responsibility sat there—cold and demanding.

Coach Hale's gaze softened but remained unwavering. "I'm offering you the co-captaincy, not just because you're tough in the trenches, but because you've shown what it means to rise again and to bring others up with you."

Brick swallowed; his throat constricted as a bitter knot tightened low in his chest. Pride clawed upward, sharp and raw, tangled with the ache of doubt that settled like a cold stone.

He wasn't sure he deserved this—not yet. The ghosts of past explosions flickered behind his eyes—the nights spent wrestling with guilt, the accidental crossings of limits that almost cost him everything.

"Leadership is never about being perfect, Brick." Coach Hale's voice lowered, steady as the earth beneath their feet. "It's about how you get back up and who you lift while you're at it."

His fingers squeezed briefly on Brick's shoulder before the contact broke away.

Then, with an unspoken finality, Hale extended his hand.

Brick met the gesture and gripped it solidly. He felt the calloused strength and the trust in that brief handshake.

"I want you to take it." The words hung heavy in the air, charged with expectation and possibility.

The door opened behind them, inviting but indifferent. Brick turned, stepping out with Hale's charge thundering in his mind—a knot of apprehension twisting tight beneath the rush of unfamiliar pride.

The corridor stretched ahead, hallways of pressure and promise.

The echo of the coach's voice trailed through the quiet, steady and true: "It's about how you get back up and who you lift while you're at it."

The hum of cleats against tile and low conversations swelled as Brick stepped into the locker room. The air hung thick with sweat and the sharp tang of liniment, mixed with the earthy musk of freshly cut grass carried in on the players' boots.

The familiar clang of metal lockers suddenly opened into a roar.

Heads turned. Teammates broke off from scattered groups, surging toward him.

A cheer erupted—raw and loud. It crashed against the narrow walls like a rising tide. "Brick! Co-captain! That's the man!" Jaxon's voice sliced through the clamor, high with pride. The others echoed the sentiment, slapping his broad shoulders and clapping heavy hands against his back.

A grin cracked Brick's jaw—real. But his eyes held something else—a cautious gleam, like a soldier waking to a new kind of battle.

Brick stiffened, fingers tightening on the cool steel locker. The room's noise dimmed in his ears as a hard weight pressed down on his chest.

From the edge of the swarm, Caleb approached, his gait hesitant. The fingers around his water bottle twisted nervously. His gaze flickered upward, searching Brick's face as if trying to decode a secret.

When he speaks, his voice nearly drowns in the noise.

"I've got that media thing Friday," Caleb said, his voice cracking under the clamor. "Any, uh... pointers? I don't want to mess it up."

Brick's hand drummed against the cold steel of his locker. Steady. Sure.

"Keep it simple. Stick to your points. Remember, they want you to slip up—don't give them the chance. Breathe before you speak, like you do before the snap. Make your words count." His tone was firm but patient, shaped by years of trial and error.

Caleb nodded, swallowing a dry laugh. "Yeah, yeah. Slow and steady. Got it."

At the periphery of the room, DeShawn slipped toward the exit, pressing his phone to his ear with a guarded expression. The faint scrape of his cleats against the floor grew quieter. His jaw clamped tight, lips pressed into a line as his words drifted in muted urgency. His eyes darted around briefly, shadowed with strain.

Then he disappeared into the hallway.

The clack of his cleats faded, replaced by the low thrum of muffled laughter and the occasional clang of a dropped helmet. The scent of liniment mingled with stale sweat—comforting yet harsh, like the unspoken demands of the day.

Jaxon caught Emma's eye across the room—a glance loaded with shared understanding.

Emma's lips curled into an approving smile, a subtle nod affirming the changing winds of clubhouse power.

"He's stepping up, huh?" Jaxon murmured, his voice low enough for only Emma to hear.

"These guys need a steady hand," Emma replied, warmth threading through her calm gaze.

The locker room's pulse shifted—a mingling of celebration and cautious expectation. The reckless cheers of victory were tempered by a new weight. A silent undercurrent tugged at the edges of the camaraderie.

Brick sensed it all: the eager scrutiny and the unspoken questioning of what he would carry now.

Caleb leaned a little closer, his voice dropping as he tucked the water bottle under his arm. "How do you stay focused when it's all eyes, all the time?"

Brick's reply came without hesitation.

"You don't look at the eyes; you look past them. To the game, to the team—that's your rock. Everyone's watching, yeah, but none of them live in your cleats but you."

Around them, other players shuffled past, stealing glances. A blend of respect and curiosity painted their faces.

Brick wasn't just one of the guys anymore; he was the anchor, the line cast in shifting waters—a man expected to pull the group through storms both on and off the field.

The chatter rose again—laughter, friendly ribbing, and the sudden earnestness of athletes realizing the gravity beneath the jargon. Brick listened as Caleb replayed his fears in quiet murmurs, offering quick, grounded advice like a seasoned craftsman guiding an apprentice.

"Own your story, Caleb. The media is just another kind of crowd noise. Control what you can. Keep your edge, but don't let it sharpen into fear."

Caleb's shoulders loosened. A flicker of confidence threaded through his movements.

Around him, the locker room hummed—a discordant harmony of old rhythms and new disciplines weaving through the air. The smell of sweat mingled with faint hints of cologne and the metallic sting of adrenaline, the scent of hungry men on the edge of something greater.

Brick's gaze drifted over the room. He was now aware not only of his teammates' cheers but also of their watchful eyes, anticipating leadership and waiting to see if the temper behind the temperance would hold firm.

A quiet gravity settled into his bones, a promise whispered beneath the noise: this was more than a title; it was a charge.

He leaned against his locker, steady as the steel beneath his palm. The room's warmth pressed in but also invited him—a battlefield reshaped into a brotherhood. The past and future danced in the shifting light beneath the flickering fluorescents.

Voices rose and fell in the ongoing rhythm of fight, fall, and rise again.

The locker room pulsed with life and possibility, alive with the quiet tension of a man stepping into his new role—as both warrior and guardian—while those around him watched, waiting for him to lead.

The stadium media room hummed with distant echoes of practice—the rhythmic thud of cleats on turf and coaches' clipped instructions carried faintly through the glass. Natalie paced the length of the sleek room, her mind circling the same words again and again.

The screen of her phone glowed in the dim light. The email subject blinked like a beacon: *POSITION OFFER – Head of PR, Dallas Lightning*. She stopped at the floor-to-ceiling window. The sharp scent of pressed suits and stale coffee lingered in the air. She pressed her fingertips into the bridge of her nose.

The sky outside pressed cold and gray, mirroring the tight knot forming in her chest.

The silence broke as Nina slipped quietly inside, a small foil-wrapped cupcake cradled like a peace offering. She placed it gently on the glass table, all business and smiling warmth. "Congrats are in order," she said, her voice low but steady, her eyes bright with encouragement.

Natalie absently nods, turning back to the glowing screen, her fingers hovering. The quiet pressure of the stadium buzz feels miles away here, trapped in this still, sealed room.

Then the phone buzzes—sharp and insistent. Emma's name flashes. Natalie answers, a wry smile slipping past the tight seal of anxiety.

"So, it looks like the Dallas Lightning is trying to swipe you out from under our noses," Emma says, her voice light but tinged with genuine warmth. "Cutthroat much?"

Natalie's laugh softens the tension. "Yeah, it seems like it. I swear I'm not actively hunting for new scandals."

"Hey, no judgments," Emma counters smoothly. "But seriously, you're a catch. If you leave, just know you're bleeding the whole league dry of talent."

A pause stretches between them. Then Emma's tone shifts into something steadier, more grounded.

"Whatever you do, keep your head clear. Make the choice that feeds your fire, not just your résumé. You know I'm in your corner, no matter what."

Natalie lets the words settle, the warmth of friendship a faint balm against the whirlwind in her chest.

Back on the screen, she scrolls deeper, eyeing the fine print—relocation requirements, a hefty salary bump, and a start date crammed between months filled with their current season's chaos. She drags her finger slowly along the calendar. The dates glare with cold certainty.

A pulse of excitement rippled beneath the caution. The chance to step into a national spotlight, to seize a career-defining role—it tempted her with sharp electricity. But the underlying price loomed large: the cracks in the life she and Brick had stitched together with sweat and stubborn love.

Her breathing hitched. The room seemed to close in, a heavy weight tightening around her ribs.

She set the phone down, screen up but reply unopened. The cupcake beside her, frosted delicately with blue and silver swirls, remained untouched—a symbol of celebration too complicated to savor.

Her gaze drifted back to the window. A couple of players trudged from the field, their figures halved by shadows and light. Brick was out there somewhere, immersed in the rhythm they had built together—early mornings, late nights debriefing over cold pizza, and the quiet understanding that came from building something side by side. If she left, she would be stepping away from all of it.

The pull of loyalty tugged like gravity.

Her fingers twitched restlessly in her lap. A low hum thrummed beneath her skin—part thrill, part dread twisting tight in her stomach.

"What's it like," she finally murmured to the empty room, her voice barely above a breath, "to choose between the future you've dreamed of and the one you're building?"

The silence answered nothing.

The soft click of the glass door signaled Nina's return. She carried a steaming cup of coffee, placing it carefully near the cupcake. "No matter what, you're not facing this alone," Nina said gently, her eyes steady. "We'll work through it together."

Natalie managed a nod, but her fingers remained poised above the phone's keyboard, a battleground of hope and hesitation. The reply box blinked—a silent invitation and risk.

She sank onto the media room's low couch. The cool leather contrasted with the heat pooling at her temples. The air carried the faint tang of cold concrete and slightly stale upholstery. The sun-drenched noise of the practice field filtered through the tinted glass—life moving forward regardless of her pause.

The cupcake's sugary promise remained unclaimed. Natalie stared at it a moment longer before swallowing—a nervous, tight swallow.

The room held its breath with her, clutching the fragile tension between ambition and love.

Outside, the afternoon light waned, the day tipping toward unknown turns. Inside, Natalie sat caught between the pulse of possibility and the anchor of what was already hers, the unopened reply balanced like a fragile tide waiting to turn.

The stadium gleamed under a pale, slanting sun, its vast emptiness swallowing the faint echo of distant footsteps. Concrete stairs ascended beside the stands, worn smooth from years of countless fans and players. Two flights up, Natalie perched on the edge, her silhouette outlined against the endless emerald stretch of turf below.

During games, this field roared. Thousands of voices crashed against these walls, shaking the very air. Now, the quiet felt almost accusatory—a mirror held up to the weight pressing down on both their shoulders.

The air holds the faint scent of cut grass, mingled with the distant hum of city life slipping beneath the stadium's shadow.

Brick's footsteps hit heavier now, each one measured, grounding the hollow calm around them. He climbs the steps, his breath even, muscles relaxed but taut beneath his tracksuit. Reaching the landing, he brushes a stray lock of hair from his forehead, taking in the way Natalie stares quietly at the field, her fingers loosely clasped in her lap.

Without hesitation, he settles down beside her, the concrete cool beneath them. His hand curves gently around hers—firm, steady, a touch meant to anchor.

"So... what do you really want?" His voice is low, raw with an undercurrent of urgency. "Not what you think I'd say yes to. What's right for you?"

He meets her eyes, unwavering.

Natalie's gaze dips back to the turf, the clean lines and empty goalposts suddenly sharp in the fading light. She lets out a slow breath, her fingers tightening then loosening in her lap. Her eyes flicker toward the copper-edged horizon, betraying a storm beneath the calm.

"It's everything... what I've worked for," she admits, her voice soft like a confession slipping through cracks. "But I'm scared. Scared that the miles will stretch between us, and we'll unravel like threads too weak to hold."

Brick's jaw tightens. The confession hanging between them cuts deeper than he expected. Part of him wants to promise her it won't happen—that they're stronger than distance. But he knows better. He knows what losing her would feel like, the slow ache of watching someone slip away. Yet he also knows this: letting her go would destroy them both more than any number of miles ever could.

His next words come out roughened but steady, weighted with the truth that has been clawing at his chest for days.

"I don't love the job or the team. I love *you*—who you are, not what you do." His thumb brushes a slow circle against her palm, a silent promise amid the quiet. "Anywhere you go, that's who I'm running toward."

A heavy pause hangs between them, the empty field stretching as a silent witness to hopes and fears unspoken. Natalie folds her legs beneath her, leaning her head briefly against Brick's shoulder. The simple contact bridges the uncertainty—fragile but real.

The late afternoon sun dips lower, gilding the horizon with a copper glow. Brick's arm snakes around her shoulders, a protector's embrace loaded with promise.

"I'll support your ambitions," he assures her, his voice roughened but unwavering. "Whatever comes, we'll figure it out. Together."

They rise slowly, the stairwell's concrete cool against their legs—a tableau of hesitant hope framed by the vastness of the game's coliseum.

Side by side, they descend the stairs—tentative and linked—carrying in their silence the fragile, shared understanding of everything that might change and everything they're willing to fight to keep.

The cool concrete beneath them absorbs the fading warmth of the afternoon light, casting long shadows along the stadium stairwell. Natalie's fingers curl tightly around the rough edge of the step as she lifts her gaze, meeting Brick's steady eyes. Her voice breaks the silence, hushed but sharp, no longer hiding behind polite deflections.

"It's not the job I'm afraid of," she said, her voice raw enough to catch on the breeze. "It's whether we can trust each other to hold on when distance stretches between us."

Distance. The word hung there—a familiar ache that traced back to her last relationship, to late nights spent waiting for calls that came too late, to the slow erosion of connection across time zones. She had learned then that proximity wasn't just geography; it was presence, choice, and a deliberate turning toward each other.

Brick's gaze didn't waver. His breath caught in a slow rhythm, the weight of her words settling deep in his chest. "Trust," he repeated, his voice gruff but earnest. "It's been a long road for me. Dreams used to be simple: win the game, prove I'm not just a hothead." He paused, swallowing hard. "But now there's more—responsibility, real stakes."

His eyes traced her face as if he were searching for the courage to say it all out loud.

"I want your dreams to matter as much as mine," he confessed, his fingers brushing against hers without hesitation. An unspoken promise lingered between them. "But damn, sometimes I'm scared I'll screw it all up."

Natalie's breath hitched. Her fingers curled into fists on her knees as vulnerability pressed against the walls she had built for years. The tremor in her voice spoke louder than words. "It's not the job, Brick. It's whether we trust each other enough to build something real—no matter where we are."

His eyes darkened.

Memories flashed through his gaze—the nights she stayed when everyone else turned their backs, the steady anchor she became when his world threatened to unravel. His jaw clenched, muscles taut, but not with the old rage. This was different. This was the fear of losing something that mattered.

He had felt it before, years ago with his father—that moment when you realize someone is walking away and you can't stop them. The helplessness had carved something sharp into him then. He had learned to fight back with fury instead of vulnerability. But she had stayed through the fury, even when it would have been easier to leave.

"You were there," he said quietly. "When the rage took over. When I thought I was done. You didn't walk away."

Natalie's chest tightened. Tears burned behind her lashes. She swallowed the lump forming like a stone. "I'm still here."

The air between them thickened—raw, unfiltered truth laid bare beneath the expansive sky. Both were aware that pain could follow, yet neither was willing to let fear carve their path.

Brick exhaled. A low rumble vibrated in his chest. "We won't let fear run the show. No frozen futures. We will test it and see where the road takes us."

Her fingers found his, entwining in a pact made without fanfare or grand declarations—a quiet covenant to face whatever came.

"We face the changes," Natalie agreed, her voice steady now, "without holding each other back."

Their breaths mingled in the cooling air, a fragile truce wrapped in resilience—a promise forged not in certainty, but in the fierceness to try anyway.

The fading sun dipped below the stadium's jagged skyline, casting long shadows across the concrete steps where Brick and Natalie sat, wrapped in the heavy hush between words. The stadium loomed around them—not just a structure of steel and stone, but a monument to the battles they had fought and the expectations that had carved grooves into their bones. Even as daylight fled, the weight of unfinished games and uncertain futures lingered in the air.

He turned toward her, boots scraping softly against the concrete, his voice low and steady—a rare softness threading through the usual edge that accompanied him everywhere else.

"Maybe we try it like this instead: take the Dallas offer." He paused, letting the words settle. "But not for good. Not right away. We make it a trial. See what happens. See how we hold up, how we bend without breaking."

Natalie's breath caught; her lashes fluttered like hesitant wings before a shaky laugh broke free, warm tears tracing trails down her cheeks. Relief slid through her like water thawing frozen ground, breaking the tension that had clenched so tightly around her chest for weeks.

"You really mean that?" Her voice wavered. "Not just a safety net if everything falls apart?"

Brick reached out, brushing a stray lock of hair from her face. His touch lingered—deliberate and grounding. "I mean it. You deserve to chase your damn dreams. But I want us to be more than a footnote in your story. Or mine."

Her hand found his. Their pinkies curled together in the subtle, secret handshake only they understood—a gesture that hung between them, fragile and fierce in the evening light. Both smiled then. Small smiles. Genuine ones. The kind that unspooled years of fought battles and quiet hopes.

Natalie stood slowly, her eyes bright but calmer. She slipped her phone back into her bag without the usual urgency. There was no rush, no snapping back to the world of urgent replies. Later—when they could be sure of what words to wield—she would answer. For now, she simply let steady breath fill her lungs, grounding her in the uneasy clarity of their compromise.

Brick rose beside her, the rhythm of their steps syncing as they moved down the stairwell toward the facility's entrance.

Their arms brushed now and then—a subtle electricity humming where skin met skin, a familiar comfort in the chaotic orbit of their lives.

Around them, teammates and staff drifted past, unaware of the fragile pact they carried just beneath the surface.

"You really think this can work?" Natalie's voice cut through the quiet.

"If we're honest—and patient—yeah." He met her gaze, steady and unwavering. "We can build something real. Something that doesn't need perfect conditions. And if it hurts, we will deal with it. Together."

Natalie nodded slowly, hope threading through the cautious weight in her chest. "Promise?"

"Promise." Brick's pinky twitched in hers, sealing the vow with a warmth that lingered long after their fingers unclasped.

They reached the threshold of the locker room, where the hum of voices and distant laughter spilled outward like a promise of normalcy. Side by side, they stepped across the line—not fully certain where this new path would lead, but united enough to start.

The plan was no longer a distant possibility but something they carried between them: tentative, precious, alive. In the days ahead, neither would know if strength meant holding on or letting go, if trust could survive the distance Dallas demanded, or if this gamble would shatter like everything fragile eventually does. But standing here, at the threshold, they chose to build anyway—knowing that sometimes love isn't about certainty; it's about showing up when the outcome remains beautifully, terrifyingly unknown.

Brick leans against the worn locker beside Caleb's, his eyes steady as he watches the younger man fidget with a water bottle. The hum of chatter and the clink of cleats on tile fill the locker room, creating a low roar behind their quiet bubble. His voice drops smooth and calm, seasoned like a coach's—soaked with quiet authority born from hard-earned lessons.

"Alright, listen." Brick's gaze locks onto Caleb's. "When you step up for that interview, take a deep breath first. Slow it down. Nobody wins by rushing. Memorize your key lines, but don't sound rehearsed. Make them yours. And pick a ritual—something small. Tap your wristband. Whatever flips that switch from nerves to focus."

Caleb nods. His eyes don't leave Brick's face, soaking in the advice like it is a map through his restless mind. His fingers tighten around the wristband—small but deliberate. The crease between his brows softens, and his posture straightens just enough to matter.

"That actually helps," Caleb says, a grin tugging at his lips, hesitant but real.

Brick chuckles—low and rough. "Boss Lady would kill me if I didn't share her playbook."

"Thanks, Brick." Caleb's voice steadies as he says it.

Outside the locker room, near the exit archway, DeShawn's voice dips low into his phone headset—measured but tight with urgency. Sweat beads along his jawline and doesn't dry. His eyes flash with something buried—conflict, secrets he doesn't want to carry.

He slipped a small, crisp envelope from his pocket, the edges sharp between his fingers. He slid it into the narrow locker gap without meeting a single teammate's glance.

Something heavy settled in the silence beneath the casual noise of the locker room. DeShawn's jaw tightened. Whatever was in that envelope, whatever the call had meant, clawed at him from the inside—a weight he couldn't set down, couldn't share, and couldn't escape.

He closed his eyes for a breath, then turned and walked away.

Near the doorway, Natalie leaned lightly against the frame, her posture relaxed but her gaze intensely fixed on Brick. A soft smile curved her lips, her palm pressed flat against the cool metal of the frame. The flickering fluorescent light caught her face, etched with something more tender than pride—relief, maybe, or a quiet recognition of what he was becoming as captain. Watching him steady Caleb like this, without any fanfare or need for credit, meant something. It meant he was ready. It meant she'd made the right call, even when the front office had doubted her.

Brick's laugh rolled across the room, rough and genuine, pulling attention from teammates near and far—the kind of laugh that carried the grit of past battles softened into brotherhood. He caught Natalie's gaze.

He tilted an eyebrow—half question, half affection.

His grin was a secret promise, only hers to catch.

Natalie caught it instantly. Her laugh was a soft murmur, barely shading the background noise. Her eyes sparkled, the cool professionalism she wore like armor cracking just enough to let the warmth through.

"Don't get cocky now, Turner," she said, her voice low enough for only him to hear.

"You'd miss me otherwise," he replied, his eyes gleaming.

Caleb cleared his throat, and both their attention shifted to him. He stood taller now, his wrists steady as he adjusted his band again. The difference was subtle but unmistakable—an unspoken nod to the invisible scaffold Brick had helped him build.

Meanwhile, DeShawn's quiet exit left a ripple that was less visible but equally charged. The tension in his jaw and the tightness behind his eyes spoke volumes behind the carefully guarded mask. Nobody questioned the retreat; it was part of the unspoken code at the edges of this brotherhood.

Brick glanced DeShawn's way once, his expression unreadable—half concern, half respect for the boundaries not to cross. He knew the weight of carrying things alone and wouldn't push.

The locker room's soundtrack morphed around them: teasing banter, the rustle of gear, and the occasional shout from someone nowhere near ready to pack up.

Natalie stepped fully inside. The doorframe framed her like a quiet sentinel. The scent of her perfume—something fresh, green, with a hint of jasmine—mingled with the musk of sweat and leather. She absorbed the scene: Brick's easy camaraderie, Caleb's newfound poise, and the unspoken struggles threading through the room's undercurrent like a current that nobody could quite name.

Her hand fell away from the frame.

A slow inhale steadied the quiet beat between moments.

Across the room, Brick's laughter folded into a grin. His gaze locked with hers, lips parted slightly in a playful challenge—an unspoken promise of battles won and battles still to come.

Natalie's smile deepened. Her cheeks lifted, though her eyes remained guarded—until a flicker of warmth finally softened their usual sharpness. A light chuckle escaped, barely audible but enough to bridge the gap between them.

The locker room pulsed around them: voices rising, footsteps pacing, and cups rattling against lockers. Amidst the chaos, a fragile new order was taking shape: Brick, now co-captain, quiet strength wrapped in raw edges; Caleb, stepping into the light with shaky but steady hands; DeShawn, carrying shadows in silence; and Natalie, the calm eye in the storm, watching it all with a breath held between past and future.

Brick's voice broke the simmering energy as he drew Caleb's focus once more.

"Remember, kid," his tone was granite. "No matter how loud the crowd gets, control the space around you. Own your moment. And when it gets too much, you breathe again. You don't run from it."

Caleb's nod was firm this time. The weight of responsibility settled like a steady flame.

DeShawn slipped past the last cluster of players and disappeared down the corridor. The quiet clack of his cleats matched the rhythm of secrets that hadn't yet found the light.

Natalie watched Brick's back as he glanced her way one last time. He raised an eyebrow—half challenge, half silent vow.

The room hummed on, carrying them all forward, threaded tight with promise and tension. This season wasn't just about the game anymore; it was the start of something raw, real, and fiercely alive.

Controlled Fire

The locker room thrums with summer energy—off-season electricity crackling against the stale weight of sweat and worn leather. Players shed pads and helmets, their voices jagged between grins and shouts. Near the benches, a battle erupts over music. One player cranks a track while another demands a change. The sharp crack of cleats on tile cuts through the stereo's hum—a grating mix of locker slams and jerseys dropped carelessly on benches.

Caleb's voice cuts across the room by the speaker. "Seriously? '70s funk? How is that even in your rotation?"

DeShawn laughs—a dark, easy sound—and drapes his towel around his neck. He leans against the stereo, a sly grin spreading across his face. "That's pure soul, man. Your pick is just static crackling between plays, whining louder than the ref's whistle."

Caleb bristles, not just at the song but at always playing second fiddle. He twists toward DeShawn, his eyes narrowing. "Soul? More like stuck in the past, Price. Time to catch up—or stay benched."

The words hang sharp in the air. Across the locker room, heads tilt, and eyes sharpen with curiosity.

DeShawn's smirk twists. "Benched?" He steps closer. "Just like your moves out there. Are you scared to step up next season?"

Heat floods Caleb's jaw, and his muscles bunch tight. "Watch your mouth."

DeShawn shoves him in the chest—quickly. A spark ignites.

Caleb shoves back—harder this time. "Keep talking, and I'll put you on the ground."

Two teammates move forward, semi-ready to intervene. But the tension only coils tighter. Others cluster closer, whispering and watching. Some bite their lips to hold back cheers, while others shift, ready to jump in if needed. The ring tightens, pulsing with contained energy. Music is swallowed beneath harsh breaths and strained stares.

From a bench near the far wall, Brick's posture snaps. He rises—no rush, no noise. Slow, deliberate steps bridge the space between them. His shadow stretches across the tile. The fluorescent light catches the jagged scar above his right eyebrow—a map of battles fought inside and out.

His voice drops low—steady and iron-strong.

"Stop."

Caleb and DeShawn don't budge, their eyes burning into each other like stones thrown into fire.

Without breaking stride, Brick plants himself between them, arms open wide, palms flat. Steady. There is no threat in his stance—only the quiet command of his presence. His jaw clenches beneath the surface, control masking something restrained and taut. He names them, his voice steady and low, a tether pulling at the edges of their rage.

"Caleb. DeShawn. Do you want your season on the bench? Because this? This is how you lose the team's trust and the coach's patience."

Silence spills thickly. Tension hangs like a film ready to snap.

Brick's gaze locks onto each man, sharp enough to cut through stubborn pride and patient enough to hold them accountable.

"Hands off. Step apart. Shower. Cool down. Now."

Words, not questions.

Neither Caleb nor DeShawn replies, but their lips tighten. Grudging murmurs resurface. They slide apart like colliding planets moving back into orbit. Muscles retract from the fight. Heavy eyes flick toward Brick and then away. Grudging respect settles into the cracks.

Coach Marcus Hale leans against the doorway, his broad frame silhouetted against the sterile hallway light. His nod tilts—subtle, unspoken approval. His eyes linger on Brick with a mix of relief and challenge. This co-captain is no longer just a hothead but a man trying to hold the line.

The energy in the room shifts. Whispers ripple among the players. Tension loosens like a tide pulling back after a storm. Low voices exchange words—the kind that speak of surprise and long-standing hopes. Brick, the volatile force, is now a steady vanguard.

In the hallway just beyond, Natalie watches, arms folded and lips pressed into a faint smile. Her sharp eyes catch Brick's steady gaze, and for a moment, words fall away between them—a silent pact forged in understanding. Trust sharpens like a blade between calm and chaos.

Caleb and DeShawn disappear toward the showers. The locker room exhales. The clatter of lockers closing blends with softer conversations, the scrape of benches, and distant laughter. Brick settles back onto the bench, calm authority holding firm as the newly tempered air hums around him.

Natalie and Brick emerge from the locker room's long hallway. Behind them, cleats scrape against the concrete, and laughter fades. Players and staff swirl in chaotic energy—voices overlapping, equipment clattering, and the sharp bite of sweat and liniment hanging thick in the recirculated air. Sunshine spills through the wide glass doors ahead, painting long shards of light across the concrete like a path.

Brick walks beside her, his steps measured but steady. The new co-captain carries his quiet strength the way some men wear cologne—it radiates off him, undeniable.

"So," Natalie draws out the word, her smirk knowing, "Zen master Brick. Who knew peace could be dressed in sixty-five pounds of muscle and a game face that could shatter glass?"

Brick rolls his eyes, and the corner of his mouth twitches.

"Don't get used to it," he says. "The second I slip, you'll be the first one calling me a ticking time bomb again."

"That's what makes this act so convincing." She bumps her hip against his as they navigate through shoulders and duffel bags—easy, natural.

They trailed behind a cluster of players debating off-season plans, some elbowing each other over smoothie flavors and others jostling for the last towel. The tension in the locker room evaporated in the warmth of their exchange. A fragile truce hung between them, but it held.

A flicker of doubt chased the steady beat of his steps. This wasn't just about controlling a fight; it was about proving to himself that he could hold it together.

Outside, the sharp scent of gasoline and crushed pavement hit them as they reached the parking lot. Brick paused by his sleek black SUV, the late afternoon sun catching the silver badges on the back doors.

He pivoted toward the rear hatch and reached inside, emerging with a brown paper bag. Lemongrass and chili escaped from the crease in the paper like a promise.

"Look what I snagged before we left." He held it out. "Your favorite Thai place still delivers after practice."

Natalie's eyebrows shot up. She squinted through the shadow of her cap, a slow smile tugging at her lips.

"Thoughtful boyfriend move? Should I be scared or swoon?"

Brick grinned. The scar above his eyebrow twitched with unspoken pride. "Neither. Just making sure you don't go hungry dealing with me."

She snatched the bag, the paper crackling softly between her fingers. "I might throw you under the bus to the media just to score free dinners."

"Try it. See where that gets you."

They fell into step, the early afternoon warmth wrapping around them. The sounds of the parking lot faded under their easy exchange.

"Seriously, though," Natalie said, tilting her head, "how did you keep that confrontation from blowing sky-high today? Has new media training got you practicing Jedi mind tricks?"

Brick snorted. "It's hard to flip out when there are a dozen pairs of eyes on you. Plus, you hovering by the sidelines didn't hurt."

"Hovering is supervision," she countered, arms crossed but a smile sneaking through.

Their laughter mingled with the muted hum of engines and distant cheers echoing from the stadium. Brick unlocked the doors while they joked about his newfound 'discipline.'

Inside, leather seats held the faint ghost of cologne and sweat from hours on the field. Natalie unwrapped a container. The sizzle of warm rice filled the confined space as the car doors clicked closed.

From the window, Brick's eyes caught movement: a figure pacing near the side entrance. DeShawn, hoodie pulled tight, phone pressed to his ear. The tight set of his jaw wasn't new—when things spiraled, he was the first to crack. Brick held his breath, waiting for the fallout.

Neither Brick nor Natalie broke their stride to interrupt the moment's gravity.

Caleb sat a stone's throw away on a bench beside a cracked curb, his head bowed and phone in his hands, not reading. A silent weight pressed down on his shoulders. The autumn light brushed his face in gold and shadow, casting him as a solitary figure amid the day's chaos.

Natalie's hand found Brick's, giving it a quick squeeze—solid and grounding. No words were needed.

Brick turned the key, and the engine purred to life, vibrating through the chassis. The tension from the locker room fight slipped behind them like fog burning off morning grass.

Laughter and easy conversation rose between them, and the promise of the evening ahead softened their edges.

As the stadium shrank in the rearview mirror, the world narrowed to shared glances and the scent of Thai spices hanging between them.

Outside, DeShawn's low voice continued its urgent cadence, while Caleb remained alone, shadows lengthening over the empty bench.

Brick pulled the vehicle smoothly onto the street, and the rhythm ahead unfolded with quiet certainty.

The door clicked shut—a soft but decisive sound that sealed away the hum and grit of the stadium. Brick's fingers found the lock, turned it with practiced ease, and then kicked off his cleats. The worn leather thudded against the mat, and a faint musk lingered on his socks—old turf, dead grass, the smell of a thousand games compressed into fabric.

Natalie set the takeout bag on the smooth kitchen counter with gentle care. Plastic containers rustled beneath her hands. Lemongrass and spicy basil spilled into the air, cutting through the staleness of the day.

Their movements unfolded without rush. Brick hung his jacket on a wall hook, the subtle creak of leather against metal accompanying his actions. Natalie peeled open the bag, retrieving steaming boxes and a foil packet. The kitchen's dim light pooled warmly across the polished island. Stainless steel gleamed faintly. Outside, the sun had folded into dusk. The city's pulse was quiet but present—distant sirens, the low hum of traffic, life continuing without them. The apartment felt like what it was: a refuge. Small. Contained. Safe.

Brick grinned. "Remember that first locker room blowup?"

"When DeShawn almost put Caleb on the floor over the playlist?" Natalie pulled out containers of jasmine rice, her smirk already forming. "It was like watching toddlers fight over a toy."

He chuckled, low and easy. "Coach Hale's face afterward. I thought he might call a timeout just to coach us through breathing exercises."

"That's when you knew." She set the containers down and met his eyes across the island. The shared joke softened the space between them. "The team was either doomed or about to turn a corner."

Brick sank into the moment. His voice dropped to a whisper. "I can't believe how far we've come. You. Me. Us." He paused, letting the weight settle. "Never saw this coming, huh?"

Natalie's smile slipped briefly. Her gaze dropped to the floor, lingering there before flickering back up. A quiet hesitance lived in her eyes now. "I've never trusted anyone like this before. It scares me more than I expected."

Brick's expression softened. The usual blaze dimmed to a steady flicker—like embers glowing against the dark. "And I've never felt so safe in my own skin. It's new territory." His voice roughened slightly. "But it feels right."

Without hesitation, he reached out. His large, calloused hand engulfed hers. He laced their fingers together and steered her toward the living room. The subtle warmth radiating through their clasped hands felt like the only real thing left in the world.

The couch welcomed them. Soft cushions creaked under their combined weight. Cedarwood from a diffuser mingled with the remnants of their day—sweat, the spicy leftovers waiting in the kitchen, and the faint salt of skin.

Their lips met slowly and deliberately. Teasing at first. Feather-light. Brick's jaw shifted beneath the brush of Natalie's touch. His breath hitched as his fingers traced slow patterns along her knuckles. Between each kiss, they pulled back slightly, their searching eyes locked for permission.

"You good?" Brick murmured.

Natalie nodded. "I'm more than good."

He grinned, and tension eased from his broad shoulders. The silent give-and-take spun a delicate rhythm, and their mutual consent wove an unspoken pact.

"Think all that media training paid off, huh?" Brick's teasing voice broke the hush. "I'm practically charming now."

Natalie's smirk deepened. "Charming? Lucky for you, I'm not your teacher. You'd be getting a solid 'needs improvement.'"

He nudged her shoulder. "Ouch. Tough grader, huh?"

"In your dreams."

Their smiles softened into something warmer. Lips met again with more hunger but steady hands. Pauses filled with soft questions, whispered assurances, and easy laughter. Time slowed, stretched, and folded them further into quiet exploration, where trust was the only rule.

When the moment felt right, they rose together and drifted toward the bedroom. Their movements blended—now Brick led, now Natalie—with a fluency born of respect. Shirts peeled away slowly, breath mingling with the scent of sweat and skin. Buttons were undone, and fabric slipped free. Every step was deliberate, an exchange of control and surrender. Soft gasps punctuated the quiet as they navigated this shared space of vulnerability.

In the low amber glow, their touch deepened from playful teasing into something raw and real. Brick held back with fierce tenderness, anchoring himself to Natalie's responses and reading her needs like a well-worn playbook. She drew him close when doubt flickered in her eyes, her fingers threading through his hair and grounding him with whispered words.

"Are you okay?" she breathed.

"Yeah." His voice came out rough and low. "With you, I am."

The night swelled with a tenderness that knifed through their defenses. No roar. No fury. Just the steady pulse of joined hearts in a quiet fight against their haunted pasts.

Afterward, limbs tangled beneath soft sheets, breaths slow and rhythmic, they drifted into conversation. Shadows curled around their voices, cradling the raw fears they dared not speak of in daylight.

The looming off-season.

The fragile promise of tomorrow.

The team's uncertain path stretched ahead—like a horizon swallowed by fog.

Natalie's head settled against the solid warmth of Brick's chest. Her fingers traced lazy circles over taut skin. The steady thump beneath her ear was a balm for her ragged edges. It grounded her in a way nothing else could. For someone who had built walls so high, this—his heartbeat, his presence, his quiet steadiness—felt like the first real anchor she had ever allowed.

Brick's hand ghosted through her hair, fingertips light as feather strokes, willing her into calm. "We'll get through it. Together."

Her eyes fluttered closed. The tension dissolved in the sanctuary of his steady heartbeat. The room contracted to the small space of quiet breathing. Soft lamplight painted golden arcs over skin and soul.

Natalie drifted off, carried on a tide of warmth and trust. Brick watched over her, their breaths mingling in the silence that hummed between them. The night held them gently—a fragile peace wrapped in shadows and whispered promises.

The clock's hands sliced through the silence—3:14 a.m. He couldn't sleep.

Brick's eyes fluttered open, shadows crawling behind his eyelids. A restlessness coiled in his chest, tightening and refusing the easy surrender of sleep. His bare feet met the cool oak floor; the apartment exhaled around him, a slumbering beast wrapped in faint hums and distant city whispers.

The kitchen door creaked softly when he pushed it open. Dim light from the street lamps spilled through the blinds in thin stripes, painting silver lines on the counters. The distant hum of traffic mingled with the soft click of the blinds as he pushed them wider, the faint aroma of jasmine curling in from the living room. Brick's throat scratched; he reached for a glass, the cold water sliding down rough and steady.

His gaze fell to the phone lying facedown on the granite countertop. The screen flared suddenly—a new message. His hand curled instinctively around the device: it was from DeShawn. The text read: "Need to talk. Shit's getting real."

Brick's jaw tightens. DeShawn didn't reach out lightly—not after months of silence, not after everything that had fractured between them. Whatever this was, it carried weight. The words hang in the air, raw and urgent, a summons Brick isn't ready to answer.

His lips twitch into a faint, unreadable smile—a crease in the night's quiet. He flips the phone face down again, like closing a book he's not yet ready to open. His footsteps retrace the path to the bedroom, each step measured and deliberate.

He pauses just inside the doorway, catching sight of Natalie asleep—her chest rising and falling, slow and even, framed by the soft folds of the navy sheets. He hesitates, as if afraid to break the quiet trust in her steady breath. His fingers twitch but stop—the distance between them feels smaller, fragile.

The faint scent of her lavender shampoo lingers in the air, mingling with the earthy weight of his own skin nearby. He breathes in, grounding himself. His hand trails absently over the bedspread, tracing small, slow circles on the cool fabric, a silent rhythm to steady his pulse.

Miles away, light pulses from Caleb's phone on the cluttered nightstand, casting snatches of blue across the dark walls of his apartment. He sits at the edge of his bed, shoulders hunched and eyes fixed on a message he's yet to answer. The glow illuminates the tight line of his jaw, the brief flicker of hope shadowed by hesitation.

His fingers twitch above the screen but do not move. A silent reckoning in the quiet—fear tangled with the possibility of something new, a hope half-formed but not yet committed. The air is thick with the scent of worn denim and the faint hint of brewed coffee left from earlier, cold and bitter. Around him, the apartment holds its breath.

Back in Brick's apartment, stillness stretched thin between two unsettled figures: one calm and deliberate, the other caught in anxious pause.

Brick lay in the dark, weighing what came next: DeShawn's message and Caleb waiting. The responsibility of both pressed against him like hands on his chest. He couldn't protect everyone, but he could try not to abandon anyone either.

"You're not gonna leave it on read forever, are you?" His voice rumbled softly into the darkness, breaking the silence without the need for light.

Caleb's reply came through the phone's speaker, distant but clear, as if the words traveled through the darkness itself.

"I'm not sure what to say. It feels like every word might change everything..."

Brick's laugh was low, almost a murmur, threading through the quiet like a tentative promise.

"Sometimes the best words are the ones you hold back. Just don't ghost me."

From across the night's expanse, Caleb's eyes flicker with cautious resolve, marking the first tentative step toward what waits beyond the screen.

Brick rolls onto his side, the mattress dipping beneath him. His fingertips find Natalie's hand, brushing it gently—a tether in the dim. The world shrinks to the slow cadence of breathing and the whispered surrender of sleep.

He glances toward the counter where the phone rests, still face-down—silent now, waiting.

Every new season starts with one controlled fire, and somewhere out there, the next spark catches.

Epilogue

A pale dawn spills across the practice field, quiet except for the gentle hum of floodlights flickering off one by one. The sharp scent of freshly cut grass mingles with the earthy dampness of turf still holding the night's chill. Mist laces the edges of the green, curling in delicate tendrils around the white yard lines, giving the stadium an almost otherworldly glow before the sun asserts itself.

One by one, figures emerge from the shadows of the nearby parking lot. Players lug heavy bags, their breaths casting fleeting clouds in the cool air. Staff shuffle about, clipboards in hand, their voices low yet precise amid the calm buildup of a new day. The stadium's vast steel ribs catch the early light, cold and imposing.

At the front of the semicircle, Brick stands like a sentinel. His silhouette is broad and solid against the dawn, his powerful frame a stark contrast to the uneasy energy crackling among the rookies gathered around him. New faces, flushed with nerves and anticipation, have eyes wide beneath the weight of freshly issued helmets and pads. The air hums with silent questions, fists tightening over grips on cleats that keep shifting under anxious feet.

Brick's gaze sweeps over them—quiet, measured. Each rookie's expression registers: some confusion, others raw determination. His eyes drill down to the skin, the set of the jaw, and the flicker of doubt barely masked by bravado. In that moment, something shifts behind his own gaze—a recognition of their fear that mirrors his own from years ago, when he was raw and uncertain. He remembers the paralysis of those early days, the voice in his head screaming that he didn't belong. That memory, worn smooth by time but never forgotten, softens something in his chest. This is why he's here: not to break them, but to show them what lies on the other side of that doubt.

His breath is steady, and his stance is unyielding. Step by deliberate step, he closes the distance.

When he stops beside the nearest rookie—a lanky kid with too much gear and far too little experience—Brick's hand settles on the young player's shoulder, firm but not crushing. The touch is grounding, like an unspoken promise that he has the rookie's back in this crucible of steel and sweat. That rare curve of Brick's lips—a small, genuine smile—breaks the usual storm cloud he carries. It doesn't erase the tension, but it softens it just enough to let the rookies breathe a little easier.

From the sideline, Caleb and DeShawn move with the ease of men who have earned their place on this team through years of proving themselves. Caleb, a cornerback whose instincts are legendary, and DeShawn, a linebacker whose intelligence reads plays like scripture—they are the thread that stitches veteran and rookie together, their easy rapport a bridge between worlds. Everyone knows they belong here. More importantly, everyone knows they remember what it felt like when they didn't.

Caleb's teasing call trails between the players—a jab wrapped in brotherly mockery. "Better watch yourself, Tyrell. Brick's going to turn you into a wall you're going to wish you never bumped into."

Wide receiver Tyrell grins, playfully shoving Caleb back, the tension lightening. DeShawn's laughter ripples out like warm sunlight, chasing away the last shadows of anxiety. Their easy banter stitches the group together with threads of familiarity, carving out pockets of relief in the looming pressure cooker.

Caleb winks at the group, rattling off, "You rookies look like fresh meat at the butcher's. Don't worry, Brick's got a soft spot under all that grit—sometimes."

DeShawn catches the ribbing with a grin, snorting. "Soft spot? The man's got scars to prove otherwise. But yeah, he's the best damn teacher you'll get."

Eyes slide back to Brick, whose presence feels like iron tempered by fire—unyielding authority without the bite of menace. The rookies straighten, their shoulders sinking a fraction as if Brick's calm is a tide pulling their nerves under and out the other side.

The coaches, moving with the precision of seasoned generals, bark the start of the day's first drill. Calls break the morning stillness: footsteps pounding on the turf, whistles shrilling, pads shifting.

The rookies exchange quick glances, the weight on their chests lifting, if only a little.

Brick steps back into position, his gaze locked forward, steady as the rising sun.

The pattern of practice begins.

The line of scrimmage hums with shifting energy under a sky sharpened by mid-morning light. Brick crouches low, shoulders coiled, ready to snap.

His breath puffs white, misting the crisp morning air as he launches forward, feet drumming against the damp turf with practiced precision. Muscles ripple beneath taut skin. He barrels into the thickly padded tackling bag with a controlled surge, halting just shy of overwhelming force, hands clasping the bag firmly yet without aggression. The bag shudders. Brick's expression holds steady—a silent lesson in power tempered by control.

From the side, a rookie suddenly charges in, reckless fire burning behind his eyes. He thrusts forward, hips driving with too much force, shoulders squared in hurried desperation. Brick steps swiftly, slipping between the teen and the bag, looming large as he cups the rookie's wide chest between two hands. The rookie's momentum crashes into Brick's solid frame.

It stops the surge without bruising the spirit. Brick's hands remain steady, palms firm but gentle against the quaking rookie's jersey.

"Power isn't rage—it's restraint."

Brick's voice drops, rough but steady. His eyes lock onto theirs with hardened kindness as rookies and a few returning players cluster tightly, forming a ring of raw energy and fresh determination. He pauses, jaw tightening slightly—as if recalling battles won and lost—before pressing on.

"When you lose control out here, it's not just you who gets hurt; it's the brother next to you. Discipline keeps the whole line standing."

Shadows flickered through his mind—faces of coaches, snarled and disappointed. The echo of the crowd's gasp when his rage spilled over. Those moments when fury blinded him cost more than just pride. The sting of regret curled tightly in his chest as he exhaled, his shoulders sinking as he shook the weight off.

He turned back to the rookie whose chest he still steadied, his voice softer now, more patient. "Let's try that again. This time, breathe it out. Control your power. Stay sharp." His hand found the rookie's back, pressing lightly, fingers spreading warmth. Brick counted slow breaths aloud, each inhale and exhale marking a measured beat. The rookie nodded, his chest rising and falling in a steady rhythm, the wild heat behind his eyes tempering into a focused flame.

Calm revived, the rookie repositioned—less like a charging bull, more like a deliberate force. He spiked toward the bag, arms wrapping, feet grounded solidly, shoulders sinking into impact with controlled grace. Brick watched deliberately, his eyes narrowing and then easing in approval.

From the sidelines, coaches leaned against metal railings, nodding once, twice—small signs of respect for the lesson unfolding. No shouts, no angry commands—just the taut silence of focus and progress. Brick's hands lingered at his sides, steady as the rookie straightened, breath ragged but eyes bright.

The rookie looked up, searching.

Brick's gaze met his—sharp but not harsh. The nod Brick offered was slight, almost reluctant—approval earned, not given.

"You got it," Brick murmured, his voice a gravelly rumble that cut through the hum of the field.

The group broke apart, the energy shifting now—less frantic, more intentional. The lesson settled into flesh and bone as drills began clicking into rhythm, controlled and sharp.

The air tasted faintly of fresh-cut grass, with the musk of sweat mingling with leather and dusty earth beneath cleats. The sun climbed higher, casting calves in dust-speckled light, shadows pulsing gently as the day's pace picked up yet remained measured. Even in this hard, physical world, discipline settled in like a cool hand on frayed nerves.

"Breathing, huh? Like that's a game-changer," a voice called from the group, tight but edged with doubt.

Brick didn't flinch. His jaw tightened slightly, but his voice remained level. "Better now than when it counts. One bad hit can ruin lives. It ends careers." He let that hang in the air, his gaze steady on the rookie's face.

The rookie's cheeks flushed with exertion and something unreadable—hope? Fear? Determination? Brick didn't answer. He caught the subtle shift in the rookie's stance and let it stand.

"Look," another voice chided, casual but sharp, "have you ever thought that anger gives you an edge? It dulls the pain and sharpens reflexes?"

Brick's jaw clenched. His eyes flicked toward that voice, cool and unmoving. He stepped forward, the field pulsating underfoot. "Edge comes with control, not chaos. You lose your head, you lose the game." He paused, his fingers flexing once at his sides. "And maybe yourself."

Surrounding players exchanged glances, sensing the weight behind the words. Brick's presence commanded attention without bluster, the raw intensity of a man who knows the cost of losing control and now teaches discipline like gospel.

The drill resumed, each movement sharper, minds tethered to the lesson. Brick stayed close, walking beside the rookies, adjusting stances, and whispering corrections. With a steady hand on a back and a firm grip on a shoulder, he shaped them—not just as players, but as brothers entrusted with each other's lives.

A ripple moved through the sideline coaching staff as they exchanged subtle nods, impressed by this rare patience. Brick's usual storm simmered down into quiet authority. It was a different kind of fire—the one that holds rather than burns.

Finally, the drill slowed, and the rookies panted but remained focused. One lineman squared off and drove in, wrapping his arms just so, planting his feet with calm aggression. The follow-through was clean, and the bag barely shifted.

The rookie's smile broke across his dirt-streaked face.

He looked back at Brick, searching.

Brick met his gaze. His lips tightened into a fierce nod, heavy with unspoken praise and trust. The rookie's shoulders straightened, pride blooming in the set of his stance.

The coaches glanced away, giving space to the moment.

Brick exhaled. The breath was a quiet release of tension that had been knotted tight all morning.

"Good job. Keep it tight. Control is everything."

The line prepared for the next move, the rhythm steady and sure now.

The bench by the practice turf creaked softly under Natalie's weight as she sank down. Sophie slid next to her, fingers tightening around a clipboard bristling with draft notes.

The dawn stretched thin across the field, casting shadows that lengthened and flickered as players shuffled through their drills in neat, purposeful chaos. A faint tang of fresh-cut grass mingled with the sharp bite of early morning dew, the air still cool against skin flushed with exertion. The snap of cleats on turf punctuated the yells of instruction and the distant thud of padded tackles.

Sophie's pen bounced a little too quickly against the clipboard's edge. Her gaze flicked from the inked lines to the swirling motions of rookies stumbling through their first tackling drills and back again. "I'm afraid I'm... too soft," she murmured, as if hearing the words for the first time. Her voice trembled, barely louder than the rustle of practice gear around them—fragile as morning light.

She had seen it before, this kind of pressure. Years ago, a rookie's arrest had spiraled into a media feeding frenzy, and she had crumbled under the weight of it, issuing statements so carefully bland that they had only fueled more speculation. The fear of repeating that failure sat like a stone in her chest.

Natalie's gaze lifted, meeting Sophie's with steady calm. She pointed to a clause in Sophie's draft press release, her finger tracing the words like a choreographer guiding a dancer's steps. "See this part here? It's good—acknowledging fault—but the phrasing lacks heart. Replace 'we regret the incident' with something that balances accountability with empathy."

"So... empathy actually builds trust?" Sophie asked, almost as if testing the idea. "I always thought firm lines and public apologies did the heavy lifting."

"Firm lines are the skeleton," Natalie said quietly, leaning back on her elbows, her voice unwavering. "Empathy? That's the muscle that holds everything together."

In the world of professional football—where toughness was currency and vulnerability was seen as weakness—this approach felt counterintuitive. But Natalie had learned that fans didn't just want accountability; they wanted to believe the organization actually cared about the humans inside the uniforms. That's what shifted narratives.

"The fans and the players need to believe we care, not just that we're sorry," Natalie continued, gesturing toward a paragraph Sophie had drafted about the team's new rookie engagement initiative. "This line here—mention the well-being programs alongside performance standards. Let the public know we invest in the whole player, not just their stats. That makes a narrative sustainable, not just reactive."

Sophie's pencil scratched swiftly across the margins. While she worked, Natalie's eyes drifted to the far side of the field.

There, brick by brick, Logan "Brick" Turner molded the fledgling linemen. His posture was a study in quiet command, with broad shoulders squared beneath his jersey and hands precise as they demonstrated tackling posture. His voice cut through the morning air—deep, calm, steady, without a trace of the fury his reputation would suggest.

Natalie's walls softened as she watched him. The rookies seemed to breathe differently around him, their jittery uncertainty transforming into quiet focus. Order bloomed amid chaos. The clatter of pads and labored breaths wove into an almost gentle rhythm.

Sophie cleared her throat, breaking the spell. "Okay," she said, flipping pages with fresh determination. "Let me try again." Her pencil scratched as she read aloud: "'The team remains committed to fostering both accountability and empathy, recognizing that true strength lies in supporting every player's journey, both on and off the field.'"

Natalie's eyes brightened. "Much better."

"Really?" Sophie's shoulders eased, tension draining from her frame.

"Really. Now, think about timing." Natalie turned to face her fully. "This release needs to drop once the rookies finish their drills. The media's watching; the story's alive. Hit while the iron's hot, but don't rush—it's about setting a tone, not just firefighting a headline."

A smile crept across Sophie's lips. She closed the clipboard with a soft snap—small but triumphant. Natalie tucked a loose strand of hair behind her ear, her fingers brushing against her cheek as she matched Sophie's smile.

Together, they turned back to the field.

The rookies' gasps and grunts rose and fell with the rhythm of drills—a symphony of effort woven through the hot morning. Between the lines of practice, Natalie sensed something fragile taking shape: strength tempered by care, rage shaped into leadership. Somehow, both she and Sophie were part of it, sending ripples outward from this patch of emerald turf.

"There's no 'too soft,'" Natalie murmured, her voice wrapped in the weight of countless battles and quiet victories like this one. "There's just the question of how you harness what you have."

###

The sharp whistle cut through the morning air. Water break. Brick's eyes locked on Natalie across the field.

Pale sunlight glinted off the dew-soaked turf. Around them, rookies panted and clattered their water bottles. His gaze held hers—that spark flickering beneath the grit—and he swiped the back of his hand across his cheek, wiping away dirt and morning sweat in one sharp gesture.

He staggered forward, limping with an exaggerated wobble toward the sideline. "Hey, Natalie—any media coaching tips? I might need a miracle to survive this next round."

She rose instantly, her heels clicking against the concrete as she stepped into his path. Her eyebrow quirked. She took in the staged hunch of his shoulders, the mock grimace tugging at his lips, and a teasing smile that curved at the corner of her mouth.

"Look at you—turning on the charm and the limp. What's next, a motivational speech?"

Her fingers reached out, quick and certain, brushing his jersey collar at the shoulder. They lingered a beat longer than necessary, smoothing away a tiny crease.

Brick caught the scent of her—peppermint mixed with something faintly sweet, threading through the dusty air—and his chest tightened, his breath hitching as he reached for her hand. A low chuckle rumbled in his throat.

The crowd dissolved into background noise: restless rookies, echoing whistles, and cleats slapping against the grass. All of it faded into the periphery.

He tugged her toward the gap behind the equipment shed. Empty sleds lay there like dark sentinels, their steel frames casting long shadows across the cracked concrete. The air was cooler here, quieter, and scented with oil and old rubber from the sled runners—a rare refuge within the chaos, a place where they could breathe.

They closed the distance, leaving no space between them.

"The rookies are tougher than I thought," Brick said, his voice roughened by morning exertion. His eyes found hers. "I saw one, Jace, catch himself before diving in wild. He's hearing what I'm saying about control." He paused, vulnerability bleeding through the usual storm. "I didn't think I had the patience for that anymore."

Years of clenched fists—frustration, focus—had left his knuckles rough. Natalie's hand drifted up, her thumb ghosting over them. Soft. Grounding. A silent promise.

His shoulders eased. Tension slackened. He breathed her in again, slower this time, as if memorizing the space she filled.

"You're changing," she murmured. "Walking that line. You're not just surviving anymore, Brick. You're coaching."

He looked up. A rare, genuine smile tugged at his mouth. Then he leaned in, his lips brushing hers—tentative at first. The kiss deepened in a heartbeat. Soft heat bloomed in the quiet shadows behind the shed. Only the press of breath, the pulse against his chest, and the faint scrape of concrete beneath their feet.

Then laughter bubbled up from somewhere deep, breaking the spell. They pulled apart, still caught in the afterglow, their eyes shining with shared secrets and stolen moments.

"Caught," Brick breathed, his grin crooked. "Guess we better get back before Coach Hale sends a search party."

Natalie smirked, her fingers sliding from his knuckles back up to tug at his jersey collar with mock sternness.

"Your new zen energy is showing. Don't let it get too comfortable—you've got rookies to scare into shape."

"Right." Brick grinned, brushing turf dust from his forearm. "Like you need me to remind you to keep your clipboard tight." His voice softened. "Ready?"

"Always," she said, tucking a loose strand of hair behind her ear.

They stepped out from the shadows, the sun striking their shoulders and casting sharp silhouettes across the practice field. Their hands brushed briefly—faint contact, a tether in the wide-open space teeming with noise and energy—before sliding away.

Natalie returned to her bench, clipboard in hand, her eyes sharp and watchful. Brick squared his shoulders and faced the group, his voice low and steady.

"Alright, rookies. Let's get back to it."

The whistle blows sharply. It slices through the quiet that has settled like a soft skin over the early morning's heat. Rookies explode into motion, sprinting through conditioning drills designed for agility—quick feet churning over the turf as they zig and zag beneath watchful eyes.

A young lineman's cleats catch on the slick grass. His body topples. His elbow scrapes raw against the dirt as he pitches toward the turf. The rough scent of earth rises, mingling with the sharp snap of fresh sweat in the humid air.

A heavy hand shoots out, catching the rookie around the elbow before impact. Brick's touch is firm but steady, his wide palm grounding the flailing energy. The lineman looks up, breath hitching in surprise, into Brick's narrow, steadying gaze—a gaze that carries the weight of a man who has learned control the hard way, through fire and failure and the long climb back. This moment, this small intervention, matters more than the rookie could know.

"Restraint, remember," Brick's voice cuts low, clipped with hard-earned lessons. He shifts the rookie's stance with practiced fingers at the shoulder and wrist, adjusting the posture like a sculptor refining his form. "Control the force, not just the fury."

The rookie nods, swallowing past the flush of embarrassment. Brick releases him with a brief, commanding nod. "Back in. Slow it down—own it."

Along the sideline, Caleb leans against the metal fence, his grin wide and playful. "Don't sweat it, guys. Coach Turner's gonna scare the hell out of you... in the best way." His voice carries warmth beneath the teasing.

DeShawn's chuckle rolls deep and easy, his eyes sparkling with mischief. "And if you start getting soft, well... that's when I step in. Game on." The words hang lightly but promise the depth of camaraderie that threads through the team like a hidden current.

Near the practice tents, Natalie and Sophie clap in rhythm. The sound is muted against the field's rough roar. Sophie's pen drums a jittery rhythm against her clipboard. Her eyes flicker bright—too wide for just fatigue, something closer to exhilaration beneath the exhaustion.

Sophie leans close, a conspiratorial glint in her gaze. "It's crazy, right? How this madness somehow feels... almost sweet? Like a strange, twisted family reunion."

Natalie's lips tug into a tender smile as she flicks through Sophie's notes. "Football life," she murmurs, her voice even but laced with fondness. "Harsh. Demanding. But it's also about trust. It's about shaping people into something they wouldn't become without the fire." She pauses, setting the clipboard down. "That's what we do here in PR too, you know. We manage perception, sure. But really—we're helping men be vulnerable in a world that demands they be stone. It's harder than it sounds."

Sophie nods, scribbling the new phrasing down. Their eyes meet briefly, forming a silent pact of understanding amid the chaos.

Across the field, the players' heavy boots grind into the turf as practice winds down. Brick's voice rings out above the clatter, steady and sharp.

"Circle up!"

Bodies shuffle toward the center hash marks. The sun leans in diagonally, stretching shadows long across the grass.

A mix of raw rookie nerves and seasoned resolve gathers. Brick's dark eyes sweep over their faces, drawing them tight into the moment.

"Trust isn't just earned in the bedroom or the locker room," Brick says, his voice calm but edged with steel. "It's built in sweat and setbacks. Every mistake you make—own it. Learn from it. And never forget, we've got each other's backs. No one stands alone."

His tone softens just enough for the vulnerability to slip through—a man who's lived through the cost of losing control and has clawed his way back.

Natalie stands slightly behind the group, her arms crossed but relaxed. Her gaze lingers on Brick. Pride flickers in the quiet crease at the corners of her eyes. Their eyes find each other across the circle. A small smile is exchanged—a private acknowledgment of battles fought side by side, victories both on the field and within.

The team begins to scatter, laughter and chatter filling the cooling air as they file toward the locker room, their footprints marking the dew-streaked turf.

Brick and Natalie stand close in the middle of the thinning field, their shoulders almost brushing. Their hands graze briefly as players pass, a silent promise exchanged in a touch. The field's clatter fades into soft stillness. Brick and Natalie remain rooted together, watching their team disperse, a quiet strength folding between them like a shield—calm readiness for the battles still ahead.

The players drifted toward the locker room. Shadows stretched long beneath the stadium's steady hum—a deep, primal pulse of anticipation that never quite faded.

Caleb stood with DeShawn near the turf's edge, their laughter low but charged with something electric. Caleb nudged DeShawn with an elbow, his grin tilted like a secret. Part of him wondered if that was what he wanted—someone to build a future with, someone who would fight for the story they would write together. But that was a thought for another day.

"So, who's stepping up next to snag their storybook ending?" Caleb's voice carried a teasing edge. "Do you reckon Sophie locks someone down before the season closes?"

DeShawn chuckled, shaking his head. The sharp tang of damp turf mixed with salty sweat clung to the air between them, adhering like a second skin. "Man, don't look at me. I'm keeping mine buried deep. But if someone wants to step up and play the hero?" His eyes flicked toward the practice facility, playful heat sparking beneath the surface. "I'm game."

Caleb threw an arm over DeShawn's shoulders—a weight that felt like belonging. "Better watch out, or Brick will put a hex on you for stealing the spotlight."

DeShawn threw his head back. Laughter spilled free—deep and unguarded. "Bring it, Iron Wall."

Across the field, Brick and Natalie held their ground—a quiet island amid the ebbing tide of bodies. They caught snippets of banter, and Brick's eyes narrowed just a fraction, the corners crinkling as a small smile tugged at his lips. His rough fingers reached out, ruffling a passing player's helmet with a fondness that betrayed his fierce exterior. His gaze found Natalie's, and in that glance, a conversation unfolded that no one else could hear—an acknowledgment of shared purpose and trust built through a hundred small moments like this one.

Sophie walked past, her clipboard hugged like a shield against the roaring world. She offered Natalie a smile bright enough to split the noon sun. "Thanks, Natalie."

Relief nested in that brief exchange—a momentary unburdening.

Natalie touched the side of her mouth, her voice low and clipped but kind. "Remember—keep the tone measured for the follow-up. Confidence, not desperation. They'll bite if we sound like we're scurrying." Her eyes flickered toward the disappearing draftee and the stadium's shadows stretching long and lean.

Sophie nodded, the weight of the learning curve softened by Natalie's steady hand. She tucked the clipboard under her arm and hurried on.

The field emptied. Cleated feet whispered across the turf, and jerseys rustled softly as breath.

Brick and Natalie remained, silhouettes softened by the early light fading behind steel and concrete. Their fingers brushed—a silent jolt of recognition. Hands clasped briefly, warm and steady. In that grip lived something deeper now: the knowledge that they had navigated this morning's chaos together and that they had emerged on the other side still solid. Still certain.

Together, they turned toward the practice facility, side by side. Their steps synchronized, unhurried.

"Do you think any of those rookies will surprise us this year?" Natalie's voice was soft, reflective, barely louder than the echoing clatter from the locker room beyond.

Brick's grin slid across his face—rough-edged but genuine. "They're tougher than they look. We just have to teach them to channel it right."

Natalie smirked, her eyes twinkling. "We'll see who writes their own story—and who gets stuck on the sidelines."

Brick's laugh rumbled low. He slid his hand to the small of her back, the gesture firm but gentle—an anchor. A promise.

The stadium hummed behind them, alive with anticipation and quiet promise. As they disappeared into the practice facility's hollowed corridors, the future whispered just beyond reach, full of potential and the steady pulse of something new—a playbook still being written.

Final Thoughts

The Final Blitz is a story about what happens when strength is mistaken for control—and when control is learned the hard way.

Brick's anger isn't random. Natalie's discipline isn't cold. Both are survival strategies shaped by pressure, expectation, and the fear of losing everything that defines them.

This book explores the quiet battles behind the spectacle of professional sports—the moments no camera captures, where choices matter more than touchdowns, and growth is earned one hard decision at a time.

If this story resonated with you, I hope it reminded you that redemption isn't loud.
Sometimes, it's choosing restraint when chaos feels easier.

Thank you for reading—and for stepping into the storm with them.

Review Request

Thank You for Reading!

Your support means the world. If you enjoyed this book, would you leave a quick review? Even one sentence helps other readers discover the story.

★★★ *CLICK HERE TO LEAVE YOUR REVIEW* ★★★